THE DRESSMAKER'S SECRET EARL

A DOUBLE-DILEMMA ROMANCE

SUSANNE DUNLAP

DEDICATION

For my daughters

ALSO BY SUSANNE DUNLAP

Stay informed about forthcoming books and get free content! Sign up for my newsletter.

CHAPTER 1

*T*ired, travel-weary, determined Augusta Hastings descended from a grueling ride on the London stage clutching all she could carry of her possessions in a single valise in one hand—and in the other a slip of paper that she hoped would lead her to her future. She had just given her rumpled skirts a straightening twitch when a man's voice screamed from behind her, "Out of the way, damn you!"

Two galloping horses pulling a high-perch phaeton bore down on her so fast she hardly had a moment to think. She leapt to the side just in time to avoid being run over, and— *splat!* Heart plummeting, she looked down. As she feared, she'd landed plop in the middle of an an ankle-deep, foul-smelling puddle, and the moisture was fast wicking up her best pelisse on its way to her knees. "Oh, blast your—" Augusta stopped herself before uttering the vilest curse she could think of. Which, being well born and gently bred, would not have been very vile. Not enough, anyway, to express her utter dismay at being mud-spattered and drenched when it was imperative that she look well-dressed and highly presentable.

Not the way to appear when entering on a career in fashion.

Before she could gather her wits enough to decide what to do next, a curricle wheeled around the corner nearly as fast as the phaeton had moments earlier. Augusta prepared to shrink even farther back against the brick wall of the coaching inn. This time, though, the much more skilled driver pulled his spanking pair of chestnuts to a halt in front of her. Instead of simply driving on, he touched the handle of his whip to the brim of his hat and said with a chuckle, "Did that rascal Lewiston nearly flatten you? He didn't mean it."

He was laughing at her. How dare he! She drew herself up, craned her neck and shielded her eyes from the bright sun behind the gentleman. A man of fashion, clearly, but the expression above the expertly tied neck cloth and many-caped drab driving coat was kind rather than haughty. A smile lifted the corners of his mouth, and he looked her over with a shake of his head. "Gudgeon!" he said.

"Sir! I—"

"Not you! The marquess!"

She pressed her lips together and lifted one eyebrow. After all, she couldn't deny the absurdity of her situation.

"But truly, have you suffered any lasting injury?" he asked.

"As you see, I am unharmed."

The gentleman's gray eyes softened, searching hers. This sudden shift caught her unawares, and she found herself struggling against the urge to cry. No one had looked at her that way since the last time she'd seen James over a year ago, resplendent in his dragoon's uniform.

"I see you're traveling, Ma'am," the gentleman said, suddenly all crisp politeness, nodding at the valise dangling from her hand. "Have you just arrived on the stage? May I direct you to your lodgings? Or better still, convey you there? Plenty of room for you, and we could squeeze in a chaperone if need be."

A bell of warning clanged in Augusta's mind. She must look like a bedraggled waif, ripe for plucking and ruining, all alone without a chaperone in sight—and she was exhausted. The constant sounding of the yard of tin at numerous toll gates, the rocking of the stage coach on rutted roads, and being squeezed in among five other passengers had made it difficult to get so much as a wink of sleep. She said, with a sigh and a note of reluctance, "I thank you, no. I am traveling alone."

"Ah. You are wary of trusting a stranger. Quite right. But truly, I would be very happy to help you on your way and lend you my paltry protection. My friend has done you a wicked turn." The spark of amusement leapt back into his eyes. "He's doing his best to become a top sawyer!"

She couldn't help smiling at this and saying, "Those poor horses! But I beg you not to trouble yourself." Then she remembered the paper she held crushed in her hand. She'd read it over at least a hundred times, hoping it would reveal a morsel of information that might help her find her way in London, but to no avail. "However, if you would be so kind, you could render me assistance by informing me which way I must go to reach Madame Noelle's establishment in Curzon Street."

"Hah!" he said, his face brightening, "I know it well. I've shepherded my sister to that door more times than I can count. It's too far to walk from here and you'll find a hackney very uncomfortable. You might as well let me take you there. It's the least I can do to atone for my friend's folly."

He reached down with one gloved hand, gazing at her with a look of entreaty. "Well, don't leave me stopped in the middle of Piccadilly," he said with a quick glance over his shoulder, where several carriages and barrows had stalled behind him, their drivers leaving Augusta in no doubt of their feelings on the matter. "I'm a much better driver than the marquess, I promise."

Before she had a chance to decline the offer, the gentleman bent nearly in half so he could grasp her hand and held it too firmly for her to get out of his grip. He smoothly lifted her as she took a step onto the board, drawing her up and into the open carriage with a little too much force. As a result, Augusta landed heavily on his lap and nearly lost hold of her valise. Laughter erupted among the curious bystanders, and a little boy pointed at her and said, "Look Mama! She nearly took a toss!"

Mortified, Augusta slid herself to the seat next to the gentleman as far as she could without tumbling down into the road. What must he think of her? She straightened her back and lifted her chin, stowing the leather valise firmly between her feet. "I do beg your pardon, My Lord," she said, deciding to over rather than underestimate his rank.

"Please do not trouble yourself. As you see, I am unharmed."

A choked laugh escaped her as she recognized his teasing echo of her own words. "I am relieved to hear it!" she said.

"Now that we have established that we have both survived the hazards of London carriage travel, allow me to introduce myself," the gentleman said, bowing slightly in her direction. "George Lanyon, Earl of Bridlington, your servant. Whom do I have the pleasure of escorting? I assume you've come to order your gowns for the season?"

"Augusta Hastings, My Lord," she answered. "And I am not here as a customer of Madame Noelle but as an employee. I am a seamstress." And as a seamstress, she hoped, it was entirely expected that she would travel sans chaperone.

"Hastings—any relation to the Earl, or any of the Grantleys?"

A quick flush spread up from her neck. "Of course not! I mean, no," she stammered.

This time Lord Bridlington's appraising gaze was unmistakable. Thankfully, he was forced to look away in order to maneuver his horses through a crush of crossing traffic. That accomplished, he said, "I am sorry. From your voice and your carriage, and under the mud on your ensemble, I assumed you to be a gentlewoman."

I am a gentlewoman, more's the pity. A gentlewoman with no desire to acknowledge it. A gentlewoman with ambitions more suited to a bourgeoise, and education appropriate to a bluestocking. A gentlewoman well aware that she should not be alone in a smart curricle with a man she does not know. "I would be grateful if you would set me down a short distance from Madame Noelle's. She has never met me, and I don't want to give her the wrong impression."

"Of course," he said.

They progressed in uncomfortable silence for a while. Augusta could hardly bring herself to look around at this hurly burly city she was hoping to make her home, afraid of accidentally meeting Lord Bridlington's disturbing eyes.

He pulled up the horses after they had traveled about a mile. "The address you seek is just there."

Augusta expected he would jump down and help her out of the carriage, but he remained seated. Perhaps the revelation of her assumed station in life had made him think he needn't treat her with further courtesy. So like a member of the *ton!* She supposed she must accustom herself to different manners in this world she was entering where, because she labored for a wage she would be beneath consideration. Yet Bridlington's expression told a different story. It was no less kind than it had been at the first. Definitely a contradiction.

Well, if he couldn't be courteous, at least she could. She stood and put out her hand for him to shake. "I can't thank you enough, Lord Bridlington. You see, I've never been in London before."

"And look how we've welcomed you!" He shook his head and took her hand just as the horses gave a little start of impatience and the carriage rocked.

Augusta was thrown off balance and had to brace her other hand on Bridlington's shoulder to avoid once more falling into him. For a moment, they were close enough that she could see the faint lines that led from the corners of his eyes, which deepened as a smile spread across his face.

And then he frowned, and his gaze shifted from her eyes to her mouth. Before she could guess what had caused this sudden alteration, he lifted his hand and touched the corner of her lips with his index finger, wiping gently. "There," he said, and held up his glove for inspection.

A dab of mud stained it. Augusta's cheeks flamed. "Oh Sir!"

He laughed and helped her stand upright and regain her balance. "I hope you will find the metropolis more to your liking once you've found your footing."

Again, he was laughing at her. But she couldn't help laughing at herself, too. Lord Bridlington held onto her until she'd climbed down to the flagway. Augusta drew her hand out of his with a little reluctance. It had felt for a moment like an anchor, something solid in her recently tumultuous life. She curtsied without meeting his eyes, then hurried toward the elegantly painted sign up ahead that indicated she had at last arrived to face the future she had chosen for herself.

Augusta took a moment to settle her nerves. She refused to admit that she'd been the slightest bit afraid of traveling all that way alone, so far from the places she knew well. She wished she were in better fettle for announcing herself to Madame Noelle, but it couldn't be helped. She had been presentable enough for a handsome young nobleman to come to her assistance—and he was handsome, in a quiet way, so different from James's dashing figure.

She had no choice but to brazen it out. So she marched up to the door, took hold of the handle, lifted the latch and pulled, setting a cluster of small bells tinkling.

"You should have seen the look on her face! It was pure terror!" said a lady's voice.

Then another lady added, "But you know—"

The talking ceased as soon as Augusta came within view. Before her on a low platform stood a striking woman of perhaps twenty years, and on the floor next to her a tall woman in black twilled silk with a tape measure around her neck. Both of them turned to stare at her. The two girls crouching at the feet of the fine lady looked up in unison, eyes widening. The entire tableau multiplied comically in the many long mirrors placed around the room, and Augusta barely suppressed a laugh. The same mirrors reflected a riot of colors and textures of gowns and draped fabrics, trailing ribbons and laces and plumes of feathers, looking for all the world like an enormous, luxurious nest.

"Madame Noelle, I presume?" Augusta said, recollecting herself and dipping a curtsy. "I am Augusta Hastings."

Instead of giving her the polite welcome she hoped for, the proprietress swept her eyes from Augusta's head to her hem, lips pursed as if she'd tasted something sour. Her irises darkened, she drew her brows together and flared her nostrils dramatically. "You have no business in here! Pauline, show this girl to the trade entrance. She can start today."

At that, one of the girls, a pert brunette with an up-tipped nose, bustled over to Augusta, taking a firm hold of her upper arm to turn her around and head her back out through the door. Before they fully passed through and it closed behind them, Augusta caught the tail end of a conversation between the two women in the shop. "A country bumpkin! Doesn't know any better, my Lady, but she's supposed to be good with a needle. What can one do?"

"Still, she had a bit of an air," the other lady said in a voice cut from the cloth of nobility, "Under the dirt, that is!" A musical laugh followed them out the door.

"You've landed in it!" Pauline said in a hoarse whisper as she led Augusta down an alley almost too narrow to pass through without brushing against the grimy bricks. They stopped at a low door, which Pauline opened with a bit of effort, and entered a small workroom lit from above by a skylight. Three seamstresses crouched over work in their laps—sprig muslin, figured silk, and gauzy nets pooling around their feet. The floor was scrupulously clean—unlike the one window, dirty to the point of opacity. A door on one side appeared to lead to the showroom Augusta had just left, and another one bore a crude sign that said *stairs.* None of the seamstresses looked up when Augusta came in.

Pauline cleared her throat. "This is Augusta. Don't know what she'll do here, but if she's handy with a needle she'll find plenty o' work to keep 'er busy." Her voice softened as she spoke, perhaps having some sympathy for Augusta's awkward entrance into that world.

"Help, hah! Divvy up the wages even more, I don't doubt," said a woman with a thick London accent, wisps of graying hair peeking out of her widow's cap.

The other two seamstresses were younger. Much younger. One hardly more than a girl. That one looked up with frank curiosity and paused with her needle in midair to stare at her from top to toe. Then she burst out laughing.

"Shhh!" said Pauline, "Madame will hear you, and then

we'll all be for it. Augusta, this is Molly, Bernadette, and Miss Carp."

They nodded in turn as they were introduced. So, these were to be her compatriots. "I should like to take my things to my room—there are lodgings with the position?" Augusta said.

"Hoity-toity!" said the old lady, the one called Miss Carp, "Lodgings is a bit rich. A shared room in the attic, and a bit of a parlor off it. But no one can take you there til the day's done, so might's well get stuck in with some work—if it ain't beneath you." She jerked her head toward an empty work table without ceasing her stitching. "You'll take Prudence's place. She didn't last long!" A silent laugh shook her.

Augusta's initial reaction of affront at being addressed in such a crude fashion gave way to curiosity. "Why didn't she last long?" No one answered. They all cast furtive glances in the direction of the showroom door.

"You can just tuck your things under the table for now," Pauline murmured.

Augusta looked down. The mud had now dried to crispness. She sighed and removed her pelisse, hanging it on a hook Molly pointed out to her. "Where shall I start?" she asked.

So it began. This was the life she had chosen, and whatever menial tasks she must perform in order to work her way up to creating her own designs she would embrace gladly.

Augusta was aware that her learned father had been disappointed that she appeared to have more genuine interest in the Mirror of Fashion than in the *Iliad*. The truth was that she valued both. Every day, she sketched evening gowns and day dresses and riding habits in the little pocket book she kept in her reticule. And every day, she read something from the well-stocked library at Crossley Grange, her former home. The pocket book was easy to bring with her in her hasty flight, but she had no room in her one valise for even a single volume from her small collection of books, the ones she'd kept when she moved in with her aunt.

Circumstances had forced her to make a decision within hours that she'd been agonizing over for months. She knew that all the education in the world would gain her no more than a position as a harassed governess. But her skill with a needle, her eye for fabrics and style, might open a door to something more creative and sustaining, something that could support her in London. So she decided on that course of action, and here she was.

Besides, she possessed a magical key to thousands of volumes of all sorts, a veritable treasure trove of books to read to take her away from whatever trials and frustrations she might face in pursuit of her new life. This was her father's subscription to Hookham's, the largest lending library in London. As soon as she settled in, she would go there and select something to read in the quiet hour or so before bed. Choosing one life need not mean abandoning the other altogether, need it?

The only thing she wished to put firmly behind her was that "respectable" future in a detestable marriage, which her aunt seemed to believe the single choice open to a penniless, well-born female.

Augusta was determined to prove her wrong.

CHAPTER 2

*B*ridlington drove the chestnuts into the stable yard behind Lanyon House. As soon as he pulled them up, Philpot, the head groom, bustled out to hold their heads.

"Did his lordship enjoy his drive?" Philpot said.

"I hardly noticed! I spent the time rushing around after Lewiston and mending his disasters." A very pretty disaster, he had to admit, recalling the delicate blush that suffused the lady's face when he'd pulled her up into the curricle.

A stable boy came and took charge of the horses from Philpot, who approached the carriage and reached up to help the earl descend. George said, "Not necessary! I can manage." He stood with the help of an ebony cane tucked next to the carriage seat and stepped down, his weight fully on his left foot, with as much as he could bear on the side of his right foot. Once planted on the ground, he stood tall—and at over six feet, he was tall by any standard. "I take it Lewiston is here?"

"Yes, My Lord. That's his phaeton there and this time

only one bit of damage to a spoke." Philpot's eyes twinkled. "Pity he's not the whip you are, My Lord."

"He doesn't need to be," Bridlington said with a wry smile, and set off toward the back entrance of the house putting weight on the cane with each step of his right foot.

That was the truth of it, he thought as his valet, Craggins, opened the door before he reached it, then relieved him of his hat and gloves and helped him out of his coat. "The marquess is changing, and said he would meet you in the yellow saloon before dinner," said Craggins.

As Bridlington climbed the stairs to his dressing room, his adventure earlier that day was still fresh in his mind. The young lady, Miss Hastings. Funny coincidence about the name, but he supposed it wasn't an uncommon one. He'd easily pulled her into the curricle, thanks partly to hours of training at Gentleman Jackson's boxing saloon, partly to the lady's slender frame.

Only one thing disturbed him about that episode. He should have jumped down to hand her out of the carriage when they arrived at her destination. Although he might have done so, the climb in and out was awkward for him, and so he had decided not to in that instant. He could see in her steady, golden-brown eyes that she half expected him to behave as any gentleman would, and was likely insulted that he hadn't.

What was done was done. Better she should simply think him rude than pity him.

An hour later, Bridlington met Lewiston in the saloon as planned. His oldest friend had spent his childhood at the neighboring estate to Bridlington Priory and they'd been at Eton together. He was among the few boys in school who hadn't made George the butt of cruel jokes. The ease of their friendship meant that the marquess hardly noticed Bridlington's decided limp and never offered to help him.

"What took you so long, old man?" Lewiston said, gazing out of one of the long windows to the street—still sunlit at that time of day.

Bridlington took a seat on a jonquil-silk-covered divan near the fireplace where a roaring blaze warmed a room so large that it was apt to be chilly at any time of year. "Unlike you, I take care not to terrorize pedestrians and chairmen by racing everywhere."

Lewiston flashed him a rueful grin. "I've decided I'll never really get the hang of it. Mostly because I'm not sure I want to. Better not to try than to come up so utterly unfit."

"You have other talents, Lewiston. It isn't necessary to aspire to the Four Horse Club."

Lewiston sighed. "If only the things I valued weighed at all with ladies in the *ton*." He sat himself in a chair opposite Bridlington, the twist of a crooked smile lighting his face. "Still, you didn't simply lag behind me. I waited a full half hour for you before I went up to change. Did you stop at Brooks's on the way?"

"No. As I said, I had to do a little mending after your dash through town!"

The saloon door opened to admit Allsop, the butler, bearing a tray with a decanter and three glasses.

"Ah, you see, I'm truly not cut out to be a whip. I'm much better at wielding a bow than the ribbons," Lewiston said, having poured them each out a glass of Madeira and brought one over to Bridlington.

It was hard not to like Lewiston, however badly he drove his teams. A friendship like theirs was rare enough. "In actuality I took my time. The day was fine," George said by way of explanation. He had no intention of recounting his episode of gallantry. His friend would doubtless tease him about it. What could he say, after all? The lady had said she was going to work for the modiste, which puzzled him. She certainly didn't have the air of someone accustomed to laboring for a wage. But it was her eyes that had impressed him the most. A warm brown color that came alight in the sun. Something hidden in them, though. Sorrow? She hadn't been cowed by his notice, although her discomfiture when he mentioned the Earl of Hastings and the Grantley name struck him as odd.

When he'd pulled her up into the curricle with a little too much force for her delicate frame, the weight of her body on his lap had surprised a response deep in his gut. And when she moved off and sat on the seat as far away from him as possible and so upright, he had to suppress the highly inappropriate urge to draw her back toward him. What was it about her?

"… and what a turnup! That blackguard trying to poison the horses at Newmarket. Think we need to go and stand buff, so I propose a jaunt there together for the next subscription race. I may not be much of a whip, but I can stand and watch with the best of them!"

Bridlington hadn't been listening, but quickly caught the gist of Lewiston's one-sided conversation. "If you wish," he said, without much enthusiasm. He sighed. Why could he not stop thinking about a lady he was unlikely ever to see on again? Although he occasionally drove his sister to Madame Noelle's if he happened to be going in that direction for a purpose of his own, of course he never went inside. Besides, she likely only tolerated his light flirtation because she had no idea he was a cripple.

"What's got into you, Bridlington?" Lewiston asked. "You look positively pudding headed!"

"Nothing! Just thinking about those races you mentioned. We should engage rooms early. All the inns are likely to be booked up for a race with such a handsome purse."

The two friends conversed lightly on the merits of different carriage horses, the best racing stables, and who had the best-matched teams and drove them with the softest hands. Lewiston, as Bridlington knew, appreciated the finer points of driving, even if he could not master them for himself.

"I say, where's your sister?" Lewiston said, nodding toward the third, unused glass on the tray.

"I haven't the least notion," Bridlington said. "Perhaps at one of her charitable enterprises. She does as she pleases, and no doubt will breeze in just in time to change before the Skinley's rout party, having already taken her dinner elsewhere without informing any of us."

At that moment, Allsop announced dinner and they both stood. Bridlington could easily read Lewiston's disappointed look. He knew his friend harbored hopes of winning Mari's affections. But although Mari had a decided fondness for the marquess, she had made it clear that she had no intention of becoming his marchioness. *He's too dull,* she'd told her brother. *We have no interests in common.* Besides, they'd known each other so long and had settled into easy bantering more like siblings than lovers. Mariana's fortune, as well as her inclination, entitled her to be selective about a husband.

And selective she certainly was.

Despite a plethora of eligible offers, Mariana had not settled on a match. Something was holding her back. Bridlington believed she wished to marry, not remain an eccentric spinster—like the middle-aged Lady Elkinson who raced around the park in a high-perch phaeton and hosted a faro bank in her own house. When he asked Mariana why she had refused everyone, what it was that she truly wanted, she evaded the question. As children, they had told each other everything. Now that they were adults, she had become closed off to him, full of secrets.

But he, too, had secrets. Secrets he did not want to divulge to Mariana. At least, not until he was ready. Everyone would think him mad, and perhaps they'd be right. Not for him the hands-off world of politics. Not for him the superficial society of the *ton.* Noble or not, he had chosen to get his hands dirty grappling with the reality of a world that had been unkind to him when he was at his most vulnerable. He had a plan, ideas, and the means to carry them out.

What he didn't have was the certainty that he could make any difference at all, and so he would keep his counsel until such time as he was ready to bring others into his schemes.

CHAPTER 3

*L*ady Mariana was an accomplished liar. Oh, she told the truth about the little things. She only lied about what mattered.

To be fair to herself, Mariana thought, the fact was not so much that she lied as that she carefully selected the truths she would tell. Although her mother regularly lectured her about accepting one of the several eligible proposals she had received, convinced that a good marriage would ultimately lead to happiness, Mariana had learned to smile sweetly and let the torrent of words glance off her, responding with an inane comment about a new parasol, or the need for another visit to Madame Noelle's, or deprecating some new mode in the latest number of the *La Belle Assemblée*.

These thoughts playing through her mind, her expression was fixed in a distracted scowl when she alighted from the town carriage and climbed the steps to Lanyon House not long after midnight, having made her obligatory appearance at yet another rout party.

"The earl is in the small saloon," Allsop told her after relieving her of her evening cape and muff.

This surprised her. George did not normally feel he must wait up for her. So rather than go immediately to her room and let Jennings, her abigail, divest her of her finery, Mariana joined her brother as he sat nursing a brandy, his bad foot resting on a gout stool. "So, here you are," Mariana said, taking a seat in the chair opposite.

Both siblings stared into the flickering fire and maintained a desultory conversation consisting of pleasantries for a few minutes. When it dwindled, George cleared his throat and said, "Bainbridge came to talk to me this morning."

Mariana screwed up her face in distaste. Viscount Bainbridge had plagued her all last season. She'd done everything in her power to prevent him offering for her, short of being rude. "What on earth can that have to do with me?"

"Don't be obtuse. Of course he asked my permission—again—to make you an offer. He's a good match, Sister. A splendid fellow, not at all high minded. A member of the Four Horse Club, you might be interested to know."

"Really! You think his being a decent judge of horseflesh and a skilled whip can atone for his appalling sense of humor, his unbearable high laugh, and his jowls? Not to mention his odious politics. And what makes him think I have changed my mind in a year?"

"He is an intelligent man—"

"Not if he believes all women are fickle and one might as well ignore what they say and assume they will merely assert the opposite the next time they're asked! Really, George, you know you dislike the man as much as I do!"

"That is unfair. He is not someone I would choose to number among my close acquaintances, but that does not mean I dislike him. He could well be in line for a ministerial post, if he stays in with the Tories. Oh I know you'd rather he were some radical Whig—as would I—but you would make a dashed brilliant political wife and you know it. You could have much more influence than you think in that capacity."

I could do better as a politician, Mariana thought, but knew better than to say. If only the estate *had* been entailed, enabling a distant cousin to inherit so she would no longer be pressed to fulfill not just her own role in the family but that of her brother, she could attach herself to someone less high born, someone who might not expect her to merely act as hostess. Someone willing to consider her a true partner. Someone she could all too easily picture, having met him last season. "I still don't see why I have to hear him out. Couldn't you just refuse for me?"

George grimaced. "I'd offered to do that, but Mama wouldn't hear of it. You know what she's like. 'At least she should give him a chance. It takes courage to make an offer.'"

He mimicked the dowager's voice so exactly that Mariana erupted in a peal of laughter.

Once both of them had wiped the tears of mirth out of their eyes, George said, "For me, I don't see that there's any hurry for you to marry."

"So why didn't you stand up to Mama?" she said, exasperated, and stood and paced across the luxuriant carpet in front of her brother.

"I assure you it wouldn't sway her. Besides, you can refuse him yourself. You know she'd never force you into a match you didn't want."

Yes, Mariana thought, *but she'd never approve the match I do want.* "That may be true. But why does it have to be I who marries into an exalted position and adds more shine to the Bridlington coronet? Can I not persuade you to let go of this ridiculous notion that you are ineligible for marriage? Your bad foot in no way disqualifies you for producing an heir!"

George couldn't help laughing at this. "A hit. But how do you know? How does anyone know that a son of mine wouldn't be similarly afflicted, or that I wouldn't end up being just as cruel and abusive as our father was?"

"You speak as though you had no will of your own, which I know is not the case. Won't you at least take the chance?" Although they'd had this conversation many times before, Mariana dearly hoped she could get George to see reason. He needn't condemn himself to a lonely life, with his only relief what could be got from casual, meaningless flirtations or seductions. She couldn't entirely blame her brother for feeling as he did, whatever the consequences for her own life. He had indeed suffered because of his foot, and not just physically.

She stood behind him so she could rest her hands on his strong shoulders. "Think about it," she said in soothing accents. "I know I won't be able to persuade you to act against your will, especially at this time of night. But I beg you to consider it."

"Wise girl," George said, "All the same, you will be at home to the viscount the next time he comes."

"You can't force me!"

"No. Nor would I try to. But I know you wouldn't be so rude as to go out when a visitor is expected. Do it for mother's sake, at least. And for his. Although he may not deserve to be successful, he deserves to be heard."

THE NEXT NIGHT, GEORGE WAS OBLIGED TO MAKE HIS ONCE-A-season appearance at Almack's to reassure his mother that he was at least trying to find a suitable companion for his future life. Lewiston accompanied him up the back stairs, saw that he stood comfortably out of the way but with a good view over the guests in the ballroom, and went off in search of dance partners. Poor Harry—once on the floor, his feet refused to obey the dictates of his head, and debutantes scattered when he approached, fearing for their toes. It made no sense, though, because the marquess was a true connoisseur of music and had a remarkably acute ear. George suspected it had something to do with his lack of self-regard. In boxing terms, he did not display well. One had to come to know him before his real value could be discerned.

Once he was alone, George sighed. *The same old crowd*. At least the same types, if a few new faces intermingled. Yet without even speaking to the ladies, he knew exactly what they would say, the flirtatious manipulation of their fans, the shade of their becoming flushes. That the ever-hopeful Lewiston still found entertainment among such unpromising company was a matter of wonder to him.

George shifted to place his weight more comfortably on his good leg and repositioned his cane—the ebony one with a chased gold handle that looked as if it could be an elegant accessory rather than a necessity. Not that it fooled anyone.

Before he had time for any further reflection, Mariana's voice sailed over the ever-surging crowd of bachelors, come-outs, and duennas. "Brother dear!" she said, waving to him indelicately and threading her way through the chaperones and their charges. When she arrived at his side, she gave him an appreciative glance up and down. "You look quite the thing! Is that a new knot? The waterfall, or some such?" She did not wait for his response but said, "I must introduce you to some of my new friends."

"You mean, there are ladies here I don't already know?" He lowered his voice so as not to insult anyone nearby.

Mariana squeezed his arm, not altogether gently. "You are too cynical, Georgie. I will see you settled if it's the last thing I do!"

He cast a skeptical look in her direction. Her zeal, he knew, was an attempt to save herself the same trouble. "It's a hopeless case, as you well know! Unless they're teaching more than embroidery and bad singing in the nursery these days."

"Pity me if you must pity anyone. I swear most of the gentlemen of the *ton* have more hair than wit. I half expect their brains to rattle in their heads like dried nuts if shaken!"

George quickly turned his laugh into a cough. "A leveler! But I wish you'd stop trying to get me riveted."

"Nonsense. One of us must take up the challenge. Look, here's Lady Mack with her niece, Lucy." She lifted her chin in the direction of a matron who had just entered the ballroom in the company of a pretty young girl in pale blue figured muslin, her head crowned with a cascade of golden curls.

"She's just out of the schoolroom!" Bridlington whispered in his sister's ear.

"I prefer to call it unspoiled." Mariana gave his arm a vicious pinch. "Besides, perhaps you would be happy with someone who believed all your utterances unquestioningly and busied herself only with running a home and pushing out brats at regular intervals."

Bridlington raised his eyebrows. "I thought that's what mother hoped that you would do?"

In the time it took for them to exchange these biting remarks, the formidable duenna had made her stately way to them, carving a wide path through the company, her determined expression scattering those in her way. When she and her niece arrived before them, Bridlington extended his hand in greeting, lifting hers and bowing over it at exactly the right angle to indicate respect but not subordination. A waft of powdery scent threatened to make him sneeze, but he mastered the impulse and avoided looking at Mariana, knowing he would laugh if he did.

To his relief, Lady Mack turned her attentions to his sister. "Lady Mariana! So good of you to take an interest in dear Lucy. This is her first season, and she is quite anxious to make the best of it." Bridlington was not insensible to the veiled dig at Mariana, still no accepted offer in her second season. As she spoke, the elderly lady's several chins waggled in a way that reminded George of a jelly. Once again, it was all he could do to resist the chuckle that threatened to burst out of his throat.

Poor Lucy still hung a little behind her aunt, smiling and blushing shyly. "Come forward, girl!" Lady Mack said, a little brusquely, and all but thrust her in front of Bridlington.

"Your most obedient," Bridlington said as he greeted the girl. When he looked up from his bow, he caught her gaze fixed on his cane, and then watched as her eyes traveled down to the leg that ended in a shoe at an awkward angle to the floor. When she managed to tear her gaze away from this disconcerting sight and meet his, the maidenly pink of her cheeks bloomed into blotchy crimson. *Next she'll look sorry,* Bridlington thought. It was a progression he had become all too familiar with over the years. "I would ask to lead you out in the quadrille, but as you see, I do not care to dance." He'd found that such disconcerting frankness usually sent girls like Lucy scurrying away.

"Of-of course, My Lord," Lucy stammered. "Might I help you—"

The poor creature had said the one thing guaranteed to set George against any possibility of further acquaintance. He turned to Mariana, pretending he had not heard Lucy, and said, "There's Lewiston, making up to Miss Jameson. Her fifty-thousand would go a long way toward repairing the marquisate's damaged fortunes."

"Was it the Peninsula?" Lucy said, surprising Bridlington by addressing him directly and daring to lay a hand on his arm. "Did you receive a bullet? In a battle?" Her hopeful eyes betrayed her ignorance and inexperience.

"It was not, and I did not," said George, without offering any other explanation. Her eyes registered hurt. She lifted her chin and looked away.

George knew he'd been unpardonably rude. But the one advantage to his disability was that allowances were made. He wished they weren't, in fact. As that evening, when he wanted nothing more than to have his behavior send Lady Mack and her niece far away, and yet they remained. He feared they were discouraged, but not altogether deterred.

GEORGE WAS RIGHT, MARIANA THOUGHT AS SHE WAITED FOR her chaise the morning after the Almack's assembly. It would have been crueler not to face Bainbridge than to send him away in no doubt of her feelings—as she had done earlier that morning. She knew what she wanted and who she wanted. And although the dowager would never force her to a match she abhorred, having had a miserable marriage of her own, it was a far cry from that to approving what she would see as a truly unsuitable husband for her only daughter. Her mother, Mariana honestly believed, wanted her children to be happy—within the confines of the society she knew. Unlike the late earl, she treasured her daughter and worshiped her imperfect son.

All at once, a memory flashed into Mariana's mind, of screams echoing in the night through Lanyon House during what must have been the long vac. She was still in the nursery, a room on the third floor of the mansion, and distant sounds of discord sometimes filtered up to her there. But these had been different. She'd leapt out of bed and run to the door, only to be stopped by the nurse who would not let her go no matter how she squirmed and fought.

The next morning, her brother was confined to his room.

He had a fever, she was told, and on no account should she disturb him. He'd remained there for weeks, and when he finally emerged, he was no longer the mischievous, lively older brother she adored. He also wore a contraption of leather and steel that encased his foot. Even through his stockings, she could see the swelling, and his face had been streaked with pain.

Mariana shuddered and shook the memory away. Much had changed since then. George was now the head of the family, and respected throughout the *ton*—if accused of being a bit of a misanthrope with a tongue that could cut mercilessly.

He would not be so forever, if Mariana had anything to do with it. Finding a way to push him into the world where he belonged was a mission second only to her own desire to be allowed to follow her heart and her mind. He might satisfy his cravings with light dalliances, flirt outrageously with married women, even take an opera dancer under his protection—although to her knowledge he had not done so. But she knew he had more heart and soul than that. He deserved more. Just as she deserved a husband who would appreciate everything she had to offer, inside and out. Who didn't see her as a means to social acceptance and wealth. Who wanted a true connection. A meeting of hearts, minds, and souls.

Such a person didn't exist in the closed circle of the *ton*. She had met him, however, quite by chance. He had no rank, no fortune, no great position; only brilliance, integrity, and a warm heart. Who was this unicorn? He was Jeremy Thorne, private secretary to Prime Minister Spencer Perceval. And he was tall, handsome, witty, but most of all, incredibly smart. He approved of her ambitions and principles. Such she had learned through their secret meetings, which had started last season. Secret, but not private. She sighed.

One of the drawbacks of being in London for the season was her mother's insistence she be chaperoned when she went out into the town, no matter the reason. It was a bit of a challenge, but she'd managed to find ways to trick the young maid, Maddy, who willingly came with her to shop or visit. One of her principal subterfuges was convincing Maddy that she had no need to follow her into Hookham's library, because no one expected ladies to be accompanied by a chaperone in that staid location.

The chaise pulled up at the front steps of the mansion, and the footman handed Mariana into it, her two borrowed volumes in her hands, followed by Maddy. Although it would be an easy walk, Maddy vastly preferred riding in a handsome, crested barouche to navigating the busy flagways. Once they arrived, she suggested Maddy stroll along Bond Street while she exchanged her books. Then she nodded to the officious porter and entered the library.

As was her usual practice, Mariana ambled aimlessly at first, perusing the shelves, catalogue in hand, until she judged that no one was paying any attention to her. This was the most difficult part of the operation because, like it or not, she attracted notice wherever she went.

Thankfully, at that time of day Hookham's was not very crowded, and she soon made her way to the shelf on which she knew she would find the missive from Jeremy, having sent a note around to his lodgings in Duke Street the day before telling him to leave the document inside a copy of Fordyce's Sermons. She took down the volume and casually flipped through the pages. A single sheet of paper fluttered to the ground, and she swiftly bent to pick it up and read it.

All it bore were three words: *I am here.*

Warmth spread from her middle up into her cheeks. That meant he had managed to get away from the House and time his visit to the library so that they could meet, rather than having to simply trade letters. Keeping herself to a languid pace, she walked on to the alcove between two shelves where she knew she would find him.

Her heart always jumped a little when she caught sight of his tall, elegant form, dressed fashionably but not fussily. He reached out his hand to grasp hers and pull her a little into the shadows. They were careful not to stand too close together, in case a passing patron caught sight of them.

"Have you got what I asked?" Mariana whispered, trying hard not to respond too obviously to the melting look in his limpid dark eyes.

He reached into the inside pocket of his coat and drew out a sealed bundle of papers. "Not even the newspapers have this information yet, although there's nothing secret in it. It's just the debate about punishment for Luddite rebels."

She took the sheaf from him, their gloved hands touching momentarily and sending a tiny shock up her arm. No doubt she would find herself livid when she read how the Tory government was planning to deal with the weavers in the north, who saw their jobs being eradicated by machine-powered looms that produced an inferior product. But that would be later. For right now, she must take advantage of the few minutes to simply be in Jeremy's company.

"My Lady," Jeremy began, and stopped.

"What?" Mariana asked, wishing he would call her by her name and drop this formal nonsense.

"It's nothing," he said, and she saw the flicker of something in his eyes withdraw, a barrier go up between them.

How vexing it was! She didn't care about the difference in their stations, but he did. He'd never openly declared himself to her, and unless he did so, she could not speak. At least in this she felt constrained by the rules of propriety. Realizing that whatever he'd meant to say would remain unspoken between them, she said, "I shall read this and write to you again. I wish you didn't have to work for Perceval."

They shared a zeal for reform, and that had been what initially drew them to each other. Thus Jeremy's position with the Tory prime minister conflicted with his own beliefs. It had been too lucrative and influential for him to turn down, as he'd explained to her when they first met at an evening of cards at Lord Lister's house. His advancement would depend on impressing powerful politicians of which-ever party.

The attraction had been instant and powerful then. At least on Mariana's part. And she couldn't believe in her heart that Jeremy felt any different. Still they danced around each other, meeting out of sight and by chance, making their mutual interest in liberal politics the excuse for it all.

"I'd better get back," Jeremy said, and took her hand, pressing it and lifting it to kiss.

Even through her kid glove, Mariana could feel the warmth of his shapely lips. "Yes. Until next time," she said, reluctantly drawing her hand out of his, turning and wandering away, feeling his gaze like a ray of sunshine against her back.

She had a scheme in view that would enable them to come into closer contact, and for him to believe that an offer for her would not meet with opposition, if she could carry it off. It was bold to the point of insanity. But if she wasn't to spend her life bored and unfulfilled, now was the time to take a chance.

Her thoughts were so disordered after their meeting that she completely forgot to change her books. Maddy, too busy gazing at the parade of pinks and elegantly dressed ladies, did not appear to notice.

CHAPTER 4

*A*lmost all thoughts of her disquieting first hour in London were soon driven out of Augusta's head by constant activity. After a long, tiring few days bent over her needle, she found herself unable to think of anything except the allure of escaping into the pages of a good book—something to elevate her mind above gowns and fripperies and the latest gossip of the *ton*, important though all that that was for her ambitions in the world of fashion.

It was hardly surprising, then, that instead of keeping her mind focused resolutely forward, she couldn't help obsessing about the events of the past year or so which had brought her to this place. When she recollected sweet scenes with James —scenes that, after more than a year since she'd last seen him and ten months since he'd died were fading from her memory—she tried to push them aside. Sometimes, though, the exquisite pain of recalling the way he looked at her, how handsome he had been in his regimentals, the brief moments they'd shared before he had to go to fight in the Peninsula proved too strong, and she went over it all again.

Too often, though, an altogether less pleasant scene

forced itself into her imagination. It was the one that had immediately precipitated her flight from her aunt's house. And because it involved someone whose name had been inadvertently thrust into her mind almost as soon as she'd arrived in London, she had little hope of being able to forget it.

She'd been out on the moor on a brisk spring day, gathering wildflowers and thinking about what she could do to take charge of her future and somehow release herself from her aunt's cloying protection. She entered through the door to the garden and was scraping the mud off her shoes, preparing to go to her room and lose herself in reading a book before dinner, or making a sketch of a gown she'd conceived on her walk, when her aunt's brisk step approached from the direction of the parlor.

"Augusta! Augusta! Where are you?" She came down the back corridor with the determination of a rat terrier on the scent. "Oh! There you are! Your shoes, Augusta, your shoes!"

Augusta looked down at her feet. "Yes?"

"And your hair! Oh, I suppose it will have to do. You're wanted in the parlor."

With no explanation, she whirled around and strode away, only throwing over her shoulder a quick exhortation for Augusta to follow her immediately.

Augusta found her aunt's commanding ways annoying in the extreme, but knew it would be fruitless to resist, and so she went after her—at a much slower pace.

When she arrived in the best parlor expecting she knew not what, she stopped before taking more than three steps into it. A slender, foppish man stood in the center looking around him through his quizzing glass as though what he saw did not please him at all.

Aunt Phyllis said, "Mister Grantley, Sir, allow me to

present my niece, Augusta Hastings, daughter of the late Sir Alastair Hastings of Crossley Grange. An old family—"

"Enough," the man said in a lazy drawl, accompanying his words with a dismissive wave. "I know all that." He again lifted his quizzing glass to his eye and peered at Augusta from top to toe. "I suppose," he said, as though he were examining something to purchase, something that he found not quite up to the mark, "she would do."

"I beg your pardon," Augusta said, bristling, "I have not the pleasure of your acquaintance, Sir." She lifted her chin and stared straight into the heavy-lidded eyes that showed evidence of dissipation in their slightly red rims.

"Grantley, as your aunt says. My father is Hastings. I need a wife."

"Sir!" Augusta said, her temper flaring. She recognized the disreputable younger son of the Earl of Hastings, her aunt's near neighbor, whom she had once seen on a public day. She knew a little about his circumstances, that he was deeply in debt and needed to marry in order to gain access to a fortune he'd been left by a distant uncle. But could he be suggesting that she should marry him? Preposterous! Once she was certain she could speak without spewing venom, she said, "I wish you all good fortune in finding this wife," and curtsied, intending to leave the room as quickly as she'd entered it.

"You can hardly object to my fortune," said that same lazy voice. "I understand your choices are—shall we say, limited?"

Augusta turned a shocked gaze to her aunt. "What exactly is the meaning of this, Aunt?"

Lady Bagley minced over to Augusta, a false smile on her face and said, "You see, against all the odds I've found you an eligible match! It's so much more than you could ever have hoped for. You'd be an influential lady in the county, and be able to afford all the elegancies of life. The contract has already been drawn up, and the settlement is most generous."

Fury welled up in every bit of Augusta's body, but she did not want to unleash it in front of a stranger. "Mr. Grantley, I beg you would excuse us. My aunt and I have a great deal to talk about."

He could not have misinterpreted her words, and with a facetious little bow and a mirthless smile, he turned and went out of the parlor. Augusta waited until she heard the carriage drive away before turning to her aunt and screaming, "What have you done!"

That had been the beginning of the worst twenty-four hours of her life. Worse than learning of James's death from a servant at the breakfast table many months before. Worse than realizing after her father's death that his estate was so encumbered by debt that she had no choice but to sell it—leaving her with nothing after the debts were paid—and move to her aunt's house.

Having long had an idle dream of going to London to try her skill and imagination in the world of high fashion, once she was apprised of her aunt's machinations, Augusta put her hazy plan into action as fast as she could. She forged a letter from Lady Westleigh to a modiste she'd once heard her mention and sent it express, then ran away the very next day, taking only what she could carry—including the precious Hookham's card.

But that card remained untried in her reticule. Because Madame kept the seamstresses fairly chained to their worktables from early in the morning until dinner time, a walk to Hookham's hadn't yet been possible. Even if it were, she could hardly imagine having any quiet time for reading. The attic rooms she shared with the four other seamstresses were in constant chaos. Barely permitted to talk in the workroom, they made up for it by twittering and tattling in the hour or two after dinner until everyone fell into an exhausted sleep.

The chatter, which might have been aggravating, Augusta

soon realized contained potentially important information about the *ton*. It took only a couple of nights for her to commit to memory such details as the identities of all the patronesses of Almack's and the rules governing that most exclusive of enclaves; the names and titles of those who brought their business to Madame Noelle's and which families were already in town and which would come soon; who was in her first season and who in her third; which peer was hanging out for a rich wife and which heiress had the biggest fortune. Along with her workmates, she eagerly perused the Post and the Gazette for social notices and the *Mirror of Fashion* and other journals for anything that could give a clue as to what styles would soon be à la mode.

But she also found herself scanning the papers for any mention of the one *ton*-ish name she could associate with a face: the Earl of Bridlington. She felt a bit disloyal to James for having this interest. Not that she had any expectations, or desired to ever see Bridlington again. Her purpose in coming to London had nothing to do with finding a husband—even supposing the earl were eligible and interested. He intrigued her a little, that was all. He had been kind and obliging—but at the same time dismissive. He said he had a sister, and that she was a customer of Madame Noelle. Augusta therefore persuaded herself that her interest was purely businesslike, that it was with the goal of gleaning yet more information about a fashionable come-out. She did not mention the earl's name to Pauline and Molly, however. She had no desire to recount the story of her ignominious arrival in London. They knew as much of it as they needed to, and Augusta hoped that the memory of her standing before them covered in muck was fading fast.

ON AUGUSTA'S THIRD MORNING AT THE ATELIER, AS THE seamstresses hastily dressed, they took up the subject of one of Madame Noelle's best customers, continuing from the night before as if there hadn't been hours of sleep in between. This customer was the Lady Mariana. She was beautiful and wealthy and despite a plethora of eligible offers, still unclaimed in her second season. From their vivid descriptions of her, Augusta guessed that this very lady must have been the striking witness to her undignified arrival her first day, and for some reason she could not guess, she was sorry for it.

"She torments all the most eligible bachelors!" Molly said as she braced herself while Bernadette tightened her stays.

Not to be outdone, Bernadette piped up, "They call her bewitching, but I think she's simply a witch, and puts some potion in their punch to make them besotted with her—just so she can disappoint them."

Lady Mariana, by their description, sounded a little like someone she would respect. "Surely she has a right to choose her future husband. Perhaps none of the gentlemen is worthy of her?"

A cacophony of "Outrageous!" "Of course not!" "You wouldn't think it!" erupted until Pauline shushed them all and spoke. "It's true she's the daughter of an earl, and her brother has inherited the title, but that don't make her better than every beau in the ton! There's plenty higher. There's dukes and marquesses, and earls as date back to the Conqueror. She's a prime catch sure enough, but it's her second season already. If she don't settle soon, she'll end an old maid."

Augusta's curiosity was piqued. If the lady had the means and the beauty to attract an eligible husband yet resisted accepting anyone, what could her motives be? Did she have a rebellious nature and simply wish to thwart the hopes of her family? Or was there truly no one amongst her acquaintance who met with her approbation?

"She's got a fitting today," said Molly, her eyes betraying less scorn than admiration. "Pauline'll tell us what she chooses and where she's planning to wear it. She's already had three new silk gowns in different shades, and I believe Madame ordered the silver lace specially for her next ball gown."

By now they'd tumbled down the stairs and settled into their stations at the worktables. Pauline went through to the showroom to take up her role as assistant. The murmurs of Madame's discussion with Pauline and the other girl regarding customers filtered into the back room. Augusta usually ignored them and lavished all her attention on her needle. But that morning, something intruded most startlingly on her ears.

"We have Lady Mariana Lanyon this morning. She wants a dress for Almack's Wednesday. Something completely new, she says. A bit of foreign lace, a ruffle or two and a belt with a jeweled buckle ought to be sufficient."

What did she say? Augusta's ears tingled to attention.

Pauline said, "Yes, Madame. But wasn't she here not long ago?" Madame did not answer, and so she continued, "Shall I fetch the new lustring? The color would be very fetching on Lady Mariana."

Could it be? Augusta gripped her needle and held her breath the moment she heard the name *Lanyon* coupled with *Lady Mariana.* That surname had been seared on her memory ever since her very first day in London. And Lady Mariana had only minutes ago been the topic of conversation. Could she be of the same family as the earl? He had mentioned a sister, and that he knew this modiste's establishment quite well. Please God let her never encounter the famous Lady Mariana! Yet she couldn't help thinking back to her first day there and trying to recall if the lady she'd seen then looked at all like the earl, whether her eyes also danced, and whether her smile could disarm her potential suitors the way Lord Bridlington's had unsettled her, quite against her will.

Her mind was occupied with these disturbing thoughts until it was rudely interrupted by a fracas emanating from the showroom.

"How dare you! I should take you down to Bow Street to be clapped in irons! Thief!"

All the others looked up, eyes round. What thief had breached the velvet confines of the showroom, Augusta wondered? And what could he have tried to steal?

But there was no intruder. Madame's shoes tapped back and forth across the floor as she cursed and railed against one of the fitting assistants. Augusta couldn't tell which one, but prayed that it wasn't Pauline.

"Out! Out! And I shall not write you a character. No other modiste will employ you, mark my words."

"But Madame!" cried a tearful voice—not Pauline's, but the other assistant who arrived each day from east London and was unknown to her, Augusta noted with relief—"How shall I buy my mother's medicine? You didn't want it, you said so!"

"Ungrateful wretch! So you took that as an invitation to steal, did you? Now leave at once before I send for the constable."

Sobs faded away as the door to the street opened and slammed shut. No use wondering what the girl was accused of stealing. Pauline would enlighten them later.

But the day's surprises were not at an end. The door into the workroom burst open, and Madame stood like an obsidian pillar in it, eyes flashing and lips pressed in a thin line. She surveyed each one of the seamstresses in turn, stopping to examine Augusta more closely. "You! What's your name again?"

"Augusta Hastings, Ma'am." Augusta stood and lifted her chin, ignoring a queer feeling in the pit of her stomach.

"Miss Hastings, kindly put down your work and attend me in the fitting room." She swiveled around on her heel, slammed the door behind her, and left the seamstresses staring at each other.

"Well!" said Miss Carp. "Don't sit there like a lump. Get to it girl! I collect it's yer fine ways that's done it."

In a daze, Augusta entered the showroom for the second time since she'd come to London, this time by invitation. Could this mark the beginning of her ascension from the workroom to having some influence on design?

"Don't stand there gawking!" Madame said. "I suppose you'll have to do. Put on this apron."

She tossed a starched white pinny to Augusta, who caught it with one hand and awkwardly removed her gray sewing room apron with the other. Pauline scurried to her side, took the discarded apron from her and threw it behind a small chest of drawers before taking the opportunity to murmur quickly in her ear, "Just do as I do, you'll be fine. And put some pins in your bib." She jerked her head toward a pretty porcelain dish that held a quantity of straight steel pins. Augusta did as she said.

Before she'd worked ten of the pins into the stiff fabric of her apron, the bells that signaled the arrival of a customer tinkled, and Madame glided out of the room and into the vestibule.

"My Lady! How delightful to see you again so soon!"

While Madame continued her obsequious greetings, Pauline said so quickly Augusta could hardly follow her, "Don't look at her, don't say anything, just do. You should disappear. It all happens by magic, y'know."

Augusta caught the sardonic jest in Pauline's voice and was hard put not to let a nervous giggle burble up.

A moment later, Lady Mariana Lanyon strode into the showroom and took her place on the pedestal as if she knew she belonged there. But remarkably, she didn't preen at all, never glancing in a mirror or touching her hair to make sure it had stayed in place when she removed her elegant poke bonnet.

And it took only a moment for Augusta to recognize her. With a sinking heart, she realized Lady Mariana had not only seen her covered in mud, but was definitely Bridlington's sister. Had to be. The same slightly mocking expression and glittering eyes, although hers were a deep blue rather than a clear gray. She had ample opportunity to study those eyes because, to her surprise, rather than examining the luxurious wares draped on chairs and wrapped around columns, Lady Mariana turned her attention first to Pauline and then to Augusta, smiling and looking back and forth between them as Madame chattered on about the newest gowns and trims and what would My Lady want? How could she fulfill her merest whim?

"Sorry, what were you saying?" Lady Mariana said, glancing over her shoulder at Madame's simpering face. And then, as if she knew without having to have it repeated, she said, "Oh! Just another ball gown, if you please. My brother tells me I've worn my others too often, and need to lead the way in fashion, especially since it's my second season. You know, *plus ça change...*"

Without thinking, Augusta picked up Lady Mariana's thread and said, *"Plus c'est la même chose,"* while she continued to stick pins in her apron. She turned and took up her position against the wall next to Pauline until such time as she was needed to drape some fabric or pin a flounce, and was met by the searching gaze of the most eligible heiress of the season. *Yes,* she thought, *the very same eyes,* and then felt the heat of a blush rise up her neck and into her cheeks. She instantly looked down at the floor, but not before seeing Lady Mariana lift one eyebrow ever so slightly and purse her lips to suppress a smile.

As Madame snapped her fingers at Augusta and Pauline to bring her lengths of fabric and yards of trimming to drape over Lady Mariana's supple body, Augusta couldn't help feeling as if what her employer was suggesting for this tall, elegant lady wouldn't make the most of her natural attributes. The color she insisted was all the fashion—Pomona green—would not flatter Lady Mariana's pink-toned complexion, deep blue eyes, and dark hair with auburn lights. Augusta walked over to where a length of soft violet gauze lay tossed over a marble bust, lifted it and said, "Madame, if I might suggest—"

"Augusta, you are new to this position, and so I will overlook your impudence in this one instance," Madame said, turning her steely gaze on Augusta. "It is no part of your job to suggest anything."

Augusta clamped her lips shut and re-draped the gauze. She glanced up quickly and met Lady Mariana's wide eyes and it was all she could do to prevent herself from laughing aloud.

THE REST OF THE DAY PASSED IN A HAZE. AUGUSTA'S PEACE HAD been seriously disturbed in her new life. First had been Bridlington and his mention of Grantley. Now Lady Mariana, Bridlington's sister, and her apparent interest in her. What could it mean?

Yet by far the most disheartening part of a day that had started out with the promise that she might be on her way to climbing to a higher position than menial seamstress was Madame's brutal shutdown of her attempt to offer an opinion about fashion. Although she had already realized that the seamstresses were little more than beasts of labor to the modiste, she had hoped that Madame would be grateful for someone who could do more than pin and stitch. Clearly, she had been mistaken. What she had seen as a promising future, what she had congratulated herself on having been a fortuitous choice, suddenly seemed less so.

Toward the end of the day, Pauline took Augusta aside after Madame retired to her office behind the showroom and said, "Now, Gussie, I think it's time you told me why you're here. You don't gammon me. Your work's fine—no question o' that—but you ain't one of us. And don't come off telling me it's just that you come from the country and don't know London ways. What's brought you here like this? You get in trouble with your beau?"

At first, Augusta didn't understand what Pauline was implying. When she did, she opened her eyes wide and formed an "o" with her mouth, just managing to stop herself protesting in the strongest terms. Pauline put her finger to her lips, and Augusta swallowed down her retort. "Certainly not," she whispered instead.

"But still. It's something, innit. You with yer book learnin' and gentle ways—no doubt Madame will see she can turn 'em to account and raise the tone here. But she didn't know that about you when you come, I c'lect. Mind you, it was none too smart to think Madame would want you to stick your nose into her business like you did!"

"I see that now," Augusta said with a shake of her head. "As to the rest, it's a long story, and there's not time to tell it now." She also wasn't certain how much she wanted to confess to Pauline—or anyone.

But Pauline wasn't put off. "Let's you and me take a walk in the park for a few minutes. There's time before dinner."

Augusta wanted to demur, but the idea of fresh air—at least, as fresh as one could get in London—appealed to her, and so she let Pauline lead her out the door and down Curzon Street in the direction of the park.

"Because you're pretty, you know," Pauline said once they were wandering on a foot path, picking up right where she left off. "Not that you make much of it. But I see gents lookin' at you when you don't notice."

"Doubtless they're looking at you," Augusta said, threading her arm through Pauline's. Her fellow seamstress's pert face and bright hazel eyes held more allure than they ought to, Augusta thought, and privately believed it would not be many months before Pauline found herself carried off by some worthy artisan or shopkeeper.

"Na, they don't take my fancy. I've got my own beau, though we don't see each other much."

Augusta welcomed this change in topic, and asked Pauline to tell her more about him. It seemed he was a shoe-maker's apprentice, who was in his final year and would soon be able to work in his own right. "He's got 'is eye on a place in Cornhill, if he can manage it. Once he's got it going, we can be married."

"Will you continue with Madame Noelle?" Augusta asked.

Pauline stopped and turned to her, eyes wide. "Course not! My Jimmy'll support the family, he will. Leastways, it don't make no sense for me to continue in that miserable place."

Augusta smiled and let the matter drop. She would be sorry not to have Pauline in the workshop. Although the girl was minimally educated, it hadn't taken long for Augusta to perceive that she had a quick mind and wits to match. How dull it would be without her. But perhaps she herself would not have to remain in the workshop for long.

"One thing, that minds me of," Pauline continued, "See, Jimmy has nights off Saturdays, and it's been a bit since I've been able to go out with him. Just to walk about, although once he saved and took me to Astley's."

Augusta wondered where this turn in the conversation was headed. She didn't have long to wait.

"Madame, she don't like us going out at night, 'cept for emergencies. And then, she locks the door at ten o'clock. So I been thinkin' I could tell her I have to go see me mum, who's sick with something, and take care of her overnight. Only, I'm not sure she'd believe me. If I was to rush off, sudden like, and you could tell her I got a message I had to go, then maybe she'd take your word."

It seemed a lot of trouble to go to, but Augusta had a tender spot for those whose love faced obstacles of any kind. "Of course I can help you. You just tell me what to say."

Pauline squeezed her arm. "I knew you was a right one! Happen I can do something like that for you one day. You're so pretty, I don't doubt but what you'll have someone sweet on you in no time, if you don't already. Is that why yer here? Your beau come to London?"

This was a line of inquiry Augusta had no intention of permitting. "Far from it!" she said, with complete honesty, and added a little more invented detail to her story of penury and grief over the loss of her parents, her lack of fortune, and no relations willing to take her in.

Hookham's, she thought. Her own fanciful tale brought to mind the pleasure she took in reading. All she needed was a good book. That would set her to rights, adjust her outlook. Perhaps give her some inspiration. Or at least, a few hours of escape, now that she realized her initial hopes for advancement had been premature.

CHAPTER 5

A fortuitous result of Augusta's new role in the showroom at Madame Noelle's was that, in addition to the pinning and draping, Madame sent her on errands to the silk warehouse and the linen drapers, and to the different haberdashers that sold trimmings and notions. While Madame gave detailed instructions as to what she wanted her to procure, Augusta relished the opportunity to see the raw materials for herself and imagine how she would use them in her own creations.

Thus she found herself in a crush of customers at Harding & Howell, where she had to compete for attention with ladies purchasing single gown lengths to make up themselves. She waited for one of the attendants to finish with a matron who kept insisting that a rose-pink satin would be the very thing for her ball dress when he tactfully suggested a less girlish camelopard. Augusta had to admire his obvious taste and knowledge. In the end, the lady had her way, and Augusta exchanged a wry look with the attendant as he turned to cut the necessary yardage.

"How may I be of service to you, Ma'am?" he said when

the lady moved her bulky form from taking up most of the available space at his counter.

Augusta took Madame's list out of her reticule and handed it to him.

"Ah…you are new at Madame's establishment?" He raised his eyebrows along with his voice.

"Yes. Only a few days since."

He laid out some of the fabrics for her to look at. She cast a critical eye over them and said, "Does Madame not require better cloth than this?" She pointed out a catch in the puce satin, which was very thin.

He smiled at her. "What was I thinking? Of course. This would be more suitable to Madame's needs," he said, reaching for an altogether finer bolt of fabric.

Had he been trying to sabotage her, Augusta wondered? Or cheat Madame Noelle? She looked directly into his eyes which, rather than being evasive, stared back frankly with a hint of merriment in them.

"You know your material, Miss…"

"Hastings. Augusta Hastings," she said, guessing that it would be a good thing to be known for her discernment so they didn't try to pass off inferior goods on her. "And you are Mister…"

"Gordon, Miss Hastings." He gave her a small nod. "I'd give you a week."

Augusta looked up at him in surprise. "A week? For what?"

"That's how long Madame's assistants normally last, with the exception of the redoubtable Pauline, and there's an old lady there, too."

She laughed, remembering the abrupt departure of her predecessor, and said, "You mean Miss Carp. I look upon this position as a means to an end. I intend to be a modiste myself one day."

He shook his head. "I hope you have a private income. She won't pay you enough to save for as much as a new hat. But judging by your manner, I assume perhaps you do."

She thought this was none of his business, but his words disturbed her, both because he could so easily guess her station in life, and because, if there was no way to advance while in Madame's employ, her dream might be even farther away than she thought. She decided to ignore his comment. "We'll have twenty yards of each shade of blue satin, and twelve each of the sarsenet and the gauze. Put them on Madame's account. When will they be delivered?"

Instead of answering her, Gordon said, "Beg pardon, Ma'am. I hope I didn't offend. I hear a great deal about what goes on in the dressmaker's establishments in London, and would be more than willing to keep you informed if I happen to hear of a better position."

He certainly had a nerve. "I've been here less than a week. I think I need to glean what I can from Madame Noelle before I look for another situation." Besides, Augusta thought, a different dressmaker would not be patronized by Lady Mariana.

Why had she thought of that? What possible importance could that have to her?

She flashed a sympathetic smile at Mr. Gordon and turned to leave, noting that she had just enough time to get to Hookham's at last if she hurried, and her absence would not be noted since she'd gone out on Madame's business. As she walked away, she passed another young gentleman standing near the counter—but not apparently looking to purchase anything—and caught a glance between that gentleman and Mr. Gordon. They both smiled shyly, as in affection. Could they be brothers? She wondered. They didn't look at all alike.

Augusta made her way as quickly as she could in the

direction of Bond Street, which meant a brisk walk around St. James's Square and then north on Duke Street before reaching Piccadilly. All she had in her mind was that at last she would be able to make use of her father's extravagant first-class subscription. At a borrowing fee of a shilling for each book, Augusta figured she could afford to take out two that day. Ironically, her father had never used the subscription for himself. Why he even subscribed, she didn't know. He surely had plenty of books of his own, although not the newest ones. Still, she believed her father would have been gratified to know this one extravagant folly of his would end up benefiting his daughter, that although she'd rolled the dice in favor of fashion, the life of her mind would not be forgot.

While she was in the warehouse, the weather had turned and a light mist had begun to fall. Augusta pulled her woolen shawl tightly around her and wished she'd worn a more protective hat than her cotton-covered poke bonnet trimmed with a scrap of blue ribbon that even Madame could not justify selling to the girls. She quickened her pace, hoping the rain would not become more persistent.

Crossing Piccadilly, she couldn't help remembering her first day in London, when Lord Bridlington took her up in his curricle. She had been deeply mortified, but he had been kind enough not to make her feel it too keenly. So her mind was occupied and she didn't notice an urchin nip out of the shadow of a doorway and grab her reticule—breaking the ribbon that held it to her wrist—and dash off in the opposite direction to where she was headed.

"Stop!" she yelled, and not paying any attention to her dignity tore after the boy, pumping her arms and yelling "Stop! Thief!" She needed that bag! It not only contained what little money she had, but also the Hookham's subscription voucher. She dodged pedestrians, interpolating *pardon me* and *so sorry* with every near collision in her pursuit of the rascal, who scampered like a rabbit through the throngs of people. She had almost caught up to him and was near the end of her breath when a horse cantered past her from behind. The rider pulled the reins up and wheeled his mount, placing the animal in the way of the boy, who had looked back over his shoulder at the sound of Augusta's pounding feet.

She stopped herself just in time to see the rider reach down, grab the boy by his collar and lift him right off the ground. The boy's arms and feet flailed wildly and his eyes were round and terrified.

"I'll just take that," the gentleman said, relieving him of Augusta's reticule, then dropping him unceremoniously to the ground. "Now off with you, or I'll call the constable!" the man growled, but the boy had already taken off toward an alley between two buildings as fast as his feet could carry him.

By this time gasping, Augusta lifted her eyes to meet those of her rescuer. Gray, cool, amused. Bridlington. She tried to curtsy to him, but her knees were shaking, and she was almost too breathless to speak. "I th-thank you, My Lord," she managed to squeak out.

"I believe this belongs to you, Ma'am?" He dangled the drawstring bag toward her. "Miss Hastings! You do get yourself into scrapes. I was quite impressed with your speed, I must say."

Augusta wished the cobbles beneath her feet would open so she could drop through them to obscurity. Bridlington was struggling not to laugh, which seemed to her a bit unkind. With as much self-possession as she could muster, she walked sedately up to him and reached for her reticule. One glimpse of the merriment in his eyes turned her self-consciousness into self-deprecation. "All right, I'll allow that I was a bit carried away," she said, "yet it also seems you do enjoy playing the knight in shining armor." She took her bag out of his hands and tied the torn ribbon so she could loop it over her wrist again. "But I think I would have reached the thief only a moment later, so your efforts on my behalf were not necessary."

He uttered a bark of laughter and looked as though he wanted to say something else to continue their repartee. But instead, he touched his whip to his hat brim and said, "Your servant, Ma'am," then turned his horse away from her and trotted back in the direction from which he'd come.

Well! Clearly he was too high in the instep to bother himself about a lowly seamstress. Why, then, had he gone to so much trouble to reclaim her reticule? Come to that, she surely didn't expect any other courtesy from him beyond the return of her stolen property. So why had she felt the need to answer him with such raillery?

She squared her shoulders. It did not matter what Lord Bridlington thought, although Augusta raised a self-conscious hand to her hair to see if it had been disarranged by her mad dash after the young thief, and discovered to her dismay that a long curl had loosed itself from its pins.

THE SIGHT OF THAT LADY TEARING AT FULL SPEED ALONG Piccadilly, heedless of stares and with no concern for the dignity of her person, was something George would remember for a long time. When she came to an abrupt halt a few feet away from him, her cheeks were rosy with exertion and her eyes flashed with outrage. He fancied he could see gold lights burning in the midst of the brown, and one soft curl of her hair had come loose from under her bonnet and lay becomingly over her shoulder. It was her slightly parted lips as she took in great gulps of air that most drew his attention, however. Quite unbidden, the idea of kissing those lips flooded over him so powerfully that he took refuge in teasing.

And she rose so delightfully to his teasing. He wished he could improve his acquaintance with the lady.

Then again, perhaps not. What had she said? He was a knight in shining armor? What knight needed a cane and walked with a decided limp! Better to leave her with an imprecise image in her mind.

In any case, the timing of this second encounter was not conducive to further discourse. His mind had been much occupied by a circumstance he had only minutes before been made aware of, and he was on his way from Brooks's in the greatest haste to stable his horse back at Lanyon House and hire a hack to take him to Soho. As a result of this, once again he had failed to accord Miss Hastings the courtesy she might have expected.

He had no more time to consider, though, because he had arrived at the discreet door of Madame Agatha's Corinth, had tapped out the appropriate knock that would alert her it was he, and was being ushered into the bordello's plush parlor by a dour liveried porter.

Moments later, a waft of strong violet scent announced the arrival of Madame Agatha herself, who emerged—supported as always by a single crutch—through the dusty velvet curtain that separated the two halves of the large parlor. Underneath her silk taffeta skirt, George knew, was an elaborately carved wooden leg strapped to the stump just below her left knee.

She stretched out her right hand to take George's. "M'Lord!" she said. "I knew I could depend on you, young Georgie!"

Agatha was one of the few people in the world George

suffered to use his childhood name. "You required me urgently, you said. How may I be of service?"

Agatha lowered her voice. "It's Hortense," she said. "She's had her brat, and now she's threatening all sorts of trouble over it. Says she'll expose the father, who—she claims—is well blunted enough to pay fer its keep."

"A boy?"

"A fine, healthy lad, and no mistake."

"Well, at least we can be grateful for that." George's shoulders relaxed, and he took the seat offered him by Agatha, resting his cane against the cushion. "What do you want me to do?"

She cocked her head on the side and with a shrewd light in her eyes said, "I know you got an interest in this brat. Can you see he's cared for?"

George frowned. "He's not my responsibility. However, it may be that I can make some arrangement. Are mother and child safe?"

"For now. But I can't keep 'em here above a se'nnight. Nothing worse for business than babies yowling."

"Heaven forbid we men are reminded that our actions can have consequences!" There was a bitter edge to his laugh. "I'll take care of that matter and let you know what I've arranged. Your note mentioned that there was something else, as well. Another unfortunate?"

Madame Agatha reached into the cleft between her ample breasts and drew out a folded—and somewhat sweat stained —letter. "Youngest of eight. Been surviving on scraps, poor mite. You'd think he was no more'n five years old, but from what I can make out of what he says he's really ten. Hare lip. It's a miracle he's survived this long. Saw him rooting around in the rubbish. Mum's deep into the blue ruin, and there's another on the way." She shook her head and tsk'd, handing him the folded paper.

George opened it and glanced at it before saying, "I'll go there tomorrow and see if I can remove him to Marylebone."

Mademoiselle Agatha gazed at George with affection. "You can't save every poor creature in St. Giles, M'lord."

"No," George said. "But I can at least try to help the ones you find for me. It's hard enough to survive in poverty when you have the unfettered use of your body."

That the abbess thought he was out of his wits to exert himself in this way George well knew. They had a long-standing friendship that had begun when his Eton "friends" decided it would be great fun to have him initiated into the mysteries of sex by a lightskirt who was similarly disabled to him. After getting him thoroughly bosky they led him to a dingy bagnio where a whore by the name of Maggie scraped together the meagerest existence because, although decent looking enough, her physical deformity disgusted the higher-toned patrons. George had quickly sobered up when he realized what his friends intended and, instead of merely satiating himself in Maggie's capable arms, he ended up talking to her about her affliction and how it affected her.

That had been the first time in George's life that he had truly felt himself fortunate. No expense had been spared to try to fix his clubfoot, whatever his father's twisted reasons and however painful. And when nothing worked, he had special boots and shoes made that—although they did not eliminate his difficulty walking—made it considerably easier for him to get around in the world. And instead of bulky crutches, he had a selection of the finest ebony and Malacca canes to lend distinction to his affliction.

No poor child born without full use of all his limbs had a hope of doing more with his life than begging in the street, or ending up in a brothel.

Bridlington visited Maggie often after that when he was in London. Not to satisfy his carnal desires, but, through her, to help other poor disabled children. The illusion of his patronage increased the fortunes of the house, Maggie became Madame Agatha, and she worked with George in secret to find and help children in the poorest parts of London.

After a glass of Agatha's excellent Madeira, George left a purse full of sovereigns with her along with instructions to find a nursemaid for the newborn. He didn't relish the letter he must write to the babe's father and knew that in all likelihood it would be his own resources that would support the infant in the care of some worthy childless couple.

He promised to return the next day to fetch the older boy and see what could be done for him.

HER COMPOSURE RECLAIMED, AUGUSTA RESUMED HER BRISK pace for the final short distance to Hookham's. The light rain had persisted, and in addition to being a bit disheveled she was a little damp by the time she reached the library. A liveried porter stood and nodded to the patrons who arrived in a steady stream both to escape the unpleasant weather and to peruse the fine collection of books and journals within. Augusta's heart pounded in anticipation—at the same time as a tiny spasm of sadness caught at her throat. How her father would have loved to be there!

After brushing droplets of water off the shoulders of her brown serge pelisse and fishing the subscription card out of her reticule, Augusta took a deep breath and approached the door. She smiled as she showed her card to the middle-aged porter, who clearly enjoyed his importance as gatekeeper. As she drew near, the wear on his coat showed plainly, and Augusta's seamstress's eye noted that a bit of silver braid had come unfastened from his shoulder. This detail distracted her for a moment, so she didn't immediately realize that, far from allowing her to enter, the porter was telling her to go away.

"Your name is not Sir Alastair Hastings, I presume?" He lifted his chin and peered down at her from over his bulbous nose.

"Yes, I mean no, of course not," she said, a frisson of embarrassment traveling down to her fingers, which now trembled. "He was my father."

"I am afraid the subscriptions may not be transferred to another person," he said and handed her back her card, looking up at the patron just behind her. "Your father may select volumes and share them with you."

She couldn't believe it. Had she heard him correctly? Surely they wouldn't deny her entrance! It simply wasn't right. Recovering a little from her confusion and disappointment, she stood her ground and said, "My father purchased this voucher only weeks before he died. It entitles the bearer to gain entry to the library and borrow books for an entire year. The bearer! And I now bear this card in my hand. He bequeathed it to me that I might continue to read improving texts while I was in London." She struggled to maintain her calm.

"Please, Miss, kindly remove yourself so that others may pass by," the porter said, his voice icy.

"I don't think you understand," Augusta said, speaking a little more loudly and taking a step toward him, her hackles well and truly up. "My father's membership here should be honored, since he has not had—indeed, could not have had due to his illness and death—his entire year." To her shame, her voice quavered at the end and she felt the sting of tears behind her eyes.

"And the card would certainly be honored were he to

present himself instead of you. How do I know you didn't steal it or find it discarded somewhere?"

The man was infuriating!

"Potter, what seems to be the difficulty?" said a woman among the patrons grouped behind her.

Augusta turned and, to her immense surprise, there stood Lady Mariana, arrayed in a stunning day dress of Indian muslin, holding an umbrella up to protect the chip straw bonnet perched becomingly on her head.

"It's this young miss here, My Lady," said the porter, tipping up his hat and tilting his head in her direction.

Lady Mariana then looked at Augusta and recognition flickered in her eyes. "Why, Potter, this young lady is a friend of mine! Surely you can let her inside. I see she has a card."

"Yes, My Lady, but it is not hers. She claims it is her father's. This Sir Alastair Hastings."

Augusta wanted to sink into the ground. Now Lady Mariana had heard her father's name, and would know something about her that she wished to keep hidden. No use fretting about it now. She looked steadily into Lady Mariana's eyes and said, "My father is deceased, My Lady, and I wish to use the rest of his subscription, since he is obviously unable to!" She dipped the smallest curtsy, her indignation at her treatment overwhelming any reticence she might have felt at that moment in addressing someone who was not only far above her on the social ladder but who was a valued patroness of Madame Noelle's establishment.

"Oh Potter, don't be so fastidious!" Lady Mariana stepped forward, and to Augusta's immense surprise, threaded her arm through hers and drew her through the door and into the library. "If there is any trouble with the librarians, refer them to me," Lady Mariana said over her shoulder to the stunned porter.

Lady Mariana's presence acted like a magic elixir on

everyone in the library. Smiles came to previously sour faces, curtsies and bows followed them in waves. The other patrons—almost all of whom belonged to the more leisured classes—glanced with some curiosity at Augusta in her drab clothing being guided around by her fashionably attired escort, and then returned to their perusal of the shelves. Perhaps they thought she was a maid, or a paid companion. But Augusta saw no others in the room who might have been described as such.

"What good fortune to meet you here, Miss—Hastings, I collect? And you are from..."

"Yes," Augusta said. "Augusta Hastings, lately of Crossley Grange near Bideford, in Devonshire." As soon as she uttered these words, she regretted them. It made her old home sound so much grander than it was and as if she was trying to puff off her consequence—which was the opposite of what she intended.

A flicker of amusement passed through Lady Mariana's eyes. "Ah yes, I believe we met when I was with my brother for a hunting party in Leicestershire."

This nearly brought a laugh to Augusta's lips, since the idea of herself being part of the hunting set was patently ridiculous. She had an image of the sturdy cob, good only for trekking around the moors and galloping on the beaches, lumbering along behind blood cattle worth hundreds of guineas. Struggling to control her mirth, she said, "Yes, My Lady," and exchanged a glance with Lady Mariana that assured her the joke was shared.

In a neat redirection of their conversation, Lady Mariana said, "What is your taste in books? Do you favor novels? Or are you a devotee of Keats?"

"I like to read history, and biographies of great men. Some novels. I'm afraid I'm not very fond of poetry, but I do love the classics—Aristophanes is a particular favorite. "

At this, Lady Mariana cast a surprised look in her direction. "I was unaware of any translations from the Greek into English."

Realizing her accidental slip in revealing her excess of education, Augusta blushed and stammered out, "I don't—there aren't—"

Lady Mariana laid a hand on her arm and lowered her voice. "Please don't be anxious. Your secret is safe with me. Or perhaps I should say *secrets.*" A twinkle of amusement enlivened the lady's eyes. "I shall show you where you may find your dull histories and other improving volumes, although if you know the titles you might first peruse the catalogue to be certain they are here. For myself, I come for no other purpose than to borrow the latest bloodcurdling romance! At least, I am told I must."

"How brave of you!" Augusta said, smiling.

"Nonsense. You're the brave one." Lady Mariana leaned close to Augusta and whispered in her ear, "I, too, have a taste for such serious subjects, but I must disguise them within an assortment of light reading or my mother will despair of me. Indeed, she already has." She let go of Augusta's arm and said, "You intrigue me, Miss Hastings."

"I don't know why I should, My Lady" Augusta said, thoroughly confused as to why Lady Mariana should take the slightest interest in her.

"No, I see that you don't. There must be dozens of modistes and seamstresses in London who eschew the fashion journals for serious reading and who have enough knowledge of Ancient Greek to read it with pleasure. I shall bid you adieu. Perhaps we may meet again."

She put out her hand to Augusta, who took it briefly then watched her walk to greet a young woman who had nodded to her in passing.

Augusta's heart beat faster and when she reached up to

take a volume down from a shelf her hand shook. How could she have been so careless? But she had an odd sense that she was in no immediate danger of being unmasked by Lady Mariana. She clearly had a strong sense of the ironic, not dissimilar to that of her brother. Augusta had to admit, she liked her.

It didn't take long for Augusta to put her initial embarrassment over gaining entrance to the library behind her and to allow herself to sink into the pleasure of being surrounded by books. She lost all track of time. The smell of leatherbound volumes, the comforting ranks of spines with gilt lettering, the thought of all the wisdom and solace to be found between their covers—it recalled to her mind the many pleasant hours spent reading in silent companionship with her father. The thought should have made her sad, but instead she felt hopeful. Cheered. As if just knowing a place like Hookham's existed opened up possibilities she hadn't anticipated.

After she knew not how long, she had chosen Southey's *Life of Nelson* from among those biographies up on a high shelf and was scanning the catalogue for another book to borrow when a voice broke into her concentration.

"Are you perhaps lost, Ma'am?"

Augusta turned to see a tall young man dressed unstudiedly in the latest style. She couldn't help noticing, though, that his coat of superfine was expertly tailored, and that his starched collar and neck cloth gleamed crisp, bright white. Was he employed at Hookham's? Surely not. He vastly outshone the other denizens of the library. Although some of the younger librarians cut a dash in their skin-tight pantaloons, any attempt at being a la mode was thwarted by the aprons they wore. This gentleman did not wear an apron. In any case, he seemed willing to help her, whoever he was. "I had thought to borrow one of Madame d'Arblay's novels, but

I cannot find any beyond *Cecilia*, which I have already read, since the catalogue lists books by title." This vexing feature shouldn't have surprised her, but it did.

"Ah! I see you have excellent taste, Ma'am." A smile lit the gentleman's eyes, which appeared an indeterminate color in the dim light of the circulation room, and coaxed a dimple into one of his cheeks. He didn't have the polish of a dandy. In fact, the lines of his face spoke rather of having faced some difficulties, of having seen much. Nonetheless, it was a handsome face. Handsome in a rugged, well-proportioned way. "Hookham's also possesses *Evelina*, I believe, if it is not already in some other reader's hands. Although these older novels languish sadly neglected by those seeking more sensational reading material."

Augusta smiled. "Then *Evelina* it is. Thank you, Sir."

He put out his hand. "Jeremy Thorne at your service."

So, he wasn't employed by the library. Why had he approached her? "I am most grateful," she said, curtsying rather than giving him her hand, and wishing she did not feel the creep of a blush in her cheeks. She drew herself up. "I shall request the volume, and then I must be on my way."

Mister Thorne lowered his hand and cocked his head on the side. "Have I offended you in some way?"

His suddenly serious expression caught her off guard. "N-no Sir!" she said. "I'm just... it's simply... I haven't been in London long and..." Her tongue tripped over itself in an effort to alleviate this awkward situation.

A broad, slightly rueful smile lit his face. "I'm sorry. I shouldn't tease, especially a pretty young lady who doesn't know me and might well think me impertinent! Allow me to atone by getting one of the librarians to help you find your books and seeing that the dragons behind the desk don't make you wait too long."

Before she could protest, he'd turned away from her and

strode up to the circulation desk, filled out two slips and signaled to one of the librarians who scurried over and said, "Of course Mister Thorne!" The librarian looked at the slips and frowned. "Are you certain, Sir?" he said.

"Do you question my judgment, Curtin? Not that it should matter, but I am merely performing a service for this young lady, who is new to Hookham's." He glanced at her, and Curtin peered around Mister Thorne's tall form to follow his eyes. Augusta gave the man a weak smile, and he nodded and went away in search of the d'Arblay.

Mister Thorne came back to Augusta's side. "I shall leave you in the capable hands of the redoubtable Curtin, Miss…?"

Should she trust him with her name? It would be impolite not to, after his kind intervention. And after all, what harm could there be? "Hastings. Augusta Hastings."

"Miss Augusta Hastings." He once more put out his hand. This time, she knew she shouldn't ignore it, and so she took it in a firm grasp.

But instead of simply shaking hands with her, Thorne lifted it to his lips and pressed a light kiss on her glove.

Her glove. The kid was shiny with wear. Would Mister Thorne notice? Whether he did or not she couldn't say. It was odd of him to kiss her hand. A rather old-fashioned gesture. What did he mean by it? She looked up at him quickly. He simply gave her a crooked smile and a brief bow, turned away and walked off toward the door without any books at all in his hands.

When she accepted her own volumes from Mister Curtin, neatly wrapped in paper and string, she was surprised to note that the doors of Hookham's were closing for the night. Had she really spent so much time there? Indeed, few patrons remained, and Augusta, not wanting to call any more undue attention to herself, hurried out, her acquisitions tucked under her arm.

Such an odd day, Augusta thought as she wandered back through the lamp-lit streets. First, Mister Gordon with his rather impudent assumptions. Then to encounter Lord Bridlington again in such a way, with his strange combination of chivalry and distance. And soon after that his sister. Finally, Mister Thorne. All these occurrences unsettled her. But it was meeting Lady Mariana in Hookham's that made her the most uneasy. She had inadvertently revealed things about herself she had hoped to keep hidden. This one fact altered her perception of the library, which she had envisioned as a place where she could hide away, where she would not meet anyone and could indulge her own fancy for reading and study with no one to tell her she would end with a squint, or chastise her for choosing unsuitable material. But encountering Lady Mariana there had caused her two worlds to collide. Already she'd had the uncomfortable experience of discovering that Bridlington had some acquaintance with the Earl of Hastings and might—with very little effort—unearth the secret of her disgusting intended betrothal. Would Mariana mention their encounter to her brother? Augusta wasn't certain whether she wished for that or not.

And then there was Mister Thorne. Something in his eyes, an expression, drew a reminiscence from her of a stolen moment with James. They'd been at a public assembly in town and she'd broken the heel of her shoe. James had come to find her as she hid discreetly in an alcove to try to mend her slipper. With a mischievous gleam in his eye, he'd asked for her other shoe and broken it to match its mate. And then he'd kissed her—so lightly and quickly that she hardly believed it had happened.

Mister Thorne seemed at first glance to be someone who would dare to effect a shameless remedy to the difficulty of a broken heel. And through his handshake, and the cut of his clothes, she deduced he had wiry strength that was not unlike James's. A reminiscence. That was all it was, Augusta thought. Nothing more. She would never see Thorne again and could tuck their brief acquaintance deep into her store of memories, to be forgot, or at least buried. Besides, although she could hardly avoid encountering Lady Mariana in the course of her life, Mr. Thorne would be unlikely to present himself at Madame Noelle's.

She climbed the stairs to the seamstresses' rooms with the ghost of a smile on her face. The others were already in bed, if not yet asleep, and she crept to her corner to undress for the night and then blow out the candle.

But sleep eluded her, and she puzzled over the events of the day for hours.

CHAPTER 6

"*Y*ou done with that slip yet, Gussie?" Pauline said as they sat busy in the workroom between customers the day after Augusta's jaunt to Hookham's.

Augusta looked down to the fall of pink satin in her lap. She'd been hemming it for a young lady who was going to be presented at court that season and had finished that task, but sat in a daze without reaching for the scissors to snip the thread. "What? Oh, yes."

"Well get on then! There's loads more to do before tomorrow!"

All four seamstress's heads were bent over their work, and Augusta quickly set to on the next project—a pelisse of gold twilled silk lined with pearl satin, frogged and braided from neck to hem. She might have chosen to adorn it less liberally, but she could do no more than execute her employer's designs at that point.

And there was plenty to do of that sort. The season was now in full swing with balls, rout parties, assemblies, and dress parties every evening, always several in one night. By noon, the streets overflowed with fashionable carriages bearing the quality on morning visits, footmen overloaded with parcels following ladies parting with large sums as they shopped, and urchins running here and there delivering messages and generally getting under everyone's feet. This crush had been Augusta's excuse for taking so long over her errand the day before. It didn't stop Madame from ringing a peal over her for it first thing that morning.

After sewing bleary-eyed for two hours before the fittings began, Augusta took up her position in the atelier with Pauline, struggling to suppress her yawns. Madame sent Augusta to answer a ring on the bell of the atelier while she consulted her appointment book, and an urchin handed her a letter sealed with a lavender wafer and addressed to Augusta Hastings in a very elegant hand. After a moment of heart-stopping panic that she had been discovered by her Aunt Phyllis, she stuffed it into her pocket. It could not have come from her aunt, whose hand was usually a spiky mess. Not to mention that she would have had to pay postage on receipt if that purse-pinching lady had discovered her whereabouts and decided to write to her.

"What did he want?" Madame asked, a disapproving scowl on her face.

"Oh, nothing. Just a note … about the latest shipment at the linen draper's."

Fortunately, the proprietress was too distracted to inquire further, and Augusta kept the letter safely out of sight through three dress fittings and several hours of sewing lace trim on ball gowns until her fingers were numb.

When at last she could turn her mind to that unusual missive, something told her it would be a mistake to let any of her compatriots know she'd received it. "I need a breath of air," Augusta said after she finished a particularly delicate task, and stood and stretched her arms above her head. "I won't be a moment."

Only Pauline raised her questioning eyes. Augusta smiled back at her, snatched her bonnet and wrap from the hook behind her chair, and swept out to the alley next to the atelier.

A glance around assured her she was completely alone. She drew the letter out of her pocket and looked it over carefully, tracing the direction with her finger. The paper was exceedingly fine—smooth and creamy—and the ink had stayed obediently on the surface rather than bleeding as it dried. Lacking a pen knife, Augusta used a stubby fingernail to lift the wafer, trying not to tear it, and unfolded the note to read.

Miss Hastings,

Please forgive the presumption of writing to you at your place of employment, but I know of no other address. I have a commission for you that I would like you to undertake in the greatest secrecy. You will be handsomely compensated for it, but you may not work on it chez Madame. If you have any interest in aiding me, I beg you would consent to meet with me tomorrow evening. I will take care in the morning to request the delivery of my new gown from Madame and ask that you be the messenger so that you may perform any final adjustments before I go out that evening—which will give you ample excuse to absent yourself for longer than might be expected. There is no need to accept this commission until you are made aware of exactly what it is, so do not be afraid that you are agreeing to something whose nature is as yet unknown to you.

I hope I haven't mistaken your character in thinking you would be amenable to what I propose.

I will expect you at Lanyon House in Berkeley Square at seven.
If you do not appear I will assume you have chosen not to take part
in my scheme.

THE LETTER WAS SIGNED WITH A FLOURISH, MARIANA LANYON.

Emotions warred in Augusta's breast. Although she had
told herself that coming to London was her chance to be
settled and calm, to move beyond the grief and disappoint-
ments of her life and be quiet and industrious, to turn her
back on the empty and meaningless future everyone but she
seemed to desire for herself and work toward a different life,
she had a naturally inquiring and curious disposition. Her
vision of becoming quickly recognized as someone with a
keen sense of fashion and being able to work her way up to
designing clothes herself was clearly a pipe dream as things
stood. Surely becoming better acquainted with one of the
most influential come-outs might serve her well when she
found a way to advance her real ambitions. Besides, she
craved relief from days that had already become
monotonous.

In short, Augusta's fingers were constantly occupied but
her mind and heart were not engaged, and she found herself
unceasingly busy but unconscionably bored. Here was the
possibility of something that could enliven her with its air of
mystery and secrecy. Perhaps Lady Mariana wanted her to
design a gown? The lady had witnessed her attempt to offer
an opinion about the fabrics when she was there for her
fitting. Yet if the desire for a new gown were her object, such
a thing did not seem to warrant so much secrecy.

The one matter that checked Augusta's enthusiasm was
the connection between Mariana and her brother, the earl.
Both of her encounters with him had had disturbing effects
on her equilibrium. When she had grasped the earl's hand as

he pulled her into the curricle so effortlessly, it had been the first time she'd felt a man's grip since James. It should have given her a strong and painful reminder. But when the recollection of that sensation tingled in the palm of her hand, James's deep brown eyes weren't the ones that came into her mind. Instead, she recalled Lord Bridlington's soft, flecked gray gaze, bent upon her with warmth and curiosity. The second time, he'd acted with haste and sureness, but had barely given her the time of day. Such treatment suggested that he had no interest in someone as lowly as she. With hardly a glance, he'd ridden away—proving that he was no different from any of the other dismissive members of the *ton*.

Enough! she thought, driving the image from her mind. What did Lady Mariana's brother have to do with the matter before her now? He'll no doubt be out at his club at that hour, and she would not risk encountering him. She was to present herself at a back entrance, in any event, where he would be unlikely to stray.

Still, the question plagued her: Why me? Why not Pauline, who had no doubt served Lady Mariana on many more occasions and therefore was more familiar?

But in her heart, Augusta knew the answer. Lady Mariana had seen in her someone closer to her own station, someone educated. The very qualities Augusta had sought to hide. For whatever reason, these qualities mattered for Lady Mariana's mysterious project. With that in mind, Augusta decided she might as well find out more, certain that she could extricate herself if necessary.

As Lady Mariana had predicted in her letter, at around midday the next day, Madame Noelle told Augusta that she would be needed to make a delivery and do a final fitting that evening, after all the other work was completed. She did not ask if she had any objection to this, as it was not her custom to consult the wishes of her menials. As having the experience of working for that lady would provide entree to any other house in a more advantageous position, or into a fine lady's service as a well-paid dresser if any of them had such an ambition, no one dared express the slightest objection to the conditions of employment there.

To Augusta's surprise, though, when Madame gave her the satin ribbon-tied box that contained the evening dress she was to convey to Lady Mariana, she put a hand on Augusta's arm and said in a low voice, "I must warn you of something." Madame looked behind her as if to ensure that no one was within hearing. But Pauline had hastened out of the showroom as soon as she could go and was no doubt upstairs with the others, eating the dinner that had been sent up from Madame Noelle's kitchens and trading gossip about the day, so they were alone.

"Yes, Madame?"

"Lanyon House is the home of Lord Bridlington, Lady Mariana's brother. Although of the first respectability in rank, he is well known to have rakish tendencies. Surprising considering... Well, the less said about that the better." She lowered her voice even more and leaned toward Augusta. "I have heard that he has several barques of frailty under his protection, which is no more than one would expect of a gentleman of his rank. Of course no one high born. In fact, quite the reverse. But be on your guard, Miss Hastings."

"I fail to see how this could affect my delivery to Lady Mariana," Augusta said, unaccountably dismayed by this information. "In any case, likely it's simply idle gossip."

Madame raised her eyebrows yet higher. "I think I know

which rumors to trust and which to dismiss. He has been seen, you see. His chaise takes him to the most disreputable places. I have it on the best authority."

"Surely he's just going to his club, or to a gaming house," Augusta said, her spirits sinking a bit more, hoping Madame was wrong about Bridlington.

Madame shook her head and pursed her lips, a spiteful gleam in her eye. "You haven't been here long enough to know. But trust me. I've been in the world a bit more than you, girl. Bridlington is very secretive and his temper is by no means easy, so one of the undergrooms at Lanyon House says."

Could it be true? She was very little acquainted with him. And she well knew that men in the *ton* frequently dallied with courtesans. Even married men, who sometimes kept mistresses in a most flagrant manner. The possibility that Bridlington could be just like so many other gentlemen of rank disappointed her more than she cared to admit. Such tendencies made him seem more like the despicable Grantley, whose reputation formed a not insignificant part of her decision to flee from him—that and the fact that her skin crawled at the thought of his touch.

But her skin did not crawl at the thought of Bridlington's touch.

With a sigh, Augusta bundled the unwieldy dress box into the hack Madame had grudgingly paid for to take her the short distance to Berkeley Square. It was the hour after the strut, when the gentry would be at home preparing for their evening engagements, and the streets were relatively empty. She had hardly had time to consider more deeply what Madame had told her before she found herself approaching a servants' door to a fine mansion. She needed both hands to hold the dress box and, for a moment, could not figure out how she would manage to knock and alert someone that she had arrived.

But as soon as she reached the door, it opened to reveal not a servant, but Lady Mariana herself, who must have been watching for her arrival.

Augusta tried to curtsy despite her load, but Lady Mariana said, "Never mind that! Come in quickly before anyone sees you."

Why it could be a matter requiring secrecy to have a gown delivered by a seamstress was beyond Augusta's ability to guess. Still more mystifying was the fact that Lady Mariana relieved her of the box as soon as she was through the door and put it on the floor without so much as a peek, as if she had no interest in what it contained.

"Follow me," Lady Mariana said, and hastened down a short, dimly lit hallway to a back staircase. Without pausing, Lady Mariana started up the stairs with Augusta close on her heels. They went up and up until the stairs ended at a low door. "Mind your head," she said as she opened the door and ducked to pass through it and into an attic.

Augusta stopped just inside the door. Madame's warning suddenly seemed not quite so nonsensical, and she was about to protest and say she was expected to return to the atelier immediately when Lady Mariana reached out and laid a hand on her arm. "We used to play up here when we were children," she said, her eyes full of a combination of kindness and mischief. "I'm sorry about all the mystery, but I assure you I will not get you into trouble. It's cold, and I apologize, but soon the fire will warm us a little. I laid it myself, so it's not so efficient as the ones the housemaids kindle."

She walked toward a small fireplace at one end of the open space punctuated with stout wooden supports. Scattered among these were numerous trunks of different sizes, broken furniture and old rolled-up rugs. A branch of candles on a rough table by the fireplace made that portion of the room welcoming in contrast to the rest of the attic. Two threadbare upholstered chairs had been placed across from each other near the fire. Close by stood a small writing desk, equipped with paper, ink, and quills, and a stack of disordered periodicals next to it threatened to topple over at any second. Augusta sat in the chair Lady Mariana bid her to and then listened as one of the wealthiest heiresses in the land described what she needed of a secret seamstress.

LADY MARIANA HAD NOT ENTIRELY DECIDED HOW MUCH TO take this interesting young seamstress into her confidence. Seamstress? The daughter of a baronet, if what she'd let slip at Hookham's was true. In fact, she wasn't certain at all why she had determined to involve this particular girl in her schemes. Yet there was just enough serendipity in their several meetings that some connection seemed fated, and it hadn't taken long for her to discern that she had encountered a lady of superior intellect and education, whatever she was trying to hide. It remained unfathomable to Mariana what she was doing earning her keep as a menial dressmaker. But no doubt there would be time to discover this—if she consented to participate in what was a very daring plan.

"First," Lady Mariana said, once Augusta had settled herself in the chair and stopped scanning the open attic as if she was looking for an escape route, "I must ask you to keep what I am about to divulge to you a secret from everyone you know. It is nothing against the law or—for you at least— the bounds of propriety, I hasten to add. Not against the laws of the land, I mean, only against—well, you will not get into trouble for helping me. But if my proposed actions are discovered, they could prove ruinous to me and my family, as well as to other individuals who I am not at liberty to name."

Lady Mariana paused and looked directly into Miss Hastings' eyes. What did she read there? A flicker of panic, certainly. But beneath that, a little flame of interest. "I think you are not afraid of taking risks, if I've judged you correctly. The way you stood up to the porter at Hookham's, for instance." She paused to give Miss Hastings a moment to recall the scene, and to realize that Mariana was in possession of some knowledge about her that she hadn't divulged to her employer. "You felt as if your rights had been denied you. Am I correct? You are accustomed to certain expectations."

Miss Hastings slowly nodded, but said nothing.

"That is to the purpose here. For I find myself at the mercy of forces not in my control and that prevent me from leading a life of purpose." Mariana's pulse quickened. "I could say more, but perhaps another day. Would you care for some refreshment?" She picked up a small bell from the desk.

"No, thank you My Lady."

"Very well. And if you agree to help me in this mad scheme, I shall insist on you dispensing with this *my lady* business and calling me Mariana. But let me continue."

AUGUSTA SAT IN UNBELIEVING SILENCE FOR A FULL HOUR AS Lady Mariana talked to her about the Luddites and the injustice of the mill owners placing so little value on the lives of the weavers. She mentioned Lord Byron's impassioned address to the Upper House, and spoke of movements in government to persuade the first minister to soften his draconian approach to domestic unrest.

"I have a connection in the House, someone who keeps

me informed of important matters, but I want to know more, I just want to have the experience..." Was it her imagination, or did Lady Mariana blush? Whatever the case, she suddenly stopped talking and took a turn around the room. "I can't explain it exactly now, but I need your help in order to achieve my fondest dreams. I can honestly say that I will not be able to do it without you."

Augusta was at a loss. What on earth could Lady Mariana need her for so desperately? She had no clear idea of the political forces at play in Westminster, and as to how a seamstress could be important... "I'm afraid I don't understand, My Lady. I can't see what exactly all this has to do with me."

"Of course not, because I haven't explained it yet. Although the matters being debated in the House have to do with all of us—like it or not—I feel as if everything is hidden behind a veil, as if everyone thinks my knowing about it would endanger my feminine sensibility. It's maddening beyond anything. But that is not to the purpose right now. I have asked you here because I would like you to alter a suit of fine men's clothing for me to fit someone for whom it was not intended."

Men's clothing? "I'm sorry, My Lady, but I am a dressmaker, not a tailor." Although she had mended her father's shirts, Augusta doubted she had the ability to refit men's carefully tailored garments.

"I cannot, for several reasons, enlist the help of a tailor of any skill. Surely simple alterations would not be beyond your capabilities?"

It did not surprise Augusta that Lady Mariana had an imperfect grasp of the different techniques required to make ladies' clothing out of soft, malleable materials and in lines that flowed over a body rather than formed themselves around it. And men's suits, with their more precise lines and robust fabrics, and the need for judicious padding to achieve the ideal fit—could she do it? And what if she failed? "You may think me bird witted, but I find myself unable to come to a decision about this, My Lady." She failed to see how undertaking such a project could in any way advance her toward her ultimate goal as a modiste. "If you could perhaps give me a clearer idea of why you are asking this of me."

"For now," Lady Mariana said, sitting once again in the chair and picking at its arm distractedly, "let us say I wish to aid a young man out of charity. It is not far from the truth. It's what I tell my brother when I take away his slightly worn coats, breeches, and pantaloons."

At the mention of her brother, Augusta's heart skipped a beat. What had he been wearing when she last saw him? Riding dress, of course. She hadn't looked closely. She'd been too embarrassed to notice anything beyond his mocking eyes. With an effort, she drove the image out of her mind. "Will the young man come here to be fitted?" Augusta asked, unable to imagine how such a thing as Lady Mariana described could possibly be accomplished—and how improper it would be if it were.

"Eventually, I don't know. It doesn't matter. But there is another part of my scheme, for which I will need your help in a different way."

The intense expression on Lady Mariana's face raised the hair on the back of Augusta's neck. "Yes, My Lady?"

"I do wish you'd call me Mariana! If you become my partner in this, you will need to accustom yourself to it."

Her partner? Were they to be on an equal footing? Clearly Lady Mariana did not disdain a seamstress, or think her beneath her notice, as her brother did. But then, Augusta reminded herself that Lady Mariana had discovered that she was gently bred and well educated.

Not waiting for a response from Augusta, Mariana

continued, "You see, I should like you to play a role yourself in raising my friend out of his lowly state."

"I?" Now Augusta didn't know what to think, and began to regret her impulse to respond to Lady Mariana's summons.

"I'm not a snob. I think all human beings deserve to be valued and respected, whether they shovel coal or sit on the bench. But the *ton* has a different view. To help me in my project, I need someone unknown to society, but who could creditably move in the first circles, who has enough breeding and education to be accepted without question—and who can also do the necessary alterations."

Oh no. Augusta's pulse quickened as she perceived danger ahead. What had she walked into? "I shall have to think—"

"Please say you will help me! I perhaps should have said I am willing to pay you handsomely."

Ah. So much for being on an equal footing. She would be a hireling still. But wouldn't extra money be good? Lady Mariana had leaned forward in her chair, poised with both hands on the arms as if to spring up. Her eyes shone with such intense fervor that Augusta had to look away. This lady was a force to be reckoned with. Having her goodwill, however, might be important if she ever found herself in a position to set up her own modiste's establishment. But something told Augusta the risks of this project might well outweigh the rewards, which in any case were at this point very far out of reach.

Augusta had learned, though, that working for Madame Noelle alone would not be enough to assure her future in the world of London fashion. She would have to be more assertive. She'd already taken a bold, perhaps foolhardy step toward a new life. To be cowardly now would not answer. After a deep breath, Augusta said, "Yes, I think. I mean, I know. I will help you, My Lady."

A moment later she found herself pulled up from the chair and engulfed in Lady Mariana's scented embrace.

She let go of Augusta after a moment and held her at arm's length. "Mariana. You *must* call me Mariana, as I said, because I now transform you into a school friend newly arrived in London from Ireland, I think. Or perhaps the Indies? No, that would be less believable. Perhaps it need only be Bath."

The depth of the deception Lady Mariana was proposing began to dawn on Augusta, and she opened her eyes wide.

Mariana said quickly, "You won't be alone! You will have a cousin who has come with you."

"Is he the young gentleman who needs this clothing?"

"Yes, yes, of course." She waved away the question. "You must think me a shameless plotter. But I have very good reasons for everything, I promise you. And I won't let you suffer for it, even if everything goes all in a toss. Admit it: You squirm under the redoubtable Madame Noelle's silken yoke."

Was it so obvious? "It has not been precisely as I had hoped."

"What had you hoped?" Mariana cocked her head on the side with a little smile, then continued. "You needn't tell me all now. But you should know that I will ask you to engage in a few evening activities as part of my plan. I assume you have suitable gowns for such things?"

Without thinking, Augusta laughed. "I am afraid, My—Mariana, just as the cobbler's children have no shoes, the seamstress has very few clothes. I left all except my most ordinary gowns in—well, that does not signify."

Mariana did not at first say anything, and Augusta worried that she had perhaps revealed too much about herself.

"I have been rattling on talking only about myself and my

plans. I know nothing of you except what I have observed. Another time," said Mariana, "you shall tell me your story, for I know you must have one. I see it in you, the desire for more out of life. As to the question of gowns, I have more than anyone has a right to, and I'm certain you could easily make over one of mine to fit and suit yourself. But you still haven't answered me for certain: shall you help me in all my schemes? Dare to throw your lot in with me?"

CHAPTER 7

*T*he day after his visit to Madame Agatha, George sat down in his book room to write a letter to the gentleman—if he could be considered one—responsible for the infant that had just been born under Agatha's roof. It took some time. He had to curb his impulse to take him severely to task, since what, after all, had he done in this case that so many other gentlemen of the *ton* didn't also do as a matter of course? If it had simply been an isolated, unfortunate circumstance, it would have been a different matter. But George had reason to know that the gentleman in question had a habit of seducing friendless girls and leaving them to bear all the consequences of his actions.

Having drafted a satisfactory letter, signed, and sealed it, George rubbed his eyes, stretched, and went up to his dressing room where he met Craggins, who had already laid out his tail coat and breeches, and had a ewer full of hot water waiting for his master to wash his hands and splash on his face.

Once dressed for the evening, George made his way to the back stairs that led down to the mews and his waiting carriage. He wondered idly what Mariana would think of his activities earlier in the day. Doubtless she assumed that he passed his time idling in the club, or dining with his equally idle friends. He'd only once taken his seat in the Upper House—something Mariana often took him to task for. To her, government was the only way to work toward changes that would benefit society. The problem was, it was so damnably difficult to make his way into the warren-ish halls of Westminster and take his seat, and the debates went on for hours. Although he applauded his sister's interest and zeal, such things were not for him. Instead, he'd found his own way to act on his principles.

He gave a mirthless laugh. That wasn't the only reason for his avoidance, he knew himself well enough to admit. Being amid a crowd of men instantly transported him to his days surrounded by boys who teased and tormented him, goading him to try to run fast and imitating his pronounced limp, calling him names and generally being as cruel as young people could be. It was silly to think of the House as anything like the playing fields of Eton. Nonetheless, he contented himself with following affairs of the government by means of the newspapers and through the pamphlets and intelligence Mari brought him. George often thought she should have been the boy. She would have made an exemplary earl.

It was remarkable, he thought, that with so profligate and heedless a father, both he and his sister cared deeply about their fellow beings and the state of the world. He supposed it was their mother's steadying, loving influence that had won out in the end. He thought fondly of the dowager, who was also charitable in her many quiet ways. She also took a benevolent view of her children and meddled as little as possible in their daily lives.

By the time his mind had roved over all these matters, he'd reached the back stairs that led to the stable yard and started down them one step at a time, leaning on his cane to take the pressure off his bad foot, not paying much attention to his surroundings.

He had just rounded the last landing and prepared to negotiate the final flight to the mews door when he stopped short. A woman stood on the landing at the bottom of the stairs, peering out the half-door to the stable yard as if to ensure there was no one there to see her. An intruder? He thought it unlikely. Not so early in the evening. And hardly probable such a person would be a woman in any case. A woman who—if he wasn't mistaken—he had seen before. George's heart started to race, and he held his breath. Should he make himself known? He never felt more vulnerable, more exposed, than on a staircase.

As he watched, the lady suddenly stepped away from the door and pressed her back against the wall as if she'd seen someone in the yard. Which she no doubt had, because Philpot had been alerted to watch for his lordship's arrival and ready the carriage.

The sight of her face confirmed his suspicion with a jolt. A gasp escaped him and, startled into incivility, he said, "What are you doing here?"

Her face went scarlet as her eyes met his. Those same, warm brown eyes, full of latent laughter, that he had seen most recently in pursuit of a thief on Piccadilly. Her hair was neat this time, and the color in her cheeks was no doubt the result of embarrassment rather than exertion.

"I beg your pardon, My Lord, I was just leaving." She dipped a quick curtsy but said no more.

He'd taken her completely by surprise! No saucy quip, no challenging look. She must know this was his house, so it would be hardly wonderful that he should be there. Perhaps not so likely that he would be descending via a staircase normally used only by servants, though. "It seems we are destined to meet in the oddest circumstances," he said, seeing that she'd quickly regained control of herself.

"Nothing odd about this particular circumstance, My Lord. I have just delivered a gown to Lady Mariana. She is your sister, so I believe." She smiled in a way that turned up the corners of her pretty mouth and lit her face.

"I see that at least you have not met with any accidents this time, and your reticule," he pointed, "is safely in your hands."

"Indeed, Sir. I have lately learned to take prodigious care of my belongings and my person. You see, I am waiting for that pair out there to be harnessed to your chaise and driven out so that I don't risk having dirt tossed up onto my pelisse. Being no better than a seamstress, I have only the one, and it took me hours to brush out all the mud on my skirt the day I arrived."

He had the fleeting sensation of a small, firm hand in his, and saw the glint of a challenge in her expression. "Had you entered by the usual tradesmen's door, you would run no such risk."

After an almost imperceptible hesitation she said, "Lady Mariana said this would place me more directly on my route."

"A happy bit of advice as it has resulted in our paths crossing once again."

The tint in her cheeks deepened and the expression in her eyes altered just slightly. Embarrassment? "My Lord Bridlington," she said, "I gather you are going out to your evening engagements. I assure you I shall be content to wait here until you've departed and the horses are safely out of my way." She cast a quick glance back up at him and gave a rueful smile.

She wants me to continue down and go past her. She will see me descend the stairs, a cripple, a babe, taking one step at a time. She must be aware of it. Mariana might have told her if she hadn't noticed before. But her eyes had not traveled down to look at his right foot, at the way it bent even when encased in a cleverly constructed boot, remaining at an awkward angle to the floor. And she hadn't taken any apparent note of his cane, which he rested on quite heavily.

No, he would not continue down the stairs. "On no account would I delay you from your business," George said, maintaining the light, bantering tone they seem to have agreed upon.

At that moment, Philpot came through the door, and upon seeing Miss Hastings, doffed his cap and said, "Beg pardon, Miss."

George said, "Philpot, there's a good fellow. Could you hold the horses' heads while Miss Hastings makes her escape through the yard?"

She cast him a grateful glance. "Thank you, My Lord!"

"Not at all. My horses are deeply ashamed of the behavior of their acquaintances, the unruly pair belonging to my friend, and will stand aside willingly to let you pass!"

Her smile broadened and she shook her head. "I had no idea your horses were so well trained as to be courteous as well as capital-goers! But indeed, I am ashamed to recall how I must have appeared to you that day, Sir. As I am equally mortified to remember the manner of your timely assistance the other day."

Philpot, looking a trifle confused, shrugged his shoulders and said, "Come this way, Miss. Those beasts won't bother you. They're gentle as lambs." He held the door open for her and she swept through, head high.

Once she was completely out of sight, George limped down the rest of the stairs. He could not account for his strange reaction to Miss Hastings. As to exactly why she affected him so that he felt he had to school his tongue, say things calculated to make her laugh—or at least smile—remained a mystery to him. Perhaps it was the contradiction she so clearly embodied. Her protestations that she was just a seamstress seemed a little too rehearsed. She was a lady, he had no doubt. Aside from her genteel accent and correct address, she knew something of carriage horses. What had occurred to send her to London to pursue a menial occupation? Respectable families lost fortunes every day and left indigent females to fend for themselves. But rarely did any of the daughters in straitened circumstances seek employment at something he guessed was laborious work with long hours. More often they became paid companions, or governesses—which could be equally demeaning, he thought. But somehow society deemed such servitude vastly more acceptable. It puzzled him.

Similar thoughts swirled in his mind all the way to Brooks's. After a knowing footman directed him to the back where he could descend his carriage and mount the stairs unseen by casual passersby, he entered the safe confines of the dining room, met Lewiston and Newby for dinner, and then settled in for an evening of cards.

He'd had a good two hours' play, his fortunes ebbing and flowing and the brandy merely flowing, and was about to start another rubber when in walked a group of gentlemen that included the Honorable Desmond Grantley, second son of the Earl of Hastings. Grantley, after tossing his coat and hat to the porter, scanned the company until his eyes alit on George.

"Bridlington!" he said, striding forward to shake his hand. "Haven't seen you since last year! How the devil are you?"

George stood, wondering at Grantley's ability to greet him with such composure and thought perhaps he hadn't yet received the letter he'd written to him earlier. "I was surprised to hear you were in town this season. Rumor was that you were to go abroad." In fact, the rumor had been that his father had refused to honor his debts and that he had to flee to the continent to avoid the consequences. That he was on the hunt for a lady of suitable birth to marry him so he could fulfill the conditions of a handsome bequest from his uncle was well known. The gossip was that he'd found one, someone unknown in London but of good enough family to satisfy the conditions of the will.

"No, managed to avoid that. Not so purse pinched as I thought."

If he wasn't at that moment, he no doubt would be soon. Grantley was unlikely ever to outgrow his unbridled ways. His older brother, the viscount Knightford, was as steady and dull as Desmond was depraved. The idea that the self-contained Miss Hastings could be related to this n'er-do-well seemed patently absurd. In any case, she had not owned it. People on the fringes of nobility rarely disavowed their grander relations, so he was inclined to believe her. Yet there was a certain something, the shape of the eyes, perhaps? That slightly quizzical upward tilt? Absurd. He was considering it only because he'd just seen the lady a few hours earlier. Besides, Grantley's skin had a swarthy tinge, and he had hazel eyes and almost black hair.

"Shall I join you for a rubber or two?" Grantley said, having greeted the other players.

The idea of sitting at cards with him was insupportable. "I'm off for the evening. You can take my place," George said with a quick smile and reached for his walking stick.

Before he could grasp it, Grantley spotted the elegant accessory and picked it up, holding it and pretending to examine it so that it was just too far away for George to reach without taking a few steps. "I say, Bridlington! Still gimping, I see, but nice bit of Malacca! Ought to get one of those sword sticks, though, don't you think?" He made a playful gesture of pulling on the handle as if it would come free of the shaft and reveal a blade.

"Not in my style, Grantley," George said, with a smile that did not reach his eyes.

Grantley nodded, twirling the walking stick, and then turning around and showing it to another acquaintance at a different table as if marveling at its clever construction. There was nothing unusual in the stick. It was simple and serviceable, of the finest Malacca polished to a high sheen and a chased gold handle engraved with George's crest. George stood rooted to his spot, his smile fixed but his eyes growing darker with every moment that passed. It was just like Grantley to still revel in the kind of cruel jokes he used to play on George when they were both at Eton.

"I really must be on my way," George said, but Grantley paid him no heed.

"I've a fancy for a stick like this," Grantley said to no one in particular.

Everyone within three tables of the two men had stopped talking and playing cards. All eyes turned expectantly on the scene being enacted before them.

"Next thing you'll be expecting me to call you out for stealing my perfectly ordinary walking stick!" George said, inwardly seething but making an effort to lighten the heavy atmosphere that enveloped them.

At this, Grantley whirled around. "What did you say, Bridlington? I wouldn't accept a challenge, you know. Wouldn't be sporting."

The muscles in George's cheeks twitched as he kept his lips closed, teeth clenched. Whatever his handicap in walking, his pistol hand was steady as a rock, and his eye true. But what folly it would be to rise to this bully's bait, no matter how he insulted him.

Suddenly Lewiston rose from his seat and approached

Grantley, saying, "That's enough, old fellow," took the stick out of his hands and restored it to George.

"Ah! Sorry Bridlington! It really is a fine piece." Grantley gave a wicked grin—which made his face appear almost unnaturally triangular—as if to bring the company in on his joke. "I'll call on you! Must pay my respects to your mama and Lady Mariana. Berkeley Square, isn't it?"

George nodded and took his unhurried leave, grinding his teeth and suppressing his urge to plant Grantley a facer. He determined never to use that particular walking stick again. The conversations resumed behind him. Whispers of *shame* and *gammy foot* skittered among the company. He was used to it. But the idea of Grantley calling in Berkeley Square, of taking up space in his house, filled him with loathing. Would the fellow dare? Not after he read the letter George sent him earlier, surely. He fervently hoped it was all posturing, or that if he were so bold as to call, that Mariana would not be there when he did. Grantley could be charming when he chose—as his trail of abandoned fair victims attested—but his streak of cruelty ran deep, and George's deformity brought out the worst of it.

Chances were he wouldn't turn up, though, since he had nothing to gain by doing so. Mariana had already rejected him in her first season, well aware that his interest in her went no further than her fortune and that he'd no doubt treat her as shamelessly as their father had treated their mother. Mariana had made her feelings quite clear, as he recalled. Still, something made George uneasy about Grantley's unexpected presence in London. It was absurd, but he couldn't help feeling it had something to do with Miss Hastings. The earldom was Hastings, after all. But the surname could just as easily have been adopted by an old dependent and passed down through generations in no way connected to Grantley.

Beyond the coincidence of the name, Miss Hastings, as he saw earlier that day, had become in some way connected to Mariana—or had insinuated herself into Mariana's life. This thought both disturbed and intrigued him. He knew his sister's penchant for pushing the boundaries of acceptable behavior, of finding ways to move among the lower classes in an impulse of charity. But Miss Hastings hardly seemed like someone in need of charity. Could she have different motives? Did she aim to entice Mariana to behave in a yet more outrageous way than she already was by thumbing her nose at the many brilliant offers she'd had? If so, it might be necessary for him to intervene.

On reflection, though, he realized that where Mariana was concerned, intervention would be fruitless. He would have to try a more subtle approach. Perhaps that should start with finding out everything he could about the mysterious, contradictory Miss Hastings.

And after his uncomfortable experience in the club, he decided to start with the font of all knowledge about British nobility: his mother. No need to tell her all, but he could at least count on her for accurate information about the Hastings family tree.

CHAPTER 8

*W*hat have I just agreed to? Augusta thought as she made her way back to Curzon Street, too late for the dinner provided by Madame Noelle that all of them ate together after work was finished. Her stomach complained, and she bought an apple from a cart so she would at least be able to fill it with something.

She had told Lady Mariana that she was willing to return and stay long enough to at least begin the alterations to her brother's clothing. Lady Mariana had not said who would be wearing the garments, but she claimed to possess accurate measurements. Having never attempted to make a man's coat or pantaloons before, Augusta feared her work would come up short, and she would have taken the risk for nothing.

Having had some anxiety about how she would manage to return to Berkeley Square and remain out for many hours in the evening, Augusta was relieved when the next day, the same urchin who'd delivered Lady Mariana's letter to her arrived with a missive for Madame Noelle. Augusta and Pauline, after finishing the arrangement of the showroom for the first appointment of the day, occupied themselves smoothing invisible wrinkles out of lengths of muslin and re-coiling silk ribbons that they'd already neatened earlier that morning. Augusta kept one eye on Madame as she stood ramrod straight in the middle of the room, holding the recently opened letter as far away from her eyes as she could.

When she finished her perusal, Madame sniffed and lifted her handkerchief to her somewhat prominent nose. "Miss Hastings, you are required once again by Lady Mariana, although why she must needs have you jauntering to Berkeley Square rather than coming here herself for necessary adjustments to her gowns, I cannot guess. I wouldn't allow you to do it for anyone else, mind you. She asks for you later this afternoon. If Her Grace of Tewksbury had not changed her fitting to tomorrow morning, I would not permit it. However, you had best go and see what the lady wants."

Augusta curtsied. "Yes, Madame. May I take my work basket with me? I may need the large scissors, and I know not what else in the way of needles, pins, and thread."

Madame saw nothing amiss with the suggestion, and so Augusta found herself bound for Lanyon House again, work basket over her arm, this time on foot since she knew her way there through the busy London streets.

Spring was in full bloom. Even in the city, at times when the clatter of carriages was not too loud, bird song reached Augusta's ears. She had a vision of meadows purpling with heather, swallows wheeling overhead, the breeze off the sea running its fingers through her unbound hair as she ran joyfully along the cliff path hand-in-hand with James, out of sight of prying eyes. Seized with a sudden desire to see green things growing and stand in the shade of overarching trees, Augusta decided she could take a longer walk to her destination and dip south to the Green Park. Not so fashionable as Hyde Park, this expanse of lawns broken by stands of trees was more often the haunt of nurses and their charges than fashionable promenaders. Augusta's neck ached from her hours sewing and trying unsuccessfully to sleep on her uncomfortable cot, and she longed to stretch out her arms, fill her lungs with scented air, and move her limbs freely. She was a fast walker. She could make up the time and arrive at Berkeley Square no more than a minute or two late, allowing herself the indulgence of a few moments alone in the nearest thing to country within her reach.

She dashed down Clarges Street and across Piccadilly—this time taking care that she had secure hold of her basket and reticule—picking her way between carriages and horses as quickly as she could, and entered the park through the north gate. As she walked farther away from the road, she luxuriated in the fresh new green of plane trees and lindens clad in a vibrant shade that glowed in the sunshine. The chestnut trees displayed their conical blossoms, giving off a faint perfume that she inhaled with delight. Conscious of the time, Augusta soon put down her sewing basket, took a deep breath and looked up at the sky. Just in that place, she could almost imagine herself in Devonshire, having run across a field to escape her governess. In sheer joy, she spread her arms wide.

"I'm afraid no matter how hard you try you won't be able to fly away."

Augusta gave a start and a little shriek and whirled around to see who the voice behind her belonged to. It took her a moment to recognize the young man she'd met in Hookham's the other day, Mister Thorne. She put her hands up to her face to hide her flaming cheeks. "I beg your pardon, Sir, I must go."

The amusement in Mister Thorne's thick-lashed eyes did nothing to soothe her, and she stepped forward quickly to retrieve her basket, which was nearer his feet than hers. He picked it up and held it out to her. "Thank you," she murmured and tried to walk past him, but he took hold of her arm and stopped her. She looked down at his hand, and he let her go.

He spoke hurriedly. "Wait, a moment please. I'm glad I've met you here. In truth, I'm ashamed to say, I followed you. I believe you are acquainted with Lady Mariana Lanyon?"

In an instant, Augusta felt her world close in on her. The momentary freedom of believing herself completely alone and unobserved fled, and unaccountably she felt like crying. "Yes, I am acquainted with that lady," she said, forcing her voice to sound flat but courteous.

"Then I wonder…" Mr. Thorne paused and cast a quick glance around him before reaching into his pocket to withdraw a folded and sealed note. "Would you be so kind as to deliver this into her hands?"

She hesitated. Was he asking her to abet a clandestine romance? He was a lowly Mr. Thorne. This was dangerous territory. It was one thing to humor a noble lady in her desire to help the unfortunate, another thing altogether to agree to be a courier of secret messages.

Clearly sensing her reticence, Mr. Thorne said, "It's nothing unseemly, I assure you!"

"Then why can you not deliver it into her hands yourself?" Augusta lifted her chin, hoping to convey that she was no witless innocent, but well acquainted with the ways of the world.

He had the good grace to appear a little abashed. "Lady Mariana has reasons for keeping her association with me private at present. I cannot explain more, but if you are unwilling to do this for me, I completely understand."

He withdrew the letter and was about to return it to his pocket when Augusta said, "Not at all. I am on my way to her ladyship's house at this moment and will happily give her your message."

Before once again holding out the folded note to Augusta, Thorne cocked his head on the side and his mouth curved up in a mischievous smile. "I perceive, however, that you have mistaken your way."

Augusta stammered, "The weather... so fine, and—"

"No need to explain to me. Those of us who must earn our keep have few enough opportunities to steal some leisure time."

In the days since she'd been in London, this fact had been impressed upon Augusta, who had not been much aware of the freedoms embedded in a situation where she had not had to work—whatever the undoubted restrictions. The luxury of choosing her activities based on the vagaries of weather or her own moods had never seemed of much value. Her opinions had altered when faced with the reality of her changed circumstances. She took the proffered letter and slipped it into her workbasket.

So Mr. Thorne was not a gentleman of leisure? Then what—or who—was he? She had no time to inquire, as he had bowed to her and strode away towards Piccadilly.

JEREMY HADN'T AT FIRST BEEN AT ALL CERTAIN HE WISHED TO participate in the schemes of a noblewoman whose probable only aim was to forestall boredom. Yet even before he knew her well, before he had been so captivated by her that he could think of no other female, he had had to admit that Mariana Lanyon's quick mind and vivid imagination had more substance than that of most of the members of the *ton*, and even than those who haunted the halls of government. When she had approached him at Hookham's the previous season a month or so after they'd been introduced at a card party at Lord Lister's home, she'd surprised him by striking up a conversation with him. He had thought she would hardly have noticed him, his station in life being so far beneath hers.

But she had paid attention enough to know that he was private secretary to Spencer Perceval, the prime minister. They spoke the first time only briefly, ending their conversation before they could attract the curious stares of other visitors to the library.

"Do you ride?" she had asked.

"Yes, of course, but—"

"I shall be in the park tomorrow afternoon with no one except my groom, and I usually manage to outride him. We may continue our conversation there."

He had been about to tell her that he had no horse of his own in London, stabling fees being above his touch. But he hired a hack and met her, knowing she took one look at him astride a broad-barreled bay gelding and guessed in an instant what he had done.

She said nothing about it, though. Their conversation had been brief, but her fervor, her bright, intense expression, pierced through his innate caution and at the end of a quarter of an hour he was ready to do whatever she required of him. At that time, it was simply to provide her with information she desired concerning the activities in the House.

"For my own reasons, I wish our association to remain unknown to my family—or anyone with whom I am acquainted," she had said.

He had not inquired further, but accepted the need for secrecy, attributing it to the caprice of a lady with few demands on her time. He was not so naive as to imagine she had any interest in him personally—the humble son of an attorney who had distinguished himself at Oxford, and whose uncertain future depended on successfully scaling the treacherous rungs of a political career. He knew from the start she was using him for her own ends.

"You shall bring me news of the important debates as seen through your eyes. I don't want to have it through the filter of official channels. Do you understand me? Or do I ask too much of you?"

At that, gazing into her keen, sparkling eyes, he would have said she could ask anything at all of him and he would move heaven and earth to do it.

"All that remains is to decide how we shall manage these communications," she'd said, glancing around at the other riders, a couple of whom were heading in their direction.

"A note sent round to my lodgings will find me, if not immediately, within a few hours. And I might simply have a letter delivered to your house."

"Perhaps," she said. "But if it should fall into the wrong hands…"

Soon they'd settled on Hookham's as their place of rendezvous.

And so they had gone on for a number of months last year and from the moment Lady Mariana had returned to London for the season this year. Jeremy looked forward to those days when he received a note in her distinctive, hasty hand with an ache in his heart, knowing that he might see her later and, for a moment or two, bask in her extraordinary presence.

A few days ago, however, contrary to their usual practice, she had drawn him aside for a longer conversation. Always a little disconcerted by her proximity, at first he hardly attended to what she was saying, until he realized she was pointing out to him the presence of a modest young lady he later knew as Miss Hastings. She explained who she was, and desired him to make himself known to her, and to find some way to see if he thought she was a person to be trusted.

He had at first believed that no prattling seamstress could ever be persuaded to keep such a tantalizing bit of gossip to herself as that the sister of the Earl of Bridlington had a keen interest in politics and was on friendly terms with a mere private secretary. She was bound to jump to the wrong conclusions, he was sure. At least, the wrong conclusions from Lady Mariana's viewpoint, if not his.

But his opinion altered when he realized that Augusta Hastings was no common modiste's assistant. She was well educated and had the kind of manners and address that assured him that if not well born, she was at least gently bred. Perhaps the daughter of a country parson. It had not taken him more than a few minutes to deduce that she had secrets of her own to keep. Something in her eyes. While they were ready to light up with humor, they were guarded, cautious, even a little sad. It was his experience that people anxious to keep their own secrets could often be trusted to keep the secrets of others.

After he'd made Miss Hastings's acquaintance, he assured Lady Mariana of her probable trustworthiness. And two days later, that very morning, he received a note from Mariana asking him to find a way to make his acquaintance with herself known to Miss Hastings. The seamstress was to be included in the project they had been planning for some time. They could hardly meet at Lanyon House, and so Jeremy strolled in the direction of Curzon Street in the afternoon, hoping Miss Hastings would emerge to go on some errand or other so he could intercept her and ask her to take a letter to Mariana.

He'd been somewhat surprised that she turned south and entered the Green Park. But it was fortuitous, because it gave them an opportunity to talk without being observed by anyone.

So he had accomplished what Mariana had asked of him. He could not do otherwise. He had long ago relinquished all power to refuse her, his heart having taken control of his head. He knew he was nothing compared with the high-born suitors who no doubt vied for her hand. With such brilliant matches to choose from, she might easily laugh at his pretensions, if he ever dared to express them. And as to approaching her brother the earl—Bridlington would no doubt reject his suit out of hand.

Knowing all this did nothing, however, to diminish his infatuation. He found himself thinking of Mariana throughout his days at the House, doing Perceval's bidding, attending boring and unruly debates, ostensibly taking everything in with his keen analytical eye for the sake of his employer. But in reality, he saw and heard the world in relation to where Lady Mariana's interest lay, looking for ways to cull the bits that she would find absorbing, and hoping to inspire one of the mischievous gleams that lit her face so beguilingly.

Thorne gave himself a mental shake. It would behoove him to focus on his career, on advancing his own interests in the halls of Westminster. That would be wise. But he'd long since abandoned wisdom as something to be pursued in old age.

CHAPTER 9

*B*y the time Augusta reached Berkeley Square and was met once again at the door by Lady Mariana, she'd had ample time to puzzle over her encounter with Mr. Thorne and intended to question Lady Mariana about it. But as soon as she entered the mansion, she found herself swept up into activity with no immediate opportunity to ask a single question.

"I have everything ready upstairs, but only an hour to devote to you, I'm afraid. My mother has decided to entertain this evening and requires me to be in attendance, so I shall have to go and dress betimes."

Lady Mariana said all this over her shoulder as she hurried up the back stairs to the attic with Mariana struggling to keep up with her, laden as she was with her rather heavy work basket.

"You see, I have my brother's discarded coats—one suitable for day, another for evening—a pair of pantaloons, a pair of knee breeches, two shirts, and a waistcoat. The stockings will not need to be altered, of course." She bustled Augusta close to the fire and the bright candles. "I see you've brought your work basket. I have taken care to assemble such tools as I thought you might need, and the garments have been marked as they must be altered to fit."

Augusta picked up the pair of breeches to examine, deciding she should start with something relatively simple.

And then, she dropped them. Without thinking, she rubbed her hands on her skirt, as if to clean them off. These breeches—they had recently covered Lord Bridlington's thighs, been next to his skin. She had exchanged words with him, shaken hands, and sat next to him in a curricle. The only skin she had seen was his face. The rest of his body had been covered, as was fitting. But, she thought, his naked legs —and parts of his body no lady should imagine—had been encased in these exquisitely made items. She found it difficult to wrestle her mind away from that image. The intense intimacy of handling his cast-off clothing made the heat that had started in her fingers spread up and into her body. For a moment, she didn't know what to do.

How silly! she thought. These are just clothes. The superb quality of the silk and the expertly sewn seams were to be admired. That was all.

"Whatever is the matter?" Lady Mariana said.

"Oh! Nothing!" Augusta shook the disturbing thought of unclothed male thighs from her mind—not that she'd ever actually seen any. All in a rush, she understood why tailors were men and modistes were women.

After a few deep breaths, Augusta picked up the breeches again and cast an expert eye over them, focusing on details of construction, and examining how they'd been pinned, trying to divorce her thoughts from their previous wearer. Whoever she was meant to fit them for now must be very slim, she thought. This brought tall, slender Mr. Thorne to mind, and she remembered his note, which in the bustle of hurrying up to the attic she'd forgotten. "I've a letter for you,

My Lady," she said, and took the missive out of her work basket.

"Please call me Mariana! I do wish you would relinquish such formality."

Augusta cast a searching, pleading gaze at Lady Mariana. "I wish, My L—Mariana—"

"Don't worry! I won't betray you. I won't tell anyone how intelligent and ambitious you are. Heaven knows, I envy you." She took the letter, but did not open it to read then and there.

"Envy me? Why?"

"Oh, not having unpalatable expectations foisted on you, I suppose. Although I daresay I should be grateful for my privileged position. In any case, I don't trade on it. So please, no formality!"

This reassured Augusta, so she steeled herself against a vision of Lord Bridlington's skin and set to work as quickly as she could, opening seams and trimming the breeches to the right size before sewing them back together with her tiny, neat stitches.

This took her the better part of two hours, since she had to mimic their original construction and ensure that the seams were strong enough to withstand being stretched by the muscles in men's legs. Dresses, petticoats, pelisses—these were all constructed carefully, but without any particular need to guard against undue stress. Only the demands of long sleeves that needed to bend at the elbow gave her any technique upon which to model her work.

At the rate she was sewing, Augusta anticipated that it would take her several lengthy evenings to accomplish her task. And she was still uncertain about tackling the much more complex coats. She wanted to ask someone who knew more about it than she did, but who? She knew no tailors in London, and she could hardly ask anyone at Madame's.

Of course! She thought. Something told her that, gossiper though he was, Mr. Gordon at the silk warehouse might be a source of valuable information in this regard, and if she gave him a few shillings for his discretion, he might be trusted to keep a secret. But what would she say? Why would she—a dressmaker—be altering men's clothing? Perhaps she could say she was altering it for her brother, and he couldn't afford to hire a fine tailor. She could bring the coat to him and show him what needed to be done, if that wouldn't raise too many questions. If Mr. Gordon didn't know enough to be any help, she would just have to do the best she could.

THE LAST THING MARIANA WAS IN A MOOD FOR WAS ONE OF her mother's dinner parties. It would be a small gathering—no more than thirty people—and of course the guest list included several of the most eligible gentlemen of the season. It would undoubtedly be a magnificent meal, concocted by the French chef who ruled the kitchen with expertise and a temper to match, followed by cards—no doubt for stakes that would not encourage the gentlemen to stay very late, thank heavens. But she was doomed to sit between Lewiston and Sir Edmund Beresford, so her mother had told her that morning.

"And although Sir Edmund is only a baronet, his family is ancient, his estates unencumbered, and his fortune intact. He's also kind and personable." The dowager had informed Mariana of this as she sat in front of her dressing table, her abigail arranging her slightly graying hair into attractive curls.

"He could be a prince of the blood and I still would not care to marry him," Mariana said.

"A prince of the blood would be a disastrous match," her

mother said. "It would be far more congenial to know that your consequence is such that a husband would not be tempted to fancy himself superior in all ways."

Mariana knew her mother referred to the most unsatisfactory relationship between the late earl and herself. The dowager had been from a respectable but undistinguished family, rendered desirable because of her great beauty and because of a fortune that was long-standing enough for its origins in trade to have been conveniently forgotten. Mariana had witnessed many a tense interchange when her late father had thrown her mother's relatively common origins in her face, if his wife had the audacity to question his extravagance.

At least, Mariana thought, it seemed that her mother's own unfortunate experience had inclined her to be more open to approving a match for the sake of her daughter's happiness, even if it were one that many in the *ton* might believe unsuitable.

As undoubtedly was the case with Mr. Thorne. All the while Jennings fussed over her, arranging her hair, selecting her gown, choosing her jewels, that man's disturbing yet adorable image kept a slight smile on Mariana's face.

"Is my lady pleased?" Jennings said.

"What? Oh! Yes. You've outdone yourself." Jennings had chosen perfectly for her, as usual. Lady Bridlington would not be able to find fault with the figured silk gown of Maria Louisa blue that brought out the color of her eyes, a necklace and earbobs of sapphires and pearls, and fawn silk evening gloves that showed her long, elegant arms and slender hands to advantage. Mariana was conscious of owing her mother the courtesy of looking her best, whether or not she intended to look with favor upon any of the hopeful gentlemen invited to the dinner.

When a short while later she entered the saloon where

most of the guests were already gathered, several conversations stopped and almost all eyes turned in her direction.

The dowager glided forward and drew her into the room, immediately steering her toward Lord and Lady Castlereagh.

"So this is the lady who refused Bainbridge!" Lord Castlereagh said after bowing over her hand.

Mariana couldn't stop the hint of a blush from staining her cheeks. "I did it for the sake of his happiness, My Lord," she said, earning a chuckle from the earl.

"No mystery he should want you, I should say," Castlereagh said before his influential wife could send him a withering look.

The rest of the hour before dinner went off without any further embarrassment. Castlereagh escorted the dowager in to the table, and Lewiston drew Mariana's hand through his arm to take her in to dinner once the higher ranking ladies had gone in front, led by the Duchess of Wilmington and her daughter, followed by Lady Castlereagh. Behind Lewiston and Mariana came the viscountess Ambrose and her daughter, not yet out, but permitted to come to a dinner with close friends. Mariana sat an unsociable distance away from Perceval, making it impossible for her to listen to what he was saying. He spoke politely to the ladies on either side of him, but reserved more animated exchanges for the gentlemen seated nearby.

"I say, Mariana, just because I know you well doesn't mean you can cut me at dinner!"

Lewiston's words jolted her out of what she realized must be an impertinent stare at the prime minister's end of the table. "Oh Harry, don't be offended! You know I like you better than everyone. Tell me about the opera season." She deftly nudged the conversation to a topic she knew could occupy the marquess for hours. Her other neighbor, Sir Edmund, apparently had a taste for opera as well and happily entered into the subject. The two young men argued good-naturedly across Mariana about the latest diva from Italy, the cost of subscriptions, and the operas on offer that season. This allowed Mariana to simply nod and smile, contribute the odd "Oh really?" or "You don't say!" without ever actually engaging her mind. She kept wondering how Augusta was getting on with the sewing in the attic, hoping she had remembered to leave her enough candles and extra wood for the fire. She'd promised the seamstress that she would come up to her before she retired for the night.

A sudden worry rose to her mind: would Augusta be permitted to stay out so late? She kept forgetting that, despite her impeccable manners and ladylike air, she earned her livelihood in a modiste's shop. The dinner party was unlikely to break up before at least one in the morning. She should have told her to leave when she must! Perhaps there would be an opportunity to run up and see her before they all sat down to cards. Glancing at the end of the table where her brother sat, she caught him glaring at her and immediately erased the frown that must have darkened her expression. She cast him a beatific smile, which nearly surprised an inappropriate laugh out of him as the Duchess of Wilmington said something meant to be serious.

When the final course was cleared away and the covers removed, the ladies went through to the saloon, leaving the gentlemen to their port and brandy. This was Mariana's least favorite part of any dinner. She too often found herself conversing with a starchy dowager, or a simpering miss more concerned with fashion and gossip than with anything of consequence.

Her worst fears were realized that evening, and she had the most awful time maintaining an interested expression before the men finally came in to join them. She looked for her brother among them and noted that although he leaned heavily on his cane, none of the gentlemen took it upon themselves to try to help him—for which she was glad. They were all too full of whatever they'd been talking about.

Mariana breathed a sigh of relief, but it was premature. Miss Elkins, eighteen-year-old daughter of Sir Ponsonby Elkins, flew up from her seat on a small settee and approached George. "My Lord!" she cried in an irritatingly high voice. "Please permit me to help you to a seat."

Mariana could see her brother's jaw clenching from where she sat, and cast an anguished glance at her mother. George was too polite to rebuff the pretty—but obviously heedless—young girl. He said in a low voice, pitched to sound soothing but its intent was anything but, "I thank you, Miss Elkins, but I find it's better to manage on my own."

"Of course, My Lord. How difficult it must be! Pray do not hesitate to ask for my assistance if—"

"I've had tables for whist set up in the Chinese saloon," the dowager announced, putting an abrupt end to the debutante's insensitive display of ignorance. "I know you don't like to play, George, but Lord Lewiston, perhaps you'll join my table?"

Mariana sent a grateful look to her mother, who had soon persuaded the requisite number of guests to occupy the tables—including the irritating Miss Elkins. Excusing herself from a conversation about the perfidy of housemaids, Mariana strolled over to a small group of gentlemen near the pianoforte that included Perceval. Her intention was to stand close enough to listen without being noticed. Conversations among men often abruptly changed their direction when ladies were about, and she had a particular reason to attend to the prime minister. Jeremy's note to her had conveyed the information that the house debate that evening concerned the Luddites in the north.

"...It's deuced puzzling," the prime minister said.

"Wellington's delaying making any direct attacks on the French—don't know quite what he's waiting for—we're heading into conflict with the United States, and those troublemakers up north force us to attend to their petty demands and take resources away from where they're more essential."

Murmurs of general agreement followed this. Mariana itched to raise her voice and ask them what they expected, when the populace had been taxed so heavily and weavers were losing their jobs to machines that were cheaper but produced an inferior product, but she bit her comment back. Her mother would never forgive her.

"Ah! It's the beautiful Lady Mariana!" said General Woolcraft, who had turned away from Perceval to signal a footman for another glass of wine and saw her. "Won't you favor us with a song?" He gestured grandly toward the pianoforte.

She could not in all politeness refuse. She smiled. "I shall play, but I beg you will not ask me to sing. I am not in good voice at present." There was something about singing for company that Mariana disliked of all things. She could not abide having to stare out at a sea of faces—some bored, some adoring, some not attending at all—and maintain a pleasing expression. Whyever were young ladies taught to sing? At least seated at the instrument she could look down at the keys, or up at the music—which that evening consisted of a Mozart sonata she'd propped on the desk against just such an eventuality. A footman hurried over to open the lid of the beautiful Clementi pianoforte, tuned only that day. Mariana took her seat, turned to the final movement so she would not be encouraged to perform the entire work, and played as quietly as she could, hoping to still be able to overhear the interesting conversation that had resumed a small distance away from her.

Unfortunately, they'd moved just far enough away to

make it impossible for Mariana to hear any more. That, and the need to concentrate on her playing, thwarted her efforts. Desultory applause greeted the end of her performance, and she stood. However, once the entertainment had started, one or two mothers pushed their daughters forward to take their turn playing and singing an air, and Mariana was obliged to appear attentive to the mediocre musicians.

When the third one had bowed and there seemed to be no others, a disagreement arose from a far corner of the room. "I have told you before, Mama, I will not sing in a drawing room! Besides, I'm not yet out." It was the Honorable Olivia Fontenoy, daughter of the Viscountess Ambrose.

Lady Ambrose shushed her and spoke to her in a low voice that everyone could hear, "But your voice! Your tutor says it is quite exquisite, yet you will not allow anyone to hear it."

Poor girl! Mariana thought. She needed no explanation to account for Miss Fontenoy's reluctance. She wandered over to inhibit the argument, and when she approached, the viscountess nodded and walked away, doubtless looking for more congenial conversation.

"I applaud your resistance," Mariana said quietly after the viscountess was out of hearing.

Miss Fontenoy shook her head. "You are possibly the only person who does. Please don't feel you have to chat with me. I may go and join one of the card tables."

Mariana curtsied to her and glanced at the clock on the mantel. A few minutes past nine. She had momentarily forgotten about Augusta, and all at once worried that she would think she had to wait until the end of the dinner to leave. Doubtless she must return to Curzon Street before Madame locked the doors. She must find an excuse to go up and tell her to leave whenever she must.

"Dear me, I see a small tear in my lace," Mariana

murmured, in case anyone was near enough to hear her. Creasing her brow in pretended vexation, she lifted her skirt just slightly and frowned down at its hem as she went out into the stairwell, intending to climb to the next floor before dashing to the back stair entrance, when someone knocked on the street door.

Very odd for anyone to call at that time of night, Mariana thought. She paused and looked down at the entrance hall. Allsop made his stately way across the foyer from his office on the floor below and opened the door wide to admit someone carrying a briefcase.

"I have an urgent message for Mr. Perceval."

"I shall ask the prime minister to see you in the book room," Allsop said, gesturing toward that chamber on the ground floor.

The voice was unmistakable. *Thorne!* Mariana started down the stairs, but paused. She scampered around a corner out of Allsop's sight and waited for him to ascend the stairs and enter the saloon. Jeremy hadn't looked up in her direction and so didn't realize she had seen him. She peered over from the gallery, enjoying the sight of him unconscious of her presence. He pulled himself up to his full, impressive height and took a few steps around the entry hall, his eyes roving curiously around him. Ever since first meeting him, Mariana had wished so to see him standing there, in the entrance to Lanyon House, but not as a messenger. She wanted him to be paying her a call as an accredited suitor. Her heart gave a lurch. Would that ever happen? She'd told herself again and again that the cause was hopeless, that she must enjoy their light association while she could, on whatever terms possible. But every time she saw him she could not make up her mind to it. Surely her mother and brother could be made to see his excellent qualities and approve a match.

Collecting her wits, she tripped noiselessly down the stairs. Thorne looked up and saw her, and the joy that lit his face made her want to rush into his arms. What folly!

"My Lady!" he said.

She put her finger to her lips and motioned him to follow her into the book room. He placed the briefcase he'd brought on the library table and she held her hands out to him, walking toward him. "Why have you come?" Mariana whispered when he caught both of her hands in his.

"Things are evenly split in the voting. Perceval must attend and help the whip to carry the motion."

How she wished she could have taken off her evening gloves and felt the touch of his skin as he kept her hands in a firm grip! But it was enough for now. This was the first time they'd ever been alone in private and they'd never done more than shake hands politely. Her pulse raced. "Would that it didn't!" Mariana said, with an effort at focusing her attention on what he'd said.

"You knew it was bound to." Jeremy gave her a rueful smile, all the while letting his eyes roam over her face. "The Tories hold the majority."

"I know. But I wouldn't have found out until tomorrow at least. How fortunate that it is you who have come!" She cast a dazzling smile at him, her eyes alight with excitement. "You cannot know what is going on in this very house, quite unbeknownst to anyone but me." *And you cannot know what's going on in my heart even as we stand here,* she thought.

Thorne knit his brows but still smiled. "What can you mean? Surely you are not up to any mischief."

"Oh, nothing so terrible. But it will be a great lark. And I must do such things before I am—" She didn't know what to say. To mention marriage raised the specter that her husband would be other than he. The thought wiped the smile from her face.

They continued to face each other. Mariana searched Thorne's eyes, wishing with all her heart that he could be at least the son of a baronet, or of a merchant who was rich as Croesus, instead of the brilliant son of a prominent but impecunious attorney. That he had distinguished himself in his knowledge of the law and had become indispensable to the prime minister weighed heavily in his favor. At least in her eyes. But she feared it would never be enough.

At that moment, the door flew open, and Spencer Perceval strode in. Mariana and Jeremy let go of each other and Mariana whirled away from him. "Are you certain I cannot persuade you to take a glass of port?" she said, her voice cheery, as if they had been discussing only that.

"As I said, My Lady, I must deliver my message and hasten back to the House." Jeremy gave her a respectful bow.

"I shall leave you to talk about your gentlemanly matters!" she said, sending one more speaking glance at Jeremy and deliberately acting the coquette as she glided out of the room. She carelessly left the door ajar, but Perceval crossed the room in a few firm footsteps and pulled it shut with a decided click.

Alone in the hall, Mariana pressed her hand to her heart. She had not expected this. But she had no time to dwell on it. She must not forget Augusta! As quickly as she could, she made her way to the back of the house and the stairs to the attic.

She found Augusta in a state of agitation.

"My—Mariana!" Augusta said, standing and rushing to meet her. "I have done all I can this evening, because I must leave! Madame has a strict curfew of ten o'clock for us, and although there are ways to circumvent it, I had not planned it so this evening."

"Of course you must go," Mariana said, casting her eyes over a pile of garments stacked on the table. She had expected Augusta to finish only one of the pieces that night, but to her surprise, both the breeches and pantaloons appeared to have been altered, as well as one of the shirts.

"I'm afraid that's all I've managed. I did not want to begin the coat when I was tired. If I lose concentration, I could make a terrible error that cannot be fixed. I'll start that the next time."

"Of course, if that is what you think best. Quite honestly I am amazed at all you have done so quickly. Are you able to come back tomorrow? Or the next night? I need the evening clothes ready by the time of the opera masque on Monday. Which reminds me that there's something else I need you to alter, but I daresay you will find it much easier." At Augusta's worried look, Mariana said, "I cannot explain more just now —I must return downstairs. But do you go back to your lodgings, and return as early as you can. I shall ensure that Jennings knows you are to be given admittance whether or not I am here to greet you."

"Jennings?"

"My dresser. She is in my confidence to a degree and will not question you." At least, Mariana hoped not. She did not want to tell this devoted servant more than she had to, nothing that would force her to lie if questioned.

The more real her scheme became, the more Mariana became conscious of the risk involved. But she was in it too far to turn back now. She began to have some qualms about what she'd planned, knowing that if she were discovered it would not only be her reputation that could suffer irreparable damage. People were bound to criticize her mother and brother for allowing such behavior. And she wasn't yet confident that she would be able to perform her role well enough. She felt a bit guilty for involving Augusta, who likely had much to lose should everything go awry. But she could not act alone. She would offer her enough payment to make it well worth her while. She hoped to God that her instinctive trust in this girl would be rewarded. If not, so be it.

Having talked herself into a state of relative confidence about what was ahead, and with Jeremy's warm grip still making her hands tingle, Mariana returned to the party in high color. She dismissed her mother's inquiry as to whether she was sickening for something. "Just the heat, Mama," she said, fanning herself. "I shall be better presently." She looked around. "Where is Mr. Perceval?"

"He has been called away for a vote," the dowager said. "Most vexing."

"And Mrs. Perceval?"

"A headache, she said."

It seemed Mariana's glowing cheeks and bright eyes did nothing to deter any of the gentlemen from paying court to her that evening, and by the end Mariana knew her mother could find no fault with her behavior. She was in such high spirits that she even flirted with Lewiston, who no doubt thought he had done something to break through her resolve not to find him charming.

CHAPTER 10

The morning after the dinner, George went to his mother's room ostensibly to talk over the event. Lady Bridlington enjoyed such chats, and it was the least George felt he could do to appear as though parties mattered to him.

"Come, my dear boy," Lady Bridlington said, dismissing her haughty abigail with a wave of her hand. She was still clad in a luxurious brocade dressing gown, as was her custom, although her hair had been prettily coiffed under a lovely lace cap. She never went downstairs until she had breakfasted, dressed for calling, and perused the early post, which was spread out on a small table by the daybed where she lounged.

"I thought the dinner was a great success, Mama," George said, bending to plant an affectionate kiss on his mother's scented cheek.

"Yes, indeed. Your sister was in her best looks and behaved very prettily, much to my astonishment." She raised one eyebrow slightly and pursed her lips in an expression George knew was an attempt to suppress a smile.

He smiled back at her and pulled up a cushioned stool.

"You, however, appeared quite distracted the entire evening. It's not like you to present such a moon-calf face to the world."

This startled George. He was not conscious of appearing any different in company. Perhaps he wasn't as good at regulating his thoughts as he presumed. "I don't know what you mean, Mama."

"I know you too well, George, to be put off like that. Who is she? Who have you met? I know she wasn't at the dinner last night. You were hardly there yourself."

This was not the way George intended his conversation with his mother to go. "Now you're being fanciful," he said.

She sighed. "Is it fancy to hope that my son has at last fallen in love? My son who has so often declared his intention of remaining solitary all his life because he was born with an affliction that sets him apart from the world?"

He laughed. "And yet, I doubt you would want me to marry in a way that disobliged you."

"Where did you get that idea? Frankly, between you and Mariana I am almost willing to accept any in-laws with true affection and a modicum of intelligence. I don't understand Mariana. She has half the eligible men in the *ton* dangling after her, yet wants none of them."

"Perhaps, Mama," he said with a smile, "Your insistence that we must marry for love *and* to suit the family is an unreasonable expectation."

It was too true, what the dowager said. He wondered if she suspected—as he did—that Mariana was hiding something from both of them. It wouldn't do to inquire, though, in case it raised a suspicion she had not previously entertained. "Can you blame Mariana, though, Ma'am? She has been the catch of the season two years in a row, and is beset by fortune hunters. It is hard to know whether in such a case affection is real."

"You can't fob me off with your sister," Lady Bridlington said, a note of amusement in her voice, "You know I worry about you just as much. I fail to understand why you haven't settled on any of the delightful girls of sense and breeding—not to mention beauty and fortune—who have set their caps at you."

"Must we go over that again?" George said, scrambling to figure out how to direct the conversation along different lines. "You well know my feelings. I refuse to be pitied or settled for."

Lady Bridlington picked up the coffee cup at her elbow and took a sip. "And yet, I see in your eyes that maybe, just maybe, you have found someone who will do neither."

There was no arguing with his mother's intuition. He some-times thought she saw things she wished to see, that her desire for them brought them into being—especially when they pertained to her children. But in this case, she was mistaken. He had no such intentions with regard to Miss Hastings, the only lady he had met recently. They had not spent more than half an hour in each other's company. As to why she continued to be of concern to him—that, he told himself, was simply an accident of circumstances that kept throwing them in each other's way, and now he could blame his unease about her relationship with Mariana. "That is not to the point. You would be better served turning your attention to Mariana. I was minded of the many suitors she has rejected by running into Grantley at the club."

At this, the dowager wrinkled her nose. "An odious fellow. That was an offer I had no expectation of Mariana's accepting and, indeed, thought him most impertinent to make. He could bring nothing to the alliance. The advantage would have been all on his side."

"He has no scruples. He behaved true to character at Brooks's the other day, I can assure you. I wonder how it is that he has fallen so low, with such depraved morals, having so estimable a father and elder brother." George hoped this would inspire his mother to explore the family's history.

And she did not disappoint him. "True. It's an old family, with many branches. But I believe his grandfather was a shocking rake. A gamester as well."

"What were the other branches? There were numerous sons, I believe."

"Yes. I think a few inherited lesser titles from other relations, although the earldom has come down in a direct line for centuries."

This was promising. "Their estates are in the West Country, I believe? Cornwall, is it?"

"No, Devonshire, as I recollect. I think quite an unexceptionable baronet has—or had—a small estate on the north coast. The kinship is remote, but there nonetheless."

"And this baronet had sons too?"

She paused, looking up at the high ceiling with its pastoral frescoes as if she could draw a memory from it. "No, I don't believe so. At least one daughter however." At this observation, the dowager narrowed her eyes. "What is your interest in the family?"

"None, aside from curiosity." He wasn't entirely sure she believed him, but she didn't press him for more.

After that they discoursed amiably on the events of the previous evening and spoke a little about the dress party Lady Bridlington was planning in Mariana's honor in early May. "We shall invite everyone, of course, although who knows how many will come."

George was confident that few would decline an invitation to a rare party at Lanyon House, even though the daughter was in her second season, and reassured his mother on that score before taking his polite leave of her.

THE INFORMATION GEORGE HAD EXTRACTED FROM HIS MOTHER both reassured and alarmed him. Miss Hastings must be the daughter of the insignificant baronet she had mentioned. Judging by where she'd landed in London, she'd come on the stage from the West Country, and of course, the coincidence of the name. But the checkered history of the family, the preponderance of unsavory characters in the lineage—evidenced by Grantley—forced him to consider that he might do well to suspect her motives in befriending his sister. And then there was the mystery of why she took pains to conceal the connection.

He would have some time to think over what he had learned when he rode out to Richmond that day with Lewiston. Harry wanted to give his trusty cover hack an airing, and it had been some time since George had given his spirited bay gelding decent exercise. The weather was fine, so the plan agreed with him. The ride would provide ample time for private reflection when conversation was impossible, since they both wanted to have a few good gallops.

That settled, Bridlington returned to his room to don riding dress and send a note down to the stables.

BOTH THE HORSES WERE FRESH, PRANCING IMPATIENTLY WHILE the city streets imposed a sedate pace on them. George had a hard time reining Galahad in when they rode along Rotten Row to the carriage drive, through Kensington and then over Putney Bridge to the wilds south of the river. But he always felt confident in the saddle, and his spirits rose as they alternately raced each other and dawdled, enjoying the fine spring weather.

At one such moment of ambling, as they rode at a walk on loose reins and the gentle clop of hooves was broken only by the occasional snort, Lewiston asked, "What's on your mind, Bridlington? Are you put out by Grantley's behavior at the club?"

"What? Can you doubt it? But there's not much I can do about it at the moment."

"Then what's taking you so far away from here? Don't think I've ever seen you so distracted." He pulled up his horse as they reached the top of a rise that revealed a magnificent vista over rolling green fields.

"The usual matters. What will become of Mariana. Whether Mama will want to move to the dower house at Bridlington Abbey. Although she needn't, since there's no mistress to take her place." George played with the handle of his whip, not looking at Lewiston.

"There! I see that look. There's something else, isn't there. The last time I caught that expression was when you fell into calf love with that girl down at Oxford, daughter of the bagwig."

George had forgotten that brief, embarrassing episode, and laughed. "No! Nothing like that. Although…"

"Out with it. It'll go no further. You must know that."

"It's foolish," George said, trying to decide what to say to his friend. "I don't even really know her."

"Opera dancer?"

He tapped Lewiston lightly with his whip and Galahad lifted his head up with a jerk. "No indeed! Far from it." But was it? he wondered. "You remember I told you about the seamstress, the one you covered in muck so shamelessly, and I had to drive her to Madame Noelle's?"

"I don't recall such a thing. When did you tell me? And a seamstress! Might as well be an opera dancer," Lewiston said.

So he hadn't mentioned Miss Hastings to him. He remembered that he'd decided against it at the time. "Except I am convinced she's in fact a gentlewoman. She said she had no family and was penniless, but I think I've discovered that's not the case."

"You've discovered—you mean, you've been so interested in her that you've been making inquiries? After just that one chance meeting?" Lewiston's voice dripped with sarcasm. "I never would have thought it."

George took a deep breath and released it slowly. "Nor would I. But it wasn't just one meeting. And I think she's involved in something to do with Mariana. That's really why I've been trying to find out more about her." He looked at Lewiston and saw that he didn't believe him. "It's the truth!"

"So, a seamstress, who would know Lady Mariana because she works at the modiste she favors has something to do with her. I fail to see just why that would spur you to inquire into her life history."

"I can't explain. If you'd seen her as I had, you'd likely know what I meant. There's a mystery. I can't help thinking she's running away from something. I also have a growing suspicion she's in some way related to Grantley."

"Now you have me. What in blazes? Obviously, this mysterious girl must have a name. May I know it?"

"Shall we start back?" George said. "I don't want to end this fascinating conversation, but it looks likely to rain in the next hour or so." He turned his horse and urged him gently forward to pick his way down the rather steep slope.

George waited at the bottom of the slope for Lewiston to catch up with him.

When he did, Lewiston said, "Her name?"

"It's Miss Hastings."

"A name isn't much."

"Not unless it's allied to countenance, manners, and education."

"Beauty?"

George looked off into the distance and said quietly, "That too."

Lewiston gave a low whistle. "You're in it for sure, George. Don't deny it. What are you going to do?"

"I don't exactly know. But I can't leave the matter. If you could just see her, meet her," he said.

They rode on in silence for a few minutes until Lewiston said, "Here, she don't know what I look like. P'raps I could find a way to talk to her and she wouldn't know there's any connection between you and me."

George laughed. "You don't know what she looks like either!"

"I've a fair idea, from what you've told me. My Mama's in town for the season, just came down yesterday. I collect she's been to this Madame Noelle's, probably wants some new togs for the balls. I could offer to take her there."

"Wouldn't she think it strange? And what excuse would you have to talk to Miss Hastings if you did?"

This silenced Lewiston. "There's got to be a way. Let me think on it."

"I don't see what good it would do. Maybe a better idea is for you to try to find out from Grantley if he has any cousins in North Devonshire, girls of about twenty, perhaps as much as twenty-two. With golden brown eyes and a sharp wit. And a graceful figure." He stopped himself, although other descriptions came to his mind. "I would wonder, would like to know in particular, if she shares Grantley's abhorrence of physical deformity."

"Doesn't she know about your foot?" Lewiston asked, incredulous.

George shook his head. "I don't believe so. The three times we met I never walked. Once when I was seated in the curricle, another time I was mounted, and the third time I took care not to walk or lean on my cane, and she never looked at my legs." Mixed up with his desire to see Miss Hastings and speak to her again were unavoidable feelings of deep anxiety about how she would react to his clubfoot. He wondered if anyone had told her about it yet, if she happened to have mentioned their encounters to someone. If perhaps Mariana had told her. Somehow, the idea of a pitying look from her, or worse, a sudden expression of disgust, would be insupportable. "Race you to the copse over there?" he said, bringing the conversation to a precipitate close.

The two friends rode back to Berkeley Square in mutual silence, broken only by a few comments on the weather and the roads. They arrived in the stable yard just as the first fat drops of rain stained the ground.

CHAPTER 11

*A*fter taking apart the seams of the coat and seeing the many layers of construction between the outermost superfine and the lining, Augusta realized she would absolutely need help taking it in. And she didn't think she'd be able to simply describe her problem to Mr. Gordon sufficiently so that she could manage it on her own. So, without asking Mariana, on the second afternoon after Mariana had left her alone in the attic, she rolled the coat up into a ball, stuffed it in her work basket, and scampered down the stairs and out to the street. She thought she had less than two hours to accomplish her errand, and because the warehouse was all the way on Pall Mall, she had to spend a precious shilling and hire a hack to take her there.

Augusta strode into Harding & Howell, which was even busier than it had been the first time she was there, and cast her eyes around looking for Mr. Gordon. At first, when she didn't see him, she worried that he wasn't there, that her jaunt had all been for nothing. But she waited, and soon enough, his slim, well-dressed form emerged from an almost-hidden door. He marched up to the counter where

Augusta had seen him before, lifted a section of it and let himself slip behind it. Before any other patrons could occupy him with their requests, Augusta hurried over.

"Mr. Gordon!" she said as she approached.

He looked up, at first alarmed, then his expression settled into a practiced smile. "Miss Hastings! I didn't expect to see you so soon. Was aught amiss with your order?"

"No," Augusta said, and leaned partway across the counter. "I need your help."

His smile broadened. "Madame tormenting you already!"

"No, nothing like that. At least, not exactly. I have an alteration to do that I don't know how to accomplish. I've brought it with me. I thought you might be able to tell me how to approach it. You see, I have no experience sewing men's clothing." She opened her work basket and drew out the coat.

Mr. Gordon laid it flat on the counter and ran his hands appreciatively over the fabric. "Weston," he said. "This is extremely fine." He looked closely and saw the chalk marks where the alterations were to be made. "Why do you have to make it so small? Surely it would be better for a new coat to be made."

Augusta glanced around her to make sure no one could hear what they were saying. "It's for my young cousin. He couldn't afford a new coat and asked me to alter this one, which was given him by the gentleman he works for." She was spinning a tale that she knew would soon run out of thread.

Leaning close to the garment, Mr. Gordon examined every seam, and stopped at the inside of the collar, peering even more closely.

Augusta saw, with a start, what he was looking at. A tiny embroidered crest. She looked up and their eyes met.

"Your brother works for the earl of Bridlington? I know

the household. There are no young servants who would fit in a coat as small as you intend to make this one."

Her pulse suddenly pounding, Augusta said, "No. He doesn't. Not exactly."

Mister Gordon grabbed her wrist. "Have you stolen this, Missy?"

Shocked, Augusta said, "No! Only, I can't explain to you what I'm doing with this coat. It isn't my secret to tell." She felt near to tears. Why had she taken this chance? "I came to you because I thought perhaps you could be trusted. I'm willing to pay for your help. Or rather Lady—my partner is willing to pay."

After what seemed like an eternity, Mr. Gordon spoke again. "It could be that we might help each other. You have no experience of men's clothing…" He leaned closer and lowered his voice. "And I am not very good at working with ladies' clothing."

What was he suggesting? "I don't understand."

"We can't talk here," he said, smiling and nodding to a woman who was approaching the counter. "Meet me in the Green Park in ten minutes."

She could do nothing but agree at this point. She'd already been gone from the attic for nearly an hour, but Mariana had said she would be out until later in the evening. She sincerely hoped that would be the case.

Augusta waited for Mr. Gordon just inside the Bath Gate. He came promptly at the time he said he would, and he had a satchel with him. It took only a few minutes for Augusta to discover that it contained an old-fashioned lady's court dress that needed not taking in, but letting out. He'd brought her extra silk to use for this purpose.

"Why do you want this?" she asked.

"Let's each of us keep our secrets," Mr. Gordon answered. "I can make the necessary alterations to the coat by tomorrow. Will that be enough time for you to do the dress?"

"I'll make sure of it," Augusta said.

They traded garments, nodded to each other, and went their separate ways.

How Augusta managed to keep the arrangement she'd made for the alteration of the coat and her work on the voluminous silk court dress a secret from Mariana, she did not know. She could only attribute it to the lady's lack of interest in the details of the work. To account for her long absences from the modiste's, she simply said Lady Mariana had requested her again, saying—on Mariana's instructions—that it was the lady's intention to order at least three more gowns from Madame in the coming weeks. Madame accepted this with equanimity, but Pauline's eyes grew increasingly suspicious.

On the third night, Lady Mariana examined the finished pieces with admiration. "You are indeed very skilled!"

"The evening coat will be ready tomorrow afternoon. It was a little more complicated than the other garments."

"I can imagine," Mariana said as she reached into a small reticule she had brought up with her and took out a number of gold sovereigns, which she placed on the table. "You will find that I am most appreciative."

Augusta caught her breath for a moment, then was aware of a sick feeling deep in her stomach. The payment should not have come as a surprise. Lady Mariana had mentioned that she would compensate her for her work. But although in becoming employed by Madame Noelle she had joined the ranks of those who were paid by the wealthy for services rendered, it had not been very long ago that she would have been the one doing the paying. A wayward ray of sunlight through the small attic window chanced to glint off the gold coins, accentuating their brightness, mocking her. Augusta made no move toward them. This was not the same as taking her modest wage from a woman who engaged in business. Augusta had no compunction there, especially since Madame subtracted several shillings for room and board from the meager amount she paid her seamstresses. The transaction here, in Lady Mariana's home, in its very magnanimity, had a sordid air. It was all wrong. Augusta continued to stare at the coins, transfixed, mortified.

At last she said, "I find, Mariana, that I am unable to accept payment for my work here."

"Whyever not? You have surely earned it! Don't be squeamish. It's only money. And I assure you, it is no hardship to me to pay it."

Augusta looked up at Lady Mariana's puzzled face. Of course she wouldn't understand. Nonetheless, Augusta said, "It has been an honor, and a welcome challenge. Besides, we have become…" Her voice trailed off. It would be too much to presume on friendship, no matter what Lady Mariana asserted. If they had met when Augusta was still in Devonshire, still in her situation as a daughter of a respected baronet, she would have assumed such a friendship despite the difference in their ranks. But now, Augusta didn't know how to account for her feelings on the matter. Her ambitions to be a modiste would require her to exact payment from ladies like Mariana—much more than a few guineas.

After a brief silence, Mariana said, "I see. Yet you have put me in the position of feeling uncomfortable about asking for further assistance from you, which you must know I had every intention of doing."

Augusta did not break away from Mariana's steady gaze. She longed to confess all to her, to explain how she came to be in London and in such a position. But although Mariana clearly sympathized with her ambitions, she might not be so understanding about her flight from her aunt's efforts to marry her off to the younger son of an earl. Yet here she was, starting to feel some regard for a different earl's son, and finding herself hopelessly entangled in that earl's sister's life. "Nonetheless, I shall not allow you to pay me. Humor me in this, I beg you. I remain at your service, My Lady, with no expectation of remuneration." She dipped an ironic curtsy, lifting her skirt with two fingers and cocking her pinkies, hoping to lighten the atmosphere, which had become suddenly laden with unspoken thoughts.

Mariana gave a short laugh, then sighed. "Very well. I won't presume to question you further, or insist. I see in you someone very like myself, someone whom I would delight in knowing better. And I can see that the question of money between us complicates things. But no matter. Let us leave that subject and come to the additional service I dare to ask of you." She turned a little away and strolled to the crude hearth, resting her wrist on the knotty wood mantel. "I ask you to do something more than just sewing. I hinted at this before, but now I must secure your participation. I would like you to accompany me to the opera masquerade in Covent Garden Monday night."

Had she heard correctly? "I'm sorry, My Lady, I mean Mariana, you want me to do what?" Augusta's mind reeled. What could she be thinking?

"It will be such an adventure, if nothing else. Aren't you curious? It's a masquerade! No one will see who you are. And we won't be without an escort." At this, the faintest blush tinted Mariana's cheeks. It was gone as quickly as it came.

The mischievous, hopeful look in Lady Mariana's eyes almost made Augusta laugh out loud. What a lark it would be indeed, if she dared. But to adopt such a role, to appear in society when it hadn't been long since she'd turned her back on such things—it was utterly counter to everything she had decided about her life, to everything she had determined to do in London, to all the safeguards she had thought through and put in place so that no one would discover where she was. To go out in the evening to a social event—even one not frequented by the *haut ton*—to exhibit herself in society of any level, had not in any way been her intention. It reminded her a little of the pranks she and Amelia used to play, one in particular. But she was no schoolroom miss anymore.

Lady Mariana said, "I do have a little additional bit of sewing to ask of you, too. You see, over there, under the holland cover is a garment that needs what I believe will be a very small amount of skill from you to make it serviceable for your needs. Would you kindly release it from its hiding place?"

Augusta walked over to where Mariana pointed. She picked up the corner of the heavy white fabric and lifted it away, revealing an exquisite silver and white evening gown. A gown she easily recognized. It was one she had delivered to Lady Mariana a few short days ago. She had wished she could make some slight alterations in the design, but of course had been prevented from doing so.

Mariana said, "It's for you. I already wore it to Almack's, so will not appear in it again. I want you to alter it to fit yourself, although we are not so very different in size. I'm taller, but we are both of a slender build. And since you will not accept my payment, if you would take this dress instead, honor would be satisfied."

It would indeed. Augusta knew that Mariana had paid much more for it than the few guineas that still glinted on the table nearby. She touched the delicate silk with the back of her hand, taking care not to allow the calluses on her fingertips—calluses she was only just developing—to catch on it. Although her condition in Devonshire had been comfortable, she could never have expected to wear such a magnificent gown. For evenings, she was more used to wear sprig muslin, with only a few knots of ribbon to decorate it and a single flounce at the hem. She'd always made the best of her gowns and was much admired for their stylishness. But this was far beyond anything. To go out in such raiment. Did she dare? Not only to appear in public, but clad in one of Madame Noelle's creations?

"This is madness," she said, but she smiled. It would be bold indeed, and it laid her open to thoughts she had vowed to put behind her. But Augusta knew enough about the masquerades at the opera house to believe that no one of her remotest acquaintance would be there. At least, she was in a fair way to persuading herself it was so. And masked, and perhaps covered with a domino—it was still a terrible risk. "But my lady—"

"When you say that, I can hear the refusal in your voice," Mariana said, wilting onto a chair like a daylily at sunset. "I wouldn't ask if it weren't important. I cannot go without you, and I can't explain it all now. Don't you want to help me see it all through?"

See *what* all through? There was no question that the stark contrast between Mariana's world and the back chambers of a dressmaker's showroom had stirred up feelings of discontent in Augusta's breast. More than that, it had stirred up her desire to exercise her own creativity, to make clothes that flattered and made the women who wore them feel uniquely beautiful, not just fashionable, because every detail would be suited particularly to them. She knew now that Madame Noelle's atelier would not be her route to such a future. Who was to say that Lady Mariana would not prove instrumental in her future success? And was she enough of an opportunist to press that advantage?

Mariana rose and took Augusta's hands in hers. "I don't

know where you've come from, what you've left behind, but I know there's more in you than a common seamstress. You say you want to be a modiste. I have no doubt you could be. But perhaps you could be even more. Don't you want to reach for a life you deserve? Don't let it slip through your fingers. You, Augusta Hastings, are not in the common way."

The conversation had shifted from simple persuasion to take part in a bold prank to something dangerously close to getting at a tender place in Augusta's heart. Before she could stop them, tears sprang to her eyes. She freed one of her hands from Mariana's and wiped them away. "I'm being so foolish! I don't know why…"

Mariana laid her hand on Augusta's cheek. "Put on the gown. Let's see how it looks. Then you can decide."

Augusta knew that to do so would seal her involvement in Lady Mariana's plans, but she could not resist. The feel of the fine silk against her body, the swish of it as she walked across the wooden floor, a demi-train softly trailing behind her, the cut of the gown that dipped alluringly to expose her white breast—with a small alteration, which she would make when she took it in to fit her—made her lift her chin and straighten her spine, showing her long, graceful neck.

"I don't think you can possibly know how beautiful you are," Mariana said. "I dare say you are well able to dance. You move as though that is the case. And not just country dances, I'll wager."

Augusta closed her eyes and felt the press of James's gloved hand on the small of her back as he twirled her around in the waltz, shocking the country matrons at the assembly rooms. And then, she realized that the hand she imagined did not belong to James. It was one that she knew from her own experience was strong and sure, that could pull her right off her feet and into a curricle. She smiled. "Yes. I can dance."

~

THE NOTE FROM LADY MARIANA REQUESTED JEREMY TO RIDE in the park again. Although he welcomed the opportunity to have a longer, more private conversation with her, he did not relish having to hire another hack. In addition to the cost, the poor animals were not up to the mark, and he felt a bit foolish astride an aged cob in an environment where one's horses were under as much scrutiny as one's dress. But it couldn't be helped.

He found her in the same secluded spot as before, her groom nowhere in sight, as usual. She dismounted on the pretext of picking up her dropped whip, and he slid down from the saddle and joined her, ostensibly to lend his aid. They stood close together. A little closer than necessary, but Lady Mariana did not step away. The fresh breeze had brought color to her cheeks, and when she looked up at him, her eyes shone. If he could believe it was for the joy of seeing him, he would have rejoiced. He suspected, though, that she was simply excited about some new project for which she required his help.

Which indeed turned out to be the case.

Without preamble, she said, "Would you be willing to accompany me to the opera masquerade on Monday?"

He didn't at first know what to say. "I-I would gladly accompany you anywhere, but—"

"Yes yes, it's not a respectable place for a lady. But I won't be a lady!"

He knit his brow, perplexed. "I don't understand."

She threw her mare's reins over its head, gathered them in her hand and nodded toward Jeremy's hack, indicating that he should do the same. "Walk with me and I'll explain it all."

For the next quarter of an hour, they strolled slowly

through the trees as Mariana told him of a plan so outrageous he could hardly believe it.

"Of course, you may choose not to go, if it's too reckless for your taste," she said, a mischievous dimple in her cheek.

"If you think for one moment I would allow you to attend such an entertainment unescorted by a gentleman, then you have clearly misjudged my character!" He became more heated than he intended, but the thought genuinely filled him with horror.

She drew herself up. "Allow? You presume to have the authority to dictate my actions?"

"No, of course not My Lady." *Poor choice of words!* he thought "I misspoke. I only meant that I would have grave misgivings, and think myself a shabby fellow if I didn't lend my protection to you, no matter how you intend to appear."

Her smile returned. "Of course. And your instinct does you great credit. I should like to know you were there, in case anything unexpected occurs." She glanced up at him with such a look of entreaty in her eyes that it was all he could do not to take her into his arms then and there.

"What must I do?"

"I have it all planned. You simply need to meet us there, masked of course."

"Us?" he said.

"Miss Hastings and myself. I have already secured a box. Won't it be a grand lark!"

The delight in her voice made him laugh out loud. "If you say so!" But he couldn't help having some misgivings about so preposterous a plan. If anyone could carry it through, though, it would be Lady Mariana Lanyon.

All that remained was for him to go to a costume warehouse and hire something suitable. Unlike many gentlemen of fashion, he did not own a domino. He'd never been to a masquerade before, and was inwardly rather excited and intrigued at the prospect.

NOW THOROUGHLY EMBROILED IN LADY MARIANA'S SCHEMES, Augusta had to hope Madame would give her permission to stay away for an entire night. It would be far too late when they left the masquerade for her to return to Curzon Street, so Mariana insisted she stay at Lanyon House, in one of the empty servants' rooms. So Augusta invented a school friend and her family who were in town to buy wedding clothes, saying her friend wanted to have dinner with her and go out, possibly to the theater, and had invited her to stay on a truckle bed in her room. Madame did not withhold her permission, but Augusta could see that her employer was beginning to lose patience with her.

Not so easy was it to satisfy Pauline's bursting curiosity. After her final night of alterations for the masquerade the next evening she'd tiptoed into the attic bedchamber on Curzon Street just before ten, the sound of her steps covered by the rhythmic breathing of the exhausted seamstresses, and thought she'd managed again to avoid having to talk to Pauline. But before she could take off her bonnet, Pauline sat up. She must not have been asleep.

Pauline put her finger to her lips and gestured for Augusta to go with her into the adjoining parlor. Once there, she lit the oil lamp with a screw of paper dipped in the dying fire, and whispered, "Out with it. There's something smoky going on here, and I won't rest until I got the whole of it."

It was clear to Augusta that Pauline wouldn't be satisfied with anything less than a romantic story. So she stayed as close to the truth as she dared in saying that she planned to go to the opera masquerade ball the following night, inventing a sweetheart from the country who would meet her there.

"But what'll you wear?" Pauline asked. "You got nothing here that'd serve."

Thinking quickly, Augusta said, "I've rented a simple costume. Been saving my pennies." Then she invented a complicated tryst, full of secret signals and single roses, stolen kisses, sighing promises. It was worthy of a three-volume romance, Augusta thought.

"'Ere, you better be careful. Those masked balls can be a little rough, truth be told. All sorts mix there."

"But I'll have Albert to protect me," Augusta said.

"I thought you said 'is name was Alfred?"

In a panic, Augusta said, "His second name is Albert. It's our special signal, when he calls me Jane and I call him Albert."

"So, are you betrothed?"

"No...not exactly."

Pauline tsk'd. "Don't you go trustin' 'im not to get you into trouble! I can tell yer innocent as a babe. What'd he persuade you to?"

"Oh it's nothing like that!" But what was it like? Augusta was running out of ideas, and afraid that at any moment the absurdity of the tale would send her into a peal of laughter. She coughed and tried to control herself. "We've known each other such a long time. Only our parents wouldn't let us marry, so that's why we're here. We can't announce a betrothal."

This sad circumstance mollified Pauline a little. "Well, I'll keep mum. Those others are chatterboxes. I wouldn't trust 'em with sixpence. Only you got to tell me all about it when you come back. Mayhap I'll get my Freddy to take me to one o' them masquerades. Wouldn't that be a spree!"

By now completely exhausted from hours of physical

work sewing and mental work inventing a Banbury story, Augusta followed Pauline back into the bedchamber.

MONDAY AFTERNOON ON HER WAY TO BERKELEY SQUARE, Augusta had stopped at Harding & Howell to pick up the coat, which Mariana said would be needed by her young friend that evening, and delivered the antiquated gown she had worked on into Mr. Gordon's hands. She didn't have time to examine his work then, but prayed it had been satisfactory. She knew she'd done a creditable job with the dress.

Her longer walk gave her ample time to become nervous before she entered through the servants' door of Lanyon House, nodding to a scullery maid who had become familiar with her from her other visits. Her mood alternated between a thrill of excitement and apprehension that something would go wrong. But what could go wrong, she asked herself? When did she become so chicken hearted? She had taken part in pranks and adventures aplenty in her childhood, rambling with the farmers' children over the rocky shore and sneaking into the kitchens to steal tarts. But in those cases no real danger threatened. At most a scolding—her nursemaid and her governess never beat her, and when she had outgrown both, she had been left to be her own judge of propriety.

Oddly, she had never done anything to raise the slightest concern in her father, or engage the provincial gossips, until she met James. The son of a local squire, he came down from Oxford after his uncle bought him a pair of colors, near the beginning of the Peninsular conflict. They met at a public assembly. All the dragoons attracted notice, in their scarlet uniforms and gold braid, and gleaming, tasseled Hessian boots. But for her, it was more than a passing flirtation. Augusta's eyes had met his, and she was completely smitten.

She had never seen anyone so handsome. They danced the cotillion, hardly exchanging a word when the figures brought them together—and Augusta had nearly wept thinking that would be the end of their story. But the ensemble struck up a waltz. This drove most of the well-bred young ladies to sit demurely fluttering their fans, forbidden by their mothers to engage in such an indecent dance. Augusta had had every intention of joining them in the supper room, but a gentle hand on her arm stopped her. One bow, one look into his deep brown eyes, and she was powerless to refuse this tall, magnificent soldier.

They'd been one of only five couples daring enough to dance the waltz, and whispers skittered around the assembly room. But Augusta was too full of joy, too drunk with happiness to care one jot what anyone else said.

The bittersweet remembrance fogged her mind throughout the young maid's ministrations as she donned her evening dress in the attic in Lanyon House. Her hair done in becoming ringlets, Augusta pulled on her evening gloves, draped the sarsenet scarf over her elbows, cast her eyes around the room—which by then was so familiar to her it held no intimidating dark corners—and said, "Where is Lady Mariana?"

"My Lady said she will meet you in the carriage, which should be waiting in the street behind the mews by now," the girl said, standing back and cocking her head on the side for a last critical look at Augusta.

"Thank you, Jane," Augusta said. She fished in her reticule for a coin to press into the girl's hand.

"Oh, no Miss! Lady Mariana said you wasn't to feel obliged." The girl dipped a quick curtsy and opened the door to the staircase for Augusta.

It was already dark, with no moon, and no one saw her at that hour. As Augusta approached the hired chaise waiting, as promised, in the lane behind the mews, the door opened and a smart young gentleman climbed down, holding his hand out to her. She stopped abruptly. Mariana had said nothing about a gentleman accompanying them, only that Mr. Thorne would meet them there. And judging by his height and build, this was not Mister Thorne.

She was about to turn around and go back into the house when a light, cultured, somewhat familiar voice said, "I await your pleasure, Miss Hastings."

She walked slowly forward. As soon as she was within arm's reach, the gentleman grasped her and pushed her quickly into the carriage, following close on her heels before snapping the door closed and knocking on the roof. For one brief moment, Augusta feared she was being abducted.

"You didn't recognize me! Famous!"

It took Augusta a moment, but when the gentleman removed his beaver hat and placed it on the seat next to him, she exclaimed, "Mariana!"

Lady Mariana erupted in a ripple of laughter. "The look on your face! Oh this is marvelous. If you didn't recognize me I have every hope no one else will."

"But…but…" Augusta was at a loss. Why would a lady do such a thing?

"You wonder why the secrecy, why I have gone to such trouble for a silly opera masquerade. You can be forgiven, and I must apologize for treating you so abominably by having you participate in a scheme you can have had no suspicion about. But you see, this is a test. I want to be able to pass as a young man, at least for a while, so I may gain admittance to a particular place women may not go before I'm to be bound in a marriage where my influence in matters of importance will be at best indirect, at worst nonexistent. And I want to know, just for a little while, the freedom of being able to go wherever I desire to without risking irreparable damage to my reputation. Oh, I know I must face a future in keeping with my station. I truly have no choice. But I am taking steps to ensure that at least I will have a hope of happiness, of being allied with someone who understands me, who knows my very soul. If I must destroy my own reputation in the process, so be it."

Augusta let Lady Mariana spill out all this pent up fervor without interruption. After all, who was she to criticize? Hadn't she, in her own way, taken charge of her future in defiance of all that the world expected of her? She, however, had none but the most remote claims to nobility and was not an heiress—two circumstances that she had the good sense to see made Mariana's situation more complicated than her own. "So, I can call you neither My Lady nor Mariana this evening. Who are you?"

"I am Malcolm Thorne, cousin to Jeremy. And you, too, are our cousin. Augusta Thorne, to make things a little easier."

"Why—"

"Oh, perhaps I should explain: Jeremy will meet us there, as I said. I at first thought to make my initial appearance as a young buck on my own, but, foolish boy, Jeremy insisted I wasn't to be unescorted. Of course, you are with me, but an opera masquerade is—as you may know—not always a very safe place for females. And oh yes, of course! A mask. Here…" She reached into the folds of her cloak and drew out a gilded lady's mask with black satin ribbons to tie around her ears. "I have one of my own. A little extra protection against being found out."

Augusta's head reeled. She didn't know precisely what she'd expected. She knew she would face an evening of pretending to be someone she wasn't—that much was certain from the moment she donned the evening dress. But that she was assisting in such extravagant folly, such a daring escapade—she never imagined. The alterations she'd been asked to make, the diminutive size of the breeches and coat—now it all made sense.

Should she beg off? She could demand that the carriage turn around and return her to Lanyon House. But she had to ask herself, why? What had she to lose in all this? No one at such an event would recognize her as the quiet, bookish seamstress. No one from Bideford was at all likely to turn up in such a place, and her acquaintance in London could be numbered fewer than ten persons.

It didn't take long for *why* to become *why not?* Augusta became all too easily infected with Mariana's spirit of bold defiance. "Tell me what I must do," she said, her eyes alight with the mischief reflected in Lady Mariana's face.

Mariana reached out and took both her hands. "I knew I was right about you! Whatever happens, however things go from now on, promise me you will remain my friend?"

Her voice sounded so small, almost childlike. It was an appeal Augusta found herself unable to resist. "Of course. It would be my honor."

CHAPTER 12

*M*ariana was up to some mischief. George knew her too well to doubt it. A certain look in her eye, an edge in her voice, were sure signs that she had got some scheme in her head, and wanted to keep it hidden from his mother—and from him.

George, Mariana, the dowager, and Lewiston had been the only ones at the table that evening. It was a rare night when none of them had dinner engagements and were entertaining no one at Lanyon House. When the covers had been removed, Mariana said, "I'm very tired from all the activities this past month. Perhaps I'm getting old, but I think I shall retire early this evening," and pretended to suppress a yawn.

Lewiston had looked crestfallen and said, "I thought for certain you'd go to the Mandeville's rout party this evening."

"Ugh, I detest a rout party. Such a crush. Impossible to have any conversation. One only goes there to be seen."

This had made George stare at his sister, noting that the expression in her eyes was at odds with her claim to be exhausted. If anything, she sparkled.

He, too, had no engagements, although for him, such a case was not unusual. Lewiston soon left the house in a desultory fashion to go to the rout and afterwards to Watier's for cards, failing to persuade George to accompany him.

George was determined to discover what game Mariana was playing. Half an hour after Allsop brought in the tea tray he and the dowager both went upstairs, ostensibly to bed.

He had no intention of retiring, however. He first thought of going to Mari's room and seeing if she was there, but decided it would be futile and waste what might be valuable time. No doubt, she would go out unseen. They both knew the secrets of the house, the hidden passages and stairs and back entrances, and it was an easy thing to leave or come back without anyone knowing.

It would be so like Mariana to get into a scrape. Their childhood and youth had been rife with games and secrets. George recalled with a grimace the time when she'd dressed him in clothes borrowed from one of the stable boys and taken him to the market in Harrogate, where she made him lean on a rustic stick and stand near a cap that he laid on the ground, telling him to exaggerate his disability. She walked by him, followed at a little distance by her maid, dropped a coin in the hat and passed on, then hid amid the crowd and watched as others did the same. Each time, he pulled his forelock and nodded and said, "thank-ee," struggling not to burst out laughing as the pennies and sixpences piled up in the hat.

But when he wanted to use their gains to buy a new whip, she'd refused. "We'll give this all to old Mistress Bundy, who has the rheumatism something terrible you know, and can't afford the doctor."

At other times, he would pretend to have tripped on his way out the kitchen door to the gardens so that the cook and kitchen maids would fuss over him, terrified that he'd injured himself, thus enabling Mariana to run in undetected and steal a ham, or some tarts, from the larder. These, too, were usually destined for stomachs other than their own, though.

Such memories made him smile. The pranks were innocent enough. But now, Mariana was a grown lady, an heiress. She had ample money of her own to contribute to charitable causes if she wanted to help out some poor orphan or downtrodden menial, so he didn't suspect her of stealing pies to take to the poor. But when he saw her face that evening, he'd known it as a sure sign that mischief was in her heart.

George's bedchamber was on the same floor as his sister's but at the other end of the long corridor. When he reached this chamber, he did not ring for his valet to help him undress, but sat in a chair by the fire leafing through a book, not paying any attention to it, his ears tingling with alertness. At every tiny sound, he held his breath. Mostly there came nothing beyond the scrabbling of a mouse, or the soft, padding footsteps of a servant passing on the way to attend the dowager.

His patience was rewarded when, after about an hour, he heard the unmistakable click of a door opening far down the hall. He listened for footsteps to come nearer and go to the main stairwell, but didn't hear them. She must have gone the other way, toward the entry to the back stairs beyond her room.

George quickly hoisted himself up with his cane and limped to open his door just far enough to see down the hall. The door to the back stairs was just closing. And unless he was much mistaken, whoever closed it had taken prodigious care not to make even the smallest sound.

It wouldn't do to follow after Mariana down those stairs —for he was certain she had gone that way, and could trip down them so quickly and quietly that she would no doubt be outside by the time he'd got halfway there. To follow in haste, he would have to use his stick, and that would make too much noise. Instead, he let himself out of his room, having thrown a coat over his arm and picked up his hat, and made his way to the carpeted softness of the central stairway. Quite possibly he wouldn't reach the servants' entrance before she did, but he had to try. If anyone saw him, he could simply say he'd decided to go and join Lewiston for cards after all.

The house was quiet. The servants had retired early as well. So he arrived at the ground floor without meeting anyone, and then headed toward the back of the house.

As he came in sight of the door that led to the mews, he saw the flash of a white dress just disappearing as the door closed behind it. That must be Mari. One of her most elegant new gowns was white, she'd worn it at Almack's. She would hardly be going out to the rout Lewiston had mentioned in a gown she had so recently been seen in, and that was the only *ton* party that night, as far as George knew. So where was she going? What evening was it? Monday. Aside from private parties, the only entertainment offered regularly on Monday nights were the opera masquerades. But that was absurd! Those wild and carefree events were not in Mari's line at all.

Unless… could it be that his sister had developed a *tendre* for someone not in their circle? Someone she'd somehow met out of his or his mother's sight, and whom she would want to meet somewhere their friends and acquaintances would be unlikely to expect her to be? The masquerades were open to anyone who could afford the price of a ticket costing as little as ten shillings. All that remained was to either hire a costume from a warehouse or throw a domino over one's evening clothes and hold a simple mask over one's face. Everyone from dukes to clerks could attend them, masked, so you never knew who you might be dancing with.

By this time, George wasn't only not tired, he was brimming with energy. Oddly, the one social occasion where he felt inconspicuous was a masquerade. If he could disguise himself enough that no one would recognize him as the Earl of Bridlington, his limp ceased to be of any consequence. Anyone who saw him could interpret the limp as part of his disguise.

What Mari didn't know was that George had been to several masquerades recently. It was a place where he could meet Madame Agatha or one of her girls to exchange a message about an unfortunate who needed his help. He preferred not to go to the bordello for this information if he could avoid it, wary of being seen there too often. Even in an unmarked carriage, his foot and limp made him easy to identify. Thus he owned a domino and face mask, which he could easily retrieve and then hire a hack to take him to Covent Garden. Would he find Mariana there? Possibly not. But he could think of no other destination that would have necessitated such secrecy. If she wasn't there, he could simply leave and no harm would be done.

Ten minutes later, he sat in a hack, swathed in a black domino with a mask covering his face down to his mouth. He felt like a green youth. There was power in anonymity. He could hardly blame Mariana for wishing to taste that power. He wouldn't disturb her if she looked to be safe, just keep an eye on her until she'd had enough of the kind of raucous entertainment the masquerade offered.

AUGUSTA HAD SAID LITTLE IN THE CARRIAGE ON THE WAY TO the masquerade, no doubt stunned to find herself in such a situation. Mariana thought she probably had no idea she'd been altering the men's clothes for a woman to wear. And not only was the person she was used to dealing with as a noblewoman suddenly transformed into an elegant man, but having to perform a role herself, to become someone she wasn't— it was a lot to ask of someone unaccustomed to London ways. Yet here she was. And she looked radiant.

"Put your arm through mine," Mari whispered as they walked toward the entry to the opera house.

"Won't it seem odd that I have no chaperone?" Augusta whispered.

"Ah. So you're unfamiliar with the world of the masquerade." She freed Augusta's arm from its place in the crook of her right elbow. "First of all, now is a good time to employ that mask I gave you in the hack."

Augusta did as instructed, looping the ties over her ears, but when she finished and Mariana started to move forward again, she hung back. "What is it?" Mariana said. "Don't you trust me?"

"It's not that. It's just…"

Mari followed Augusta's glance around at the press of couples and single men in dominoes and outlandish costumes, faces flushed with wine even before they'd arrived. Yes, it must be disconcerting. To be honest, she found it so herself. But the men's clothing she wore was like a talisman. The way it hid her feminine physique shielded her from the vulnerability Augusta no doubt felt. "The trick is to enter into the spirit of the thing. You have an opportunity to be as much someone you're not as I have! Be the fine lady for an evening. Be gay and carefree. You will come to no harm, I solemnly promise."

"Of course. I'm being silly. What could possibly happen here?"

After that, Augusta quickened her pace and lifted her

chin. When Mariana gave their two tickets to the man at the door who pointed them in the direction of the first tier of boxes, she stole a glance at Augusta and saw that behind her mask her eyes sparkled with mischief.

Once they were seated in front of the red velvet curtain and behind a low banister that divided them from the mingling mass of revelers in the slightly lower pit, Mariana scanned the crowd. She didn't recognize anyone, at least not yet. Mister Thorne had not revealed what costume he would wear. When they'd met briefly at Hookham's earlier that day, she'd tried to get him to tell her, but he wouldn't. He only said she would recognize him and not to worry. He knew she would be disguised as a gentleman. She had expected him to be shocked, perhaps even try to persuade her to abandon the scheme. But he had laughed aloud and several heads had turned in the subdued library.

In any case, he would find them. He knew which box she had reserved. Most likely a simple domino would serve his purpose, as he had little need to protect his identity, not being a member of the *haut ton*. In any case, surely his work in the House had kept him too busy to visit any of the masquerade warehouses to rent a costume, and he'd just been teasing her.

"So, what now?" Augusta said as they sat watching the growing crowd enter the gaudy opera house.

"We should order some refreshments, so we have a reason to stay here and not join the throng for dancing. At least not yet."

A look of blind panic leapt into Augusta's eyes. "Dancing? We will have to do so? Together?"

Mariana burst out in a deep, full-throated laugh that made everyone within hearing distance stare at her. They all soon turned back to continue their various conversations, except for one gentleman. A tall, lean young man in the costume of a cavalier fixed his gaze openly on the two of them. Mariana was on the point of distracting Augusta and turning away when he strode over to the box, put one elbow casually on the rail that bounded it, and leaned his chin in his hand.

"May an admirer inquire as to what inspired such mirth?"

What impudence! Mariana thought, and was about to give the stranger a good set down, when he smiled broadly and winked behind his mask.

"Mr. Thorne!" she cried. "How did you find us so quickly?"

He pursed his lips impishly and put his finger to them. "Who is this Mr. Thorne? I am a wandering cavalier, and I simply couldn't help noticing the handsomest couple here. At least, I noticed the handsomest couple to have reserved this particular box, which culled the possibilities considerably."

At this, Augusta also laughed.

"We invite you to join us within," Mariana said, making a leg in the old-fashioned way. "You may simply—"

She'd begun to point to the door leading to the corridor behind the boxes, when in one smooth movement, Mister Thorne vaulted over the barrier and landed with a flourish between the two of them. "I do beg your pardon."

The strength he must have had to perform such an operation was impressive and unexpected. Mariana started to say something to him but he turned first to Augusta, took her hand and raised it to his lips. "You are a vision, Ma'am." Mariana realized after a moment that, since she had relinquished her identity as a lady, it was the polite thing for him to do. Nonetheless, she was surprised at the spark of jealousy his actions inspired.

Augusta turned away quickly. Thorne then put out his hand to shake Mariana's. "Your servant," he said, with a quick bow of his head. Their contact, so brief and so public, sent a jolt up Mariana's arm and into her body.

Collecting her wits, she said, "We were about to call for something to eat and drink."

"Allow me," Jeremy said and signaled to one of the waiters threading through the already unruly crowd. A short while later, the same waiter appeared through the curtain drawn over the back of their box with a tray containing glasses of claret cup and a plate of small cakes.

There was something so very thrilling about being there virtually alone with the man who occupied all her dreams, in a place where no one would know them. A frisson of excitement passed down Mariana's spine, and all at once she was thrilled that she had dressed as a man. Much as she longed to see what it felt like to have Jeremy's strong arms around her, the thought frightened her a little. In this guise, he would be unable to act on what she was growing more and more certain was his own inclination. At least in that sense, her reputation would be safe. And she hoped it would act as a natural safeguard to any temptation she might have as well.

AUGUSTA COULD HARDLY THINK WHERE TO LOOK OR HOW TO make sense of this outlandish entertainment. The noise of hundreds of voices talking and laughing, many in the pit, some on the stage, with an orchestra sunk in a large declivity playing music that no one was dancing to as yet. A riot of bright colors, with a hodgepodge of costumes and jeweled and decorated masks that sparkled in the glow of at least a dozen massive chandeliers. A sweet, sickly smell of sweat mingled with that of burnt sugar—the cakes, perhaps? For a moment she felt lightheaded, but shook herself out of it. She was stronger than that! And her gown and mask—they acted as a kind of armor against the world, against anyone in that place guessing who or what she really was.

She'd been mulling this over, marveling at having effected such a transformation in her outward circumstances, at the moment when the cavalier had so boldly addressed them. Her immediate reaction had been to shrink back, but she restrained herself, not wanting to appear prudish.

She was glad she had. Although Lady Mariana had told her that Mr. Thorne would be there, she had not expected him to appear like that. He was different. Somehow, in his costume, he seemed more exposed than hidden. Perhaps it was his manners. No one since James had taken her hand in that sure way and kissed her fingertips. And his treatment of Mariana as though she were a boon companion rather than the daughter of an earl should have scandalized her, but somehow didn't. Everything was upside down.

It was too noisy to talk much, so at first—once they'd dispensed with meaningless pleasantries—they just sat and watched the company. After a time, the revelers settled a bit and space cleared in the center of the floor for dancing. The orchestra struck up some lively country dances, which were rather disorganized thanks to couples joining somewhat randomly. Augusta was laughing as the chaos ended and the strains of a waltz began when she felt a hand on her gloved forearm.

"Might I request the pleasure of this dance?"

The voice was low and the room noisy, so Augusta assumed that it was Lady Mariana exaggerating the depth of her attractive contralto. She had already mentioned that they would have to take the floor together, and Augusta said, "I'd be delighted." Then she looked up.

It wasn't Lady Mariana. It was Mr. Thorne. She snapped her eyes toward Mariana, whose amused smirk was all that showed around and through her mask. It was hard to interpret her expression, but in any case it was too late to bow out now, so Augusta pasted a weak smile on her face and stood. She expected to take Mister Thorne's arm and walk around behind the boxes to gain the dance floor, but to her amazement he repeated his previous leap in reverse, and then reached into the box, held her around the waist, lifted her over the low barrier and set her on her feet.

By now her cheeks were ablaze, and she was certain he could detect it even though she kept her mask securely tied over her ears. She wished it had been one that covered all of her face!

He guided her out to join the dancers in the swirling waltz steps, some of whom had made their way onto the stage itself. To Augusta's surprise, the waltz ended up being more organized than the country dance, and the many couples managed not to collide with each other. At first, Augusta felt stiff and uncertain, almost clumsy. But soon she let the music carry her away, surrendering to the feeling of being led around the floor by a very good dancer, twirling and chasséing with the best of them. At one point, she even closed her eyes, imagining, just for a moment, that when she opened them again she would be looking up into the adoring face of a tall dragoon with fathomless gray eyes.

Except she meant brown, not gray.

Thorne's voice interrupted her reverie. "Now, Miss Hastings, I require you to tell me just a little more about yourself. I was supposed to consider you a lowly seamstress, but I find you dancing like a lady of the *ton* who has had tutors and lessons, and see you turned out as if you were born to wear such gowns."

She looked directly into his eyes. They were kind, questioning. What could she tell him? "You are mistaken. This gown is borrowed, from Lady Mariana."

"Did you borrow her manners as well? And her air? And there's something else about you I can't quite describe."

She paused before answering him. "You are right that I am not the usual sort of seamstress. But I am not much better, being penniless and with no family to protect me. However, if I have my way, I will not always be penniless."

"Surely you're not hanging out for a rich husband!"

He was joking, but the comment stung nonetheless. "No! I intend to take charge of my own destiny. Use my own wits to get by."

"Ah," he said. "I see that you and Lady Mariana are alike in that way too."

Just at that moment, they twirled past another couple, a lady in an elaborate, old-fashioned court dress and a man in the guise of a gypsy. Augusta smiled in their direction, looked away as they passed, and then looked quickly back over her shoulder so she could see them again.

No, she thought. She must be mistaken. The couple moved out of sight behind another group of dancers, so she could not immediately get another glimpse. When they movement of the couples brought them near again, she looked more closely. She wasn't mistaken. The lady wore the dress she'd altered for Mr. Gordon. That shouldn't have surprised her. After all, it wasn't a modern ball gown, and she suspected from the outset that it would be used as a costume of some sort. Her surprise had nothing to do with the dress itself. It had to do with the person wearing it.

Their eyes met briefly, and in that moment, they recognized each other. It was Mr. Gordon himself. Dancing with a man. His lips curled up in a conspiratorial smile.

In fact, Augusta had seen his partner before, too. He was the gentleman who had been standing discreetly to the side when she'd first gone to the warehouse to place Madame's silk order. So the two gentlemen knew each other before that evening, which meant Mr. Gordon's partner knew him to be a man, had not asked him to dance thinking he was a woman.

"Is something amiss?" Thorne asked.

"What? Oh no! I'm just amused by the company. It's unlike anything I've ever seen before." This was true, but inadequate to convey her deep shock. She would keep what she saw to herself and think about it. Mr. Gordon had done a superb job on the jacket that Mariana was wearing at that moment, so she was disposed to think well of him. And he appeared so happy in the arms of his partner, they danced so naturally together. In this place, in that costume, would be the only occasion when two men could do so. She wasn't so naïve as to be unaware of the real danger men like Mr. Gordon faced. Occasions like this, the anonymity, the spirit of recklessness, must be welcome to such as he.

"I detect an unwillingness to say anything more about your past, and since I am a gentleman I will probe no more. But I would like to know what that sadness is that I see lurking in the depths of your eyes."

Recalled to her partner, Augusta blushed, but said nothing.

"I see. Perhaps someday, when we know each other better."

Would there be a time when they knew each other better? Augusta couldn't imagine what circumstances might put them in each other's way again. So she simply smiled and said little beyond commonplaces until the dance ended. Indeed, she had so much else to think about that she didn't know if she could have strung together two coherent thoughts on any more subtle topics.

The music stopped, Mister Thorne gave her an elegant bow and she responded with a graceful curtsy.

"You see? Some strict governess taught you to do that, I'm

certain," he said, before putting out his arm to lead her back to the box.

When they reached it, he seemed about to lift her over the barrier again, but she backed away. "I should prefer to walk around to the corridor and come into the box the usual way, if I may." Augusta's voice was bright with suppressed laughter. Exhilarating as his unexpected gesture had been, she had no desire to repeat it. Not to mention the fact that, since the box was on a higher level than the parterre, the reverse operation would require a great deal more effort on his part, and she could only imagine herself having to climb in an ungainly fashion, thus showing her ankles to the entire company.

"Of course," Jeremy said, and prepared to walk with her to the door off the parterre a few yards away.

At that moment, Augusta glanced up at Mariana's face, and saw something in her expression that made her think she objected to the attention Thorne was paying her. Although Mariana had not said anything to her, Augusta guessed at some attraction between them as soon as she saw them together. "Please don't trouble yourself to escort me, Mr. Thorne, I shall be perfectly safe for this small distance!"

He readily gave in, nodding and once more vaulting into their box.

Although the door that led to the back of the first tier was close, by that time the pit had grown so crowded that Augusta was obliged to wait repeatedly for the path before her to clear. As a result, several masked gentlemen raised their quizzing glasses and surveyed her in frank appreciation, and she was buffeted about in ways she feared were not entirely unintentional.

By the time she reached the door, her cheeks were hot with embarrassment, and she was ready to own that— exciting as the evening had proved—she needn't ever attend another opera masquerade. With relief, she reached out to push the door open.

But her action was stopped by a black-gloved hand that came from behind and covered hers, gripping it firmly. She looked around in alarm to see a man in a black domino wearing a mask that covered all of his face except his glittering eyes, chiseled jaw, and expressive mouth. He took a yet firmer hold of her hand and drew it away from the door handle, leaned close to her ear and said in a low voice, "A word, Madam," as he began to lead her back toward the crowded pit.

Augusta's heart pounded and her mouth felt as if it were coated in dust. She didn't want to call attention to herself by struggling against this stranger, and glanced over her shoulder at their box. But Lady Mariana was deeply engrossed in a conversation with Thorne, their heads together as if sharing secrets, and neither of them were looking in her direction.

"Come, there's no need to play coy with me! I don't have to unmask you to discover your identity," the man said. He accompanied these words with a squeeze of her hand followed by a move as though he were about to encircle her waist.

In a panic, she cast a searching gaze into the almost-hidden eyes and said, with a shaking voice, "You mistake me, Sir."

He leaned slightly toward her and closely examined her masked face. Suddenly, the glint of mischief and dimple of mirth she had detected before vanished, and the stranger's expression became first puzzled, then serious. He let go of her and backed away. "I-I beg your pardon, Madam. Please forgive me. I thought you were someone of my acquaintance."

"Not at all," Augusta said, feeling far from easy. Her

unease came in part from the fact that she perceived something familiar in the tone of his voice. Could it be? Somewhat hesitantly she said, "But I think, Sir, I rather am. Someone of your acquaintance, that is, although perhaps not who you expected."

He stood to his full height and looked down at her. It was difficult to see his reaction to what she said because of the mask, but Augusta thought she could detect a tightening at the corners of his mouth, something like a frown. "I believe you are mistaken," he said with an air of finality, then touched two fingers to his brow in an ironic salute and prepared to walk away.

Before he could do so, Augusta said, "I am surely not! Mistaken, I mean." She did know who he was. She was absolutely certain now. Even through the mask and the cover of the domino, in his attitude and the way he spoke she recognized Lord Bridlington. She knew his eyes, and how thoughts played over his face, changing his expression moment by moment. And here he was again, behaving toward her with a degree of puzzling discourtesy. Why would he do so? Something about her mask and her disguise made her bold and she said with great spirit, thinking she might never have a chance to address him thus again, "We are acquainted, and yet you treat me once more without consideration. I cannot imagine why, in what way I have injured you. Now I beg you will excuse me. I must rejoin my party of friends."

She whirled around, chin up, and took a step toward the door, but Bridlington grasped her arm and stopped her, turning her to face him again. "I beg your pardon, Miss Hastings. You wrong me. I did recognize you, but at a masquerade... people don't always wish to be known for themselves. I thought, perhaps wrongly, that I might be doing you a kindness by not acknowledging our acquaintance." He paused.

"You call me inconsiderate, yet I believe I showed great consideration in alleviating your difficult circumstances on two occasions. But, as you said at the time, perhaps you did not need my help."

She wished she could see his whole face! Was he irritated or amused? Had he not wished to be recognized by her? Perhaps she had transgressed some convention of a masquerade that Mariana had not told her about. Now she wasn't certain what to say. A witty retort rose to her lips and died before she uttered it. Instead she said with more seriousness than perhaps his words warranted, "You deliberately misunderstand me, Sir. I believe you know that you did not accord me certain common courtesies on several occasions. Was that because I am a lowly seamstress who does not deserve your notice? Or is there something else about me that does not meet with your approbation?" He had retained his hold on her arm, and she felt the warmth of his strong grip, which made her think of their first meeting less than a fortnight ago. She knew she should pull herself out of his grasp, but she lacked all will to do so.

He stared at her for a long moment, "There is nothing about you I could disapprove of. And although you may be a seamstress, you are certainly not lowly. Whatever your birth, you have a lofty character and keen intelligence. So much was clear to me from the first moment I met you." He let go of her arm as if he had just noticed he still held it. "I cannot defend my behavior, or excuse what may have seemed discourteous to you at the time. I beg you to accept my belated apology." After a stiff, formal bow, he added, "I ask you kindly not to reveal to my sister that you met me here when you next see her. I will be similarly discreet and will also not tell her that when I saw you, you happened to be wearing one of her gowns. Is she here with you?"

Augusta gasped. She hadn't thought that he would recognize her dress as belonging to Lady Mariana. Of course that was why he'd approached her and was confused about her identity. Did he expect to see his sister here? "It's not—she's not—I mean—Oh I wish I could tell you, but the secret is not mine!" Her voice rose with frustration.

This stopped him. "Ah. I deduce that it must therefore be Lady Mariana's. I know my sister well, and this does not surprise me." He chuckled and his reserve melted a little. "Don't worry. I won't say anything that would betray you. I wouldn't do that. As I said, although you may not believe it, I do approve of you." He touched her cheek. "But in exchange for my discretion in that regard, I wish you to tell me something that has nothing to do with Mariana, something that has puzzled me ever since the first time we met."

He took hold of her arms and pulled her a little closer to him to let a man in a court jester's costume slip by them, but did not let her go when the man had passed.

"What is it you wish to know?" Augusta said, her voice weak and dry.

"Who are you? What are you? Although I suppose that is two things, really. And don't tell me you are a seamstress." He shook his head, as if trying to rearrange his thoughts. "What I mean is how come you to be here now, how is it that you have stumbled across my path in so many intriguing ways?"

She looked down to gather her thoughts. His intense gaze was dizzying. "First of all, I'm nobody," she said. It was true in that moment. She had lost all sense of who she was standing there in the heat of his presence and wished he would let go of her so she could think again—yet at the same time wished he would keep holding onto her forever.

"That you most certainly are not." His voice had softened, and he ran his hands down her arms and took hold of both of hers, lifting them and pressing them together. "But you haven't answered my questions."

Augusta could hardly breathe. "If you knew me, what I've done..." If he did so, this magical moment would burst like the merest bubble. For they stood there in a sort of enchantment, outside of time. All around them costumed revelers danced and laughed and talked, but they existed alone, in their own quiet center. They couldn't even properly see each other, the masks hiding half of their faces lending still more unreality to what was passing between them. Surely the sordid, unpleasant details of all that had sent her flying to London did not belong to that moment.

Bridlington spoke next. "If I could but—" and then stopped on the point of saying something, his expression—even through the mask—melting her heart.

"Yes?"

He shook his head. "It doesn't matter. Not yet, anyway. Not until you know more about me." He pressed his lips together and looked away from her across the crowd, still clinging to her.

"What is there to know?" she asked. "I think I know enough to respect you. To believe you are kind."

He lifted her hands to his lips and kissed each one gently, slowly. "We are none of us what we seem to the world. I do not want your respect, or to show you merely kindness."

By now Augusta feared her knees would not support her. She hardly knew what to think. It was surely the fantastical atmosphere of the masquerade that had led to this conversation. He would walk away, and it would all be forgotten. By him, at least. "What do you want, My Lord?"

At that moment, the orchestra struck up a raucous dance tune and couples flooded onto the floor, one of them crashing into Augusta and shoving her off balance and into Bridlington's arms. He steadied her, and in those brief moments when they were pressed together she felt the beat of his heart. But the jolt was enough to recall her to herself.

As soon as she was secure on her feet she gently pushed him away. "I must," she managed to squeak out, "I must return to my friends. They will wonder where I've got to."

He softly pinched her chin and tilted it upward. "I will see you again," he said. "The fates seem to have decreed that we continue to meet." He leaned down toward her, and for a moment she thought he would kiss her, right there, in public. But he suddenly stood upright and bowed before turning and walking away, his gait somewhat uneven.

What had just happened? Was this the same Lord Bridlington with the lively wit? The seeming unconcern? Or was he a different person, a man who for some strange, incomprehensible reason wanted to know her? Liked her. Perhaps even more than liked her. It wasn't possible. She must have imagined it. Or perhaps he was disguised—in that other sense of the word. He had no doubt come from his club after polishing off a bottle of good brandy, in search of some illicit entertainment. She watched him thread through the crowd, seeing that when it became very dense, he unhooked a gold-handled cane from his elbow and used it to clear his path.

Yet she didn't believe he was drunk. His speech had been crisp and lucid. His judgment unimpaired. She could detect no evidence of spirits on his breath, which had been close enough to her for there to have been no mistaking it. She breathed deeply a few times to slow her galloping pulse. He wanted to see her again. She'd never wanted anything so much in her life.

Coming back to a sense of where she was, Augusta pushed past a few dancers, hastened through the door, and hurried along the corridor, her progress once again thwarted by revelers going in and out of the other boxes and waiters entering with loaded trays and exiting with the same tray empty but for a few coins. When at last she reached their box and drew back the curtain to enter it, Lady Mariana and Mister Thorne stepped apart from one another, both of them with heightened color visible in the parts of their faces not covered by masks.

Mariana forestalled any comment on Augusta's part by stepping forward and saying, "You are flushed!" and laying a hand on her arm. "What happened?"

"Nothing! Only it is so warm here. I see you, too, are feeling the heat." She opened her fan and vigorously waved it in front of her face, forcing herself to smile as if she had no misgivings at all, as if her entire world had not been upended in the past hour, and as if she didn't know she was quite possibly falling in love with someone she barely knew, and didn't begin to understand.

IT WAS NOTHING SHORT OF TORTURE, JEREMY THOUGHT. HE had never spent so much time to all intents and purposes alone with Lady Mariana, and yet he could not touch her. Not as he truly wished to. At most, they brushed against each other or leaned their heads together to whisper about some particularly shocking costume or behavior. Perhaps he imagined it, but it seemed that Mariana took hold of his arm and leaned in to say something in his ear more often than was necessary. Each time she did, each warm breath that touched the side of his face, sent a spear of desire into him that was so powerful it almost took his breath away.

He'd assumed that the presence of Miss Hastings would alleviate their bizarre closeness. But after his dance with her ended—a dance Mariana had insisted he must offer—it took her a long time to get back to the box, which left them entirely alone for longer than he expected. They exhausted the light subjects of conversation and Mariana asked him about his family, his childhood, and still more personal questions. The inquiry was so unexpected that at first he hadn't known what to say. But soon anecdotes about his jovial mother, his unruly brothers and sisters, most of whom were still living at home in Wimbledon, and his father's law practice—which was barely adequate to the support of his family —flowed as easily as if he had known Mariana for years.

"I envy you," Mariana had said, a far-off look in her eyes.

"Why?"

She shrugged. "I suppose partly because your father is such a good man, and you all love him. And besides…" She smiled up at him, her eyes glittering as if they had filled with tears, but she wasn't weeping. "I always wished I had a sister. Although my brother is truly the best of men."

He wanted so badly to take her hand and hold it between his, or enfold her in a warm embrace. But that would have been impossible, and would have attracted the most unwelcome attention. It was at that moment that Miss Hastings returned, looking as if she had had a fright.

"Are you certain you're all right?" he asked her once she had taken her seat and sipped some claret cup.

"Yes, perfectly," she said, clearly working hard to smile despite whatever was disordering her mind.

"Come, Augusta! We must dance. A quadrille is next, I hear." Mariana winked and cast him a saucy smile before grabbing hold of Miss Hastings's hand and pulling her back out of the box, down the corridor, and emerging through the door onto the dance floor she had just escaped from.

He almost told Mariana to stop when he saw the look of panic on Miss Hastings' face. But Mariana was unstoppable, and he welcomed some time alone in the box to settle his own disturbed spirits. By the time the two of them had joined a group for the dance, after some initial awkwardness, they were laughing and entering into the spirit of the evening.

It was hard to decide which of them was the more beguiling: Miss Hastings with her natural grace in a gown that accentuated her good figure, or Mariana in men's breeches that clung to her thighs and her tail coat with a nipped-in waist that begged to be held between his hands. He wished they could trade costumes with each other. Then he could act as amorous as he felt toward Mariana, and take advantage of the freedom of manners only the atmosphere of a masquerade would allow.

As TIME WENT ON, THE REVELERS BECAME INCREASINGLY abandoned, laughing more and more uproariously, flirting outrageously, and generally behaving in a way no well-bred person would dare among polite company.

Augusta, however, when she was not dancing, became completely distracted by searching the crowd for sight of Bridlington in his black domino. But there were so many men who wore such dress! Besides, he might have gone, not having discovered his sister there. At one point, she thought she saw him leaning close to a woman garbed in a way that left no one in doubt of the shape of her voluptuous figure. She thought it was he because she could see the gold handle of a cane in his hand. He appeared to be saying something in the woman's ear, his intent as clear as the way she welcomed it. Madame Noelle's words of warning flashed through her mind. He had said he wished she knew his character. If such it was, why would he want her to know it? He puzzled her extremely.

All around, rough accents and ungenteel cant reached her ears. She found herself envying Mariana's disguise, which shielded her from a great deal of unwanted ogling and rendered her safe from importunity. In a diaphanous, glittering gown, Augusta did not feel safe.

Before long, it was near enough the hour of unmasking that Mariana signaled that it was time to leave. Never was Augusta more grateful for the end of an entertainment. Although it had been an experience she would always remember, the volatile emotions it inspired, the many questions it raised in her mind, exhausted her. Before the event itself, through all that had transpired during her first week in London, she had already felt apart from—outside of—every world she encountered. More educated and ambitious than the other seamstresses. Less leisured and wealthy than Mariana and her brother. More talented—yes, that had quickly become clear—than Madame Noelle herself. Where exactly did she belong? Yet there had been something about the masquerade in its non-judgmental welcome of people of all ranks and stations, backgrounds, and proclivities, that had opened her eyes to other possibilities. She had seen more in those few hours than she'd seen in her life thus far. She'd been through more extremes of emotion, too.

Thoughts of Bridlington sent her mind into a hopeless jumble. She could no longer deny to herself that he had awakened feelings in her she had never thought to know again. She had believed that no one but James could provoke a response in her that bypassed her mind and went straight to her body. Bridlington was so different from James, who had been all masculine energy and certainty, who radiated attraction from every pore. The earl carried with him some element of reserve, of doubt, that made him less accessible than James with his military panache had been. But such a character beguiled her. Would she ever be able to break through that reserve? His way of being with her was a mixture of cajolery, self-deprecation, and retreat behind a mask more disguising than the one that had covered his face that evening. Was there something he did not want her to know about him? Could the rumors recounted by Madame have more foundation than she supposed?

She shook her head. She did not want to believe it. The testimony of her own eyes had to have deceived her. Masks, the music, and an atmosphere of abandoned merriment had made her forget herself, and attribute more meaning than was warranted to the behavior of someone who was still a mystery to her.

A tantalizing mystery, nonetheless.

CHAPTER 13

A short while later, they entered the house in Berkeley Square through the door from the mews and scampered up the back stairs. Lady Mariana glowed with triumph, congratulating herself on carrying off her first appearance in public in the guise of a man. "And you, Augusta—no one would ever suspect you of being a seamstress accustomed to long hours of hard work. Especially since you had to keep your gloves on!"

Augusta couldn't help laughing, peeled off her gloves and looked ruefully at her callused fingertips.

When they had recovered, Mariana said, "I swear that dress becomes you more than it did me. How did you alter it? Whatever you did, something around the corsage I think, it appears as if it was made for you alone. You looked every inch a lady, which we both know you are. I hope you'll forgive me for putting you in the servants' quarters, a place I'm sure you've never had to occupy before." Mariana said. "I simply couldn't imagine how to account for you in one of the formal bedchambers, which would have been vastly more comfortable. Do you have all you need?" She gestured to the workbasket Augusta had brought, and in which she had stowed necessary items for an overnight stay.

"Yes, thank you. And there's no need to trouble yourself. I am quite accustomed to ruder quarters. I shall leave before you rise, My Lady."

"Oh Augusta! Surely after this evening, after what we've shared together, you will remember to call me Mariana! In fact, Mari. Call me Mari. That is what my family and my most intimate friends do. And now, you hold my secret, and you are bound by the rules of friendship to keep it safe."

"Very well, Mari," Augusta said. "You honor me with your trust." She made a mock bow, and they both laughed.

But when Augusta awoke just a few hours later, the very moment wan daylight filtered in through the small window of her modest chamber, deep misgivings assailed her. She'd had a terrible dream, of being confined to a room from which two doors led. She did not know what was on either side of them, only that her choice of which one to go through could lead to either happiness or grief. This brought all the conflicting feelings of the night before to mind, and she found herself vacillating between a tiny thrill in having acknowledged her growing feelings for Bridlington and the inevitable doubts of her worth, her guilt at how easily she could put James out of her mind, and her anxiety about the impossible situation she had left behind in Devonshire.

And yet, once the pall of her bad dream faded in the morning sunshine as she walked back to Curzon Street, her more positive thoughts began to take hold. So it was with a light step that she hurried back to Madame Noelle's, and despite her obvious fatigue, her spirits during the ensuing long day of work never flagged.

Of course, fatigue eventually overtook her. When she and the other seamstresses had lain down their needles and tidied up the workshop, Augusta's eyes itched and her eyelids felt heavy.

She was about to follow the others up to the attics, but Pauline held her back. "Let's walk in the park a little. The weather is so fine."

Augusta wanted to decline, but Pauline's expression, she knew, would brook no refusal. With a smile and a sigh, she let her workmate pull her out the door to the street. No doubt she wanted to know everything about the masquerade, and Augusta would have to carefully select which details to reveal.

THE EVENTS OF THE NIGHT BEFORE OCCUPIED GEORGE'S MIND to the exclusion of all else while he dressed. He submitted to Craggins' ministrations without a word, only nodding his assent to the clothing the valet chose for him and absently watching him brush down his dark blue superfine coat. Had he and Miss Hastings really said so much to each other? Certain of her words came back to him with startling clarity. Yet he had an overwhelming sense that they both held things back. What had she said? She spoke no words of affection. That had all been on his part. Yet she had not stopped him, and had allowed him to hold her closer than was proper, or than she would have if she did not welcome his touch. The excuse of a crowd, of having to make oneself heard over a great deal of noise or avoid being buffeted about only accounted for some of that behavior.

As soon as he had realized that the lady in the white gown was not Mariana—as much as he knew that the gown belonged to his sister and had seen the wearer leaving Lanyon House in it—the object of finding his sister and taking her home vanished from his consciousness. Almost immediately he realized that the person he had seen must have been Miss Hastings, and having been confronted so unexpectedly and in such a circumstance of intimacy with her he had allowed his feelings to overwhelm him.

He thought at first he could just withdraw, thinking she might not recognize him. But she had. And to his mortification, she made direct reference to those courtesies he had neglected to accord her on previous occasions of their meeting because he wanted to hide his lameness. Why? Would he ever really want the good opinion of someone who wasn't willing to accept him as he was? He almost couldn't bear to recall her expression, her words. They contained so much truthful reproach, but in just as many ways she was wrong about him. So why hadn't he confessed all to her then?

"Yes, that's what I must do," he said aloud, not realizing that the train of his thoughts would not be obvious to Craggins.

"Beg pardon, My Lord?" the valet said, hardly turning a hair and not pausing for a second in his labors.

"Nothing, Craggins. I just remembered something I read."

He must not put it off any longer. She must be made aware that he was a cripple, that he was a figure to be pitied and ridiculed. She might have noticed his limp the night before, but could not have been aware of its cause. How was he to broach such a subject? Could he bear it if she reacted the way everyone else did, with thinly disguised revulsion?

He could not. And in the next instant, he knew the impossibility of it. No woman could ever see past so obvious a deformity, could love him with a love not tinged with pity. Miss Hastings would hardly be any less likely to desire him for his rank and fortune alone than any of the debutantes he met at Almack's. In fact, her very modest means would possibly make it more rather than less so. He had been fooled by the unreality of the evening into thinking that something more, something real existed between them. She would doubtless see it for what it was in the brutal light of day, nothing more than a dream.

Better to turn his mind toward things rooted in the here and now, things he could control. He'd seen Madame Agatha at the masquerade, which hadn't surprised him since it was a place she often frequented with the object of luring green youths to her Corinth. Several of the more presentable Cythereans mingled in the crowd and danced with unsuspecting young bucks, under the watchful eye of their adoptive "mother." If he didn't know she took care to keep a clean house and that she poured a significant amount of her own profits into the work they did together he might be more inclined to judge her for it. As it was, he knew that so long as men existed, so would the places where they could take their pleasure outside the strictures of a very tight-laced society.

In such a setting as the masquerade it was an easy matter for him to discuss his very different business with Agatha without arousing any suspicion or interest. As George expected, no financial assistance had been forthcoming from Grantley for the unfortunate girl's infant. She wasn't one of Agatha's flock. All of Agatha's ladies were well schooled in the art of avoiding such inconvenient complications. In fact, the girl was young—no more than fifteen years old—and had been a parlor maid at Grantley House. Having been dismissed for her misstep, she turned to begging on the streets of Haymarket where Agatha found her, brought her home, and got the whole story out of her. George hadn't really expected a different outcome. It was just one more reason for him to despise the man.

Agatha had more satisfactory news concerning the outcome of George's effort to get the boy with the hare lip admitted to the home in Marylebone. When he'd left him there, George feared that the wild child, whose speech was close to incomprehensible, would find a way to escape and resume his life in the gutter. But apparently he hadn't done so, and at least for now was safe among people who would see to his well-being.

While they spoke, Agatha told him of yet another urchin who needed his help. This one had a foot that had become infected and gangrenous, which could only mean amputation. George must persuade a surgeon to perform the operation, if the child was not already too sick to make it worthwhile, and then ensure the patient had a safe place to recover. He knew nothing of the child's circumstances other than that one of Agatha's servants found him in a state near death on the bank of the river.

These difficulties were easy to solve. At least, easy to act on with a hope of a good outcome. Resolving to put all thoughts of Miss Hastings out of his mind, George sent a letter to a surgeon he'd worked with before, arranging to meet him the next day at Madame Agatha's. It was all he could do for the moment. After that, he would see if Mariana wanted to ride with him that morning. They hadn't been out together for a long time. Having not seen her at the masquerade last night he was curious as to what she had done, why all the apparent secrecy after dinner.

THE DAY AFTER THE EVENING AT THE MASQUERADE PASSED IN an unreal fog for Jeremy. He went through his tasks in Westminster like an automaton, so familiar were they—fetch the boxes, remind Perceval of his appointments, filter the supplicants who came to get the most powerful man in government to support their pet legislation. He didn't have to turn his mind to any of it.

"Thorne! Did you hear me?"

Perceval's commanding voice, the voice that had distinguished him at the bar and brought him—a poor younger son—to the notice of powerful politicians, broke through his reverie. Jeremy must have let his mind wander while the Prime Minister finished writing the memo Jeremy was to deliver to the Secretary of War. Wellington was busy in the Peninsula, building up troops to drive the French out of Spain, but the United States had started to make trouble as well, and things weren't looking good in that quarter. These matters demanded Thorne's attention so much more urgently than whether or not the object of his infatuation sincerely returned his regard—whether the magnetic attraction he'd felt the night before had been the product of his own overactive desire or had also come from her—and he colored. "Yes, My Lord. Shall you require me to take notes during this afternoon's session?"

"Late night?" Perceval fixed him with a piercing gaze. "Mind you don't go falling in love. No time for that if you want a career! Men like you have to attend to this side of things first, climb a bit further up the ladder before you go getting leg shackled."

"Nothing of the kind, My Lord!" he said, adopting what he hoped was a mischievous smile. Let the man think that he spent the evening in the muslin company.

"I trust you know what you're doing? I don't pay you enough for senseless fripperies!"

That was certainly true, Jeremy thought with a grimace, and forced his attention back to the matters at hand.

"I'LL RACE YOU TO THE CLUMP OF TREES AT THE END!" Mariana said, having accepted her brother's invitation to go for a morning ride in the park. Rotten Row was deserted at that hour. Most of the very early riders were gone, and those who rode only to show off the quality of their horses hadn't yet arrived.

Mariana wasn't at all tired after the exertions of the night before. If anything, she brimmed with energy and excitement. How delicious it had been, feeling so free and easy in her breeches, permitted to have private conversation with another man without risking scandal. And the physical closeness with Jeremy—she still recalled the smell of him, the wool of his coat, the faintest odor of sweat. He was nervous. More than once she saw his hand shake as he reached for his glass of claret cup. And the look in his eyes when he gazed into hers...

"I thought you wanted to race!" George said, breathless, when they reined their horses to a trot at the agreed upon destination.

"I let you win! You know my mare can outrun your bay easily. I didn't want to embarrass you." It felt good to joke with her brother. Somehow, in London, they lost some of that easy camaraderie they enjoyed in the country.

They slowed to a walk and rode next to each other in silence on one of the trails around the park, until George said, "Where did you go last night?"

"Go? Why, nowhere. As I said, I went to bed early." She might have known he would suspect something. He knew her too well. But she needn't confess anything to him. "Did you go out?"

"Yes, I did in the end."

Mariana waited for him to say more, but he remained silent, smiling a little. "Well, are you going to tell me where you went? Or do I have to guess?"

"I decided it had been a long while since I'd seen anyone except members of Brooks's and people with vouchers to

Almack's, and I needed to remind myself that there are other people in London. So I went to the opera masquerade."

Mariana suppressed a gasp. She wanted to know if he'd seen her there, but could not ask. "How perverse of you, George. Did you see anyone you knew?"

"Two people."

"Anyone of my acquaintance?"

"One of them."

Mariana reached out with her whip and struck George on the arm.

"Ouch! Why did you do that?"

"Can you wonder? Tell me why you're playing so coy with me. Who did you see? And why does it matter to me?" Mariana became genuinely alarmed. Had he seen her with Jeremy?

"It's so easy to tease you, Mari! I met Lewiston there. He'd come after the rout party, which he said was a terrible bore. I only stayed a moment."

Mariana wasn't fooled. George may not have seen her there, but he did suspect her of doing something forbidden last night. She would have to be careful, plan his introduction to Jeremy at the dress party so that he wouldn't suspect her motives. "We shall have to make sure the dress party is altogether more entertaining, then."

"Dress party?" said a man's drawling voice as they passed by an almost-hidden bench.

Startled, Mariana pulled her mare to a halt. *Oh no*, she thought. It was Grantley. It was hard to decide who disliked him more, her brother or herself. What was he doing here? She exchanged a glance with George, who'd set his face in a steely scowl.

"How d'ye do. Fine morning, wouldn't you say?" Desmond Grantley smiled blandly, taking no notice of their unwelcoming attitudes.

"I thought you were abroad," Mariana said.

"Didn't Bridlington tell you? Didn't have to go. Going to be married instead." He walked up to where George had stopped, having turned his horse so that he kept Mariana in view. "Your friend Lewiston was full of questions yesterday. So curious. Wanted to know all about a cousin of mine."

"I can't imagine why," George said. "Don't let us keep you from your...What is it you were doing here?"

"While you have been exercising your horses, I have been exercising my intellect. I find nothing so salubrious as fresh air."

Mariana had the impression that a conversation was going on between her brother and Grantley just underneath the words they spoke. Something had passed between them at some point. She looked a question at George, who gave the tiniest shake of his head. She would ask him once Grantley was gone.

"I say, Bridlington, I'd be grateful to talk to you about my coming nuptials, if you'd come down here so I don't have to give myself a stiff neck." He rubbed the back of his neck, then said, "Oh, sorry. I sometimes forget that you can't easily dismount and mount again."

Mariana wanted to whip Grantley's face for his impudence and cruelty.

"Your marriage is no concern of mine," George said. "I have no idea why you should think it of any import."

"No, you're probably right. About that dress party. Friday, isn't it?"

As far as Mariana knew, no card of invitation had been sent to Grantley. "We had assumed you were not in town," she said.

"No offense taken. I'll take my leave of you, until then! If I'm free, that is." He swept his hat off and gave them an extravagant bow before walking away.

"Let's get back. I have a lot to do today," Mariana said, her previously joyful mood now spoiled. She wondered, too, what Lewiston could have had to do with whatever was going on between her brother and Grantley. "But I did want to let you know that I added a few names to the invitation list."

"Oh?"

"Not Grantley, don't worry!" she said, but looked away as she continued, "Only a school friend and her cousin. She's in town for a short while. I saw her in Bond Street, and couldn't think of another way to see her before she has to go away again."

"Which friend is this?"

"I doubt you'd remember. The name is Thorne. Distant relations of the Thornes of Maplewood in Yorkshire. She's a lively, intelligent girl. You'll like her, I'm certain."

"And the cousin?"

"I believe he's something in politics, a brilliant young man apparently." At least in this she was not lying. "I'll make sure to introduce you. And I invited a few other political sorts, so he wouldn't feel out of place among all the foppish tulips!"

George would not be standing to receive guests, so Mariana was confident she could engineer a suitable, quiet introduction. From there, all she could hope was that Jeremy's innate worth and strength would carry the day.

No uneventful life was in store for Augusta after the masquerade. She had hardly returned from Lanyon House when she received a note from Mariana asking her to come to her again that same evening. *I have a surprise for you—which I hope will be to your liking!* the note said. Knowing Mariana the way she now did, Augusta couldn't help but be wary of this surprise. Wary, and more than a little excited.

Mariana had also taken care once again to send word to Madame that she required Augusta's services, so permission to leave early for that purpose was easily granted. But before she left, Madame said, "Lady Mariana is quite taken with you, I see. Mind you don't go getting any ideas. It's no good setting yourself above your station, and if I see any cause for dissatisfaction, you'll find yourself out without a feather to fly with."

Although Augusta could have anticipated such a warning, receiving it caused her more anxiety than she cared to admit. Someone who existed in such financial ease as Mariana could have no sense of what might await Augusta if she suddenly found herself with no means of earning her keep. She sincerely hoped that her decision to go along with Mariana's plans would not ruin her chances.

But first, Madame required her to return to the silk warehouse to order the now in-demand puce net. She naturally assumed her assistant would be willing to undertake the much longer walk it would entail on her way to Berkeley Square, never bothering to consult her feelings or wishes.

Although Augusta's everyday shoes were becoming worn down at the heels from all the walking she'd lately done, she was glad of the excuse to postpone her visit to Lanyon House. Not only would it give her time out in the open air to think about the previous evening, it would also provide an opportunity to see Mr. Gordon again, to tell him in person how much she appreciated his fine work on the evening coat —which she had not seen in detail when they had furtively exchanged packages on the day of the masquerade.

She had to admit to a degree of curiosity as well. It seemed that he had recognized her at the masquerade, but she wasn't entirely sure. If he had, she wanted to assure him that he only had to say the word and she would disavow all knowledge of having seen him if she were ever questioned— although she could not imagine a circumstance in which she would be. Nonetheless, on sober reflection, Augusta decided his secrets were not hers to tell, however it was he chose to conduct his life. And now she was more than certain that he could be trusted with anything she chose to share with him. Something told her Mr. Gordon might be a useful ally.

This time, she didn't have to wait long for him to attend on her. His guarded expression on seeing her suggested that he knew she had recognized him the night before. Once she had ordered the silk and a few other lengths of material, she said, "Your work on the coat was exquisite. I wanted to thank you. Did the dress satisfy your client?"

He instantly understood her intent to assure him of her discretion, and the look of relief in his eyes was gratifying. "If I can ever be of service to you again, Miss Hastings, you have but to say the word."

She smiled. "I'm glad I know who to ask in such delicate circumstances. I hope we may continue our association to the benefit of us both."

At that point, she didn't know for certain she would need to call on him again, but knowing Mariana and her wild schemes, it seemed probable.

OVER THE PAST SEVERAL DAYS, PHILPOT HAD BECOME FAMILIAR enough with Augusta not to wonder at it when she arrived and went through the door from the stables to the back staircase. She gave him a quick nod and adopted as businesslike and subservient an air as she could before dashing up the four flights of stairs to the attics.

Mariana awaited her there, an expression of suppressed excitement on her face as she stood in the middle of the room, surrounded by two chairs and a table where she had laid out three evening ensembles, a day dress, a velvet pelisse, and a dark copper velvet riding habit.

"So, here's the treat!" Mariana said, with a sweeping gesture over the selection of garments. "I'm giving them to you."

"Mari! I cannot accept such a gift!" One glance assured Augusta that these clothes were of the highest quality, and that with the exception of the riding habit, they had likely come from Madame Noelle's workshop. Augusta walked forward to examine each piece, touching the luxurious fabrics, peering at the perfect construction, but at the same time eyeing them critically for the changes she would make, given the chance. It was no good, though. "I cannot. Surely you see that?"

"Of course you can! Don't be a pea goose!"

Augusta shook her head. "No, Mariana. Indeed, where would I wear any of these? I do not attend balls and I have no horse, nor even any means of hiring one! And how would I explain—you cannot imagine how simply I live. I share a room with four other seamstresses!"

"Oh, you needn't take them away with you. Besides, I think you should make a few alterations before you actually wear any of them. I saw what you did with the gown you wore last night. A small thing, but it made all the difference. So you are welcome to play with them, remake them, take them apart if that's what you want to do. In any case, none of them would be quite appropriate for our next adventure, and I won't want them again."

To be so unconcerned with money! Augusta should have been wary, now that she knew the degree of deception Mariana was willing to practice. But her own appetite for mischief had been whetted. And in truth, she already had some ideas as she quickly looked over the items spread out in the attic. "Will we once more be in disguise—"

Mariana interrupted her. "Not this time. Here's what's next: You shall come to the dress party we're having here in a few days, accompanied by Mr. Thorne. He is your cousin, remember? His father is an attorney, but his mother's mother was an honorable. And we know each other from school in Bath."

Augusta's head was spinning. Clearly, Lady Mariana had missed her calling as an authoress of sensational romances. "Wait, My Lady!" she said.

This stopped Mariana in her tracks and she turned a wide-eyed, puzzled gaze to Augusta. "What is it? Are you not diverted by these subterfuges?"

"Very diverting, Mariana. But think for a moment." Augusta softened her voice and laid a conciliatory hand on Mariana's arm. She sounded calm but her heart raced at the idea that she might find herself in close proximity to Bridlington once again and so soon. She wanted to see him, most certainly, but not under such conditions. Not falsely claiming to be someone she was not. She well knew how that could complicate matters. So she had to think of a different reason to object to this new plan. "What if there are other ladies at the party who know me for one of Madame Noelle's assistants? I won't be wearing a mask."

With a wry smile, Mariana looked Augusta up and down. "I know my sort well enough to believe that no one who saw you dressed in the first stare of fashion, mingling among exalted company and behaving with pretty manners, would ever think you anything other than a gentlewoman."

Except that Lord Bridlington would know instantly that she was not a Miss Thorne from Bath. After what had passed between them the night before, Augusta would never be able to confront him with equanimity. The spark between them, the words he said, the way he'd held her, touched her—everything was different now. How would she ever explain to him such a deception as Mariana described? Before last night, her meetings with Bridlington had been amusing, intriguing, but inconsequential. Thus she had thought it of no importance to mention them to Mariana. Now, however. She didn't know what to do. He had exhorted her not to tell Mariana of his presence at the masquerade. Did he even know his sister had, in fact, been there, dressed as a man, occupying a box not five yards from where their intimate conversation had taken place?

She wracked her brains for some way to get out of this new scheme of Mariana's. "You are too kind. But I don't understand. Why me? Why anyone at all? Why must you go to such trouble?" Augusta thought, but didn't say, that Lady Mariana was indulging in profligacy of the most blatant sort, throwing money away for nothing more than amusing larks. "Surely you can do as you please, go wherever you like. Do you not enjoy the balls and routs? I don't see that my presence will make any difference at all at this party."

"I am not free, as I'm confident you are aware. I know it seems odd of me to thrust you into a set that it's clear to me you have either been cast out of or fled." Mariana shook her head. "Don't dislike me for it! I know you belong in that world—my world—whatever happened to send you flying away. I know how one's ambitions can be incompatible with one's situation. I know more intimately than you can guess. But you are a gift, don't you see? A completely unknown new friend who can serve as my excuse to do some of the things I feel I must do before it's too late."

"What things? And too late for what?" Augusta asked, her eyes following Mariana as she wandered around the attic workroom, clenching and unclenching her fists.

"Oh surely you've guessed at least some of it! The rest I

can't tell you right now." At this, Mariana stopped, turned, and walked over to the small window through which a patch of blue sky dotted with puffy clouds was just visible. "You think me overbearing. Spoiled. And you're right, of course. But I promise you, my purpose is honorable!" She strode back to Augusta and took hold of her shoulders. "Of course, I will not force you to do anything that makes you uneasy. I could not! But you have such a chance too! You took a brave step. I am persuaded it required a great deal of courage on your part to leave your home and come to London alone, with your only valuable asset the skill of your hands, and a dream you had no clear idea how to achieve."

This made Augusta catch her breath. She had not told Mariana anything about her past, only something about her hopes for the future. "How—?"

"I don't know for certain, truly. I only know what I see, the way you are. You can't hide your quality, even bent over a seam in poor light. Denying your essence, your heart and soul, will not make you happy in the end, no matter your reasons for trying to do so. Denying yourself will not bring anyone back, or reclaim lost opportunities. In fact, turning your back on everything you once were risks making you overlook something new and wonderful, something unexpected that could lead you to a life as remarkable as it is rewarding.

"And that's why *I'm* working so hard *not* to deny myself," Mariana continued, "not to bury who I am in a graveyard of convention. At least, not before I'm ready. In order to succeed at that, I need your help. And I hope, in taking advantage of you that way, I can help you as well."

No one had ever expressed such thoughts to Augusta. If asked, she would have said she could have nothing at all in common with a beautiful, wealthy noblewoman who moved in the first circles of London society. And yet, what Mariana said struck Augusta with the force of a revelation. They were different, and they were the same. How could she abandon Mariana now? Surely nothing to come could be more full of hazardous possibilities than the evening at the masquerade. And she *had* liked it. More than liked it, against her own inclination. Her eyes had been opened to possibilities she'd never dared hoped for. Last night had been her final rupture with a hopeless longing for a love that would never be. She was alive again. Renewed. Bridlington had opened his heart to her, tentatively, haltingly, but she could not misinterpret the things he said.

If only she could go to the dress party as herself. But after last night, Augusta also understood something she had been only vaguely aware of before. That was the deep love that existed unacknowledged between Jeremy Thorne and Mariana. Thorne was in no way a suitable match for Mariana—at least in the eyes of society. This explained so many of Mari's actions. And for Augusta to pretend to be his cousin was somehow going to smooth the way for a revelation that would be essential to Mariana's happiness. There could be no other reason for the elaborate pretense.

Augusta took a deep breath and looked directly into Mariana's eyes. "Tell me what I must do," she said, and a moment later found herself crushed in another of Mariana's enthusiastic embraces.

They both laughed. Mariana held Augusta at arm's length, beaming a dazzling smile that had the peculiar effect of simultaneously flattering, enamoring, and terrifying her.

It only remained for Augusta to decide how to act at the party. Much as she yearned to see Bridlington again, to talk to him, laugh with him, and see if his feelings for her were real, she realized her only choice would be to avoid him at all costs. She must prevent Mariana introducing her to him as

Miss Augusta Thorne. She had the sinking feeling that if she did, she would forfeit all Bridlington's trust.

But Augusta didn't have to wait for the day of the party to encounter Bridlington again. Early the next morning, Madame sent her on an errand to the linen draper's to purchase some gown lengths of calico and muslin, as the weather was becoming warmer by the day. When Augusta declared her intention of walking there, Pauline said, "You sure about that, Gussie?"

"Of course! Why wouldn't I be?"

Pauline gave her a look from under her brows. "As if you don't know! Why, it's t'other side of Soho, innit. You know what that means."

She didn't. "What are you saying?"

"Only that—though I s'pose at this time o' day it makes no difference, but nice young ladies like you don't normally walk the streets of Soho."

Augusta laughed. "I assure you, I won't let anyone accost me! Besides, isn't it better I know what it's like?"

"Yer a strange one, Miss Augusta Hastings," Pauline said. "Though there's some sense in what you say. And you look prim enough not to attract the wrong kind of notice."

Augusta couldn't imagine that, in the morning sunshine on a beautiful May day, she could ever be mistaken for a lady of the night. And she had to admit to a degree of curiosity, especially after having seen such a different side of London at the masquerade.

"'Ere. I could go with you, if Madame'd let me."

"That's not necessary, but thank you. I will be fine. I can take care of myself, and I'm getting very good at finding my way around London now."

She also didn't want Pauline's company when she

purchased a pair of silk stockings to wear to the dress party, and possibly a new pair of evening gloves. It would lead to too many questions.

The linen draper's shop favored by Madame Noelle—its proprietor being willing to sell her substantially discounted wares for which she could charge a premium—was on Berwick Street. Although the route to Covent Garden for the masquerade had taken her through this district, Augusta had had no reason to go there otherwise until that morning. She could have taken a hack, but as she told Pauline, the weather was fine, and she was curious to see a part of London that was new to her.

She soon realized that Pauline's description of Soho had been no exaggeration. Her route took her along some not very salubrious streets. Aside from the fact that they were lined with occasional houses in bad repair, more than once Augusta saw the clear signs of a few altogether different kinds of dwellings. In fact, contrary to what she believed would be the case, she found herself exposed to some pointed stares by men descending from unmarked carriages. Most of these, however, hurriedly tapped at unobtrusive doors that were subsequently opened by women whose profession was unmistakable.

Augusta did her best to keep her gaze resolutely forward, deciding that she would most certainly hire a hack to take her back to Curzon Street—if one could be found.

Just before the point at which the neighborhood began to resume a more genteel appearance, a hired hack pulled up at a door on the opposite side of the street that didn't look quite as seedy as some of the others. Augusta would have passed by with no further notice except that she heard a voice she recognized say, "Come back in an hour, good man."

She froze. She wanted to walk on, to pretend that she hadn't heard those words, hadn't recognized the cadence belonging to someone who had lately occupied her every moment of leisure, who was well on the way to becoming dearer to her than she had ever hoped anyone might be. It couldn't be, and yet it must be. Augusta reminded herself that her intense feelings were all really based on a single interview of, what? Half an hour's duration, in the unreal atmosphere of a masquerade ball. How foolish to think so strong an attraction could have developed in that amount of time. She did not know him. She must face who he was, know now, before she was any more deeply embroiled. Before she found herself involved in a way it would be difficult to extricate herself from. She steeled herself to look across the street as the hack pulled away.

There he was, unmistakable, his tall, elegantly slouched stature, his gold-handled cane resting against the ground in one hand, the other coming down to his side having just knocked on the door. She waited. Perhaps it wasn't such a place as she imagined.

But no. The door opened to reveal a woman as painted and bedecked as Augusta would have expected. What was worse, she greeted Bridlington with obvious recognition and pleasure. He answered, "My dear Madame Agatha!" She ushered him inside, and closed the door behind him.

Augusta's feet felt too heavy to lift. All her limbs resisted every attempt to move them. Yet at the same time her heart tumbled in confusion. *I must continue,* she thought. The linen draper. No time to waste thinking about this now.

Somehow she went on, finding her way without having to ask anyone, discharging her errand with a calm assurance she did not feel, and returning to Curzon Street in a hired hack, eyes closed against the glare of the day. All she could think was that she never wanted to see Lord Bridlington again, and that she was almost certain to do so in a very few days.

CHAPTER 14

*N*o sooner had Augusta declared her resolution to forget Bridlington than she couldn't help recalling the many qualities in him that had beguiled her. That these were incompatible with the behavior she'd witnessed on the street in Soho—and that she'd had some inkling of when she spotted him from a distance at the masquerade—had her thoughts in a tumble of confusion. Who was he really? Fortunately, she had little time to indulge such thoughts due to the complicated machinations required to transform her from modiste's assistant into a plausible acquaintance of Mariana and a cousin of Mister Thorne in time for the Lanyon dress party.

Mariana had quickly realized that Augusta couldn't simply wear one of her gowns—even with such changes as she could make in the allotted time—as the dowager would certainly recognize it. So she purchased something completely new from Madame Noelle, claiming that it was for herself, taking care that it would look well with Augusta's lighter coloring: her curls chestnut rather than close to auburn in color, and eyes of a golden brown instead of a deep blue. Aside from having to hem the gown to be a little shorter and take it in a trifle around the bosom, the alterations necessary would not be extensive. And she trusted Augusta to add her own touches to make it uniquely hers.

Of course, if Mariana was going through the subterfuge of purchasing a new gown for herself, she had to show up at the party in something her mother hadn't seen before, and so she pretended to need two new evening dresses instead of one. Naturally, Miss Hastings would be required to come and make the final adjustments to the fit on the day of the party itself, and to stay in order to fix any small tears. Mariana put it that her dresser was indisposed with the measles, and that, rather than get one of the inexperienced housemaids to attend to her before and after the party, she hoped it would be acceptable for her to presume upon her long acquaintance with Madame to allow her to borrow Miss Hastings to fulfill that role. And, since it would doubtless be a very late night, Miss Hastings would stay in one of the empty servants' rooms overnight and return to Curzon Street in the morning.

Thus had Mariana communicated to Madame Noelle.

Madame was too delighted by the handsome purchase—which had involved the most expensive fabrics and trimmings—to demur at all. But Pauline, in her astute way, could not let this remarkable occurrence pass without comment.

"What's the game with Lady Mariana?" she whispered as Augusta put her things into her workbasket and prepared to take the beribboned dress boxes to Berkeley Square on the afternoon of the party. "Let me help you get a hack," Pauline said aloud, which gave her an excuse to accompany Augusta out to the street, where she could continue to question her.

After a quick look around to make sure no one was listening, Pauline said, "I think there's something devilish sly going on here. I wracked my noodle but couldn't come up with nothing that would account for Lady Mariana taking you up this way. You tell me her hoity-toity dresser's indisposed—well I never. And she never needed no one to help her with the fittings before!"

Keeping up this pretense, fooling someone as canny as Pauline, trying to figure out how to avoid seeing Bridlington at the dress party—it was all beginning to wear Augusta down. Every fiber of her wanted just to tell her inquisitive coworker everything, but she had promised secrecy, and what exactly could she tell her, after all? "Please don't ask me any more!" Augusta said, frustrated.

"Hah! So there's something. I knowed it." Pauline crossed her arms over her chest belligerently and stared Augusta down.

"I'm sure it's not what you think. I am truly helping Lady Mariana with her clothes." That, at least, was not a lie.

They were still arguing over the matter when something caught Augusta's eye on the opposite side of the street a short way down. The impression was fleeting, but she could have sworn she saw a slim gentleman staring in her direction. A familiar slim gentleman, dressed in the extreme of fashion, bedecked in fobs and with an enormous nosegay in his buttonhole, and a sallow, hollow-cheeked face above it. A chill passed through her body.

At that moment, the hack Madame's manservant had procured pulled up, and Augusta started to climb in, assuming she'd been mistaken because she'd only seen Grantley once before. He was shoved out of her mind altogether when she realized she would be unable to manage two large dress boxes and her workbasket on her own, even in a hack. And, at the other end, she would have to arrive unseen around the back of the house, which was difficult even without being laden with parcels. She fixed her eyes on Pauline's, who'd pressed her lips together in a pugnacious scowl as she stood feet planted wide apart on the flagway. Softening her own expression, Augusta said, "It appears that I need your help. Would you ask Madame if you may accompany me to deliver these gowns?" At that moment she couldn't think beyond the instant of arrival, wondering if she would be able to keep Pauline out of the house, and how to explain to her the need to do so.

Pauline dashed inside and soon re-emerged from the atelier wearing her chip hat and Spencer jacket, her scowl transformed into a satisfied smirk. After she helped settle Augusta and the boxes in the hack and climbed in after, she said, "Now no one's cocking an ear over us, so you might's well tell me everything."

It was an abominable crush, thanks to the bulky boxes. The long cloak Augusta wore so she could steal out of the house the back way to meet Mister Thorne once she was dressed for the evening was far too warm for the mild day, and sweat trickled down her back. What could she do? How could she put Pauline off?

And then, she had an idea. This evening's preparations would be more complex than those on the evening of the masquerade. She had much to do in the short hours before she would have to play her role. She believed, too, that she was enough in Mariana's confidence to be entitled to make a decision about the affair on her own. For that evening, Augusta thought, Pauline could assume the guise of her abigail. In fact, she'd be quite useful. She could more accurately take the measurements for altering her gown, and the two of them could work on it at the same time. Pauline was just as good a seamstress as she was—perhaps even better.

"I will tell you, but not here." Augusta cast a knowing glance in the direction of the jarvey.

"So I was right!" Pauline practically shrieked.

"Be quiet!" Augusta whispered, and pinched Pauline's arm.

The rest of the short ride passed in an atmosphere of suppressed excitement, which only grew when Augusta bade Pauline get out of the hack with her and come into the house through the mews entrance. "Be very, very quiet."

To Augusta's relief, Philpot did not come out of the stable and no one else was around. The door had been left open, as arranged. Pauline followed her almost noiselessly up the stairs to the attics. Augusta could sense the questions building in the seamstress's mind and hoped she could persuade her not to let them come tumbling out as soon as she saw the makeshift sewing and work room, where Jennings would be waiting for her to receive the gown destined for Mariana, and she would make her own preparations for the role she would play that evening.

Pauline behaved true to character. "My—!"

"Ssshh!" Augusta said when they entered the room. Jennings stood expectantly, and then opened her eyes wide when she spied Pauline. "Jennings, please don't be alarmed," Augusta said hurriedly. "I realized I could not dress my hair, alter my gown, and array myself properly all alone in such a short time, and you will be too busy with Lady Mariana. So I've brought a trustworthy friend to be my abigail."

She had said nothing of this to Pauline, who did an admirable job of not exclaiming in dismay at the news that she was to enact the servant to Augusta. Jennings took the box away, casting a sidelong glance at Pauline, and left them alone in the attic.

"We haven't got much time, so I can only explain a little bit to you now," Augusta said, not giving Pauline a chance to ask. "Help me with the gown. You'll need to hem it up a little in the front and take it in at the sides on the top. Can you arrange hair by any chance? No, I can manage, you'll have enough with the sewing."

"For the love of—you mean, this bit of finery is for you, not Lady High-and-mighty?" Pauline had opened the remaining dress box and lifted the elegant creation consisting of an amber satin slip covered with a pale lemon gauze round gown and demi-train, trimmed with gold lace rosettes an inch or two above the hem. Smaller rosettes decorated the décolletage and short sleeves. "You're never wearing this!" she said in awed tones. "Here! Madame didn't add them rosettes. They make all the difference. It was you, weren't it?"

Augusta laughed. "Yes, I confess. I couldn't leave it entirely as it was. And it is very fine. But I'm only borrowing it," she lied, having had to submit to receiving the gown as a gift from Mariana.

While Augusta slipped out of her York tan stuff day dress, Pauline lifted the evening gown reverently, gently bunched it up to put over Augusta's head, then eased her arms into the sleeves and tied it closed. In a few short minutes, she'd taken the measure of the necessary alterations, helped Augusta out of the gown, and set to work.

"Shall I do the hem while you—"

"No. I'll be done in the twinkle of a bedpost," Pauline said. "You do something with that mop o' yours."

The writing table had been transformed into a makeshift dressing table. On it Mariana had left white satin evening gloves, a painted fan, a silk reticule with gold tassels, a hair ornament with white and primrose ostrich feathers, evening slippers, and a small box closed with a pink ribbon. Augusta picked up the hand mirror. "Oh, no!" she said, and immediately set to work twisting her hair into a top knot and coaxing her natural curls into ringlets at her temples. When she finished, assuming it must contain an ornament for her hair, she opened the box, and gasped.

Nested on a bed of white velvet lay a necklet of topaz beads, with a folded note on top.

My dear Augusta,

PLEASE ACCEPT THIS SMALL GIFT IN APPRECIATION OF ALL YOU HAVE *done for me. It's just a bit of trumpery, but I thought it would look very pretty with your gown.*

MARIANA LANYON

"WHAT IS IT?" PAULINE ASKED, HAVING HEARD AUGUSTA'S stifled exclamation. "And I don't mind saying, I've been all patience, waiting for you to explain just what's in the wind here." She shook out the altered gown and held it up for Augusta's approval.

"No wonder Madame values you so highly," Augusta said as she surveyed Pauline's immaculate work. "And I agree. You've earned the right to be told a little more. It happens that I'm attending the dress party here this evening."

"Didn't I just guess! But why?" Pauline said, momentarily burying Augusta's face in the yards of satin and net as she once more lowered it over her head.

When the gown was safely on and Pauline had gone to work with all the fastenings, Augusta said, "As you have probably guessed, I'm in everything much deeper than you could know." She then quickly told Pauline about the men's clothing, the adventure at the masquerade, and the decision to play the role of a friend of Lady Mariana's for the evening. She chose not to say anything about Jeremy Thorne, and not a single word about Lord Bridlington escaped her lips. She didn't want to excite Pauline's romantic imagination and expose herself to innuendo and gossip back at the workshop.

"You have been busy, Miss Hastings," Pauline said, a look of disapproval in her eyes. "I still don't know the whys of all this, but I guess you has yer reasons."

Augusta smoothed on the long gloves and held out her arms so Pauline could tie the satin ribbons around them to hold them above her elbows. After that, she picked up the fan and reticule, slipped the dance card over her wrist, and turned to face Pauline. "How do I look?"

"You look like a lady. A beautiful lady," Pauline said, her voice ragged with emotion. "I knowed it. You can't gammon me. Here's where you was meant to be. And don't think you can persuade me there ain't more to the story, but yer in a hurry I can see, so I won't ask. Seeing you here, I'm more like to ask what game sent you to Madame as a stitcher!"

Augusta squeezed Pauline's shoulder appreciatively. "I'm going to have to leave you here, for I'm already late to meet —" She stopped herself. "What I mean is, you'll have to let yourself out. Don't go at the same time as I do. Here's money for the hack to take you home." She pressed several coins into Pauline's hand.

"Oh no, Gussie!" Pauline exclaimed, seeing that one of them was a gold sovereign.

"You've earned it. Lady Mariana will be so grateful for your discretion. I won't be home tonight, as you know. But I'll come tomorrow and we can go for a walk and I can tell you all then. Not a word, remember!" Then she leaned forward and kissed Pauline on the cheek. "You're a good friend."

❧

MARIANA STOOD AT THE TOP OF THE GRAND STAIRCASE NEXT to her mother, looking down as guests streamed into the house. The saloons had all been opened, and the ballroom—normally swathed in Holland covers—glittered in the light of hundreds of candles in half a dozen dazzling chandeliers. The cacophony of the orchestra tuning mingled with the low murmur of voices, which grew moment by moment. It was getting to be time for Jeremy and Augusta to arrive. She hoped the rooms would be crowded enough for them to blend in, and that her strategic invitations would lend Jeremy enough consequence for her to be able to present him to her brother, along with Augusta. She wanted to do it before the dancing started, but already she could see it might be difficult. No matter, there was always the supper at midnight.

"Try not to fidget," the dowager murmured to her daughter at a slight break in the arrivals.

"I'm not fidgeting!" she whispered back, realizing that, in fact, she had been clasping and unclasping her hands together nervously.

Why exactly was she nervous? Not everything hung on this one event, but it would lay the foundation for what she hoped would end in giving Jeremy the courage to offer for her. After what had passed between them at the masquerade, she was no longer in doubt that he felt about her exactly as she did about him, and that only his perception of their difference in station held him back.

The more difficult task would be to inspire George with the willingness to agree to a match that was far from equal. She would be of age in a few months and could make her own decision then, but she would much rather go about her business as an affianced lady than have to continue the endless round of balls and routs, where she would be assumed to be available and participating in the marriage mart.

Although being Jeremy's fiancée would not open all doors to Mariana, it would, she hoped, make it easier for her to follow him into the company of influential people in Westminster as his guest at political gatherings—and to get information from him without the elaborate subterfuge of Hookham's, or meeting in secret in the park, or the very daring step she planned to take on Monday, thanks to Augusta. Surely the dowager and Bridlington would see how worthy he was? How brilliant a future lay ahead of him? If they cared for her at all, they would see that she couldn't be happy with some peer who only wanted to hunt and fish and gamble.

The clock chimed ten. They should be here soon, she thought. Would Augusta be able to manage her hair and everything else? Jennings had told her about the supposed abigail she'd brought with her, and Mariana thought that although it let another person in on the secret she could not blame Augusta for taking the step. Mariana still didn't know all that Augusta was hiding, but the fact that she had secrets to keep assured her that anyone the seamstress saw fit to introduce to their schemes must be trustworthy.

Mariana fought to play the gracious, unconcerned hostess, standing shoulders back, chin lifted next to her mother, extending her hand, nodding or curtseying depending on the relationship with or rank of the guest. Her brother's foot excused him from duties such as this. He remained in one of the saloons, where he could sit when he needed to.

Her distracted gaze merged all the guests into a faceless mass as she imagined Jeremy in high gig, his confident bearing and forthright expression proclaiming him a gentleman, if not a nobleman. By creating a cousin of her acquaintance for him, once introduced to her mother and her brother, she would be able to engineer pretexts for them to call in perfect propriety.

"Your most obedient, My Lady."

Mariana forced the daydreams out of her mind and curtsied politely to the Duke and Duchess of Anglesea, old friends of the dowager's who had known Mariana from infancy. "Duke, Duchess," she said, handing them along to her mother.

But the duchess lingered a moment and pinched Mariana's chin, turning her face gently and examining her. "You are lovelier than ever, child," she said. "And there's a glow about you. Who is he?"

The words sent an unwonted blush into Mariana's cheeks. "I don't know what you mean, Duchess! Just the excitement of the evening."

The sparkle in the duchess's eyes told her that this old friend, at least, was not fooled. But she said no more and moved on to embrace the dowager warmly.

How would she control herself when she greeted Jeremy, if the merest suggestion that she was in love could overset her so? Mariana forced her racing pulse to slow, stood taller, and decided she would have to trust to her lifelong training in comportment not to give her away.

By the time Augusta met Jeremy, as arranged, her heart was pounding, and when she put out her hand to shake his, it trembled.

"Steady on, Cuz!" Jeremy said with a laugh. "It's just a party, you know. You look splendid, by the way."

"Thank you, Mister Thorne." Augusta didn't know what else to say, choosing to pretend to be deeply engrossed in picking up her skirts so she could climb into the chaise and four Jeremy had hired for the evening. She might have told him that he, too, looked more elegant and refined than she had ever seen him, in his fawn knee breeches and striped silk stockings, his superfine long-tail coat and snowy-white cravat with a simple gold stud adorning it. She was grateful that he'd forgone the affectation of a quizzing glass.

"Remember, I'm not Mister Thorne to you anymore! It's Cousin Jeremy. We've known each other a long time. And you were a friend of Lady Mariana's at school in Bath."

"Yes, of course. I suppose I should get used to it." Augusta had spent the last few days committing to memory all the details of the story Mariana had concocted, but in the pressure of the moment, her mind felt empty of anything except the impulse to flee.

"Forgive me for saying it, but you look more like you're heading to your own execution than that you're embarking on a lark that won't hurt anyone and might help Mariana—and myself, that's the truth of it—more than you could possibly know."

She laughed. "I'm just a little nervous. I dare say I shall enjoy it well enough once we start." She was more than nervous. She was terrified. All her concentration was focused on how to avoid being introduced to Bridlington as Augusta Thorne. She knew that she did indeed look very pretty—although she attributed this more to her garments than to any beauty of her person. And although this gratified her vanity, it worked against her desire to fade into the background.

Her pulse raced. In addition to all her misgivings about the pretense of her identity, her disorientation due to her conflicting views of Bridlington added another motive for avoiding him at all costs. She longed as well to ask him questions, to honestly inquire about his actions in Soho and at the masquerade. But she could never do that in such a setting. It would be close to impossible in any circumstance. Such things were simply not spoken of among polite company.

She assured herself that he would be busy entertaining

much more important guests than some nobody school friend of his sister's, or seamstress in disguise, whichever he chose to believe, and staying out of his way might not be so difficult. Minute by minute she regretted even more that she hadn't told Mariana about her previous brief meetings with the earl. How could she have done it without attaching more importance to the events than they warranted? All except the most recent one, of course.

Augusta suddenly gasped.

"What is it?" Jeremy asked.

"Oh, nothing at all. I was afraid I'd left my fan behind, but here it is." She drew it out of her reticule, flicked it open, and simpered above it, making him laugh.

But the fan had nothing to do with what had sent the blood draining from her limbs. She'd realized that Bridlington, as host, would be forced to stand up with every young lady there. She was confident she could avoid him in a crowd. But how to do it in the figure of a dance? Perhaps she need not dance at all. Yes, that was the only solution.

"Cousin Jeremy," Augusta said, the unfamiliar greeting and her accompanying blush making her glad of the chaise's dim interior. "I-I won't want to dance much. I don't know many of the steps."

"Nonsense! You were as light and graceful as a sea nymph at the masquerade."

A flash of memory—waltzing at the masquerade, Mister Thorne's sure movements and kind attempts to draw her into conversation, brought yet another blush to her face. "Nonetheless, I find that my ankle is a bit sore. I must have twisted it running up the stairs to get to the attics this evening."

Her heart clenched. She wished the entire ordeal ahead of them were over, and that she had already either gone through the inevitable embarrassment of meeting

Bridlington or had successfully navigated the party without having to so much as exchange a glance with him. She could not imagine how he would react if he saw her. Would he take it upon himself to approach her? Or would he perhaps regret their intimacy at the masquerade and try to put as much distance between them as he could? That would be a relief, she had to confess. She didn't aspire to a countess's coronet, after all. As to what she really wanted, that was so deeply buried in her bruised heart she couldn't have articulated it if she tried.

The groom pulled up the horses, but the postilion remained mounted. "Are we there?" Augusta asked, unable to prevent her pulse from jumping around like a scared kitten.

"Not yet. We're stuck behind about..." Jeremy opened a window and leaned out to look ahead, "... seven carriages. No need to be in a fluster." He reached over and patted her gloved hand.

Augusta's few memories of balls and parties in Devonshire didn't include the urban crush of carriages having to wait their turn to discharge passengers at the door. Broad avenues and less formal arrivals had been the order of the day there. She imagined that the number of guests at this one party would easily exceed her entire acquaintance in Bideford. She leaned back and closed her eyes, willing herself to be calm. But each time they started forward again, her attempts were foiled.

At last they drew up in front of the grand house that until then, Augusta had entered only through a small door off the mews. The groom jumped down, ordered the postilion to the lead horses' heads, opened the carriage door and put down the step. *Don't trip,* Augusta reminded herself, feeling a bit unsteady on her legs as a footman handed her out to the flagway. Jeremy stepped down smartly and put his arm out to her. She laid her hand upon it, not wanting to raise her eyes to the door.

"Try not to look like so frightened!" he whispered, teasing. "No one will eat you."

He could have no idea what she was facing. Jeremy was only to be presented as himself and would do creditably, she was certain. He could meet Bridlington without a shadow of guilt or deception, except in the degree to which he and Mariana were acquainted.

But Augusta refused to let her nerves get the better of her. She had reserves of strength. She had proven to herself that she could survive alone, make a meager living from the skill of her hands, and gain the admiration and trust of a lady who might materially advance her in her chosen career.

If only that lady were not the sister of a man who could just as easily expose her as a fraud, and of whose character she had the gravest doubts. These thoughts chased each other through her mind as she and Jeremy mounted the few shallow steps to the grand front door and entered a foyer blazing with the light of dozens of candles in wall sconces and chandeliers. A footman took her cloak and Jeremy's hat and gloves and bowed them to the grand staircase. Lady Mariana stood at the top, turned away from them as she greeted an elderly guest politely. Next to her was an older woman Augusta guessed must be the dowager. The resemblance to Mariana was marked, but softened, as though the years had worn away the sharp edges like a brook over stones. For an instant, Augusta feared that Bridlington would be standing with them to welcome guests, but he didn't appear to be there.

After a moment, the dowager caught sight of the two of them, and a puzzled expression leapt into her eyes. *It begins,* Augusta thought, watching as the older lady nudged Mariana and drew her attention to Augusta and Jeremy climbing the stairs.

There was no mistaking Mariana's expression. If Augusta had any doubt that she had misinterpreted the way of things between Mari and Jeremy, one look at her friend's eyes banished it. Lady Mariana Lanyon visibly brightened, and spots of crimson stained her cheeks. She glanced at Augusta, but her gaze lingered on Jeremy, who Augusta didn't have to look at to know he was every bit as deeply affected as Mariana. At least she would be able to comfort herself with the thought that whatever happened to her that evening, the two mismatched lovers would have advanced their claims on each other. It was enough of good to expect.

"Mama, allow me to present to you Miss Augusta Thorne and her cousin, Mister Jeremy Thorne. Augusta and I were at the academy together in Bath. You remember? I'm sure I told you about her. She is a cousin of the Thornes of Maplewood, and Mrs. Maplewood is sister to Mr. Thorne's aunt Lucy. Mister Thorne is in politics."

Her explanation was just confusing enough to muddy the connection, and the dowager simply smiled. She accepted Augusta's proffered hand and curtsy with complacence and nodded at Jeremy. Mariana put out both her hands to Augusta in the manner of greeting a dear old friend and kissed her cheek. "How lovely to see you! I'm so glad you wrote to me that you would be in London for this short while."

The lie tripped off her tongue so effortlessly that Augusta didn't know whether to be awed or scandalized, and wished she had such easy command of pretense.

"Good girl," Jeremy murmured to her as they left Mariana and her mother behind and walked leisurely into the drawing room where most people seemed to be congregating.

Now what? Augusta thought. She was in a sea of unfamiliar faces, thank heavens. There was no sign of Bridlington. "What shall we talk about?" she asked Jeremy as he handed her a glass of sherry he'd taken from the tray offered to them by a footman. "We must have some conversation. The weather has been unseasonably warm, would you not say?"

"Really? Surely you can think of something more interesting than that. You are an avid reader, are you not?" He said this with a humorous gleam in his eye. "What have you to say about *Evelina?*"

That he so clearly remembered their first meeting in Hookham's surprised Augusta. It seemed an age ago, so much had happened since then. "I'm ashamed to say that I have had very little time to read since that day—was it only just over a week ago? I have to admit that I am only halfway through the first volume. I have spent hours..." She was about to mention stitching in the workroom when a lady sporting a diamond tiara and a gaudy jeweled brooch at her bosom wandered by, casting a curious glance in their direction. "...hours, choosing the gowns for my coming engagements. And I haven't had a free evening for the longest time." This was true enough, thanks to all the work she'd been doing for Mariana.

"Thorne! Surprised to see you here!" A man's voice broke into their subdued conversation and a portly gentleman of middle years strode up with his hand outstretched.

"Richard!" Jeremy said with a ready smile. "I didn't see you in the house for the last vote. How long have you been in town?"

The gentleman did not answer but turned to Augusta, lifting his quizzing glass so that what would have been a fairly small brown eye looked abnormally huge. His accompanying smile discomfited her, although she couldn't have said why.

"May I present Sir Richard Otway, Tory member for Basset Morten. We were at Lincoln's Inn together. Richard, this is my—this is my cousin, Miss... Thorne."

He'd forgotten her name! He must be nervous too. Now what would she do? She put out her hand.

"Servant, Miss Thorne," Sir Richard said taking her hand and bowing over it. "I hope I may claim you for the second set, if your cousin has not already introduced you to all the other eager supplicants to take you out to the floor?"

Somehow, in her anxiety about avoiding any possibility of dancing with Lord Bridlington, Augusta had forgotten that there might be others who would want to stand up with her. Her mind had been fully occupied with glancing around her in case the earl entered the room, so she could exit by another door. "Of course, Sir," she managed to say, years of training asserting themselves despite her panic, and reminding her to let him add his name to the dance card dangling from her wrist.

The two gentlemen chatted briefly about politics, reeling off names that meant nothing to Augusta. Fortunately, some other acquaintance hailed Sir Richard from across the room and he bowed and left them. Soon a lively dance tune filtered into the room from the ballroom, and the tide of guests moved slowly in the general direction of the music.

"May I have the honor, Cuz?" Jeremy asked, having downed his sherry.

Augusta had only sipped at her glass, but Jeremy took it out of her hand and placed it on a table, then led her through the doors into the ballroom.

On their way, three other gentlemen of his acquaintance stopped Jeremy. He was much better known than Mariana had led Augusta to believe he would be. She'd said she'd invited a few political people so he wouldn't be completely at sea among the *ton*-ish company, and all of them were in the

Upper House, as far as Augusta could tell. More disconcerting was the fact that every one of those gentlemen had requested to stand up with her for at least one dance after being introduced to her and her card was filling up fast.

She whispered to Jeremy as he led her into the set for the first country dance, "Please tell me who I've just agreed to dance with!"

"You didn't expect it, did you?" he said, cocking his head on the side as they waited for the introduction and salute to finish before joining the figure.

Augusta shook her head just as the movement of the dance separated them.

"You're creating a bit of a stir, my girl," Jeremy said when they came together again and joined hands in a circle. "You are much admired."

"I?" She glanced quickly around, and noticed that several of the gentlemen standing in knots on the side of the ballroom were looking at her. "Why?"

The dance took them away from each other again, so Augusta had to wait for Jeremy's response. "You honestly don't know? Do you not possess a mirror?"

This sent Augusta into a furious blush, but she couldn't put her hands up to her cheeks because they were at that moment clasped by two different gentlemen as they processed in a stately walk.

Fortunately some deeply ingrained physical memory took over Augusta's body in the dance because her confusion spared her no thought for her feet. She no sooner finished one dance than another partner came to claim her. Augusta tried to keep the conversations impersonal, but two of the gentlemen requested permission to call on her the next day, and all of them asked questions Augusta was by no means prepared to answer. She wasn't certain she'd told the same thing to any of them, and prayed that Mariana would come and rescue her from what became moment by moment more awkward.

At last, her hostess entered the ballroom on the arm of a man leaning on a cane. Augusta didn't have time to see who it was, having had to turn away because of the dance. By the time she faced them again, she caught sight of Jeremy approaching them and bowing.

The set was near to ending, she and her partner having traversed the entire line of the dance. At that moment, the gentleman with the cane turned around and their eyes met.

It was Lord Bridlington, and he'd seen her.

CHAPTER 15

A sensation of extreme heat and icy cold flooded
George, and he barely attended to what his sister
was saying to him. It made no sense. How could it be that
Miss Hastings had procured an invitation to what he knew
was considered the *ton* party of the season? As far as he
knew, her relationship with his sister was based on
commerce. Although he hadn't entirely solved the riddle of
her appearance at the masquerade wearing one of Mariana's
gowns.

"I'd very much like to introduce you to the cousin of a
school friend," Mariana said. "Perhaps I've mentioned
Augusta Thorne. She just happened to be in London for a
few weeks. I ran into her in Bond Street the other day. She is
visiting her aunt, who is unwell and an intolerable bore, so I
invited her to come this evening along with her cousin, Mr.
Thorne. I believe I saw her in the dance a moment ago."

George barely attended to what Mariana was saying, still
trying to keep Miss Hastings in view out of the corner of his
eye. She looked magnificent. Even lovelier than she had at
the masquerade, especially without anything covering her

face and hiding her golden eyes and creamy complexion, its color heightened by the exercise of the dance.

Never had he wished so much that he could dance, to have an excuse to gaze at her, touch her arm, press his hand into the small of her back.

"Ah, and here is Mr. Thorne! How fortunate."

Mariana recalled George's attention as she made the introductions, but George was still overset by the sight of Miss Hastings. "Servant," he said distractedly, nodding to Mister Thorne who bowed with deference.

"Can you imagine my surprise? Mister Thorne is a political man, private secretary to Perceval. How interesting, don't you think George?" Mariana said.

He forced himself to attend to his sister's words, still trying to keep one eye on Miss Hastings, who had looked away and was engaged in the final figures of the dance. He wasn't too distracted, though, that he didn't catch a glimpse of something in Mariana's eyes that he recognized as mischief. She hurried her words, voice shaking just a little, and she sounded a bit breathless. Not at all like the self-assured sister he knew so well. "Yes, of course. Although I'm surprised you find Perceval's concerns of great interest, Mari!" Bridlington strove for a lightness of tone he didn't feel. Quite apart from the very unexpected sight of Miss Hastings, he had a growing suspicion that Mariana was up to something he wouldn't like. "You said you were here with your cousin?" he said, turning to Thorne.

Thorne opened his mouth to respond but Mariana interjected, "Yes, as I said, we were at school together, in Bath. Where has she got to, I wonder?" She cast a dazzling smile in Thorne's direction and put her hand on his arm in a familiar way.

"She was dancing a moment ago," Thorne said. "She's got a full dance card, I'll wager!"

"A very pretty girl, to be sure. And such a sweet disposition. Oh! There she is! Augusta!" Mariana called and nodded toward the set that was just at an end as a couple went around the outside and stood at the top for the reverence, men with their backs to them, ladies facing.

George followed her gaze, and his confusion deepened. Mariana had called to Miss Hastings, who responded to her summons and once again raised her eyes to his. Miss Hastings's eyes. He knew them, intimately. How came she to be known as Miss Thorne? Or perhaps she'd given him a false name when they'd met. But why? Was she in fact taking advantage of his sister's good nature? Mariana had said she'd just encountered her school friend in Bond Street the other day. She could have been in London before their meeting of course. But still, nothing made sense.

In spite of Mariana's clear gesture that she should join them, Miss Hastings turned away and hurried into one of the anterooms.

"Why—perhaps she didn't see us." Mariana said.

Thorne said, "I dare say her partner has taken her to get a drink. Thirsty work, those country dances. I hope you'll stand up with me, Lady Mariana, if you are not already spoken for?"

George looked back at the two of them in time to catch the radiant look Mariana bestowed on Thorne. Ah. So that was it. He'd never seen her like that. Her face, normally either guarded or set in an aloof, somewhat cynical expression, positively glowed. The expression vanished in an instant, though, leaving George to wonder if he'd really seen it.

"You don't mind, do you George?" Mariana said. Turning to Thorne, "You see, my brother does not dance."

Thorne cast a sympathetic look at him. "With all these

lovely creatures to choose from, I heartily pity you for that, Lord Bridlington!"

At that moment Lewiston entered the ballroom from the direction of the yellow saloon and, clearly hoping to engage Mari for a dance, made for the three of them. But as soon as the music started up, Thorne nodded to George and led Mariana out to the floor.

"Who's the fellow?" Lewiston asked without preamble as he reached Bridlington.

"I'm not entirely sure. Eton and Oxford so Mari tells me, after our time, apparently. Then Lincoln's Inn. But I don't know the family name at all," George answered, still distracted by the image of Miss Hastings—or Miss Thorne, whoever she really was, and cursing his game foot for making it awkward for him to scurry through the guests looking for her.

"You look all done up, George," Lewiston said. "Foot plaguing you?"

"No. I mean a little. I wonder...what did Grantley have to tell you about his relations in Devonshire?" Perhaps Lewiston could shed some light on the mystery of Miss Hastings.

"That's an odd thing to ask, Bridlington! However, he was pretty cagey. When I tried to quiz him about his Hastings cousins, he changed the subject, as if there was something he didn't want me to know. Look here, if that girl you're besotted with is part of that family, I'd run a mile in the other direction, I would. Nothing but trouble there, I'd wager."

This was not promising. And it gave him no more information about the lady one way or the other. He refused to believe that she was like Grantley. There'd been no guile in her eyes, no hardness. But what could he know of her after such a short acquaintance?

After a final scan of the couples massing on the floor,

Bridlington relinquished his fruitless search for Miss Hastings and resumed his duties as host, moving from one cluster of people to the next, kissing dowagers' hands, exchanging inanities and false smiles. Lewiston soon found a pretty dance partner and was busy flinging her around the room in a waltz. Such a waste, George thought. Full use of his feet, a perfect sense of rhythm, and not a graceful bone in his body.

AUGUSTA HAD LOOKED UP WHEN SHE HEARD MARIANA CALL her name and felt the blood drain from her face before rushing back into her head and almost making her dizzy. He was still there. She wasn't ready. Perhaps Mariana hadn't called her Augusta Thorne. But he'd seen her and recognized her, she was certain, if not the first time their eyes had met, certainly the second time. As soon as it was polite to leave the floor, she curtsied to her partner. He had put his hand out to lead her off, but she excused herself and rushed toward the only exit she could see on the opposite side of the ballroom, through a heavy velvet curtain. Her only object was to go somewhere Bridlington would not find her. Unfortunately, behind the curtain was only a small alcove where a few chairs had been placed for quiet conversations. There was no way out of it but to go back the way she'd come. It would seem odd for her to remain there alone for very long, but she dared not emerge into the ballroom too quickly.

Before another moment had passed, a giggle and the approach of light footsteps made Augusta's concern about being alone in the alcove moot. A bright-faced young lady with a halo of golden curls stared at Augusta in open astonishment and said, "Oh!" At that moment a florid young man joined her, his matching air of mischievous glee halted by sight of Augusta.

She said quickly, "I'm sorry. It's just so warm in such a crush. Needed some air." Indeed, it was hard for Augusta to utter the words, her throat was so tight.

"I say, are you quite well?" The young man strode past his partner and walked toward Augusta.

She put up her hand to stop him and said, "I am, I assure you. A glass of water, though, if you would be so kind."

The girl—who looked to be no older than seventeen—cast a fierce look at Augusta before turning back to her swain. "Yes, Lord Herbert, and if you would also be so kind as to bring me champagne?"

He flashed her a smile and hurried away.

"I-I'm so sorry," Augusta said. "I'll leave."

"Don't bother. It would be most improper if Hector and I were found alone here anyway." Having no audience to appreciate any gracefully flirtatious gesture, she flopped onto one of the chairs and snapped her fan open, waving it languidly in front of her face.

Augusta had to press her lips together to avoid an impertinent chuckle. Oh to have such innocent concerns! "I could leave the curtain open just enough so that you wouldn't be considered alone but no one would hear your conversation?"

The girl's face brightened. "Would you? Wait until Hector comes back. I'm sorry, I'm being terribly rude. I'm Alveria. Alveria Charters."

"Augusta Thorne." She nodded politely and moved to sit in the chair next to Alveria's.

"Thorne? I don't know any Thornes. Who are your people?"

"Oh, you wouldn't know them. We're quite nobody, really. I went to school with Lady Mariana."

"Really? My older sister did as well! She must know you.

We all came this evening—no one would decline an invitation from the Lanyons. Mama thinks one of us should marry Lord Bridlington..." Her voice lowered comically at the end of this utterance.

At the mention of his name, Augusta's face paled. She soon recovered, only to be assailed with another disturbing realization. Had Mariana considered that the lie about where they'd met would be discovered if any of her other school friends were here? Dear oh dear, she thought. Can I escape from this party without being noticed by anyone else? Surely only embarrassment and disaster awaited her. What a fool she'd been to agree to it! And how could such a man—the most eligible catch in London—consider any serious alliance with someone like her?

Miss Charters had continued to rattle on, not noticing Augusta's discomfiture. "...but I refuse to be tied to anyone who's lame! What fun is it if your husband can't dance?"

This comment brought Augusta up short. "What did you say?" she asked. "Lame?"

"Yes, of course! You must know, a clubfoot. Mama said it gives him an air of distinction, like Lord Byron, but I think it's embarrassing."

"Oh, of course, I had forgotten." Only she hadn't. She hadn't noticed anything beyond his eyes, his smile, his strong arms, the way he looked at her. How could she not have known this? Mariana's brother, Lord Bridlington, had a clubfoot. He was lame. Thinking back, she realized that such a handicap would have made it difficult for him to climb down from a carriage quickly, or dismount and remount a horse, or walk easily down a long staircase. It would also account for the awkward gait she had observed at the masquerade, thinking he must be drunk. And the gold-handled cane. His disability also, as Miss Charters said, meant that he could not dance.

Augusta felt as if she had swallowed a stone.

She had been so wrapped up in her own perceptions that she'd failed to notice something that likely had given Bridlington pain and difficulty his entire life. That Mariana never mentioned it was hardly surprising. She probably thought her brother's affliction was so well known that there was no need. In fact, the two of them never really talked about Bridlington. He did not enter their plans in any way.

Was this what he'd meant when he'd said she didn't know all there was to know about him?

From feeling desperate to avoid the earl at all costs, Augusta now wanted most urgently to talk to him, to explain herself and tell him everything. She wished to lay herself open in all her imperfection so that he would do the same. To do so would require revealing her entire involvement with Mariana, thereby exposing more of her past than she ever wanted to. She had no desire to admit how close she had come to being yoked to a distant cousin she not only didn't love, but for whom she had no respect. A cousin she in fact disliked profoundly. And yet, to keep it from him seemed cruel. Just as it would be cruel not to own that she did not want to be an idle wife, with no more to do than run a household and have children, but that she yearned to make her mark in the world of fashion.

"Here you are!" said Lord Herbert, elbowing the heavy drapes out of his way and handing each of them a glass, the champagne to Augusta and the water to Alveria.

They smiled at one another and exchanged glasses, which brought an intense blush to the young peer's cheeks. Augusta sipped the cool water and breathed deeply, then stood, holding out her glass to the befuddled young man. "Thank you, Sir. I must look for my friends." She nodded and smiled conspiratorially at Miss Charters, all the while fighting for control of her turbulent emotions. Then she pulled the curtain aside and looked around the ballroom to see if Lord Bridlington was anywhere near. Since this was the ballroom and he didn't dance, Augusta did not expect to see him, and she didn't do so.

"Ah! Miss Thorne!"

No sooner had she entered the ballroom than a gentleman she vaguely recognized came up to her and bowed. She smiled at him weakly.

"You haven't forgotten our waltz?"

"Which dance is this, Sir?" She looked at her dance card, scanning it for the first waltz, hoping to see a name so she could not be impolite when she begged off.

"It's the sixth." He peered at her card. "There I am. Lord Derby. But my friends call me Darb."

"Thank you, Lord Derby," Augusta said with a slight curtsy, and, before she could form the words to ask to be excused, the music started and Derby offered her his arm. A corpulent man with a sheen of perspiration on his forehead, Derby had an unaffected smile and kind, rather protuberant eyes.

Without warning, Augusta felt the sting of something very like tears behind her eyes. She loved to dance. To feel the music in her bones, to move so freely and gracefully. How would it be to have that ability taken away? Or never to have experienced it at all? Did men feel the same when they danced? If only everything wasn't so terribly confused! Before she ran away, she'd vowed never to dance again, her heart so full of stolen moments at the assemblies with James. Those days were soft, distant memories now. Her love of dancing had been awakened at the masquerade, and since then, she couldn't help imagining what it would feel like to be held close in Lord Bridlington's arms, letting him lead her around the room, surrendering the movements of her body to his gentle direction. Now, she knew that would never happen. Although she felt her own deprivation keenly, worse by far was the consciousness that Bridlington would never know the joy of dancing.

Lord Derby, despite his unpromising appearance, turned out to be a skilled dancer, and the intricacies of the waltz came so naturally to Augusta that she soon allowed herself to luxuriate in the joy of music and movement. "Is something the matter?" he said, when she must have unintentionally allowed her expression to reflect her inmost thoughts.

"Of course not!" Augusta said, making an effort to smile.

When the dance ended and Derby led her off the floor, he said, "You dance wonderfully, Miss Thorne. Are you related to the Thornes of Yorkshire? I wonder if you might permit me to call on you, take you for a drive in my curricle one afternoon."

"Oh, I'm afraid, I'm not in London for long, just visiting my aunt."

"Not leaving tomorrow, I dare say!" he said.

"N-no, but I believe we are engaged for the next while." More lies!

"Augusta, there you are!"

Never was a voice more welcome to Augusta's ears. Lady Mariana came up to her, greeting Derby with a smile and a handshake, saying, "I must claim my friend, My Lord. A very particular person wishes to make her acquaintance."

"No doubt," said Derby, with an unwilling but nonetheless gracious bow. "But first, I would be grateful if Miss Thorne would tell me where I might find her to take her for a drive in the park tomorrow."

Augusta turned her panic-stricken eyes to Mariana, who seemed not the least perturbed by this.

"Why, she's staying at the Clarendon with her aunt, of course—although I have already invited her to spend the afternoon with me. You could call for her here." And then Mariana nodded to him and led Augusta away.

"Oh, Mariana, how could you tell such a bouncer!" Augusta whispered with a smile pinned to her face as they threaded their way through the guests.

"Because it's entirely believable. You're doing brilliantly. Of course. And I decided something so simple and it would solve myriad difficulties—and, I hope, make those I care most about happy."

Augusta stopped abruptly. She wasn't sure which of Mariana's statements to address first. "What do you mean?"

"Well, I noticed something earlier this evening. I'm afraid it's plain as day, really, although I can't for the life of me understand how it could have happened so quickly, or how I could possibly not have known anything about it."

Augusta felt as if the floor were buckling beneath her feet. Mariana's words sliced into her, broke her open. She knew what Mariana was referring to. How could she not have seen it? And now, everything Augusta was trying to keep inside had spilled out into the crowded, noisy room. "What did you see exactly?" she asked, hoping perhaps what she feared had not come to pass.

"I saw how my brother looked at you. And I saw your reaction. It wasn't the first time you'd seen him was it?"

Augusta couldn't find the words to answer her.

"I suppose, coming here almost every day, you must have crossed paths. He often chooses to go directly to the stable yard rather than wait for Philpot to bring the curricle round to the front. Still, that hardly seems enough for him to be so unsettled by the sight of you, even if you met every time you came."

No, Augusta thought, *but it was a beginning.* Without those few other meetings, what happened at the masquerade would never have been possible. Should she tell Mariana about that? Bridlington had asked her not to. And her own feelings were so confused still, she didn't trust herself to be able to explain. "As you say, Mariana, we met perchance once or twice." She tried to affect a nonchalance she didn't feel. "I don't see precisely what you mean, however. We have become friendly."

"Friendly? Is that what you call a look as though the world only exists in each other's eyes?"

Surely not. Surely they both had more command than that of their feelings.

"Your blush tells me everything."

"Where are you taking me?" Augusta said, suddenly awakening to the fact that they had passed through several reception rooms crowded with guests talking, laughing, and drinking.

"To my brother. He is in the Chinese saloon, sitting for a while. You know standing tires him, with his bad foot."

She didn't know. Or hadn't even suspected. Not until a few minutes before that. "But what shall I say? He knows me as Augusta Hastings! How will you explain Augusta Thorne?"

"That is a complication I did not anticipate, I will admit. But I don't think it will matter."

Mariana didn't appear to have an answer to this problem. Augusta stopped her. "You must tell him. You must be honest about Jeremy."

"You know, don't you." It wasn't a question.

"Since the masquerade. Even with both of you in men's clothing, it was obvious." Augusta couldn't help smiling despite herself. "Will Bridlington object?"

"Lady Mariana! You look ravishing!" A young woman dripping in diamonds draped herself on Mariana's arm. "We must have a comfortable prose. Will you take supper with us?" The lady included a somewhat embarrassed looking young gentleman in the question, pointedly ignoring Augusta.

"I am afraid I am already engaged to sit with my friend, Miss Augusta Thorne." Mariana nodded toward Augusta. The lady turned away as if her attention had been commanded by someone else and glided off. "Insufferable snob!" Mariana muttered.

Yet those were the creatures who populated Lady Mariana's world. "I fear there are many who would look askance at a marriage between you and a parliamentary clerk. Or who would find it unconscionable that an earl should cast more than a cursory glance in the direction of a seamstress."

"True enough," Mariana said, tucking Augusta's arm in her elbow and drawing her on through the rooms. "But Jeremy is not just a clerk. He is a man of brilliance. And describing you as a seamstress, even taking no account of your gentle birth, is like calling Mister Knighton a sawbones." She squeezed Augusta's hand. "I don't mind them. George's opinion—Bridlington, I mean—is the only one that matters."

"Not your mother's?"

Mariana was silent for a few moments. "My mother made a brilliant match, and she was the unhappiest woman I've ever known."

Augusta fought to master her own tumultuous feelings and consider Mariana's predicament. She could see the dilemma of her wishing to marry the appealing, intelligent young man who was anything but the social equal of an earl's daughter. He would have been a more suitable match for herself, a thought which provoked a wry smile. She was glad enough to have the subject diverted from anything to do with herself and Bridlington, and said, "What did wearing men's clothing to the masquerade have to do with any of this?"

Mariana put her finger to her lips. "I can't say here. That evening was not the culmination of that deception. Something bigger, more important is ahead. You won't know about it until afterwards, though. And I still need you to do something for me."

Secrets. Lanyon House was riddled with them. If she had anything to say to it, at least one of her own secrets would not live past that night.

By that time they had entered the Chinese saloon, which owed its name to having a few pieces of furniture in the modish oriental style.

"Ah, there he is! Come with me, Augusta."

She saw him in a chair by the fire, gazing in her direction, and she wanted to run to him. She tensed every muscle with the effort of standing still.

He planted his cane next to his bad foot and pushed himself up. She had never seen him do that before, but she gave it no more than a moment's thought. She had so many questions. Yet she would be able to ask none of them in that crowded, public room.

"I must go and see if supper is nearly ready," Mariana said, giving Augusta a little push in Bridlington's direction and then hastening away.

They met somewhere in the middle of the room. Augusta curtsied. Bridlington took her hand and lifted her out of it, drawing her toward a settee over to the side, a little away from the knots of conversing guests. "Miss Hastings," he said once they were seated. "Or is it Miss Thorne?" A little smile lifted one corner of his mouth.

Augusta wanted to sink into the floor. Of course he would ask that first of all. "I would not have deceived you. I have not known Mariana—Lady Mariana, I mean—very long, but long enough to know that she sometimes gets carried away with her own enthusiasms. It served her that I should be Miss Thorne this evening, for reasons of her own. But as you know, I am not." Augusta suddenly felt shy. She didn't know what to say. Mariana had seen the spark of attraction between them. But what of all the contradictions? What of Bridlington's presence at that house in Soho?

"My sister can be relentless." He raised a hand to a footman. "Ratafia?"

"No, thank you." She toyed with the tassel that dangled from her fan. "I don't know what I'm doing here." The words came out before she had a chance to understand why she spoke them.

"In this house? Or sitting next to me?" His voice was low. For her alone.

She looked down in confusion and shook her head. "You forget, My Lord, that before the day we met, I had never been in London before."

"I have long wondered, why did you come? Surely not to work for that tyrant Madame Noelle. I think I know something of your background."

Oh no! He mustn't know, not yet. She could no more explain it all to him in that moment than fly to the moon. "Don't ask me, I beg you!"

Perhaps out of nervous habit, or because he needed to occupy his hands to fill the silence between them, Bridlington rubbed the gold handle at the top of his ebony cane, his fingers tracing the engraved crest. Augusta watched them, fascinated. The cane. It had been the clue, the thing she should have noticed more than any other that would have revealed the affliction he'd been born with. He must have had it in the curricle. Not while he was in the saddle, but he certainly carried it at the masquerade. And of course, it had accompanied him to that house in Soho.

"It is a beautiful piece," Bridlington said. "An ornament. An essential. It is one of several things that make it all so impossible, as I'm sure you're coming to understand, now that you see me here."

"Why? What is impossible?"

"You must know. It was wrong of me to say what I did to you the other night."

"It was not unkind, or unwelcome." She'd gone over and over his words since then, pulling them apart, thinking about them. Why couldn't she make her thoughts stop whirling! The voices around her suddenly sounded loud and hollow, as if echoing in a cave.

A slight frown creased his brow, and he said, "Are you quite well?"

Fighting for control and mustering all the courage she could, Augusta said, "I didn't mind hearing it, what you said. Your words did not distress me, although they confused me a little."

She looked down at her hands, knotted together in her lap. He reached over and covered them with one of his. "You don't know me. We can never be ..." His voice trailed off.

The only thing Augusta could think was impossible was to be sitting there amid gay party goers and discussing matters that dealt with their deepest feelings. But if he was determined to discuss it, she must allow him. "What must we never be? What do you want of me?"

"More than you should be willing to give," Bridlington said, exasperated.

His words made no sense. Not after what he had said to her the other night. Then, their souls had spoken to each other. They knew each other as only two people in love could. But he seemed to be telling her she had been deceived. This was no renewal of his sentiments. He was putting her off. Backing away. Mariana must have misinterpreted his look, attributing an emotion to him akin to what she and Jeremy felt. But they had known each other for longer. She and Bridlington had spent, what, less than an hour in each other's company? Moment by moment, Augusta was coming to believe that he did not, after all, regard her with anything akin to love. He found her attractive, but he regretted what had passed between them at the masquerade and sought to extricate himself from a situation that could become an embarrassment. She was not good enough for him. Or only good enough for...

He leaned slightly toward her, his eyes full of tenderness and regret. "I would give anything for things to be different. If I could only be sure of you, sure that you were not ashamed of such things."

Different? Sure? Ashamed? And then, all at once, Augusta gasped.

He was suggesting something improper. Trying to give her a slip on the shoulder. Offering her a carte blanche. He wanted to set her up as his mistress, so that he would not have to patronize that house in Soho. Or perhaps he would continue to do that, and go to the masquerade as well and dally with lightskirts there. How foolish she had been! The spark between them—it was not love. Not on his side. It was pure desire, untroubled by affection. His words stabbed her deep in her gut.

She now had no doubt. He did not want an honorable alliance with her. He didn't even know that she was the daughter of Sir Alastair Hastings of Crossley Manor in Devonshire, that, until their fortunes had changed, she had been privileged to be educated and petted and had enjoyed a position of respect and consequence in the county. He didn't know any of that, so why would he interest himself in her for any honorable purpose?

All the doubts and insecurities of the past days, all the jumble of ideas and thoughts and experiences of her brief time in London, washed over her like a bucket of icy water.

She had been blind. Of course this privileged, wealthy peer wouldn't care about someone like her beyond using her to gratify his lust. Well, she wasn't so lost to propriety that she would ever consider a dishonorable proposition, no matter that her heart twisted at the thought that she could have been so deceived in Bridlington. She may be in straitened circumstances, but she had her wits. And the fact remained that, rich or poor, her family was as old and venerable as his.

"I see," she finally said, lifting her chin and squaring her shoulders. "I believe I have given you quite the wrong impression, My Lord. Please give me leave to forget everything you said to me the other night. You can have no interest in me, not in any way that would be considered honorable. And you have mistaken me if you think I would accept any other proposition." Her voice shook with the effort to control her anger and distress. "I am afraid it is time for me to leave. You need not see me out, and we need not ever meet again."

She stood and walked away, blinded by tears she couldn't stop, before Bridlington had a chance to scramble to his feet. He would not try to follow her, she knew. It would be too awkward for him and obvious in front of his guests. She did not turn around. She hadn't looked into his eyes, she couldn't bear to. She headed straight for the door of the saloon with the intention of going out and running down the stairs and out onto the street for some fresh air.

Just as she reached the door, a man blocked it on his way in, ushering a woman who must certainly not have received an invitation to the party. Her gown was so diaphanous as to be nearly transparent, and she'd dampened it so it would cling to every voluptuous curve of her body. Augusta stood staring in horror. All around her people had stopped speaking.

But her horror was not for the woman, who could have

been any of those loose women at the masquerade the other night. It was for the gentleman. She'd only seen him for certain once before, but there was no mistaking him. The Honorable Desmond Grantley, the man whose suit had precipitated her flight to London, stood looking down at her with his peculiar smile that lifted his lips at their corners and squeezed his eyes shut without changing their expression in the slightest. "Let me pass," she said.

He arched his eyebrows in mock surprise. "But of course, Miss Hastings," he said and stepped aside, sweeping his arm in an ironic bow, and she ran past him.

The evening could get no worse. Grantley had seen her. Where was Mariana? More to the point, where was Jeremy? She must go away, now, and not come back. She would return to the atelier, not stay overnight, end her association with Mariana. Perhaps Grantley did not know of her position with Madame Noelle. Except she knew he must. All at once she realized she had certainly seen him more than once before: her fleeting view of him earlier that same day. He'd been watching her. Would he come after her? Anger at Bridlington, shame at her naïveté, and distress about Grantley stopped each breath on its way to her lungs.

By now, the guests were streaming in to supper, and she could not make her way through them without calling attention to her headlong flight. Tears stood in her eyes, and she blinked hard to stop them falling before she could get her handkerchief out of her reticule. What had she expected? She was nothing now. Everything she'd done was in shambles.

Oh where were Mariana and Jeremy!

Could she trust Mariana, though? Crazy as she was, flighty and mercurial, Augusta somehow thought that she could. She and Mariana were alike in some deep way, however different their outward circumstances. She knew everything she'd been asked to do was somehow to help

Mariana be able to choose her mate for herself and have a fighting chance of happiness. Wasn't that what she'd attempted for herself in taking her own crazy step of coming to London? If she left now, if she turned her back on this aggravating, beguiling earl's daughter, she would be letting them both down.

The question was how to uphold her bargain with Mariana and avoid ever seeing Lord Bridlington again. She could not. She must not.

But oh, how she wished to!

GEORGE'S FIRST REACTION WAS SHOCK. WHAT HAD HE SAID TO make Miss Hastings run off so suddenly in such a state of distress? He knew he'd been expressing himself clumsily. All he meant was to give her the opportunity to separate herself from him once she understood the extent of his affliction. He struggled to his feet just in time to see her flight stopped at the door out of the saloon by someone he had no wish to see, and who he had hoped would not arrive uninvited to the party. Quite apart from the notorious, barely clad married lady he had on his arm, the way Grantley looked at Miss Hastings was as impudent and insulting as anything George had ever seen. He'd said something to her that made her go white with what, fear? Why would she fear him? But the recognition was clear. They must not only be distant cousins, but also be known to each other. The idea sickened him.

All this went through George's mind as he limped to the door, desperate to go after Augusta, to find her and talk to her so he could undo the damage his ill-considered words had done. He prayed she had not left Lanyon House. He certainly had no time to waste. His cursed foot!

"Why the rush, Bridlington?"

Just as he reached the door, so did Grantley, who had sauntered over to it and stood in just such a way that would make it necessary for George to either squeeze past him or push him aside—neither of which actions would be appropriate as host in his own house. "I find I must attend to something important. I'm sorry I have no time to chat just now, Grantley," George said, his eyes boring into his.

"Yes," Grantley said in his lazy drawl. "I saw Miss Hastings go. In quite a fury, wasn't she. She has a habit of flying off. But perhaps you didn't know that about her. Will be quite difficult to tame her, I imagine."

What can you possibly know about that remarkable woman? George thought but did not say. He could not make Grantley pay for his rudeness just then, but George vowed to find a time and a place to teach him a lesson he wouldn't soon forget. At that moment, all that mattered was finding Augusta—Miss Hastings. With a scathing look at his unwanted guest, George stepped sideways and slipped through the door around him, right into the midst of the crush of guests heading toward the supper room.

He was tall, so he could at least see over most people's heads, and he scanned the crowd for Miss Hastings' chestnut curls. He thought he saw her going with Mariana and Mister Thorne into the chamber where the supper buffet had been laid out. If they stayed there, he might be able to catch up to them, take her somewhere quiet and talk to her. But the crush was extreme and, without barging through ladies in evening gowns of delicate gauzes and men almost as gaudily arrayed, he could make little progress. It was like a nightmare, trying to outrun a demon through a bog that sucked your feet down with every step.

Or as though you had a foot you couldn't easily walk on without risking a fall.

Every curse he'd ever known how to utter ran through

his mind. Seeing the sudden hurt in her eyes—that's what it was, just before they flashed with anger—that hurt, it stabbed him. Her wound was his. And after that, the insult she'd suffered from Grantley. It might as well have been leveled at him, too.

All the while, George's bred-in-the-bone manners kept his face impassive, and he answered polite queries with a smile and rote responses. In the meantime, his opportunity to make all well with Augusta and start again was slipping through his fingers.

When he at last reached the supper room and the funnel of guests spread out so he could move more quickly, he saw Thorne and Miss Hastings leaving by the door at the opposite end of the chamber. He started that way, but Mariana rushed over to him. "Let her go," she said, not having to ask him what he was doing there. She always did know him so well, and it appeared she also knew Miss Hastings in a more than superficial way. "There will be time to talk to her tomorrow."

George nodded, suddenly weary to death. "Did you invite Grantley?" he asked.

"Grantley? No! Beyond what he discovered from us in the park, no card went to him. I thought he knew he would be unwelcome."

"He did. But he's here. With Mrs. Fitzroy, in one of her invisible gowns."

Mariana made a face. "Does this have anything to do with Augusta?"

He heaved a sigh. "I don't know. I don't know anything. Except I do know that they are cousins. What a hash I've made of it all!" Suddenly aware that a few of the guests were staring at him, he said, "I'd better go do the host bit."

"I'll help you make all right," Mariana said, laying her hand on his shoulder and squeezing it lightly. "You'll see."

CHAPTER 16

*A*ugusta was so completely distressed when she entered the supper room that Mariana could make no sense of what she was saying. Something to do with her brother, and honor, and Grantley—although what Augusta could have to do with that scoundrel she couldn't imagine. Jeremy had had no choice but to take Augusta away from the party, and thus had left earlier than Mariana hoped. She'd been left to wonder about it all for the rest of the party, and had a difficult time concentrating on her duties as hostess. More than once, she'd failed to answer a direct question, and had completely forgotten that she'd engaged herself to Lord Barton for the quadrille.

So, hours later, once the final guests had at last been ushered into their carriages, Mariana knew that she wouldn't be able to sleep until she'd talked to George. The dowager had retired just after supper, exercising the privilege of her age as well as her inclination. But her brother was still awake, and awaiting her.

She entered the Chinese saloon and cast her eye around at tables haphazardly arranged, bearing half-empty wine glasses. The servants—except those necessary for seeing the guests out—had gone to bed to catch a couple of hours of sleep before rising and setting about putting the house to rights again.

Like so much detritus from the party, George sat on the sofa near the hearth, legs stretched out before him, his neck cloth untied and coat unbuttoned, a brandy glass and half-full decanter on the table at his elbow. He raked his fingers through his wavy locks, demonstrating exactly how his hair had become so completely disarranged.

"I never saw Grantley," Mariana said as she took a seat next to him.

"I spoke to Allsop and suggested that he tell Grantley he might be happier at another party than ours. If he'd have stayed I wouldn't have answered for my actions. But that matters not at all." He rubbed his hand over his drawn face. "I'm not going to ask you to explain how you came to be acquainted with Miss Hastings. I would rather simply discover what you actually know about her. I must tell you, I have met her before this evening, on several occasions."

"Augusta owned something of the kind to me when I brought her to you. I could not have mistaken the obvious feelings between you, although how they could have arisen on what must be a very brief acquaintance I still don't know. I assume you encountered her here, when she was coming to me to help with the sewing work?"

"On one occasion, yes. But I had already met her before that."

Mariana was astonished that Augusta had said nothing to her about Bridlington in all the times they'd been together. She was a keeper of secrets, for sure.

George refilled his glass and said, "I was beginning to suspect something of her history from before she came to London, but I confess I hadn't figured Grantley into my inklings." He downed a substantial gulp of brandy. "Of course, she was already upset. Thanks to my own stupidity."

Mariana said, "I knew her father was a baronet. I found that out when I chanced across her trying to gain entrance to Hookham's on the strength of his subscription. But I made no connection with Grantley. So you think they are not only distantly related, but acquainted?"

He pursed his lips and rolled his clubfoot back and forth against the hearthrug. "The Hastings estate is in the part of the country from which she hails. They would have been neighbors as well as kinsfolk at one time, before Grantley came of age. If that is the case, what brought her to London to labor for a pittance I cannot say. Although it would also explain Grantley's impudent familiarity with her this evening."

"They saw each other here?" This explained more and more why Augusta was so overset. Mariana well knew how unpleasant a conversation with Grantley could be. "Did you speak of this with her?"

"No. She had already run away from me before her encounter with that cur. We didn't talk for very long, and I was reluctant to push her to tell me her entire history at a party."

"Do you know what Grantley said to her?"

"No, I didn't hear. But he said something to me when I followed her that still has me puzzled." He repeated Grantley's words to Mariana.

"*Hard to tame* … What can he have meant? In any case, if she was running away from you before she met Grantley, what did *you* say to send her off like that?"

He rubbed his eyes and pinched the bridge of his nose. "Curse my damned reticence! I'm not entirely certain. I barely got out what I meant to say. I referred to the conversation we'd had the other night."

"What conversation? Where?" So they had exchanged more than just a few words.

He looked up quickly. "So she didn't tell you?"

"Tell me what?" She was becoming exasperated. "Perhaps you should relate to me exactly how you came to know Augusta, because I am now thoroughly confused."

George sank his face into his hands. "I should have known I could trust her," he said. "I should have trusted my own instincts. I met her first of all when I chanced upon her just after she'd descended from the coach on her arrival in London. Lewiston had gone hell for leather by her in his phaeton and splashed her all in mud, so I took her up in my curricle and drove her almost to Madame Noelle's door."

"When was that exactly? Because I, too, saw her that very day! She came into the modiste's looking as if she'd been wading through muck. I thought it funny at the time, but she stood there so correct and confident in spite of that."

This made George lift his head and cast her a wan smile. "That sounds just like her."

Yes, Mariana thought. He is very much in love.

"The second time I saw her, a young rascal had snatched her purse on Piccadilly. I was riding, on my way to—well, it doesn't matter."

"You seem to have been remarkably useful to her." It was so unlike George to interest himself in the affairs of others. Augusta must have truly intrigued him from the beginning.

"How could I not help her in such a case? After that, I saw her at the stable yard door, when I was about to descend the final flight to get into my curricle."

"And of course you spoke to her each time. She has wit. She is educated and intelligent. She is remarkably handsome. And no doubt she did not throw her handkerchief at you." Her brother was so accustomed to receiving attention whose only design was to lure him into parson's mousetrap that it must have been refreshing to talk to a lady who had no such motives—and who had more to say for herself than simpering commonplaces. "But there had to have been more. She is remarkable, I warrant, but three brief conversations would not suffice to upend your world—and hers."

"No. We met for longer, the other evening, at the opera masquerade."

Mariana stifled a gasp. Of course he'd been there. She hadn't seen him, assuming from his brief mention in the park that he hadn't lingered there. Her attention had been all on Jeremy, on the delicious mischief of the evening. But if he'd spoken to Augusta, he must have been well within sight of their box. How much did George see? "So Augusta was the other person you saw at the masquerade. What really took you there?"

"I saw someone I thought was you leave this house that evening in a gown I recognized. You had retired early to bed, but I suspected you had some secret plan, so I listened and waited. I heard you leave your room and go down the back stairs. Naturally I assumed the lady in the white dress was you. And since this occurred on the night of an opera masquerade, I was afraid you'd taken it into your head to throw propriety to the wind and enjoy some illicit fun in that way."

So far, he'd said nothing to imply he had seen her in her men's clothes. "How is it that you know so much about the masquerades in Covent Garden?"

His face reddened slightly. "I can't tell you everything, not now. That is an entirely separate matter. Suffice it to say that I approached Miss Hastings in the pit, thinking it would be you and that I would persuade you to come home. But of course it wasn't. And then we talked."

"There's something about a masquerade, isn't there? It breaks down barriers, opens up possibilities." Their conversation must have happened before Augusta joined them back in the box after her waltz with Jeremy. No wonder she'd been so beside herself at the time, her eyes so bright, her face aglow. "Did she say why she was there?" How much had Augusta told him?

"I don't think … I never asked her. There seemed to be other things to say, and it didn't matter. I assumed she'd come with friends, perhaps those she knew from the modiste. I admit, the curious fact of her appearing in public in your gown and having departed from this house had me in a puzzle. I assumed perhaps you'd made her a gift of that dress since she'd been undertaking work on your behalf."

"Why didn't you mention this to me?" Mariana asked.

He looked up at her and shrugged. "Since I hadn't found you at the masquerade, the last thing I wanted was to make you suspect I was spying on you, following you in the evening. You would have raked me down."

"You know me well enough to believe that! How were you disguised? A simple domino I assume, as Augusta recognized you."

"My purpose was not disguise of myself, and so I took little trouble over it. And once we were known to each other, I couldn't help but say the things I'd been thinking for days—"

"You didn't try to seduce her!" Mariana cried and stood, putting her hands up to her cheeks.

"Of course not! What do you take me for?"

She sat down again. "This still doesn't give me any explanation of why Augusta dashed away from the party as if she were being chased by a demon."

"I fear she misinterpreted something we were talking about. I am such a fool! Why couldn't I just have been simple? Told her straight out?"

"What is it you are afraid of, my dear?" Mariana went and

stood behind her brother's chair so she could rest her hands on his shoulders and her chin on the top of his head. When she reached her arms down to wrap them around his neck and lean to plant a kiss on his cheek, she felt a slight dampness on his cravat. *Tears?*

He breathed in suddenly and wrenched her hands away, leaned on his cane, stood, and turned to face her. "This," he said with a sweeping gesture down his right leg to his foot. "I am afraid that she will despise me for it."

Mariana's heart clenched for her brother. She knew there was no sense trying to soothe him or tell him that from what she knew of Augusta's character, her warmth and intelligence, such a thing as his clubfoot would not weigh in determining her affections. So she simply went to him and embraced him.

What a mess he'd made of it all.

SECURE IN THE KNOWLEDGE THAT AUGUSTA HADN'T, IN FACT, left Lanyon House, but had only been taken around to the back by Jeremy so she could go up to the servants' quarters, Mariana went to bed confident that they could talk in the morning before she returned to Curzon Street. She would find out then what words George had spoken to give her such a horror of remaining in his company. And after that, she would arrange things so that they would give George an opportunity to make all right. There was no need to disturb her at that late hour. Better to give her a chance to vent her feelings. They had much to talk about, even beyond her sudden flight, and the clear evidence that George was in love with her. Augusta would have to be ready to tell her everything.

The evening had not been all disaster. George and Jeremy had had a long conversation, and it seemed as if they liked each other. George still didn't know about her intentions, but having passed that marker, her confidence in a good outcome had blossomed. It warmed her just to think about it.

And, revising history to suit her present aims, Mariana found that bringing Augusta and her brother together had been part of what inspired her to transform that lovely girl from a useful implement, a fortuitous blend of abilities and temperament that would help her achieve her own goals, to a key ingredient in the future of the Lanyon siblings. The masquerade had been a start, but although Augusta certainly acquitted herself well there, the real test had been that night's dress party. Up until its sudden ending, Augusta had risen to the occasion in a way that exceeded all expectations. She had some misgivings, however, when it came to considering Augusta's possible future. She, of all people, would not want to discourage her, or steer her to a more conventional life. But she also knew that—if the love between Augusta and her brother were to result in a marriage—Augusta could not continue her work as a modiste, let alone a seamstress.

Mariana fell asleep even before Jennings had doused the candle by her bed, aglow with the certainty that she was engaged in a noble enterprise that would be very much to Augusta's and her brother's benefit. Everything would come to rights for all four of them.

WHATEVER MARIANA BELIEVED, AUGUSTA DID NOT AWAKEN IN the servants' quarters of Lanyon House that morning. In fact, she did not sleep at all. As soon as she'd shed her borrowed finery and regained a little control over her emotions, she slipped away and took a hack to Curzon Street. Her mind reeled with conflicting feelings, everything from anger and sorrow to terror, and she needed to put some distance between herself and all the associations of Berkeley Square. Her pulse leapt and her heart twisted at the realization that she had left herself open to the most improper of advances, and worse—the despicable Desmond Grantley had seen her, knew where she was, and had it in his power to destroy all her hopes. A wave of nausea overcame her when she thought about what he might have said to Bridlington after she left. That Grantley hardly seemed like someone Bridlington would associate with did not occur to her in her disordered state. The two men couldn't be less alike. And yet it had been Bridlington who had dishonored her with a suggestion that she might enter into an improper relationship with him. How ironic that the honorable choice would have been to marry Grantley!

But she did not want to marry. She came to London for a different purpose altogether, one that now seemed as far away as the moon. She had cast her lot in with Mariana, believing that she had some sympathy for her ambitions, and was in a position to help her achieve them faster than spending endless, numbing hours pushing a needle through layers of fine fabric to assemble someone else's designs. To continue working with Mariana would inevitably throw her in the path of Bridlington. Yet in the opposite direction lay the gilded trap her aunt had set for her.

She had been cornered. She could see no way out, no way beyond.

In her desperation to get away from the disturbing scenes of that evening, Augusta did not remember that the door to the atelier would be locked at that hour. No one expected her back before morning, and her fellow seamstresses would by then have fallen into their usual exhausted and unrousable sleep. This truth came home to her as soon as she'd paid the hack and it drew away in search of its next fare. *How stupid!* she thought. She still had some money in her purse, but no idea if it would be enough to meet the cost of lodging at an inn, even supposing she knew where one would be. Come to that, what respectable hostelry would allow an unescorted female to take a room at that time of night?

The watch on the next street called the hour and Augusta knew he would soon turn the corner and make his way up Curzon Street. If he found her there alone on no particular business, he would be within his rights to take her up before a constable—or at the very least confine her to the watch house. Any excuse she could think of for being in that place at that time sounded weak to her own ears. What they would assume her business to be in that part of town at two in the morning Augusta well knew.

It occurred to her that she could probably go back to Berkeley Square, gain entrance through the stable yard, and seek shelter in the room Mariana had kindly arranged for her. But she dismissed that idea as soon as she thought it. Unthinkable. No, the only possible course was to set out walking as though she had a destination in mind. And so she began, her hood drawn up and her basket hanging from her elbow, eyes cast down and pace quick. She must at all costs avoid the streets that would lead her back to Lanyon House, as well as avoid any that were likely to take her past gaming hells or other disreputable establishments, or lead her into districts like Soho.

She circled again and again through all the smaller streets of Mayfair for what seemed a long time, not wanting to venture beyond Bond Street, and then doubled back until she reached Piccadilly, which was surprisingly busy with carriage traffic. Despite the early morning hour, revelers spilled onto the streets from private parties, and gentlemen left genteel amusements for the spicier pastimes to be had at gaming houses and clubs. Wherever she went, she drew stares. A solitary woman of sober demeanor was an unusual sight. A lewd comment from someone leaving a tavern on Piccadilly made her turn an abrupt corner, without looking to see which street it was.

Unfortunately, she'd gone down St. James's Street, site of several men's clubs—including White's, with its notorious bow window—a street down which ladies were warned never to walk alone. After being jostled unpleasantly by a few dandies reeking of spirits, Augusta hurried to the next corner, King Street. The crowd thinned here, as it was not a Wednesday evening, the night of the Almack's assemblies. But the very scarcity of other pedestrians made her feel uneasy. She imagined footsteps behind her, in her distraught state thinking Grantley had followed her somehow and would abduct her.

Such were her alarming fantasies when, in a gesture Augusta felt had been sent by fate to set the seal of misery on her evening, the heavens opened.

By the time she reached St. James's Square, Augusta's shoes—only the delicate, borrowed dancing slippers, which in her haste she'd forgotten to change—were worn through and she was drenched and chilled to the bone. She had no idea where to go next, only a sense that the Thames was not much farther south, and that to venture in that direction would leave her prey to thieves and cutthroats. The only other females she encountered in this part of town draped themselves on the arms of fashionable gentlemen or lurked in doorways.

The wet cobbles and flagways magnified every footfall or hoofbeat. Once again, her fevered fancy imagined a menacing presence following her, never quite catching up, always a threat to come. She pushed herself to walk ever faster and turned another corner, her heart beating as if it would burst out of her chest and tears stinging behind her eyes. This, she thought, had been her worst nightmare of what might await her London.

By then she had lost all sense of direction and her knees shook, dangerously near to giving way beneath her. She stopped to catch her breath, teeth chattering, wondering what time it was and how she was to pass the remainder of the night, whether she might find a doorway a little out of the rain, when a gentleman bearing an open umbrella walked by her, stopped, and said, "Miss Hastings?"

She started. No, it wasn't Grantley's lazy voice. It was a different voice, still familiar. But she didn't want to be recognized by anyone, didn't want anyone to bear witness to her despair and ignominy, and took two steps away from the gentleman. In her exhaustion, she swayed on her feet, and before she knew it, two strong hands had hold of her and were propping her upright.

"What in heaven's name! What are you doing here? I set you down at the back of Lanyon House hours ago!"

"Mr. Thorne," she said, barely above a whisper.

"I was Cousin Jeremy earlier! But see here, you're done up, and you must be frozen through. We need to get you off the street. My lodgings are just there. No one's about. I can take you in and get my man to bring you something to eat and drink, and then you can tell me all about it."

She wanted to protest, to refuse his help. But all she could think of was how desperately she wanted just to sit down somewhere. Her limbs seemed no longer in her control, and she suffered Jeremy to steer her toward a door a short way down. That she was about to enter the lodgings of a single gentleman unchaperoned did not occur to her. She'd gone far beyond investing such things with any importance at all.

Minutes later she found herself in a modest parlor being waited on by a somewhat surly but obliging manservant who brought a glass of brandy for her. "Oh no, I couldn't," she said.

"Don't refuse it. You'll find it revives you. I know you'd rather lemonade, but I'm afraid I'll have to insist." Thorne picked up the glass and held it out to her until she took it, then stood and waited until she put it to her lips and sipped.

The searing heat of the liquor did indeed revive her a little, and her senses and her faculties gradually brought her back to full consciousness. What they told her was that she was in the most improper situation possible. "I mustn't stay here!"

"Yes, it doesn't look good, but I didn't see any other answer. Don't forget, you are my 'cousin,' and it would be a poor thing if I was to let you wander the dangerous streets of London at all hours! Not to mention that you'll undoubtedly catch a chill if you don't get out of your sodden cloak and shoes. Come now. Off with them." He held out his hand.

She stood and removed the heavy cloak, instantly hugging herself when she realized the rain had soaked all the way through and made the shoulders and bodice of her dress cling to her revealingly. She gasped and looked up. Jeremy's cheeks had flushed, but his expression remained kind.

"Now your shoes. And then you will lie here quietly until I can dry your cloak sufficiently."

"Oh, no, I must go!"

"I defy you to succeed! You could hardly stand when I found you. There's no sense worrying about it. But when you're able, I want an explanation from you."

"Truly, I must beg your leave—"

"No. I think we know each other well enough to be honest, and it's clear to me that you've been bamming Lady Mariana as well as me." His tone was serious.

The truth of his words made her heart sink. She didn't want to tell anyone what had precipitated her rash flight to

London two short weeks ago. Notwithstanding her horror of being coerced into a marriage that set her teeth on edge and her very real desire to become self-sufficient as a modiste in her own right, she was ashamed of how she had done it. She was well bred, well educated, and intelligent. She should have foreseen the hazards that would attend such a radical leap from safety. Her aunt was a bully, but not a tyrant. *I should have been stronger*, she thought. Should have had the strength of character to say no to an arrangement that disgusted her and resigned herself to tolerating her aunt's ceaseless recriminations.

But that would have been an equally miserable life. "I beg you, Mister Thorne. Please don't make me say anything more. Not now!" She didn't have any strength left to stem the tears that now streamed down her cheeks.

Jeremy reached into his pocket and pulled out his handkerchief. She took it and buried her face in it. "All right, I won't plague you. But things must change," he said. "You'll have to explain yourself."

Explain. If only it were so simple. "Just let me stay here until I can return to Madame Noelle's. It won't be more than an hour or so now, if it's as late as I think. Perhaps I can leave out a back door, or something, so no one thinks you have..." She couldn't bring herself to say what it was a young woman seen sneaking out of a gentleman's lodgings at break of day might signify.

"Mariana will be worried, I wager."

Mariana! Would she look for her in the maid's room? No, she expected her to be gone by the time she rose. "Please say nothing to her! I can't go there, ever again."

He opened his mouth to say something more, but closed it.

Augusta lay back on the pillow and closed her eyes, conscious of Jeremy lifting her feet up onto the settee and draping a blanket over her before she succumbed to exhaustion.

THIS WAS A TURN UP FOR THE BOOKS, JEREMY THOUGHT AS HE settled himself in an armchair by the fire, feeling disinclined to go to bed while there was a genteel young lady asleep on his sofa. How in heavens name was he to get her out of his lodgings without arousing deep suspicion in the landlord, or anyone happening to be on the streets early in the morning?

More to the point, what should he tell Lady Mariana, who would no doubt soon discover that Augusta wasn't where she was supposed to be?

He himself wasn't entirely at his best. After leaving Augusta at the back entrance of Lanyon House, he had felt too restless to go home. In fact, he'd gone to a tavern frequented by the Parliamentary staff, who unloaded the frustrations of their strenuous days by telling stories about the members they worked for and drinking many rounds of punch. Not normally one to over imbibe, the success of the evening at Lanyon House—coupled with its precipitate ending—had put him in agitated spirits. Bridlington was a capital fellow who seemed genuinely interested in his work for Perceval. Yet he remained uncertain as to whether Mariana truly shared his passion, and whether the time was right for him to declare himself.

These turbulent thoughts soon pushed the more immediate problem of a damp damsel asleep in his lodgings out of his mind, and the warmth of the fire lulled him into a comfortable drowse. From there, it was the tip of a wink into a deep, dreamless sleep.

CHAPTER 17

*B*undle pulled back the heavy curtains and let the morning sun stream into the parlor. This woke Jeremy, who raised his arms high to stretch out the kinks in his joints from sleeping awkwardly in a not-very-comfortable chair. An instant later, he leapt up, eyes and mouth open wide.

"Breakfast, Mister Thorne?" said his servant, as if there was nothing unusual in his master's abrupt actions and the sight of a lady asleep on a sofa in his rooms.

"Oh my God!" Jeremy cried.

This exclamation woke Augusta, who sat up slowly and blinked many times before looking around her. "My heavens!" she said, jumping to her feet. "Why am I still here? What happened? What time is it? Oh this is dreadful!"

Jeremy said, "Let's not panic. There must be a way out of this. We did nothing wrong, after all. You were so wet, and exhausted." He took two steps over to where her cloak, now dry, still lay draped over a wooden chair and picked it up, then put it back down. Augusta snatched up her water-stained slippers and tied them on, fingers shaking.

The clock on the mantel chimed nine and Augusta let out a little shriek. "I'm late! I can't go back now, I'll be turned off for sure. And it's too soon for that!"

By now, Jeremy was pacing around the small parlor. "First, coffee, Bundle," he said to the taciturn servant, "And some bread and butter."

"I can't eat anything! Are you out of your mind?" Augusta's heart raced as the full meaning of her predicament became brutally clear.

"No. I will think more clearly once I've had some coffee, and there's no point getting into a quake here. We have to think carefully about what to do."

That, she thought, was right enough. She knew better than to fly into a pelter that wouldn't help anything and would likely result in more chaos. In any case, she felt faintly sick at the thought that Lord Bridlington's indecent suggestions now had all the weight of prophesy the way things appeared at that moment.

She pressed her hands against her temples. It was possible that Madame would not expect her to return very first thing in the morning, having given her leave to stay away all night. That wouldn't change the fact that emerging from a gentleman's lodgings alone in broad daylight without arousing suspicion presented what felt at that moment like an insurmountable difficulty.

But the difficulties were about to become magnified to an unthinkable degree. Bundle reentered with a tray bearing coffee and bread and butter and said, "You have a caller, Mister Thorne."

Augusta cast a panic-stricken glance at Jeremy. "Where shall I go? What can I do?"

Jeremy raked his fingers through his still disheveled hair and said, "There's only my bedroom. Quickly!"

He took hold of Augusta's hand and all but dragged her

through the door that led into that room and slammed it shut behind her. Breathing hard, Augusta took in her surroundings. She had never before entered a gentleman's private quarters. The narrow bed had not been slept in. An ivory comb and brush sat atop a dresser with only a small mirror above it. Instinctively, she went toward the mirror to assess the state of her hair and gasped. She looked like a harridan! At that moment, she wished more than anything that she could disappear, or wake up from what had surely been a horrible nightmare.

"Jeremy! I didn't know where else to come. Augusta—Miss Hastings—she's vanished!"

The words came clearly through the thin door of Jeremy's modest lodgings, and Augusta covered her mouth to stifle a cry of dismay. Mariana!

"Calm yourself," Jeremy said. "People don't simply disappear. There's likely a perfectly good explanation. Sit and have some coffee. Where did you look for her?"

"I received a note from Madame Noelle saying that she wasn't in the atelier, that she assumed she was still at Lanyon House and wished to know at what time she might expect her seamstress to return. I went to look for her, and her bed in the maid's room hadn't been slept in."

Oh no, Augusta thought. How was she to go back now, even supposing Jeremy could placate Mariana and send her away? He was doing a good job of acting cool and composed, she had to give him that. Had Lady Mariana been to these rooms before, Augusta wondered? How did she know where he lived?

For a few moments, nothing was said. Augusta heard the clink of china as Jeremy brought a cup of coffee over to Mariana.

"Hello … two cups?" Lady Mariana said. "Were you expecting company at this hour?"

"Of-of course not!" Jeremy said, his voice betraying a shade of nervousness.

Augusta followed Mariana's footsteps as she walked around the parlor. They stopped near the hearth. "What's this? I recognize it." Then a moment later, "It belongs to Augusta! What is the meaning of this?" Her voice had gradually tightened until she ended on a harsh note.

"It's—I can explain. It's not what you think—"

Augusta couldn't bear it anymore. She took a deep breath, opened the bedroom door, and walked back into the parlor.

Mariana's eyes opened wide and her cheeks flamed. "What exactly are you doing here?" she said between clenched teeth.

"I know this looks terrible," Augusta said, "but I can assure you—"

"And I trusted you! How dare you take advantage of my generosity. My innocence! You're just as bad as that disgraceful libertine, Grantley!"

Although innocence was an epithet she would not use to describe Lady Mariana's essential qualities, the mention of Grantley made the blood drain from Augusta's face.

"Mariana! Please listen!" Jeremy took two long strides to her and grasped her hands.

She shook him off and hugged herself. "I will never, never listen to you again!"

"But you don't know anything!" Augusta cried. "Jeremy loves you! I mean nothing to him, and I'm not here at his invitation." What else could she say?

"Loves me? He has an odd way of showing it!"

"It's all a mistake, a huge misunderstanding," Augusta said. "He took me around to the back of Lanyon House and left me there. But I didn't stay. I fled. I'll tell you why, I promise, and it's not what you think. And then I couldn't get into the workshop and started walking, and got caught in the rain, and—"

"And you just happened to end up here?" Mariana strode around the small parlor looking every bit as fierce as one of the caged lions at the Tower of London. "Oh, I don't know why I'm listening to you!"

By now, Mariana's face was wet with tears. Augusta exchanged an apologetic glance with Jeremy, scooped her cloak off the floor where Mariana had dropped it and retrieved her work basket from the corner. Then, heedless of who saw her, or of the impropriety of leaving Mariana alone with Jeremy, she dashed out the door and onto Duke Street.

AUGUSTA ENCOUNTERED ONLY TRADESMEN AND SERVANTS ON the street, most of the *ton* not even breakfasting until eleven let alone leaving their houses to make morning calls. She walked toward Piccadilly with what she hoped was an air of calm confidence, but her mind was in turmoil. Her most immediate worry was what to expect when she returned to the workshop. Perhaps Madame would simply assume she'd been sent back by Lady Mariana after she received the note she mentioned. Or perhaps she could enter the workshop without Madame's knowledge and pretend she had been there all along. But that wouldn't do. The other girls would see her, and they would likely say something.

If Madame had sent no message, Mariana would have assumed she'd left early as she said she would and would not have gone looking for her. Things were already hopelessly tangled after all that had happened last night, she thought. Now her life had twisted into a knot she could not imagine ever being able to untie.

Pausing to take a few deep breaths and pat her curls into some semblance of order, Augusta slipped down the alley that led to the workshop door. She hoped Pauline would be there and not in the fitting room helping Madame. After a pause to still her racing heart, she opened the door and stepped inside.

"There she—"

In an instant, Pauline's hand shot out to stifle Molly's exclamation. The three seamstresses sat staring at Augusta in mute astonishment, Miss Carp with a malevolent smirk, Bernadette with her usual wide-eyed confusion, and Molly with suppressed merriment.

"Just like I said! Miss Hastings 'as been here all along, maybe just stepped out to fetch something she forgot in Berkeley Square," Pauline said, a threatening edge in her voice as she glared at each of them in turn.

"Y-yes, that's it. I returned quite early, then thought I'd left my scissors at Lanyon House and started back. It wasn't until I was nearly there that I realized I had them all the time, they were tucked underneath a length of lawn I'd brought in case of having to mend Lady Mariana's slip." Augusta hoped what she said accounted for enough time to make the escapade believable. It sounded quite pathetic to her.

"Well, we just got started. You missed breakfast, but that can't be helped."

Augusta exchanged a speaking glance with Pauline, knowing she would have to find a way to tell her at least some of what had happened in the time since she'd finished helping her dress the night before.

Without another word, she took up her place at her worktable and set about sewing lace to the edge of a sleeve on a sprig muslin day dress. She affected unconcern, trying to smile and chat softly as usual, avoiding the looks of curious inquiry that met her whenever she raised her eyes.

❧

MARIANA WAS ONLY VAGUELY AWARE THAT AUGUSTA HAD LEFT. Although her fury had been aimed full force at her friend, she was conscious that she had been unjust. She trembled with combined rage and disgust not at Augusta or Jeremy, but at herself, at her crazy, outrageous schemes to thwart boredom and give her the illusion that she had any control over her own destiny. It served her right that such a muddle would occur. Whatever Augusta's secrets, her own actions had brought this about. She buried her face in her hands, giving full vent to the tears and frustration that had built up since the beginning of that season—no, before that, since the time she first met Jeremy and had seen in him someone who could meet her on her own terms, rise to her level, and open up the world for her.

Now what had she done? Made a complete fool of herself. In her heart she didn't think Augusta had a *tendre* for Jeremy, or he for her. That hadn't stopped her lashing out in spite and jealousy. It had been a shock, seeing her there. She wasn't sure what she'd expected, or even why she'd decided to go to Jeremy's lodgings. She knew his direction from having sent him messages, but had never before crossed the threshold. In its way, just being there was her boldest step yet. She had sworn Jennings to secrecy—not that she really needed to. Her abigail was loyal to a fault. When Mariana thought of her waiting outside in the hack, her sobs redoubled. How could she be so cruel and inconsiderate?

Just as she was about to sink to the floor in despair, two firm hands took hold of her arms and held her upright, then gently steered her and eased her down to the sofa. She kept her fingers pressed against her eyes and shuddered like a child recovering from a temper tantrum. Perhaps that's what she was, Mariana thought, the ghost of a smile flitting across her face.

"Here," said Jeremy. "Drink this." The sofa cushion dipped

as he sat next to her, so close she could feel the heat of his body.

By this time, Mariana was afraid to take her hands away from her face, knowing that her eyes would be red and her nose running unattractively. As if he had read her mind, Jeremy tucked a handkerchief under one of her palms so she could grasp it and bury her face in it without revealing the mess she knew it to be. "I'm sorry," she tried to say through the bunched-up handkerchief, but her throat was thick and pasty.

"Never mind. Be a good girl and take a sip."

She slowly lowered the handkerchief and the strong aroma of brandy tickled her nostrils, making her sneeze convulsively. She must have bumped the glass, because a moment later liquid seeped through her bodice. "Oh dear!" she said, and Jeremy took the handkerchief from her and started to blot the amber stain. He paused, his hand against her chest. All she could think was that he must be able to feel her heartbeat. And then his touch set off a reaction in her body that stirred something in places deep inside her. She looked up.

Jeremy's brimming eyes gazed at her with an intensity that took her breath away. She gave a little gasp as he slipped his arms around her and drew her to him. She looked down, suddenly shy, but he gently touched beneath her chin and lifted her face to look at him again. At the liquid warmth in his eyes, her lips parted involuntarily, and before she could think, his mouth met hers in a fierce kiss. His embrace, the taste of him, sent a deeper shiver through her entire body, and she gripped the lapels of his coat, wanting to erase all distance between them, make them become a single being.

After what seemed like a moment stolen from time, they slowly broke apart. But she remained in the circle of his strong arms, and he drew her head to rest beneath his chin.

"You don't know how long I have wished to do that," he whispered into her hair. "Forgive me."

Mariana didn't know what to say. It was exactly what she had wanted too, but how could she allow herself to do something so rash? And alone, in his lodgings? She half-heartedly tried to push herself away from him, aware at the borders of her consciousness that she could so easily allow herself to transgress the bounds of propriety, but he tightened his embrace and she melted back into him. "Please," she said, "I must go. I don't know why... How could I..."

"Yes," Jeremy said in a voice full of emotion. "You must go. Or I won't answer for what might happen next." Then he kissed her again, more deeply and passionately than before, and Mariana circled her own arms around his neck, her body alive to his every touch. She didn't want to leave. She wanted him in a way that terrified her.

A click behind them made them let go of each other suddenly, breaking the spell.

"Beg pardon, Sir, but there's a message for you from Westminster."

Though not really a gentleman's gentleman, Bundle did his best to serve his master, who instinct told him would rise to be more than a private secretary someday. Although he would keep to himself his opinions on seeing Mister Thorne alone with two different females in one morning, he was pleased to recognize a lady of the *haut ton* this time, and politely averted his gaze.

"Thank you, Bundle."

Mariana had risen quickly and turned her back. Jeremy took the folded paper out of the servant's hands, and Bundle bowed and left the room.

"I must go! Immediately!" Mariana said as soon as the man's footsteps faded away.

But Jeremy took hold of her hand and raised it to his lips. "You needn't worry about Bundle. He won't gossip."

"Yes, but what are we to do?" Mariana wanted him to tell her, to admit to everything she'd hoped for so long.

"I think you know what I want. But how can I presume? I can offer you nothing, or I would have been asking Bridlington for permission to pay my addresses to you long ago. As it is, he would think me a gazetted fortune hunter."

Jeremy's hand felt so right, so warm. She didn't want to let it go, but she knew it was past the time for her to return to Lanyon House. More than anything, she wanted to stay in his arms and kiss him again, no matter where it might lead, and the thought sent a blush rushing into her cheeks. "Are you offering for me, Mr. Thorne?" she asked.

He pulled her close to him, holding her two hands clasped together between his. "I have no right to do so. But if you would have me, I would be the most fortunate man in the world."

"Hyperbole is entirely welcome in a case like this," Mariana said with a mischievous chuckle, unable to meet his eyes. "Of course, I shall be of age in a few months, although I won't come into my fortune for four more years after that." She looked up at him to see if this information had any effect.

But he simply smiled. "Then I won't feel such an opportunist, if we manage to bring things about. And by then, I should be in a better position in the government. If I could but get out of Perceval's orbit and into that of someone whose views I agree with." Jeremy gave a short, caustic laugh.

Mariana said, "In any case, we have one more adventure, one more scheme to undertake before I'm quite ready to become a sober wife." Although, she thought, there was nothing sober about the feelings that had been awakened deep inside her that morning.

He answered her impish grin with one of his own. "And I know for a fact that you can dress the part." Mariana lifted her face to his, eager for another kiss, but he took her head and tilted it down before planting a chaste peck on her forehead.

Mariana dashed a few remaining tears out of her eyes, which now shone with happiness. She hadn't exactly doubted Jeremy, but his diffidence, his way of holding her at a respectful distance whenever they met, had made her think that possibly he didn't feel as she did, or not as strongly, and that he might never come to the point. But now, her doubts had quite disappeared.

Mariana left the lodgings in a glow, hardly noticing anything or anyone around her, and climbed quickly into the waiting hack. Aside from a single, questioning glance, Jennings said nothing, but her eyes told Mariana that she knew something important had happened. No wonder. Mariana felt as if she'd never known herself before. This was what loving and being loved in return felt like. Did this sensation come to all women at some time? She doubted her mother had had a similar experience. Unless she'd been in love before she met her late father.

But no one spoke of such things in their house. So much silence. Mariana wanted more than anything to tell Augusta all about it, to ask her if she had ever felt the same. Or, perhaps, if this was how she felt about George. Something told her that a lost love was part of what had sent Augusta out into the world alone and that perhaps made her unwilling to risk her heart again. Yet that didn't seem quite enough to provoke such a rash action. The missing piece, she worried, might reside in Grantley's unappealing hands— which would make it difficult for any of them to discover it without drastic measures.

Despite the conclusion she had jumped to when she first

walked into Jeremy's lodgings, Mariana knew that Augusta was not in love with him. Yet it was love, Mariana thought, that had driven her away from Lanyon House and out into a rainy night. Whatever had happened at the party was more than a misbegotten word from her brother's notoriously acid tongue. Augusta would have been fully capable of sparring with him in such a case. This brought up the memory of her own conversation with George. Imagine him being acquainted with Augusta even before she was! Thinking back, it all became clear. The way he spoke about Augusta, the way he'd looked at her in the ballroom and as she approached him across the saloon. And Augusta—her nervous agitation, her confusion. Mariana chuckled softly.

"My Lady?" said Jennings.

"Oh, nothing. I was just thinking how strange life can be." Mariana was not in the habit of confiding her deepest thoughts to her abigail.

But Jennings somehow always knew what they were. "Strange, but good, I hope, My Lady."

Strange, certainly, because here she was, so desperately in love with someone the world judged to be far beneath her. And there was her brother, in a fair way to being in the same state with a lady who was probably no more suitable a match for him.

Would she ever know the state of Augusta's feelings toward George? She had behaved so abominably to her that she was afraid she had forfeited her friendship and trust for good. Perhaps, though, this nascent spark between Augusta and George might give her a way to earn that trust back. The so-called seamstress deserved to reach for more in life, perhaps even more than her ambition of making her mark in the world of fashion, of that Mariana was sure. And along with her worthiness and determination came an undercurrent of pride, inculcated and absorbed over generations of privilege. Evidence of this was plain in everything Augusta said and did. She was proud and independent—characteristics Mariana now knew were what had drawn her to the seamstress from the beginning. They also meant that, whatever was to happen next would have to be on Augusta's terms.

But the first step was for her brother and her friend to make their peace with each other. She would invite Augusta to call tomorrow.

CHAPTER 18

*I*f anyone had asked him, George couldn't have said when it was he realized that Miss Augusta Hastings held the key to his future happiness. And for a while, he hardly acknowledged it himself. All he did know for certain was that her distress on the night of the dress party pained him in a place he'd long thought buried. Whatever it took, whatever he must do to win her regard, he would do without hesitation. That she thought he intended a dishonorable alliance with her pained him deeply. For that, at least, had been clear enough from her words before they parted.

First and foremost, he must find a way to assure her that he had no improper intentions toward her. How could she think from what he said at the masquerade? Yet he supposed he had not been clear. He was afraid, unwilling to tell her the real reason he held something of himself back from her. Something he said, some way he said it, had given her the wrong idea. How could she be so mistaken in his character? What had led her to think him capable of seducing a well-born lady who was a friend of his sister?

And then, he realized with a start when he thought back

to last night, she had never once looked down at his foot. She hadn't offered him any help as he led her to the settee. The only indication that she had any consciousness of his affliction was when she stared at the gold handle of his cane as he worried it with his fingers. His cane. It was quite distinctive. The gold handle could have marked him out from across a room. Across a large public space. Had she seen him conversing with Madame Agatha on the evening of the masquerade? She couldn't have known that the subject of their discourse was as far from dalliance as it was possible to be. He gave a bitter laugh before taking the length of starched muslin from Craggins and beginning the delicate process of tying his neck cloth. How on earth would he be able to make her believe something he'd taken such pains to hide from the world that his own family had no idea of his activities?

In any case, she was gone. He doubted she would ever return to Lanyon House. And without that possibility, Lanyon House offered no comfort to him. Perhaps some time away would make everything clearer. Lewiston wanted them to go to Ascot for the first meet of the season. That would take him out of London for a few days and give him a chance to think things through.

Still, the image of Grantley's sneering visage disquieted him. And what he had told him about Augusta. The family link George suspected must be a fact, yet mere kinship did not inspire those words or that look. He resolved to discover the truth of their relationship, feeling that it might in some sense elucidate Augusta's quickness to judge him based on scant evidence. As to how knowing more would help rehabilitate him in her esteem was a question he couldn't wrap his mind around at that moment.

He ate a solitary breakfast, not expecting Mariana to emerge from her room until noon at least. So when the front door opened and he heard her voice greeting Allsop, he was very surprised. She'd not only been up, but had gone out. He went down to meet her and ask her if she had any inkling of what Miss Hastings and Grantley could have to do with each other, if she had any ideas beyond those they'd talked about last night.

But far from appearing drawn and haggard after a late night, Mariana glowed. He'd never seen her look more beautiful, even though she wore a simple day dress unadorned with any jewels—not even her modest strand of pearls. "Mari!" he said, "Where in heaven's name have you been at this hour?"

She came forward and unexpectedly embraced him. "I have been setting my life in order."

"Come and tell me about it," George said, putting out his arm and leading her into the book room, not without a great deal of apprehension. He knew her well enough to fear that his idea of an ordered life might not accord with hers.

"Would you like coffee?" he asked.

A distracted look came into her eyes and she smiled faintly before saying, "No, thank you."

"Then you'd better tell me what all this is about. Did you finally meet your match at last night's party? I hardly dare hope, as I don't think there were many eligibles in attendance that you hadn't already refused."

She went to George with her hands out and took both of his in hers. "Oh, but I have met him! And I need you, my dear brother, to listen to what I say and don't dismiss him out of hand." She led him to the sofa where they sat, angled toward each other. She clasped her hands in her lap and looked down at them shyly. He'd never seen that expression on her face before, and he thought she was sincere about whatever she was going to say—which would make things even harder if she wanted him to approve an unsuitable match.

For clearly, this was her intention.

She raised her shining blue eyes to his and said, "He has no title, no fortune. His family is respectable but not distinguished. But he does have a brilliant career ahead of him. I've never been more sure of anything in my life."

Thorne. She didn't even need to utter his name. Had he not been so distracted by Miss Hastings, he might have realized where her heart lay last night. Anyone who saw the two of them together would have known it. His own failure to recognize it was more due to a wish that she had no such feelings for Thorne than anything else. He had nothing against the man. But was Mari fully aware of what a furor there would be in the *ton* if she were to marry him? "I presume you're speaking of Jeremy Thorne."

"Yes! You do see, don't you? He's already private secretary to Perceval, and is much admired in Westminster. You could talk to some of the political peers and you'd soon see how well they regard him." She grabbed one of his hands convulsively and clasped it between hers, raising it to her heart.

"Mariana, you know I can't—"

"Don't say it! Not yet! I think you must know I will never be happy with any of the vapid fops who care more about their neck cloths than the state of the country. I would die! I need to be active, I need to be involved. I could be with him. You see, I would raise him up and it would assure him of even more notice. If you permit the match, you will be showing the world that you believe him capable of earning your regard." At this, she lifted his hand to her lips and kissed it, then laid her cheek against it.

George said nothing for a while, but gently pulled his hand out of his sister's effusive grip. "He may earn my regard, but he can't earn enough to support a wife. At least, not a wife like you, accustomed to every luxury."

She drew herself up, a haughty gleam in her eyes. "But I

have my allowance, which is generous. I know I won't come into my fortune for another four years—"

"Does he know that?"

Mariana raised her eyebrows and blinked at him. "Of course! It's partly what gave him the confidence to offer for me. He didn't want to appear to be hanging out for a rich wife."

"And you think you'd be content to live in modest lodgings somewhere on the fringes of fashion, and wear made-over gowns to whichever parties you were still invited to?" George doubted his sister had seen very far beyond a wedding.

Some of the joy left her face. "It would be hard, if it came to that. But it doesn't have to, and you know it. You could easily see that we were comfortable enough."

"And if I didn't? Would you still want to marry him?"

A distant, thoughtful expression came into Mariana's eyes, and she smiled slowly. "Yes. I most definitely would."

He nodded. She was deep in it. And who was he to judge her for it? All George wanted was to assure himself that Thorne truly possessed all the virtues Mariana had invested him with. "Very well. Have him call on me. I'm not saying I will approve the match, mind you."

But he had barely got the words out before Mariana threw her arms around him and planted a wet kiss on his cheek. When she had released him, she said, "But there is something else I must see to, Brother dear." The familiar mischievous gleam leapt into her eyes. "Will you contrive to be at home tomorrow afternoon? I want to invite a caller. You will be glad to see her, I'm certain."

He knew she was speaking of Miss Hastings. "Mister Thorne's mysterious cousin, I suspect?" His heart did a little jump, and then he felt the full force of dread, of having to face what she truly thought of him. "She won't come."

"She will. I won't tell her you'll be there."

"How very flattering!"

"To be honest, after what happened between us this morning, she might not consent to visit me."

"Oh?" So Mari had seen Augusta that morning. What could have occurred? "Was she well? How did she seem? Where was she?" Could she have been at Lanyon House without his knowledge, as she no doubt had been on so many other occasions?

"It's too complicated to explain. We quarreled, and I was completely in the wrong. However, I intend to eat the humblest pie imaginable. I think she is a forgiving person, and will want to maintain our friendship. I hope that at least."

"Very well. I shall be here. And your Mister Thorne may make his case to me." He put up his hand to prevent another of Mariana's enthusiastic embraces. "Now, I must go and see Lewiston. He's found some lodgings he wants me to inspect, and we're to go to Ascot in two days." Would he still go if his meeting with Miss Hastings had any good outcome? But that was unlikely.

They stood. "Thank you, George. You are a good man, you know." Mariana stood on her tiptoes and kissed him lightly on the cheek. "Until tomorrow."

She left the room with a light, buoyant step. How wonderful, George thought, to be so happy. He hoped he would not have to disappoint her, that Thorne would live up to her exalted opinion of him.

MARIANA WAS CERTAIN SHE COULD BRING GEORGE AROUND. But she felt he'd be in a much more flexible mood if she could straighten out the misunderstanding between him and Augusta first. So she went up to her chamber and composed a letter to Augusta that she hoped would persuade her to come to Lanyon House the next afternoon. George would be off to Ascot on the day after that—the eleventh of May. This was also extremely fortuitous because that was the day she and Jeremy had settled on for her final gesture of mad independence. She would take one last daring step before having to resign herself to her destined place as a matron of the *ton*. Her hope that she would be able to do so with the man she truly loved at her side, the man who would encourage her in her desire to be active, buoyed her.

She said nothing about George in her letter to Augusta. She begged her dear friend's forgiveness, saying that she had behaved toward her in an infamous way, and wanted to make it up to her. She also suggested that the entire episode— unfortunate and painful though it was—precipitated an event that she'd longed for in her heart, and ended by saying that Jeremy had offered for her.

She sealed that letter with a wafer and wrote another, to Jeremy, saying that her brother had given him permission to see him. *I need hardly say*, she wrote, *that you must wait until after our adventure, and also until after Bridlington comes back from Ascot.* Mariana confessed to being a bit concerned about a delay, worried that if her brother happened to say anything to Lewiston, his old friend and one of her unsuccessful suitors, the marquess might persuade him to refuse his consent to their match.

After writing the requisite note to Madame Noelle requesting Augusta's presence for some made-up emergency, she could do no more that day. Too agitated to rest despite her lack of sleep, Mariana summoned Jennings to help her change into her riding habit, and sent a note down to the stables. A ride in the park would refresh her and give her much needed time to reflect on all that had happened in the last few days.

It was on her second circuit of the leafy paths through Hyde Park that she encountered Desmond Grantley mounted on a nervous-looking bay mare. Courtesy forced her to stop and accept his greeting, but she relished it not at all. She had counted herself fortunate that she had avoided seeing him the night before.

"Lady Mariana! You look charming. Positively blooming. One would never suspect this was your second season rather than your first." He'd pulled his horse up and reached for her hand.

The dig did not go unnoticed by Mariana. She gave him a frigid smile, shook his hand, and said, "We were surprised to see you at our dress party last night. I'm sorry you couldn't stay to have a chat. What brings you to London, Sir? I'd heard you'd contracted a suitable match and had taken yourself off the rolls."

"Why, kind of you to mention it! I have indeed."

"I saw no notice in the Gazette or the Post, however, so I'm afraid I have no idea who the lady might be."

A tightening around his lips was all the indication that she had hit upon a delicate subject. "No, she has been taken ill and is supposedly on a rest cure in Harrogate. It was not thought wise to announce something that could not be celebrated for some time yet." The slight narrowing of his eyes was all that indicated a problem with this match. Mariana could not imagine actually wanting to be married to such a man. Perhaps his intended was similarly disinclined, and pressure had to be brought to bear in order to make her agree.

Added to these suspicions, Grantley did not present the appearance of a man in love. This came as no surprise to Mariana, if the rumors were true, that he had been more or less forced to find an acceptable bride—a bride of sufficient rank, apparently—if he wanted access to the handsome fortune that lay just out of his reach. That he would squander it as soon as he could she had no doubt, just as she had no doubt the poor girl he married would be miserably unhappy.

"I had the good fortune to meet Bridlington in the club the other day, and we exchanged too-brief words last night before I was, uh, obliged to leave Lanyon House."

Mariana couldn't help feeling a little smug that Allsop's hint to him had been unpalatable.

"I have some further business to discuss with the earl," he said, "and shall call in Berkeley Square betimes. He is remaining in town, I collect?"

"Yes, aside from going to Ascot. The House is in session and my brother takes great interest in the debates." This was a lie.

A hard light came into Grantley's eyes. "I should think it's dashed difficult to get around in that monster of a building when you have to hobble like a cripple."

Mariana pressed her lips together. She would not rise to Grantley's obvious attempt to provoke her. "It's a beautiful day, and my horse is impatient to move on," she said instead.

"But we have hardly spoken!" Grantley said mockingly. "I hope you will be at home when I call on your brother so we can exchange more news and so that I may extend my polite greetings to your excellent mother."

"You are most welcome, of course, but I feel it only fair to tell you I am quite busy for the next few days and will have no time to receive callers." She scrambled to think of a believable excuse not to spend any more time than absolutely necessary in his company.

"Oh, my call will be of brief duration, I daresay." He lifted his hat and bowed, then urged his horse on.

During this exchange, Philpot had ridden up to be close

behind Mariana, for which she was grateful. Desmond Grantley was the last person she had wanted to see in London, and she dreaded his visit to Lanyon House. Her previous elated mood was now damped unpleasantly following their conversation, and the fatigue she'd kept at bay crept into her body. "I'm tired," she said to the groom. "Let's go home."

CHAPTER 19

$\mathcal{W}$ith her entire body screaming at her that she was doing the wrong thing, Augusta succumbed to the penitent entreaty in Mariana's note to her and found herself walking to Lanyon house on the afternoon of the day after the terrible scene at Mr. Thorne's lodgings. Mariana had implied that she alone wished to see her, but had requested her to arrive at the front door, not the tradesmen's entrance. *For we are now officially friends. I have presented you to my mother and brother, after all, so creeping in the back way is no longer appropriate,* her letter had said.

As she mounted the shallow steps to the door, Augusta was conscious of her drab clothing. She had attired herself in her best, the dress and pelisse she'd worn while traveling, which had now at least been restored to its respectable state but was no more fashionable or new than it had been two weeks ago.

The butler bowed her in politely and took her hat and pelisse before ushering her upstairs to the yellow saloon. Augusta's heart felt as though it would leap out of her chest, finding herself once again in a place where she'd felt the bottom fall out of her world less than two days before. At least it was only Mariana that she'd have to face.

However, when the door opened and she took several steps into that elegant room, she halted, frozen. Both Mariana and Bridlington stood by the hearth. Before she could summon up the strength to turn around and rush out, Mariana had advanced toward her, both hands outstretched.

"Now don't be cross with me, my dear!" she said. "I think there has been a terrible misunderstanding between the two of you, and I couldn't bear it if you were not at least friends."

The blood flew into Augusta's cheeks as she curtsied, eyes down, to Bridlington. He put out his hand and took hers, raising it to his lips. "You cannot know how delighted I am to see you again. I fear I may have led you to believe something quite untrue of me at the dress party the other night. I'm not very good at courting."

"I think," Mariana said, claiming each of their arms and leading them over to the sofa, "that the time for half truths and prevarications is over. You may think me impertinent, that what passes between the two of you is none of my affair, but if I am right I think it could well have some effect on my future life."

She rang for sherry, and once Bridlington had accepted a glass and Augusta refused one, said, "I have a small matter that must be attended to. Forgive me if I leave you for a short while." Mariana's smile could not hide her mischievous pleasure as she left George and Augusta alone together unchaperoned.

Augusta, however, was inclined rather to be distressed by such a circumstance, and sat in mute anxiety once the door had closed behind Mariana. What was it Bridlington had said? *I'm not very good at courting.* Had he been courting her? Surely not!

Bridlington spoke. "I must apologize. I won't waste time

being coy. I want you to know that I would never make an improper advance to a lady. Thinking back, I see now how you could have misinterpreted what I said to you the other night. You must think me a scoundrel."

She summoned up the courage to look into his eyes. There they were. Soft, deep, expressive gray eyes that seemed to peer inside her and reach the hidden places, the buried dreams. She couldn't help responding to them, laying herself open to his kind, inquiring gaze. "It's good of you, My Lord," she said and stopped. "But I saw you."

"At the masquerade? After we spoke?"

"Yes. And then again, in Soho."

He sat up tall, shook his head, and laughed. "I can explain it all. It's not what you think." And then Augusta listened to his narrative about the children he tried to help, how he and a woman who kept a Corinth worked together to make the lives of disabled poor children a little better. She was ashamed of herself for judging him and believing what other people said.

"I don't blame you for thinking what you did," he said. "My own family knows nothing of this."

"Why? Why wouldn't you tell them?" So he kept secrets, too.

"I can't explain, and it's not important now. What matters now is you and I. When I said I wanted to know you, I meant it sincerely. I want to know all about you, not just what you have been presenting to the world these past couple of weeks. I wish you would tell me who you really are. Oh I don't mean your name, for I know that. What I desire is to understand what has happened to bring you to this pass. What could have led a true lady to bury herself in a dingy seamstress's workshop? All I know for certain is that what-ever the truth about you, I'm in love with you."

Augusta gasped. "Sir?"

"Is there any hope that you have the slightest feelings for me? Imperfect though I am?" He looked down at his right foot, and she followed his gaze.

"I do not care a straw that you limp and use a cane," she said, looking up and into his eyes again. "But you do not know me. You can have no true feelings for me because I have done such a terrible thing. I am not worthy." She fought hard against tears and managed to keep them at bay. How she longed to tell him everything! But the habit of secrecy was hard to break, and what would he think of her if he knew all? If she told him anything, she would have to tell him everything.

"Don't be afraid of me," Bridlington said. "I will not harm you in any way, or judge you for anything in your past. I am the last person to do so. Please believe me." He reached out a tentative hand and slowly drew hers into it. She let him.

So be it. Whatever else, if his feelings were sincere, she owed him the truth. She'd summoned enough courage to take the steps that had led her to London. She must continue to be brave now. "Very well, My Lord, if you truly wish to know all." She looked away from him to a spot on the floor, then gathered her courage. "I was secretly betrothed to a dragoon. He was killed in Spain, a year ago. I was grieving him still when I arrived in London."

And so she began a recital of her life so far: growing up motherless, falling in love with James, his death, then her father the baronet's sudden death just six months ago.

"Your dragoon—did you truly love him? I am hardly a substitute for that sort of man." He lifted his bent foot and nodded toward it.

"I thought I did love him, that I would never love again. I cried for days. But it was a childish infatuation. I see that now." James had awakened her heart with his boyish fervor. Next to her now, listening to her with such deep interest, sat a man—a man who, despite his privileged situation, had suffered in a way she could not imagine.

She continued her recital, about having to sell Crossley Grange and move in with her aunt who wanted nothing more than to have her off her hands and, as a result, set about trying to arrange a match for her.

"I can't imagine she would have failed in that endeavor!" Bridlington said, having taken hold of her other hand and nested both of hers between his as she spoke. "But I thank God that she did."

Of course, this was the crux of the matter. Augusta did not want to reveal any more to him, because if the truth were generally known, it could well bring Aunt Phyllis down on her post haste.

She was about to say something to divert the conversation away from that dangerous topic when the door to the saloon opened and Allsop entered.

"Yes?" Bridlington said with impatience.

"A caller, My Lord. The Honorable Desmond Grantley."

Augusta felt the room spin around her and without thinking clutched Bridlington's hands in both of hers.

"What is it?" he asked, his brow creased in concern.

"I can't. It's just—"

Before she could say another word, Grantley walked into the room, full of disdainful hauteur as he surveyed the scene of Augusta and Bridlington seated close together, hands clasped, on the sofa. "Ah! We may continue our interrupted discourse, I see."

GEORGE'S INCREASING ARDOR FOR THIS BRAVE, INTELLIGENT lady changed suddenly to alarm when he found his hands in her claw-like grip. As gently as he could, he freed them so he could stand in order to shake the hand that Grantley extended to him—little as he wanted to after what had passed between them the night before. Grantley stood in the middle of the room as George limped over to him without his cane. Of course, he deliberately did not advance to meet him and make it easier.

"I am glad that you are at home to callers, Bridlington. I did not expect to see Lady Mariana, who said she would be occupied these next few days. But I am delighted to perceive that we have the company of the elusive Miss Augusta Hastings!" He made a move to walk over to her, but Augusta rose and stepped behind a chair.

"As you see, we have been conversing," George said, fixing him with a steely stare. "I am surprised that you have made this lady's acquaintance. She appears not to desire it."

Grantley fixed a scornful smile on his face. "I assumed—until I was disabused of that notion—that she would still be in the north, as I had been informed by her amiable aunt."

The information that Grantley was acquainted not only with Augusta but with the aunt she had just been telling him about, momentarily stunned George. When he recovered, he turned to look at Augusta, who hadn't uttered a word since Grantley arrived. She was so white and rigid he was afraid she would swoon. The three of them stood like pieces on a chess board, waiting for someone to make the next move.

It was Grantley who did it, taking three steps toward Augusta and moving the chair out of the way so that they were within arm's reach of each other. She inched backward. "What, no fond greeting from my betrothed?"

Betrothed? It was unthinkable. Yet he knew that, for Grantley, there had to be someone. It was the gossip all over town. If it was indeed Miss Hastings who had been sacrificed to Grantley's greed, no wonder she'd shrunk from telling him the whole of her story. And no wonder she had felt she must flee to a life no one would expect her to pursue, and where she could melt into the teeming masses of London and escape detection. Yet through the well-meaning actions of his sister and himself, she had been caught like a rabbit in a trap. George met Augusta's wide, beseeching eyes. She gave a tiny shake of her head.

"Hasn't she told you?" Grantley asked, taking Augusta's chin in his hand and turning her face back and forth, examining her profile. "Pretty thing. At least they did that for me."

"I. Am. Not. Your. Betrothed," Augusta said through clenched teeth.

"Oh, I think you'll find you are."

This was too much for Bridlington. Not caring how ungainly he looked he rushed over and shoved himself between Grantley and Augusta, forcing Grantley to step backward and nearly lose his balance.

Grantley's eyes hardened. "Take care, Bridlington. I wouldn't want you to fall."

"Just try to make me!" George said and planted Grantley a facer, a flush hit that sent him sprawling on the Axminster carpet. Grantley lifted his hand to his nose, and it came away streaked with blood. He hoisted himself off the floor and strode close to George, who stood his ground and met his eyes. The two men glowered at each other, Grantley pressing his handkerchief to his nose, George keeping his fists clenched by his sides.

"You have insulted me," Grantley said, fairly spitting the words. "There can be only one answer. Name your friends. We meet on Hounslow Heath at dawn."

The blood charged through George's veins. He wished he could deal with Grantley then and there. But that wasn't possible. "Agreed!" he said instead, and Grantley stalked out of the room, slamming the door behind him.

As soon as his footsteps faded down the stairs, Augusta ran to George, her eyes wide with fright, "No! It's not worth it! *I'm* not worth taking such a risk for. Please don't do this, it's insane! I'll marry him!"

Her choked words tumbled out in a rush, tears making wet paths down her cheeks. George wrapped his arms around her and let her bury her face in his shoulder, her body convulsed with sobs. "Hush, my dear. I'll make all right. You'll see," he murmured into her hair, which quickly came loose from its careful knot and trailed down her back, pins showering onto the carpet. Looking down at her like that, he could see the burnished lights in her glossy locks. He stroked them and uttered soothing nothings until she gradually quieted. And that was when he realized she had behaved as if he had no clubfoot, as if when he walked it wasn't with an ungainly limp. She never offered to help him stand or offered him a seat he did not want. He now knew without any doubt that it simply didn't matter to her.

When she had calmed enough to speak, Augusta said, "Please, for my sake, do not do this. Why would you? It makes no sense."

"On the contrary," George said. "Nothing has ever made more sense to me." He tipped her chin up with his index finger and searched in her eyes. "I will not let that man marry you."

"Don't kill him!" Augusta shrieked.

"I don't mean to," he said, his mouth set in a grim line.

"Then, how can you prevent it? My aunt—she made the bargain with the earl. She didn't want to be responsible for me. Marriage would have been my only option. That's why I ran away. At least, one reason."

He tucked a lock of hair that had fallen across her cheek behind her ear. "As I said, I can prevent it."

"How?"

"I shall marry you. If you'll have me."

She jerked her head back and gasped. "You don't mean it.

How can you? You don't even know me. You're just sorry for me because of Grantley. You don't know what I want from life, what will be impossible in a marriage such as ours—"

He pressed his finger against her lips. "I never say anything I don't mean."

She still looked doubtful and confused.

"Perhaps you'll believe me if I simply show you how I feel." He placed his hands on either side of her face and held it angled up toward his, bent his head down, and kissed her. At first she merely accepted the touch of his lips without pulling away. But as his kiss grew deeper, she returned it, and the world disappeared as she threaded her arms around his neck and he wrapped her in a fierce embrace.

An hour later, George took a rather disheveled Augusta upstairs to give her into his sister's care. He assumed Mariana had gone to her room, having strategically left the two of them alone. He didn't know how much of what had subsequently passed had come to her ears, so on their way he said, "Don't tell Mariana anything. I can't have her in high fidgets about this. There's nothing she—or you—can do."

Augusta reluctantly agreed not to breathe a word of the threatened duel to Mariana, but he could see by her bewilderment that she hadn't fully comprehended the gravity of the impending event, or perhaps didn't believe it would really occur.

George knocked on his sister's bedroom door, which she opened, her eyes full of eager curiosity. He would have to leave Augusta to explain why, mixed with the soft glow of love in her eyes, evidence of many tears still remained. He had other business to attend to,

Starting with writing a note to Harry, who would be at Brooks's.

. . .

WITHIN AN HOUR, LEWISTON ARRIVED AT LANYON HOUSE, AND after George related what had occurred earlier that day and Grantley's connection with Miss Hastings, they went through the arrangements for the meeting the following morning.

"His seconds have to ask you to apologize first. Do it, man! It's no dishonor."

George ignored the suggestion and said, "I have my Mantons. They're in the gun cabinet. If you could arrange the surgeon."

"You don't mean to say you're going through with it? Have you thought?"

"Yes. Have you? Do you suppose I would allow that black-guard to marry the woman I love? Or perhaps you think that my lame foot means I'm at too great a disadvantage to prevail." His voice was like flint, each word hard edged and uncompromising.

Lewiston stared at him open-mouthed. "The woman you love? So that's what this is about?"

"What, do you think I'd threaten to kill a man over anything else?"

"I thought it was … the other day, at the club. You know. But I see now."

"Grantley and I have been heading toward this for a while, you're right. But I don't know if it would have come to this without his insult to Augusta. I've spent my whole life being subjected to cruel and insensitive comments about my foot. My skin is well toughened against those barbs." Now, he had a curious feeling of elation mixed with the tension of his heightened nerves. It was true. The reason he gave to Lewiston. He had never uttered those words before. *The woman I love.* It had come upon him in a blinding instant, when she looked up at him with her red-rimmed eyes, pleading with him not to fight for her, and he had told her he never needed to fight for anything else as much as her, his darling girl. And her eyes lit up, and he kissed her again before she had an opportunity to protest. The memory of that kiss put a smile on his face, even though the matter at hand was deadly serious.

"He's a good shot," Lewiston said.

"I'm better." Just as he was a better pugilist, having had to overcome the disadvantage of his balance with a clubfoot. Just as he was the best horseman he knew, and better at handling the ribbons than the members of the Four Horse Club, which he had not been invited to join. So few people saw past his weakness to perceive his strength. Only Madame Agatha truly understood what he was capable of, having served as his means of righting so many wrongs dealt to unfortunate children.

The fact remained that all this would be worth nothing if he allowed Grantley to put a bullet through his heart at dawn tomorrow. He knew that on his side, much as he wanted to, he would not kill that despicable excuse for a man. He had another plan, which he fully intended to see to its conclusion.

Mariana made her peace with Augusta, a process significantly smoothed by the fact that her brother had asked Augusta to marry him, and she had soft glints in her eyes that drove out almost all unpleasant thoughts and memories. Although she could discern a thread of uneasiness underneath Augusta's rapture, Mariana had put it down to anxiety about her situation. What was to happen in the immediate future? Would she come to stay in Lanyon House? And what of her ambitions? Would she have to relinquish them entirely? They had talked on these and other light matters.

"How ironic it would be for you to return to Madame Noelle's as a customer!" Mariana said with glee.

"That I'm not sure I would have the heart to do. Nor would I necessarily want to. My opinion of her abilities is not of the highest, as you know. Speaking of which, I must return to Curzon Street now," Augusta said.

"Your color is better. You were ashen when you first came in. But are you certain? You won't be in Madame's employ much longer."

"I can't just disappear. It wouldn't be fair to the others! There's work to do."

Mariana laughed. "You are too good. But I won't stop you. Besides, we'll have plenty of time to talk and make plans when we are sisters."

Augusta smiled and her eyes glittered. "What about you and Jeremy? Has Bridlington—George—given his consent?"

Mariana felt certain that, in his amorous glow, her brother would allow the match, but she said to Augusta, "Not yet. Although he's open to it. Jeremy is to come and see him in a few days."

"I hope he does approve. Anyone seeing the two of you together would believe you were designed for each other."

"There is one more thing I need of you," Mariana said after a pause. "If you have any credit left with Madame, I need your help in modifying another coat, this one for daytime wear."

A wary look came into Augusta's eyes. "What do you contemplate now, Mari?"

"I cannot tell you. I can only ask you to trust me a little longer. I retrieved the coat from the attic, hoping you would take it away with you and see to it today." She handed Augusta a small parcel wrapped in brown paper. "This one isn't so particular as the other, and you did such a good job on that one."

Augusta's reluctance was unmistakable, but Mariana put all her pleading persuasion in her expression, and she took it. "Very well. I shall have it delivered to you tomorrow morning. I doubt I will be free to come myself, not after so many recent absences."

The two friends embraced, and she saw Augusta off through the grand front door, parcel in hand. Mariana felt a bit wistful about putting an end to the hiding and scheming in the attic, the coming and going on the back stairs. But she would always have the memory of that time, whatever happened in the future.

AUGUSTA WISHED SHE COULD HAVE SAID NO TO MARIANA, BUT somehow, that lady's entreaties were impossible to resist. She felt worse on this occasion, though, because she had no doubt that whatever it was Mariana planned, George would not approve. And his wishes, his approval, was now of paramount importance to her. She quaked a little at how he might respond to her own ambition, which—even as she basked in the certainty of his love—she was reluctant to relinquish altogether.

She was under pressure of time to somehow alter this other coat for Mariana. There was no possible way she would be able to undertake the work herself in such haste, therefore she knew her only hope would be if Mr. Gordon could do it. So rather than return immediately to Curzon Street, she bent her steps on a direct route to Pall Mall, hoping she would find him there—and that he would be able not only to do the work, but to see that the finished coat was delivered to Berkeley Square the next morning.

She was fortunate on both counts. Mr. Gordon was not only able, but willing to undertake the work—having been rewarded handsomely for his previous efforts and assured of Augusta's discretion with regard to his own personal matters.

"I will take it to Lanyon House myself, Ma'am," he said.

"There is no need for you to put yourself to such trouble," Augusta said. "Surely a delivery boy could do it." She explained which door the package must be conveyed to.

He leaned across the counter and lowered his voice. "In cases such as these..." He paused and glanced quickly around him. "... it is better to involve as few different eyes as possible." He winked at her.

It wasn't until she'd walked away and had turned toward Curzon Street that Augusta understood what he'd meant. Her first instinct was to be shocked. But then she shrugged. Let him think what he would. Anything that would guarantee his secrecy.

It was past dinner time when Augusta reached the workshop and ascended the stairs to join the others. Her heart was in such a state of mingled joy and alarm that she hardly thought she'd be able to school her face into some semblance of calm. When she met Pauline's eyes, she shook her head minutely. Although she felt she could probably trust the girl with more of the story than she'd revealed on the night of the party, now everything had grown in scope like a balloon being filled with gas. Indeed, she feared her own capacity for putting it all into words. She could tell Pauline was bursting with curiosity and furious not to have it satisfied, but she steadfastly refused to utter another word about what had happened, keeping both her elation and her foreboding to herself.

CHAPTER 20

George hardly slept. He was already awake when Craggins came in to rouse him an hour before dawn. He'd taken his valet into his confidence of necessity, in case he didn't return to Lanyon House later. He'd long ago made a will, naming Mariana his heir so there would be no fight among any distant male family members who might suddenly make themselves known.

But now, he wanted to add something. He had met the love he'd been waiting for all his life. The love he sincerely didn't believe he wanted or needed. How foolish he had been! Although she clearly had been able to take care of herself to that point, was resourceful enough to take a bold step to reject a life she did not want, he still felt an overpowering need to free her of those cares. If he perished before they had a chance to be together, before he could wed her, he wanted to ensure that she would have a life of ease. He wrote out a codicil giving Augusta a fortune of ten-thousand pounds, with Lewiston as trustee. He was strongly tempted to add a condition that she could not have this fortune if she married Grantley. But that was a circumstance that he felt confident she could easily avoid if the codicil were ever to be executed. He would not put it past Grantley to exert some other influence on her, however. Instead he put in the condition that the funds were to be used solely at her discretion, distributed by Lewiston as needed. Lewiston would ensure that Grantley never got his sordid hands on that money.

Once attired in a plain black coat and dark pantaloons, he shook hands with Craggins, transferring a gold sovereign into that worthy retainer's palm, and then crept down the stairs. Lewiston was already waiting for him in a hired carriage with no telltale crests on the panels. The doctor, he said, would meet them there.

"I wonder if Grantley will delope," Harry said.

"I don't believe so." He knew a murderous look when he saw one, and believed Grantley entirely capable of killing a man in a duel. Especially when he believed that a fortune hung in the balance. He also didn't put it past him to abduct Augusta and flee to the continent if that were the outcome. Thus he dismissed the idea that Grantley would consider doing the gentlemanly thing and firing into the air, although any triumph he might feel would be dampened considerably if it were known that his adversary was a cripple.

After that, the two men said nothing as they drove west out of London in the closed carriage.

It had rained overnight, and there was still a fine mist settling in scattered blankets over the streets. The mist grew more persistent when they emerged from the thickly settled areas into country dotted by small villages and farms. They might have to find a slight rise if they were not to be shooting blind, unless a breeze came up to blow the mist away.

The journey to Hounslow felt at once interminable and as fast as lightning. George had thought he would have time to think of things to ask Lewiston to attend to, but he found his mind completely empty, his senses painfully acute.

Grantley and his second were already there when they arrived. The ground was well soaked thanks to the rain, but the mist had cleared enough that they would be able to see to aim. Grantley's second, a man Bridlington knew only slightly, asked him if he would be willing to apologize in order to settle the matter.

George refused.

The pistols were examined and approved. The doctor turned his back. The duelists took their places back to back and cocked their pistols, waiting only for Lewiston to start the count and drop the handkerchief.

George's senses were so acute he could hear the dawn birdsong as if it were a chorus in a cathedral. His heart slowed as he focused, concentrating on what was to come. He thought of Augusta. If this were to be his final moment on earth, he wanted hers to be the face he saw, not that scoundrel Grantley's.

"I thought you'd cry off, Georgie," said Grantley over his shoulder. "It's easy to be brave in the drawing room."

George thought about Grantley's cowardly meanness toward a boy who couldn't keep up with him on the playing fields at school and wanted to say, *you are the coward in this drama.* But he knew his words would be wasted.

"I hope you can walk straight," Grantley murmured, just as Lewiston said, "One…."

Knowing Grantley sought to unnerve him, George gritted his teeth and focused his mind on his purpose, digging deeper and deeper into it with each uneven step he took. George's feet sank a little into the mud as he paced. He hoped the ground was just as sodden where Grantley had to walk. It would serve his purpose nicely.

"…eight…nine…ten!"

George turned, lifted his pistol and aimed first at Grantley's head, finger ever so gently resting on the trigger. He waited.

From a distance of twenty yards, Grantley's face was clear enough. He leveled his pistol at George, his eyes narrowed and the corners of his mouth turned down in a scowl.

George saw the burst of fire and the smoke from the pistol an instant before he heard the report, and felt a searing pain in his left shoulder, but stood firm. Grantley had lowered his spent gun and was staring at George.

"Shoot, damn it!" he said.

George slowly lowered his pistol until he was pointing it directly at Grantley's right foot. He flicked his eyes up to see the dawning fear on Grantley's face as he realized that George's intent was to cripple him just as he was crippled, make him spend the rest of his life limping. He could have stepped away, he could have run, but that would be the action of a coward, and so he stood there.

George counted to three slowly in his head. At the moment when he squeezed the trigger, he shifted his aim infinitesimally so that his bullet struck the sodden ground immediately next to Grantley's right foot, sending a shower of mud into the air and over Grantley's highly polished top boots and nip-waisted coat.

As soon as he'd done it, Lewiston ran to him. "You're hit!"

He looked down at his left shoulder. "So I am."

And then he collapsed on the ground.

GEORGE CAME TO HIS SENSES IN THE CARRIAGE. THE DOCTOR had bandaged him up quickly, saying the bullet had not lodged in his shoulder and that it was a graze that should heal relatively quickly.

"What were you thinking?" Lewiston said. "Why didn't you aim to kill? Or delope?"

"I wanted him to feel, for a moment, what it might be like to lose the easy use of his right foot. And then, I wanted to humiliate him. Imagine going to the club and boasting about besting a cripple in a duel, and being drenched in mud thanks to that same cripple's flawless aim."

Lewiston sighed. "I don't think I'll ever understand you. Do you think this will force Grantley to relinquish his claim on Miss Hastings? He wants that fortune."

George shrugged, then winced. "Whatever his plans, he will find them difficult to carry out. It's not so easy to marry an unwilling bride. And I intend to make her safe as quickly as possible."

"Special license, eh? What will the dowager think?"

George gave a short laugh. "I think she'll be relieved. I have been swearing that I will never marry. I daresay she'd given up hope. Are we there? Take me in the back way so no one sees us. I don't want to alarm my mother or my sister. I won't go to them until I'm in better shape."

GEORGE COULD NOT HAVE KNOWN THAT MAY ELEVENTH would be a momentous day for Mariana as well. It was the day she had arranged to meet Jeremy in one final, daring gesture of independence, to fulfill a lifelong ambition that would never be possible for a woman. But this day would not be possible for her either unless the requisite coat arrived on time for her to dress before meeting Jeremy.

Immediately after breakfast, she raced down the back stairs to await Augusta. What was keeping her? Had she asked too much for the work to be accomplished in such haste?

She was about to give up on her project when, to her surprise, a dapper young man appeared at the stable yard door bearing a parcel tied up with string. Her first thought was that it was a damnable nuisance to have someone arrive when she was expecting Augusta. The young man rapped on the glass half of the door, and Mariana opened it.

"Yes?" she said, too impatient to be polite.

He bowed courteously and said, "I have a package for Lady Mariana Lanyon. Am I right in thinking you are she?" He held out the parcel.

She took it cautiously and wrinkled her brow.

"You do not know me, but I am in the confidence of Miss Hastings. I helped her with a similar project. You have all my discretion at your disposal. I am Aloysius Gordon, tailor and haberdasher."

So, Augusta hadn't done all the alterations herself after all. She had said that men's coats required skills she did not possess. Her answer had been to involve another in an endeavor that was supposed to be highly secretive—just as she had involved the girl who had acted as her abigail on the night of the party. Mariana had a moment of irritation, but then realized there was no point in crying over something that had already happened. "Thank you," she said, and took the package from Mister Gordon.

But instead of walking away, he said, "Forgive me, Ma'am, but I conjecture this coat is to be worn by yourself?" He cast his eye over her in a way that would have been rude if it had contained any suggestion of desire.

"It is. But that is no concern of yours."

"I beg your pardon, but it certainly is. I would ask your leave to ensure that the fit is correct. I take great pride in my work, as does Mister Weston, who had the original tailoring of the garment. It would not do to be seen in public in an ill-fitting coat of such fine quality."

"I have little time," Mariana said.

"It will be the matter of a few moments, I assure you."

"Very well," she said, deciding that to waste any more time talking would be counterproductive. "Follow me."

She led him up the stairs to the attic workroom, and stepped behind a makeshift screen to remove the dress that covered the pantaloons and shirt she already wore and donned the tight-fitting coat.

When she came out, Mister Gordon rested an elbow in one hand and cradled his chin in the other, his stance elegantly poised, and cast a critical eye over Mariana. Without a word, he approached her and tweaked and settled the coat, removed a tiny pair of scissors from his waistcoat pocket and snipped an errant thread, and then stood back again. "It will do, provided you don't plan to be among very discerning gentlemen."

Mariana smiled. There was something about this fellow she liked. He didn't flatter. And he made no comment about the fact that she, a woman, would be wearing the coat. Then she had an idea. "I shall be gone but a few hours, and when I return, I will have no more use for this coat. Perhaps you know of some deserving young fellow who might benefit by being more elegantly turned out than he can easily afford?"

This brought a broad grin to Mister Gordon's face, and a mischievous twinkle to his eyes. "At what hour should I attend you to take receipt of this item?"

MARIANA LET HERSELF OUT OF LANYON HOUSE THE BACK WAY an hour later, wearing her fawn pantaloons and the coat that had been altered by Mister Gordon, her neck cloth tied in a simple knot. Jeremy had said that the clerks and secretaries never affected dandy dress at work, whatever they chose to wear in the evening. They were to meet outside the House and walk in together. Jeremy would give her a portfolio to carry. Once inside, they would have to part ways. She could not accompany him into Perceval's office. The debates started at midday, though, and there would be sufficient activity for her to blend in without calling undue attention to herself.

Mariana felt a thrill of accomplishment as she walked to the hackney stand with long, confident strides, swinging her arms like a young man off to his day's business. The jarvey paid no particular attention to her when she climbed into the hack and directed him to Westminster. Her mood was so buoyant that she gave him a generous gratuity when she paid the fare.

She stood still in the stream of men of all ages striding along with such a sense of purpose, some in pairs or groups of three talking, heads together and faces serious, no doubt discussing important issues. They certainly weren't talking of the latest *ton* party, or the most recent issue of The Lady's Monthly Museum. She caught only scraps of conversation, picking up isolated words—war, mills, penalty, America.

"May I walk with you, Sir?" said a familiar voice from behind her.

She wheeled around to see Jeremy grinning and had to suppress an impulse to fling her arms around his neck and squeal with glee. "Of course!" she said aloud, then in a much quieter voice, "You'll show me where to go, won't you?"

"The important thing is to look as if you know what you're doing and are engaged on important business. Do you have a pocket watch?" he asked.

"A pocket watch?"

"You can take it out and look at it periodically and shake your head, as if you don't have enough time to accomplish everything you've set out to do."

Mariana laughed. "I don't think I'll be able to keep up the

pretense for an entire afternoon. Shall we arrange to meet in say, two hours?"

"I'll have to see what Perceval has on his docket today. Why don't you go to the strangers gallery for the first debate and I'll come find you there once I know?"

Since she had no other suggestion to make, Mariana agreed. It was, after all, what she'd come for. They parted just inside the doors. At first, Mariana stood still and simply let herself take in her surroundings. When her lack of motion began to attract a few curious stares, she followed Jeremy's advice and started walking, following the general trend of the crowd through the halls, listening to bits of conversations, reveling in feeling deliciously invisible.

ON THE MORNING WHEN SHE KNEW THE DUEL WAS TO TAKE place, Augusta awoke in the attic room on Curzon Street before dawn. She had no experience to draw on in order to imagine what George was going through at that moment. She still held out hope that the two men would come to some agreement to avoid having to meet. Failing that, she hoped they would both delope.

Her mind was a jumble of conflicting emotions. One second, her heart swelled and a tingle of joy spread throughout her body as she remembered the tender words she and Bridlington had exchanged less than twenty-four hours before. The feel of his arms around her, the taste of his kiss.

And then, a piercing dread would shatter those feelings, and she would picture him lying cold on the ground, blood seeping from a horrible wound. That would be followed quickly by Grantley's looming, leering face as he claimed her, a sacrifice on the altar of greed.

No sooner had that picture left its horrifying mark on her imagination than she once more saw those clear gray eyes gazing into hers with such an intensity of love that it made her weak. And those kisses. She had to admit, James had never kissed her quite like that. They were both so young, and he was full of his soldierly pride and honor. He had been more handsome than George. But his eyes did not hold as much feeling, changing and deepening as his thoughts sped and he reacted to every nuance in her heart.

Could it be true? Could George have really meant it, that he would marry her? Mariana seemed to think it settled. How would it be to have that mercurial lady as a sister? Life would certainly never be dull. Although she couldn't imagine a greater happiness than being with the man she loved, she feared that doing so would mean relinquishing her long-held dream of being a modiste. Could she be satisfied only designing clothing for herself and Mariana—which George surely couldn't object to? Perhaps. But she had to acknowledge a desire not just to create her designs but to be *known* for creating them.

She shook her head at this thought, and tried to keep her mind and heart focused on the good things that had happened the day before, as all of them—Bernadette, Molly, Miss Carp, and Pauline—woke and dressed, drank their coffee and ate their bread and butter and then tumbled down the rickety stairs to the workroom, ready to spend another day bent over their sewing. But astute, observant Pauline was quick to see that something momentous had happened to Augusta. There were no fittings scheduled until the afternoon, so Pauline found a quiet moment to whisper that they should go for a short walk at nuncheon.

By that time, Augusta was in a state of high fidgets, hands trembling as she tried to think of some way, any way, to get news of the outcome of Bridlington and Grantley's meeting.

But of course, such things occurred under a cloak of secrecy. She couldn't even apply to Mariana, because she knew nothing. Even if she dared, Mariana had told her yesterday that she would be out all day today, so a letter would not find her at home.

"What's got you in alt?" Pauline said, as soon as they were on the flagway.

"Oh Pauline! So much has happened. I don't know where to start."

"Well, we only got a minute, so start fast! And you better get yourself under wraps before Lady Wyndham's fitting this afternoon."

As quickly as she could, Augusta told Pauline the story of her tumultuous afternoon at Lanyon House, the seamstress's eyes opening wider and wider as she spoke.

"Well! I never did! You could knock me down with a feather. Damme if I don't think it might of happened, after what I see'd t'other night, you all done up like a lady."

"I swear it happened just as I said, and now I can't bear it. What if he's dead?" The tears started in her eyes and she blinked them back as fast as she could.

"Now don't you go worriting. No use thinking the worst. That won't do no good at all."

"You're right of course. We need to go back. It's time for the fitting. Do I look all right?" Augusta doubted her ability to keep an anxious furrow from her brow.

"You'll do. Just keep looking down. You can pin the hem."

AUGUSTA HAD CALMED HERSELF SUFFICIENTLY TO PRESENT A tranquil face to Madame as they awaited Lady Wyndham's arrival. Only a few minutes late, the viscountess swept in on a cloud of ambergris that sent Pauline into a sneezing fit. While she recovered, Augusta helped Madame slip the new ball gown over the head of one of the most elegant hostesses of the *ton*. Only once did she look up and catch her employer staring at her with a frown on her face. With a customer there, however, she could say nothing.

She had just finished pinning the hem up in front when there was a sound of a carriage coming to a stop just outside the door, followed not by a polite knock but by the door being yanked violently open and setting the bells tinkling shrilly.

When Augusta looked up to see who had entered the showroom, ice trickled through her veins and her mouth went dry.

"I'm looking for my—" The large matron in an unfashionable stuff pelisse and a squirrel muff stopped speaking abruptly when her eyes met Augusta's. "You! What is the meaning of this!"

Augusta stood and rushed forward, trying to push her aunt Phyllis out the door before she said anything more. "Aunt Phyllis, I beg you!" The plea in her voice fell on deaf ears.

"I apologize, My Lady!" Madame said to her bewildered customer, "Please do not regard this rude interruption. I assure you I have no idea who this woman is!"

"She is my aunt, Lady Bagley, come from Devonshire. I beg you will excuse me!" Augusta said, shoving her aunt with all her might back through the door she'd just entered.

"Don't you touch me, you ungrateful wretch!" Aunt Phyllis said, insensible to the stares that met them out on the flagway. "You're to come with me, immediately."

"But I can't!" Augusta said, tears washing down her cheeks in earnest. "I mustn't!"

"The only thing you mustn't do is fail to honor your betrothal. You know it's the right thing, and the only way for you to reclaim what is left of your tattered reputation. So I'm taking you immediately back to Bideford, and I shall lock you in your bedchamber until such time as Grantley claims you! I had a job, I'll tell you, putting the earl off when you disappeared."

"Please, Ma'am. Let us talk in private." The only convenient place that presented itself was her aunt's cumbersome traveling carriage. A large coachman Augusta didn't recognize stood next to it. She did not want to be confined in so small a space with her aunt. "Let us walk in the park for a moment."

She took no more than two steps in that direction when she found herself lifted off her feet and, before she could utter a sound, bundled into the coach.

"Take your hands off me!" she cried, but her aunt had already climbed in after her and blocked the way. She grabbed the handle of the other door only to discover that it was locked from the outside.

"Drive on, Fitzroy!" Lady Bagley said, and the coach set off with a lurch.

Augusta's heart sank to her knees. She looked out the coach window hoping to see someone whose aid she could beg for, but the street was empty and soon they were going too fast for her to have any hope of escape. She had not thought her aunt capable of such a thing, of abducting her. That was the first time she had an inkling that there was more than her niece's reputation and well-being at stake for Lady Bagley. If she married Grantley, he would come into a large fortune. Augusta wondered bitterly how much of it would end up in her Aunt Phyllis's hands.

JEREMY CAUGHT SIGHT OF MARIANA ONLY ONCE DURING THE two hours she was in the House, and she seemed to be managing quite well, looking busy and not too overawed by her surroundings. In a different life, she could have trod the boards of Drury Lane and made a huge success, he thought. Those qualities would, ironically, help make her the kind of wife who would assure his career. Although of course that hadn't been why he'd proposed to her.

"I think that's all we need for today, Thorne," Perceval said, handing a sheaf of documents to Jeremy, which he stowed away in his briefcase. "I'll need you to summarize those for me before my address tomorrow."

"Yes Sir," he said. He couldn't help smiling, knowing that in minutes he would be greeting Mariana, feeling pleased that he had been instrumental in helping her achieve a dream she'd had for years. He and Augusta Hastings had helped her, that is, who Mariana told him was to marry Bridlington. He could never have suspected it! And yet, the one time he'd seen them together, thinking back, he could detect their attraction to each other in small looks and gestures.

Jeremy followed behind the prime minister as he made his halting way out of the building, stopping at irregular intervals to have brief conversations with ministers and lackeys who asked him questions and gave him sealed letters. Jeremy took his pocket watch out and looked at it. He'd be a little late for Mariana. He hoped she wouldn't worry.

They finally reached the doors, which the two liveried porters opened wide for Perceval and Jeremy to pass through. One of them stopped Jeremy to point out the young man waiting for him just outside.

What happened next was so sudden, so unexpected, that later Jeremy would have a hard time recreating it in his mind. All he was aware of at first was a loud crack, and then silence. He watched, frozen in horror, as Spencer Perceval collapsed onto the ground, a pool of blood flowing out of him so quickly that it spilled like a river down the steps.

Guards and members rushed to his inert form. Someone said, "There he is! Get him!" and pointed to a grim-faced man making no attempt to flee, holding a still-smoking pistol pointed down at the ground.

At that moment, Jeremy remembered Mariana and looked over to where she'd been standing moments before. She'd been so close to Perceval, close enough so that blood spattered her white neckcloth—which he could hardly distinguish from the pallor on her face. He ran to her and reached her just as she fainted.

"The boy's swooned!" someone said, seeing Jeremy with Mariana limp in his arms. "Is he hurt?"

"Get me a hack!" Jeremy screamed.

"I'm afraid we cannot let you leave the vicinity, Sir," said a burly uniformed guard. "All parliamentary personnel must remain to be questioned."

Goddamn them! "I must get this—man—to his lodgings where he can be looked after. You must know he had nothing to do with this! I am Jeremy Thorne. You'll know where to find me, and I'm happy to cooperate with any investigation. But please!"

At that moment, Mariana's carefully hidden hair came loose from its pins and fell in all its voluminous glory over Jeremy's arm. The guard opened his eyes wide and said "Stow me!"

Jeremy saw his chance. "This is no place for a lady. I must get her to her brother's house. Let me go!"

"This way, Sir!" someone said to him, gesturing toward a hack that had pulled up on the side, a little out of the way of the commotion.

"You have better things to do, surely," said Jeremy to the guard. He then carried Mariana away and the still-stunned guard did nothing to stop him.

CHAPTER 21

"*I*'m fine, damn you Craggins!" George said as his valet tried to get him to go to bed in the middle of the afternoon. "The doctor said so, and he's patched me up so it hardly shows. Now help me into my clothes."

He wanted to dress quickly, although getting his injured arm into a tight-fitting coat was no easy task. He must go and talk to the dowager. It was imperative to tell her that he had decided to marry before gossip had a chance to reach her. He hadn't decided whether or not to explain about Grantley or say anything about a duel. He would see how the interview went first.

Lady Bridlington was in her suite, having just finished her toilette as she prepared to go out shopping in her landaulet. George went quickly to her and took her outstretched hand, kissing it, then bending and kissing her soft, papery cheek.

"I'm surprised to see you at this hour, my dear," she said, looking him over carefully. "You're pale. Is it your foot? I didn't notice you limping any more than usual."

His foot. He'd hardly thought about it all day. At least she hadn't noticed him holding his left arm a bit stiffly. "No, nothing like that. Just a bad night, I think."

"I see. Why are you here?"

George knew her directness was not a sign of displeasure, only concern. "Because I have something important to tell you."

"Bad news?" Her eyebrows rose in alarm.

"Not in the least." He flashed her his most radiant smile and said, "I'm getting married."

She sat rigid, saying nothing for a full minute. "Married? You? But you haven't courted anyone! Oh please don't tell me you're elevating some lightskirt to the rank of countess!"

He shook his head and laughed. "Not at all. She's perfectly respectable, I assure you. You've even met her. I just didn't know I was courting her until yesterday."

"You strange, unnatural boy."

He stiffened.

"No, my dear, I don't mean your foot! I mean the way you've spent your whole life guarding yourself from hurt so that you even fooled yourself into thinking you were immune to love."

George still had her left hand in his and squeezed it. The dowager reached for his other hand and grasped it. A knife of pain shot into his shoulder and he gasped.

"What is it?" she asked, narrowing her eyes. "I think you need to tell me all."

George cursed himself for his weakness and for thinking he could conceal something as momentous as having been injured in a duel from his too-canny mother.

"I shall. I want to make you understand before you fly up into the boughs when I tell you who she is."

The dowager drew him down to sit next to her on the silk-covered day bed. "I was afraid there was a thorn in your story."

George suppressed a laugh. She couldn't know how close she'd come to the truth. He quickly assembled some version of Augusta's story that would be moderately acceptable to his mother. Since knowing she had been betrothed to Grantley would assure the dowager that she was of gentle enough birth to be acceptable, and since he'd been so unwise as to reveal that he had an injury, he decided he would have to tell her about the duel.

"It all came about just two weeks ago," he said.

"Two weeks! One moment," Lady Bridlington said. "I think I need to be fortified with some Madeira. I can see in your face that I will likely find myself distressed." She rang the little bell on the table by her side, expecting her abigail to come in immediately from her dressing room. But there was no response. "Where can Potter be?" she said.

From out in the hallway came sounds of feet rushing past and murmured exclamations. George made out, "Poor Lady Mariana!" and exchanged a look with his mother. He jumped up and limped as quickly as he could to open the door and look down the hall. To his horror, he saw Mister Thorne carrying what appeared to be the lifeless body of a young man into his sister's bedroom.

"I'll be back, Mother!" George said, not waiting for her to say anything, and hastened down the hall to his sister's room. He burst in without knocking, just in time to see Jennings waving a vinaigrette under the nose of a person stretched out on Mariana's bed attired in pantaloons and top boots, a Weston-tailored coat he recognized as one of his own, and a blood-stained neck cloth that had been untied to reveal a white throat. As soon as he saw the face above this raiment, he knew it was his sister.

She'd opened her eyes and was struggling to sit up. George said, "Jennings—go to the dowager and tell her all is well, that I'm just having a quick word with Lady Mariana but will return in a few minutes."

The abigail curtsied and ran off to do as he bid.

As soon as she was gone, George looked up to see Jeremy Thorne, disheveled and himself spattered with blood, gazing with dismay down at Mariana. "You," George said through his clenched teeth.

"Don't blame him, George!" Mariana said, pushing herself up on her elbows. "It was me! I did it!" Her panic-stricken eyes searched his. "Don't destroy my life! Or Jeremy's. He doesn't deserve it!"

George ran his hand through his hair and turned away, walking around the room, trying to gain control of his faculties. What had his outrageous sister done, and what did Thorne have to do with it? He circled back to them. Thorne was now seated on the bed with Mariana's hand sandwiched between his, and the two were gazing into each other's eyes. "You must know this changes everything, Mariana."

She tore her gaze away from Thorne's and looked steadily at George. "No, it doesn't. It can't. When you hear all, you'll understand."

George couldn't imagine what she could say that would change the basic impossibility of his condoning a match between the sister of an earl and a parliamentary secretary, who clearly had something to do with Mariana being clad as a man and covered in blood that didn't appear to belong to either of them.

Mariana loosed her hand from Jeremy's, swung her legs over the edge of her bed, and stood. "We'll talk. But not here. Jeremy, please wait downstairs in the book room while I change my clothes into something more suitable. George, you may join him, but if you send him away before I come down, I swear I will leave this house and never return!"

"As you wish," George said, nodded curtly to Thorne, and

went back to his mother's apartment. He must first tell her about his own adventures before revealing his sister's. If Mariana thought her escapade—whatever it was—could be concealed from the dowager, she was sorely mistaken.

AN HOUR LATER, GEORGE WAS LEAVING HIS MOTHER TO ABSORB and come to terms with the news that he had decided to marry the penniless daughter of a deceased baronet, a daughter who happened to be related to—and had been betrothed to—his worst enemy, when one of the footmen stopped him before he went down to the book room.

"My Lord," the footman said, "There's a person at the back entrance wishes to speak with you. And another person who wishes to see Lady Mariana."

"Two? Can't Allsop deal with this? I'm in no frame to talk to tradesmen—nor is My Lady."

"It's not tradesmen, My Lord. The girl says it's urgent private business. She says she comes from Madame Noelle." That the footman was repeating something he had been told but that made no sense to him was patently obvious.

"And the other?"

"A man—if you could call him that." The footman's lips curled in distaste. "Something about a coat."

It was all too tangled for him to make out. It seemed he had to go and see what it was. "Very well, send them to the—no, I'll come down, although I can little spare the time." This delay of the trimming he was planning to give his sister and her suitor vexed him. In telling his own story to Lady Bridlington, he recognized that he could hardly occupy the moral high ground compared with his sister, whatever she had done, and the longer he waited, the less bite there would likely be in his lecture.

He went down the back stairs to the servants' entrance where he found a neatly dressed young woman with what would have been an impish face, were it not for the creases of worry on her brow. Behind her, a well-turned-out young gentleman stood by, clearly discomfited. "Well, what is it?" he asked.

The gentleman gestured to the girl to go first. She curtsied low. "My Lord. I come about Gussie—Miss Hastings, that is."

The hairs on the back of his neck stood on end. "What news of her? Is she unwell?"

"No, not unwell, just gone!"

Gone? An image of an abduction by Grantley leapt into his mind. He took hold of the girl's shoulders rather roughly and said directly into her face. "What can you mean *gone*? Out with it!"

Quick tears sprang to her eyes, and George collected himself and let her go. "I'm sorry. Please, quickly, tell me what you came here to say." He had another awful thought that Augusta, in the cold light of day, had decided she could not marry him. Perhaps it was his clubfoot after all.

"*She* came. Her aunt, that is. A big ugly woman, if I do say My Lord!"

"I don't care what she looked like. Her aunt?" He was gripped by a terrible sense of foreboding.

"Like I said. She come from Devonshire in her carriage and took her right away with her. That is, the big coachman lifted her in. Gussie was beside herself I could see, only I couldn't do nothing."

The aunt. He hadn't reckoned on her at all. She was the one who arranged that cursed betrothal. No doubt there was some remuneration for her in the settlement. "When was this?"

"Just after nuncheon."

That was hours ago. "Why didn't you come sooner!"

The tears threatened again. "I couldn't! Madame wouldn't let me leave until dinner."

"Where did they go? Do you know?"

"No, I dunno where they went, I just know Augusta come from Devonshire. I think she said somewheres near Bideford."

By now George felt a bit sorry for this girl, and also grateful that she'd known to come to him. "Were you in Miss Hastings's confidence?"

She looked up at him blankly.

"Did she tell you her secrets?"

"Oh! Yes. I been here too, see. The night of the dress party. I was her... abigail."

A discreet throat clearing brought his attention to the other unknown visitor. "And you, Sir. What is your business here?"

"It's no wise important, M'lord," he said, twisting his hat through his hands. "I'd have gone away directly when Lady Mariana was not here, but then I met Miss Pauline, and she told me about Miss Hastings, and I have an interest in what becomes of her. Miss Hastings, that is."

An unknown sweetheart? No. George would not credit it. "What exactly is your interest?"

"The kind lady did me a service for which I owe her a debt of gratitude. I'd as lief not go away till I know she's safe." The high color in his cheeks spoke of embarrassment, not ardor.

George didn't have the energy or inclination to figure out exactly what either of them meant, but dug a sovereign out of his pocket and gave it to the girl.

She looked at it, and handed it back to him. "I don't want no blunt. I just want Gussie back and happy, is all."

"Keep it, girl," he said. "When I find Miss Hastings, whom shall I tell her I owe for the timely information?"

"Tell her Pauline, My Lord."

"And you, Sir?"

"I am Aloysius Gordon."

George reached into his pocket again, but Gordon put a hand up to stop him. "If you please, no, Sir."

"I suggest you return tomorrow for news of Miss Hastings," he said to both of them. Pauline dipped another quick curtsy and flushed to the roots of her hair, then turned to go out, but George said, "Wait!"

She looked at him over her shoulder. "Yes, My Lord?"

"Is there anything keeping you with Madame Noelle?"

The girl looked puzzled.

"Would you come with me to fetch Miss Hastings? She'll need a chaperone. I can't bring her away without one."

The transformation in the girl's face was instantaneous. "Yes! My Lord!"

"Can you be back here in half an hour, ready to go?"

She nodded and ran out the door.

"And you, Mister Gordon. What do you know of post houses? And are you at liberty to attend me as well?"

A broad grin spread over Mister Gordon's face. "You just say the word and I'll do whatever you want!"

George sprang into action. He went back upstairs and found Allsop. "Tell Lady Mariana and her friend that I have been called away on urgent business and will speak to them when I get back. Tomorrow, in fact." He hurried to his chamber, where Craggins was clucking over the shirt and coat that had been ruined in the duel. "Never mind that," he said, "Send word to Philpot that I want the chaise and the four chestnuts ready to go as quick as can be." Then he added, remembering his wounded shoulder, "I'll want him to drive, and a postilion. Then pack me a portmanteau for a stay of a few nights. I don't know yet how many."

"Yes, My Lord," Craggins said, unruffled. "Shall I be going as well?"

"What? Oh, I don't think so. I'll manage without you for this short time."

He didn't want to have to explain everything to Craggins. It was enough to have Gordon along with him to arrange things at posting houses. He would be bound to have to stay over at least one night, since it was already late afternoon and would be near six by the time they left. He didn't even have a clear idea of exactly where he was going other than that it would be near Bideford in North Devonshire.

In the panic of preparations, George all but forgot the pain in his shoulder and his crooked foot. He was going in pursuit of the one thing his life was missing, the one person who could make him whole.

Everything else was unimportant.

CHAPTER 22

*T*he twenty-four hours since her aunt had come to Madame Noelle's had been nothing short of a nightmare. They'd traveled in the rattling accommodation coach at a pace that surprised her. Several times she was certain a wheel might fall off, or a window blow out. They'd had several changes of horses, but hadn't stopped at any inns for the night. Aunt Phyllis had brought a hamper full of sandwiches and a few apples, but Augusta was too queasy and distraught to eat a thing.

Her aunt slept a good deal of the time, snoring heavily, and when she wasn't asleep, she harangued Augusta about her thoughtless, reckless behavior, accusing her of ingratitude for the pains she had taken to arrange a match that was more than suitable. Augusta did not say a word. All she could think was that George must have been killed in the duel and Grantley had sent to get her aunt to bring her niece to heel so he could marry her and gain access to his fortune.

By the time they arrived at Bagley Manor, her widowed aunt's modest and rather threadbare estate, all Augusta wanted to do was go to sleep and never wake up. Her aunt made good on her promise to lock her in her room, but by this time, all thoughts of escape had gone from Augusta's mind and she went without a murmur. What else could she do? *Please, George, please be alive! Please find me!* she said to herself over and over, finally giving free rein to the tears she'd been holding back. How could he find her? What if he was dead? The idea of a life shackled to a cruel man who cared nothing for her felt like a prison sentence. Somewhere in her mind she knew that no parson would perform a marriage ceremony with an unwilling bride, but she still worried that there were ways to get around that—perhaps an unscrupulous curate not averse to earning something to supplement a meager salary. In any case, if George were dead, she'd lost her position with Madame Noelle thanks to her aunt, and truly would have no way to live unless she married. And what about Lady Mariana? She might blame Augusta for his death and be lost to her as well.

Despite her agitation, Augusta fell into a deep sleep the night they arrived, and only awoke when she heard the key turn in her locked door in the morning. Sarah, the house-maid, brought in a tray with a glass of milk and a slice of bread and butter and placed it on the table near the window. "Beautiful spring day, Miss!" she said, as if serving a young woman who had been kept under lock and key was not unusual at all. "Milady says I'm to help you dress. The earl is coming this afternoon."

For a moment, Augusta's heart leapt. Then she realized that Aunt Phyllis likely meant the Earl of Hastings, Grant-ley's sullen father, and she wanted to cry.

Her stomach was so empty it hurt, and so she drank the milk and ate the bread. Thoughts of simply running away again—this time to hide in a barn somewhere and become a maid of all work on a farm—occurred to her and were then dismissed as ridiculous. Two days ago she had seen the possibility of a new life, of true love with a man she could respect and who loved her in return. An imperfect man, to be sure. But a good man. He'd told her of his secret efforts to improve the lives of disabled children, the house of refuge he kept at his own expense. He'd also explained about Madame Agatha, a kind woman who helped him in these endeavors. How could she judge a woman who had had to fight for her life and had found a way to make a livelihood on her own, without marrying? It was wrong of George to keep such a secret, to believe that those who loved him might ridicule him for it. She had hoped that her influence could help him overcome his misguided beliefs in his unworthiness. That such a man loved her enough to fight for her, to risk his life to win her—and had possibly given his life in the end— warmed her heart, and caused her unspeakable sorrow. But surely fate could not be so cruel to her. It wouldn't wrench another love, another future from her so suddenly, so violently.

Poor James. He had already been little more than the idea of happiness by the time he died. But George was real. She could still feel the warmth of his embrace. And she knew he would give her—would have given her—the kind of life that would truly make her happy. Perhaps he would even be able to condone her ambition. She'd had some thoughts about how she could manage not to give up her dreams entirely.

But that was not to the purpose now. Sadly, at that moment everything that had happened in London felt like a distant fantasy. Here she was, back again, and faced with the same unpalatable future.

With Sarah's help, Augusta half-heartedly donned a pale blue muslin round gown and a paisley shawl that had a tiny tear in it. *I should mend it,* she thought, and then thought of the workshop, and wondered what Pauline, Molly, Bernadette, and Miss Carp were doing at that moment. They would not miss her. She never fit in. She never really tried to, always having her eye on a bigger prize.

Augusta let her gaze wander around the room. It was the one she had moved into after her father's death, a small haven from grief and regret. She would remain there for the day, having no desire to go down to the parlor to sit and bear her aunt's remonstrations. So she turned to her small collection of books, which still sat in a neat row on the windowsill but had become caked with dust. She would spend her time reading, escape into the story of someone else's life, enjoy the fiction of a happy ending. She picked up *Cecilia* and blew the dust off it into a swirling cloud, remembering the day in Hookham's when, without knowing it, she'd started on the path that would eventually take her to George. But it had all been an impossible fantasy. A smile flitted across her face. Those two weeks of her life would make a good romance, if she were ever inclined to take up a pen.

With a rueful shake of her head, she turned to a page in Madame d'Arblay's book where she knew the heroine would be united with her true love and all would come to rights, and spent the next few hours living a vicarious life.

"Augusta! Augusta Hastings! Come down here at once!"

Aunt Phyllis's grating voice drew Augusta unpleasantly out of her book. She went down to the parlor where her aunt paced up and down, wringing her hands.

"What is it, Aunt?" Augusta asked, dreading her answer.

"He should have been here by now. I sent the message to Grantley Hall this morning."

The Hall was the home of the Earl of Hastings. It stood about eight miles away, and so was an easy distance by carriage. "Why did you wish to see me then?" Augusta asked.

"Because you must have done something! I can think of no other reason that the earl would ignore a message from me concerning his son's betrothal. I'm determined to find out what it was!"

"I assure you, Ma'am, I have had no communication with the earl." She wasn't going to say a word about her interchange with Grantley, who was not, after all, the earl.

"Grantley was in London, Hastings said. Perhaps you saw him and poisoned him against the suit. But Hastings assured me that no other lady of sufficient breeding would consent to marry his son."

"And so you thought that I would be content to ally myself to such a profligate rake?" Augusta shook her head in disbelief.

"You have no choice. Your situation is dire. Now, if you don't marry him, you will be an old maid, a drain on the parish, no doubt. Such an ignominious end to your father's line!"

Augusta thought that her father's line was hardly grand enough to be worth preserving—and her marriage wouldn't keep the Hastings name alive in any case. She would become a Grantley. But as Sir Alastair had been Aunt Phyllis's brother, she kept this observation to herself.

The two of them stood there regarding each other in mutual distaste when Augusta heard the unmistakable sound of carriage wheels coming up the very rutted lane that led from the turnpike road to the manor.

Her aunt's face brightened. "He's here! Took his time, I daresay. I doubt he's brought Grantley with him, he'll still be in London. But we can do all the settling without him, and I think the earl will want you to go and live in the Hall until the wedding. He told me so when he was last here, although why Bagley Manor won't do, I'm sure I don't know. It may not be as grand, but it's just as old and respectable. Tidy yourself! Your hair, Augusta, your hair!"

But there was no time to do anything except stand and wait. They listened in silence to horses champing and a postilion jumping down, a groom calling to a stable hand, halting footsteps approaching the front of the house, the knocker sounding, and Sarah answering the door.

A moment later, Sarah came in from the hall and said, "Beg pardon, Ma'am, the earl is here." She curtsied and then opened the door wide.

Augusta was sure her eyes deceived her. It couldn't be. It was the earl, certainly. But not the earl she expected. George Lanyon, Earl of Bridlington, stood framed by the doorway in her aunt's house, arrayed in a many-caped driving coat, his curly brimmed beaver tucked under his arm—a sight so unexpected she nearly shrieked with delight. Her heart started racing, and she couldn't keep the foolish grin off her face as she watched her beloved enter her aunt's parlor leaning on the ebony cane with the gold handle, not taking his eyes off her face.

"Sir! Who are you? How dare you come to my house without my leave! It is an insult!"

Aunt Phyllis fluttered around him tossing distressed comments in his direction until he said, "Silence, woman!"

She broke off with a pathetic whimper.

Bridlington continued his slow progress across the room until he stood directly in front of Augusta and took her hand, lifting it to his lips. "My darling," he said.

Augusta could bear it no longer and threw her arms around his neck. He kissed her fervently, but then pushed her away with a grimace of pain.

"What is it?" Augusta asked.

"It's nothing. I will tell you in the carriage. You're coming with me."

At this, Aunt Phyllis once more found her voice and said, "You'll not ruin my niece's reputation! A fine thing, to take her away without a chaperone!"

"Oh I have a chaperone waiting outside. My Lady's abigail. And I have a valet to make things all correct. I assure you, Madam, my fiancée will be conveyed to London with the greatest observance of propriety."

"Your-your f-fiancée?" Lady Bagley stammered.

"Yes. Grantley has abandoned his suit. With a little persuasion. He has been encouraged to go abroad. Your niece —if she will have me—is the future Countess of Bridlington." He held both of Augusta's hands and spoke softly to her. "I have engaged rooms at the posting house nearby for the night. We will return to London tomorrow."

"What's this about my abigail?" Augusta asked, her eyes dancing.

A moment later, her question was answered.

"Where is she? Is she here? Don't bother none, I'll just go and see." In swept Pauline, who, when she saw Augusta standing with Bridlington clapped her hands and said, "Oh I knew it! You couldn't be such a fine, beautiful lady for nothing!"

"And now, Madam, we need detain you no longer." George put his arm out for Augusta and led her away.

When they reached the door of the parlor, Augusta looked back at her aunt who stood stock still in round-eyed astonishment and said, "Don't look so surprised, Aunt. This is what you wanted for me after all, isn't it? Goodbye."

LATER THAT EVENING, AFTER A HEARTY DINNER IN THE PRIVATE parlor at The Swan, skillfully arranged by Mr. Gordon,

George told Augusta about everything that had happened, the outcome of the duel, and Mariana's brush with an event that was now being talked about everywhere. On his way, he'd heard the news of Perceval's assassination and realized that somehow his sister had been close enough to have witnessed the entire affair.

"I blame Thorne," George said.

She looked at him askance. "How can you? Do you honestly think Mari wouldn't have found some other way to get into the House? Besides. You could blame me as well. I altered the clothes to fit her. All except the coats."

He sat up and opened his eyes wide at her, failing to achieve an angry expression. "Oh you did, did you! Why is it that I suspicion you had a little help from a certain Mr. Gordon, who arrived at Lanyon House expecting to receive a man's coat for his troubles."

Augusta laughed. "I knew I couldn't do it all. I did, however, alter the breeches and pantaloons. And I knew they'd been yours. I felt a bit … odd, knowing they had been so close to you. Even then." She couldn't help stealing a glance at his thigh.

"Even then? So you liked me a little from the beginning?"

She more than liked him, Augusta had to admit, as she recalled the shocking sensation of picturing the breeches clinging to George's naked body. She shivered.

"Are you cold?" George asked. "Come here." He tucked her comfortably within the shelter of his uninjured arm.

"Tell me again what you did. Could it be that you deliberately aimed at the ground so Grantley would be splattered with mud, not wounded?" Augusta found it hard to believe, yet it seemed consistent with the character of the man she had so recently come to know and love.

"I have a particular fondness for mud," George said drily.

Augusta laughed and then sighed, "I can't help thinking about poor Perceval. What will happen now?"

He shrugged. "They'll find someone else to step into his shoes."

"And he has such a large family. His poor widow!"

Neither of them spoke for a moment until Augusta broke the silence. "There's one aspect of all these events you haven't considered," she said, glancing shyly up into Bridlington's eyes.

"What would that be?" he said, and brushed her temple with his lips.

"If Mariana hadn't had the mad impulse to dress like a man and see the inner workings of the House, I would never have properly met you." She let that sink in for a while, and then said, "You know, I think Jeremy Thorne is an exceptional man with a brilliant career ahead of him. Not that my opinion is of any consequence, of course."

"Gudgeon!" George said, and squeezed her all the tighter.

"So you'll let Mariana have her way?"

"I shouldn't. Lord knows what Mama will think."

"Perhaps she'll think the same of Mariana as she does of you."

George sat up straighter. "But I have been remiss. Thorne has put me to shame, in fact. There is one thing we haven't settled." He eased himself away from Augusta and stood, then knelt down in front of her and took both her hands. He said, in a voice thick with emotion, "Augusta Hastings, will you do me the honor of becoming my wife?"

Augusta paused a moment before answering, taking in the sensitive gray eyes whose moods she already knew, the arms capable of holding her so securely, and the lively mind that met hers in all the most important ways. "Yes, George. I will marry you—but I have some conditions."

He raised an eyebrow. "Conditions?"

She smiled. "I'll explain all when we return to London. I'll need Mari's cooperation in this."

The Earl of Bridlington had no trouble agreeing to wait for more information about Augusta's conditions, and set about making sure his betrothed knew exactly how much he loved her.

CHAPTER 23

The dowager cast her eye over the odd group of individuals in her drawing room—some seated, some standing—with a degree of satisfaction, although why she should do so, she wasn't entirely certain.

There was her beguiling, headstrong daughter who had captured the hearts of almost every eligible beau in the *ton*. But she knew her own mind, and that tall, lanky gentleman standing next to her with his hand resting on her shoulder was her choice, the man she wanted as her mate for the rest of her life. No family, no fortune. But Lady Bridlington could see as clear as day that he was the match for her daughter. George had taken more convincing than she had, but between her daughter and herself, they'd persuaded him.

Which brought her to George—born a cripple with a foot that could not be fixed, subjected to cruel teasing and victim of brutal efforts to straighten his foot that only made it worse. How had he turned into such a fine man with intelligence and a heart big enough to encompass as many disabled children as he could find? He stood very close to Miss Hastings—who would soon enough become the next Countess of

Bridlington. She was of a good family, although not high born enough to satisfy the gossiping biddies at Almack's perhaps. But the dowager had only to see the way George looked at her to know that only someone like Miss Hastings could have broken through his determination to eschew love at all costs. He did not want to be pitied. He did not want his wife to be ashamed of him or make excuses. He did not want to be hurt. Miss Hastings, the dowager was certain, would never hurt him.

There were two other people there as well, a saucy young girl and an overly dapper young gentleman who had been introduced to her as Miss Pauline Dawkins and Mr. Aloysius Gordon. When she'd asked who they were and what was their business here she'd been told by her daughter that all would be revealed at this peculiar meeting.

But it was Augusta who initiated the discussion of the matter at hand.

"George—Lord Bridlington—asked for my hand the other day at an inn near my former home in Devonshire. I, of course," she paused and smiled up at him, "said yes. But I said I had certain conditions."

Conditions? Lady Bridlington opened her eyes wide. What common young woman would attach conditions to marrying an earl?

"I have Mariana's support in this. We became friends because we are alike in so many ways. We both wanted more out of our lives than the world thought was our due. I have no doubt Mariana will have the opportunity to exert her considerable talents in the political realm, thanks to Jeremy.

"My ambitions were—are—different. Not so noble, perhaps, as Mariana's. But I'm equally passionate about them. I came to London not only to escape a detestable future but to try to make a better one for myself using my own skills and talents. I was mistaken in the way I went about it, but I cannot regret it because my actions resulted in becoming involved with Lady Mariana and my fiancé, Lord Bridlington."

"You are being quite mysterious, my dear. Pray come to the point," the dowager said, not without kindness.

Augusta smiled at her. "Although I was educated with an eye to intellectual pursuits, my nature led me to take great pleasure in fine materials and the way they can be made to augment a woman's beauty and comfort. Ever since I was a girl, I fashioned my own clothes not merely to mimic what was in the magazines and journals, but to suit my imagination. I came to London thinking I could become a fashionable modiste, make my mark on the style of clothing worn not just by ladies of the *ton,* but by others with less money to spend on their wardrobes.

"So, here is my condition." She stood and looked directly into George's eyes. "I want to establish a modiste's atelier that will furnish clothing designed by me. I know … " She put her finger up and turned her attention to the dowager, "I know that it is unseemly for a countess to engage in trade. I would therefore like to create an establishment known as Madame Pauline's. Pauline is the finest seamstress of my acquaintance, and she has a good eye for drape and construction. I trust her to bring my vision to life. And she will be aided by Aloysius Gordon's unerring feeling for the best fabrics, his knowledge of how to procure them and sure perception of quality, and his other connections in the trade."

She stopped speaking for a while and looked around the room. Pauline and Gordon both stared at her open-mouthed.

"Part of the mission of this establishment will be to provide decent clothing to the children my Lord Bridlington houses in Marylebone."

Pauline raised a tentative hand. "Gussie—I mean Miss Hastings, soon to be My Lady—so you don't want no one to know it's your business? You want me to take the credit for it? But no one'll come just for me!"

"They will when Lady Mariana Thorne patronizes your establishment, and brings all her *ton*-ish friends to do so as well, along with the political wives and daughters. And of course, I will be a client too, although I am not so influential in that world as Mariana." Augusta looked once more into Bridlington's eyes. "Those, my lord, are my conditions. Can you tolerate a countess with her finger secretly in a thriving business?"

The dowager saw with deep satisfaction the smile that spread across her son's handsome face, and then turned to gaze at Mariana, who had leaned her head against Jeremy's arm and closed her eyes. They were not like any other family in the *ton*. Her children had somehow come into the world with hearts and consciences—features her late husband had sorely lacked.

They were remarkable. And they would ensure that their world, at least their small corner of it, was the better for having them in it.

AUTHOR'S NOTE

This is very much a work of fiction. However, I have anchored it securely in the history of the time. 1812 was a dramatic year in British politics, with the Luddite riots, the Peninsular War, the American War, and the assassination of Spencer Perceval—the only British prime minister ever to be assassinated. This did indeed happen on the steps of Parliament on May eleventh of that year. Of course, Lady Mariana's foray into the house dressed as a man is entirely fictional. But I refuse to believe that upper-class women at the time weren't also often interested in affairs outside of their round of parties and pursuit of the perfect husband, and sought ways to have some political influence.

This belief is also at the heart of Augusta's story—and is the underlying theme of my entire series of Double-Dilemma Romances. Each of these books features parallel and equally important romantic plots. But the dual dilemma could just as easily apply to the competing desires of the female protagonists to step beyond their circumscribed worlds without sacrificing the fulfillment of love and family —something women still often struggle with today.

Of course, in my fictional world I can resolve everything to everyone's satisfaction, which, sadly, doesn't always happen in real life.

I hope you enjoy getting to know the inhabitants of my world! Book Two in the series, *The Soprano's Daring Duke*, is coming soon. For news and special extras, sign up for my email newsletter at https://susanne-dunlap.com!

ACKNOWLEDGMENTS

This book would never have come into being in its present form without the guidance and encouragement of book coach and editor Julie Artz. Thank you for your wisdom and help, and for pushing me to question, revise, and push beyond.

I would also like to thank my beta readers, authors Louise Bergin and Melissa Addey. If you liked this book, check out Melissa Addey's Regency Romances! The first two books in her *Regency Outsider* series are available now.

I owe thanks as well to my friend of many, many years and ace proofreader, Susan Babcock, who has cast her unerring eye over this manuscript and saved me from avoidable embarrassments.

Another shout-out goes to the members of Regency Fiction Writers for their unfailing generosity in sharing their expertise and knowledge.

Finally, I would like to acknowledge the many women I know—the book coaches, editors, friends, family, and neighbors—who have cheered me along the way to this novel. Thank you for your constant support.

ABOUT ME

I am the award-winning author of over a dozen historical novels set in a variety periods, all featuring strong women. For material, I have roamed through history from the middle ages in Southern France (*The Orphans of Tolosa Trilogy*) to Russia during the Revolution (*Anastasia's Secret*), passing through the court of Louis XIV, the French Revolution, Romantic era Paris, the Crimea, and early 20th century New York. I have a PhD in Music History from Yale—the spur that set me onto my career as a historical novelist. My love of Regency Romance has been lying in wait for me for decades, and I've finally succumbed to the lure of this captivating genre. This book is the first in a series of stand-alone novels called Double-Dilemma Romance.

In addition to being a writer, I am certified as a book coach in fiction, nonfiction, and memoir by Author Accelerator, working 1:1 with many remarkable writers. I also teach workshops, and have lovingly built several online self-paced courses for writers, the most recent of which is *The Heart of Historical Romance.* You can find more information about my books and about working with me on my website, Susanne-dunlap.com.